Simple Jess

Pamela Morsi

JOVE BOOKS, NEW YORK

SIMPLE JESS

A Jove Book / published by arrangement with
the author

PRINTING HISTORY
Jove edition / April 1996

The Putnam Berkley World Wide Web site address is
http://www.berkley.com

ISBN: 0-515-11837-0

A JOVE BOOK®
Jove Books are published by The Berkley Publishing Group,
200 Madison Avenue, New York, New York 10016.
JOVE and the "J" design are trademarks
belonging to Jove Publications, Inc.

PRINTED IN THE UNITED STATES OF AMERICA

10 9 8 7 6 5 4 3 2

For my daughter

LEILA

One of God's favorites.

She will never read this book
but she can recognize her name.

Simple Jess

CHAPTER
ONE

Althea Winsloe was hopping mad. Her face was red, her teeth were clenched, and she was marching down the well-worn mountain path with such determined haste that she was completely unaware of the bright blue sky, the lush fall colors of the oak and ash and elm—the beautiful autumn day that surrounded her. Her anger was a typical consequence of her morning visit with her mother-in-law.

Beulah Winsloe had apparently made it her goal in life to frustrate, subjugate, and infuriate Althea. This morning Beulah had been in fine form.

Althea couldn't still her thoughts as her hands tightly clenched the handle of the woven market basket.

"That woman! That woman!" she whispered furiously to herself. "She will not run my life. I swear my soul upon it."

Her vow offered no immediate comfort. The young woman still seethed. She made her way angrily along the steep forest path at such a pace that the little cherub-faced boy who followed her could hardly keep up.

"Slow down, Mama," he pleaded at last.

Startled, Althea halted immediately. She turned to the little fellow coming up behind her, her expression a mixture of surprise and guilt. She had been walking way too fast for the short legs of the small person who accompanied her. In her furious haste she'd not given a thought for this child, her son.

"Baby-Paisley!" she called out to him as he hurried toward her. His homespun overalls were still a bit big for him. The rolled-up cuffs at his ankles were at least three

inches wide. He was fair and freckled, sturdy and determined. His face was flushed from exertion. His short,
chubby legs had to make three strides for every one of hers.

"I'm sorry, Baby-Paisley," she said, bending down waiting to sweep him up into her arms. "I suspect I'm walking
as fast as I'm thinking. Mama didn't mean to leave you
behind. Why don't you let me carry you?"

The little boy ran up beside her. Ignoring her open arms,
he dropped to his knees, taking a grateful breath at the
respite. Looking up at her, he shook his head.

"You cain't carry me, Mama," he told her, his brow
furrowed in serious contemplation. "I'm too big."

Althea's bright brown eyes twinkled. "You are a pretty
big boy," she admitted. "But I can still carry you."

"I'm the man of the house," he stated flatly and with
considerable consequence as he stuck his thumb against his
chest.

The curve of Althea's smile hardened and sadness extin-
guished the bright stars in her eyes.

"I suppose your grandma told you that," she said.

The little fellow nodded proudly. "Gwamma says I'm the
man of the house. So I cain't be Baby-Paisley no more."

Althea squatted down next to him and set her hands
lovingly on the small expanse of shoulders so eager to take
on the weight of the world. She loved him. He was the only
thing in her world that mattered and she vowed she would
protect him. Planting a kiss on the top of his head, she
smiled down at him, her words careful but tender.

"You're a very brave little boy and you're my Baby-
Paisley," she told him. "You and me, we don't need any
'man of the house.' "

"But Gwamma says—"

Althea shook her head. "What Grandma says is what
Grandma says," she told him firmly. "But what Mama says
is the law."

"Yes, ma'am," the little boy answered, clearly disappointed but accepting the truth when he heard it.

She tousled his sandy blond curls. "They'll be plenty of

time for you to be a man, Baby-Paisley," she said. "You're only three years old, you know."

"Three and a half," he corrected her boastfully.

She nodded in agreement. "Still," she said. "Three and a half is not too old for a boy to let Mama carry him if his legs get tired."

"I not tired, Mama," he insisted.

Althea smiled proudly at her young son. "Why don't you hold my hand at least," she suggested.

Baby-Paisley was thoughtful for a long minute; finally, he nodded. "I'll hold your hand," he agreed. "So you woan get lost."

The two began to make their way along the path, Althea deliberately kept her pace slow. She smiled down at the sturdy youngster by her side. He was, to her eyes, a living, breathing miracle. From that first awful day when he came squalling into the world he was an unending source of amazement to the woman who had given him birth.

Who would have thought, Althea often mused, that two very ordinary people like herself and Paisley Winsloe would have created this perfect little human being, this bright, happy, wonderful child.

Paisley Orville Winsloe was smart and strong and tender and funny. Being all that at age three, his mother could only ponder in amazement what an estimable man he might grow up to be. It was Althea Winsloe's sworn duty to see that he realized his possibilities.

And she would do that, she swore silently to herself, without the interference of Beulah Winsloe or the Piggots or anyone else. Once more she silently seethed.

The community of Marrying Stone, it seemed, had plans for her. Plans about what would be *best* for her and for Baby-Paisley. Plans about what would be best for her farm. Plans that Althea was very intent upon rejecting.

"She cain't raise that boy without a father," Beulah had declared publicly whenever she'd been given half a chance. "My own dear Paisley has been dead half that child's life. It's time he had a man to look up to."

The whole thing had come to a head last Friday night.

Folks had gotten together for a Spelling Bee, but it had ended in a shouting match.

Her mother-in-law spoke for the Winsloe clan. Granny Piggott, the oldest woman in the community, usually the keeper of what wisdom ever prevailed there, spoke for their neighbors.

"Ever' child deserves a daddy," Granny stated with conviction. "Be he upstanding citizen or piss-poor ne'er-do-well, ever' child ought to have one."

The folks on the mountain wholeheartedly agreed with her and most of them felt compelled somehow to offer, at least, some stupid opinion of their own.

Althea did not remain a meek and biddable daughter-in-law through this debate.

"I have no intention to remarry," she said over and over again.

Granny Piggott snorted in disapproval. "Of course you'll marry again," she said. "It's just a matter of who it'll be. You can take your choice among my grandsons and nephews."

Those were fighting words for Beulah Winsloe. "You're just wanting the Piggotts to get their hands on my boy's farm."

"It ain't your boy's no more," Granny answered. "It belongs to the gal and the next feller she marries up with."

Beulah didn't argue the former. It was the latter that stuck so painfully in the old woman's craw. "That's McNees ground and always has been," her mother-in-law stated flatly. "That place is got the best corn bottom in these parts. We'd never a-given it up if we'd known that our boy was fixin' to die young."

Mrs. Winsloe made it sound as if somehow Paisley had betrayed his family when he'd choked on a fish bone and died.

"It's land up for grabs," Granny stated.

"It's McNees and Winsloe ground," Beulah snapped right back.

"It's Baby-Paisley's!" Althea shouted, shushing the both

of them. "It's my son's farm and I intend to keep it for him until he's old enough to tend it."

"It needs tending now."

Althea made every effort to remain calm. Breathing deeply, she recited the Golden Rule inside her head, a tried-and-true method for avoiding trouble.

"Perhaps I'll put in a crop next spring," she said quietly.

"You should not have ever let them fields go fallow." Beulah shook her finger at the young woman accusingly.

"And there ain't no telling where you're a-going to get game this winter," Granny scolded. "Your man's gun is a-rusting and his dogs are going wild."

"That's why she ought to marry up," Beulah said with conviction. "And she ought to be marrying up with a McNees."

McNees was Beulah Winsloe's maiden name. It was also Althea's. Besides being in-laws they were also distant cousins. And like the Piggotts, the McNees family made up a considerable portion of all the inhabitants of the mountain.

"Lord have mercy," Granny huffed. "Althea's a McNees herself. You don't want a gal marrying up too close with her kin."

Beulah raised a haughty eyebrow. "You should know well about that. It's the Piggotts that brung feeblemindedness to the mountain."

Granny's eyes narrowed, but she let the insult pass. "Who you gonna marry her up with, Beulah?" she asked. "The McNees ain't got no bachelors right now, 'cepting some babies and yer brother, Tom." Granny hooted as if she'd heard a good joke. "You gonna marry her up with that *old* man?"

The fact that Tom McNees was a whole generation younger than Granny notwithstanding, Beulah's favorite brother *was* old enough to be Althea's father.

"Tom'd make a good husband, if he were of a mind," Beulah defended. "But now that he's the new preacher, he has no time for farming anyway."

"There is always time for farming," Granny answered with certainty. "It's just that when a man's been a bachelor for close to fifty years, like your brother Tom, well I don't suspect he'd be much of a bridegroom for a squirmy gal still full of hominy."

Beulah drew herself to full height with fury. "Are you a-saying that my boy's widow is prone to rollix?"

Granny raised her chin and pursed her mouth in disapproval. "Ain't saying nothing of the sort. She's just a young woman and a healthy one. And nain brittle when it comes to man tending. The Good Lord surely meant to give her a houseful of children to raise and it's time she get at it."

"I don't need any more children," Althea declared adamantly as she stepped between the two women. "It's my life and my son is all the babies I want."

"A woman always needs more children," Beulah insisted. "And don't you be a-telling me otherwise. I birthed six and done buried ever' one, your husband was the last. I got nary a one to comfort me in my old age."

"I'm sorry for that," Althea told her. "But I don't think—"

Beulah interrupted her. "You don't need to think, Althea. You're young and the young are too busy for thinking. I'm an old woman. I got time to ruminate and consider and I've figured out what's the best for all of us."

"Mother Winslow—"

"Seems to me, Beulah," Granny stated, "that you oughter be thinking more about this here gal and less about that corn bottom you're so fond of."

"Don't you be puttin' that sin on me, Granny," Beulah snapped. "It's you Piggotts that's got your greedy hands out."

"It ain't greed to do right. This gal'll be wanting a young man. One that'll keep her warm of a cold night. One that tends toward a breeding nature. And I'll bet she likes fellers what are handsome. They ain't none finer-looking than the Piggotts, on this mountain or the next."

The argument had gone on and on. Ruining the whole evening far as Althea was concerned and accomplishing absolutely nothing. Only the lateness of the hour had finally broken up the confrontation. Althea had gratefully taken herself and her sleepy child home.

She hoped that she'd heard the last of it for a while, but this morning at her mother-in-law's that had proved not to be the case.

"I've been thinking about what that old windbag Granny Piggott said the other night," Beulah told her.

"I don't want to talk about this again," Althea answered sharply.

"No, some of the things she said is true," Beulah said, nodding. "So I been studying and studying about it."

"There is really no need—"

"Course there's need!" Beulah interrupted. "You are a-goin' to wed, sure as the world. It's just a matter of who and when. The *when* needs to be soon. You'll need a man to take care of you come winter. My Orv cain't barely fend for the two of us. And as for the *who* . . ." Beulah stopped to shake her head. "Well, truth to tell, gal, I won't be havin' no stranger coming in and takin' over our land."

"Mother Winsloe, I will never remarry. I'm willing to promise you that. I would never give Paisley's birthright to a stranger," Althea assured her.

"Sure you won't, 'cause you don't have to," she said. "We got just the right feller for you here in the family."

"What?"

"I sent word over to my cousin, Eben Baxley."

"Eben Baxley."

"You remember him from your weddin' day, don't you?" she asked.

Althea did remember. Paisley and his cousin had gotten so drunk together the night before that even by that afternoon the bridegroom could hardly stand up for the ceremony.

"That Eben," her mother-in-law continued. "He's a fine, good-looking feller with a way with the ladies, or so it's said. Don't worry about that, of course. A wife can always turn that nature into attendin' to breeding."

"Eben Baxley!"

"I know what you're a-thinkin'," her mother-in-law

assured her. "You're a-thinkin' that he likes the gals what's a bit younger and prettier than you. But don't ya give it a lick of worry. I been studyin' on it and I know that Eben sets a fine store by them dogs of Paisley's. A man'll do a lot of things to get himself a fine pack of hounds."

"Ouch, Mama! You're squeezing my hand."

Baby-Paisley's complaint brought Althea's thoughts back to the present. They had just come around the last bend in the trail. Before them was the Phillips Store and in the distance the Marrying Stone church and school.

"Mama's sorry, darlin'," she said to the little boy. "Do you think Mr. Phillips may have a bite of candy in his big store?" she asked.

The little boy didn't answer, but his eyes widened and he licked his lips.

Althea smiled at him for a moment before drifting back to her thoughts.

"Do a lot for a fine pack of dogs, indeed," she muttered under her breath.

"Sugar, coffee, cartridges," Jesse Best whispered to himself as he walked the narrow path along the ridge. "Sugar, coffee, cartridges."

It was important that he didn't forget. Being given the responsibility of going for supplies was no small thing. It was a job that a man would do. Jesse didn't want to forget anything. Of course, there was the list in his pocket. His sister Meggie always gave him a list. She had read it to him before he left home. Meggie was practically a scriber. She could read and write pretty near anything. She'd read him the list in his pocket and it said sugar, coffee, cartridges. Jesse wanted to remember that. He wanted to just tell Mr. Phillips what he was there to buy. That's what other men did. Jesse wanted to be like other men.

In many ways, he was. He was tall. Taller than most who lived on the mountain. And he was big, too. Pushing the plow, hauling water, and chopping wood had made his chest broad and his arms as thick and muscled as a pair of hams. His legs and back were just as sturdy.

"Jesse is stronger than a mule," his father would tell folks proudly.

But Jesse knew that he wasn't a mule. He was a man.

He had his looks from his mother's side of the family. The Piggotts were good-looking people. Everybody said so, especially the Piggotts. They were fine-featured and blessed with good teeth. And it was strong in the blood, those fine features. As Granny Piggott often pointed out, no matter what kind of warthog a Piggott was to marry up with, the younguns came out pretty as roses. Jesse was not a rose, of course, he was a man, but he favored the Piggotts, as did his sister and many of his cousins. He had big eyes, very round and very blue. His nose was well shaped and proportionate in size, and his smile was gleaming white. His skin was too fair, of course. It reddened up with the first hot days of springtime. Only now with autumn in the air were his arms and face the toasty brown of a man who worked outside. His hair was blond. More than blond, really. Granny Piggott said it was "white as cotton and thick as an Injun's." This morning his hair was covered by a glove cap of homespun gray as he hurried down the trail.

"Don't you dawdle!" his father had called out to him as he'd left the cabin. He had shoved his hat on his head and nodded in promise. Men didn't dawdle. And Jesse Best was a man.

"Sugar, coffee, cartridges," he said to himself once more.

The place where he lived was called Marrying Stone Mountain. At least that was what his brother-in-law, Roe Farley, called it. Roe hadn't always lived here. That's why he called it something, Jesse believed. If a person had always lived here, he didn't need to call it nothing but home.

To Jesse that was exactly what it was. He knew the mountain from the top of the tallest tree at the summit to the lowest swampy places in the hollow. And he knew the peaks that surrounded it nearly as well. It was good that Jesse knew this place so well. Because there was a lot of things that Jesse didn't know.

Something at the side of the path caught his attention and his eyes lit up in excitement.

"Mushrooms!" he said with delight and dropped to his knees on the ground next to a big mockernut hickory brightly colored in the leaves of autumn. Three big morel mushrooms stood like sentinels beside the tree, their long white stems were tall and stately and the big brown tops looked much like Jesse's own homespun hat.

His blue eyes twinkling with expectation, Jesse carefully removed the leaves and duff around the base of the tree. He giggled out loud when he found the half-dozen smaller mushrooms that had been concealed in the debris.

"Always some little fellers hiding in the leaves," he said.

He reached to pluck them from the cool damp earth, but his hand stopped midway. He jerked his hand back and pushed his hat to the back of his head as he dug his hand in his hair. Something wasn't right.

Sugar, coffee, cartridges.

Don't dawdle.

Jesse is a man.

He squeezed his eyes shut. There was something else. Another thought. It was there. It was there, somewhere in his head. Something else. Something else he was trying to remember. It was something important. It was . . . It was . . .

"Autumn," he said aloud.

With a puff of air, he released the breath he'd been holding. It was autumn. He looked down at the mushrooms again. In the springtime, morels were the best mushrooms. So sweet and tasty even his sister Meggie's bad cooking couldn't ruin them. But it was not springtime. It was autumn. In autumn, morels were bitter to the taste and could make a person sick.

"It's autumn," he said again and hurried to his feet. "Don't dawdle!" he admonished himself.

Jesse hurried down the path as if to make up for the careless minute he had spent beside it. He had almost made a mistake. He hated making mistakes. But it was so hard to keep everything in his head at the same time. It was so hard to be able to think of everything at once.

"Sugar, coffee, cartridges," he reminded himself.

It wouldn't have been a big mistake. He would have simply carried the bad mushrooms home in his pack and Meggie would have thrown them out. His sister Meggie wasn't like him. Meggie was smart. Smart people didn't make mistakes. Jesse wasn't smart. He didn't mind that so much. But he hated making mistakes.

The path before him widened and Jesse could see the church and the school. Phillips Store was just a ways past and downhill all the way. Jesse slowed his step. He mustn't dawdle, but he didn't need to hurry, either.

As Jesse made his way across the clearing he saw Pastor Jay sitting on the Marrying Stone, the big piece of bright white quartz that jutted out of the ground and gave the mountain its name.

"Morning, Pastor Jay," he called out.

The old man didn't answer, he just continued to stare out into the nothingness of the heavens, talking. Jesse's feelings weren't hurt. The old man probably didn't even know that Jesse had called out to him. Pastor Jay wasn't the pastor anymore. Folks still called him that, because they had for so long. But Tom McNees was pastor now. He did all the preaching and marrying and burying.

Pastor Jay just sat around on the Marrying Stone mostly, reading the Bible and talking to himself. Pastor Jay had lost his mind. That's what people said. Jesse didn't understand that. He could see how a man might lose his socks or his knife. But he didn't know how someone could lose his mind. Jesse's mind didn't work very well, but he'd never lost it. And since Pastor Jay could still read and talk and get his trousers on without help, Jesse figured he still had his mind, too.

It was hard to understand. But then, most everything was.

"Sugar, coffee, cartridges," he whispered to himself once more.

From the churchyard on, the pathway widened to a degree that it was generally referred to as "the road." It was a simple track through the trees, broadened by timber cutting, the remaining stumps had been sawed off as close to ground level as possible. Uneven and treacherous, "the road" was no fine thoroughfare. But then it didn't get a lot of traffic. Buell Phillips, the owner of the store, possessed the only wagon on the mountain. Wheels were just not that useful on the steep terrain. A mule-drawn skid was much more typical of local transportation. Most folks, like Jesse this morning, made their way along on their own two feet.

When he reached the curve in the road that brought the store into view, the young man's steps hurried.

"Sugar, coffee, cartridges."

He increased his pace to an excited trot as he came closer to his destination.

The store was a rough-hewn barnlike structure that was poised almost precariously upon the side of the mountain. The back of the building was cut into the ground like a cellar. There was a porch entrance to the second floor at the back. It was where the Phillipses lived. The front rose nearly shoulder-high from the slope and was supported by a half-dozen thick maple poles that served to firm its foundation. In the cool shade beneath the overhang, enjoyed in summer by dogs, hogs, and varmints innumerable, the pale dusting of last night's frost still lingered.

Jesse took the steps two at a time. Sitting on a barrel beside the front door was a rheumy-eyed old man with a scraggly gray beard that hung down to his chest.

"Morning, Uncle Pigg," Jesse called out to him.

The old man let loose a powerful wad of tobacco that cleared the porch easily before he glanced up at the young man beside him.

"Morning, boy," he acknowledged.

Jesse grinned in admiration at the distance traveled by the tobacco spittle. "That was a dang good shot," he said proudly.

The old man shrugged off the intended compliment. "What brings you to the store this day?" he asked.

Momentarily he hesitated. "Sugar, coffee, cartridges," he answered solemnly.

Pigg Broody laughed heartily as if he'd told a great joke. "No use reciting fer me, boy. It's Buell what'll take yer order."

"Yessir," Jesse answered.

"Go on in there, but stay outer trouble. Got a drummer from the city come up," he warned. "It's best to keep your guard up when they's strangers about."

Jesse nodded. But he didn't take Pigg Broody's word much to heart. His sister's husband, Roe, had been a stranger when he'd come to Marrying Stone. Jesse didn't see that folks you don't know were much different than those that you do.

Pigg took another long shot off the end of the porch. Jesse was shaking his head in admiration as he crossed the threshold into the cool darkness of the store.

He stopped just inside the door and took a deep breath, drawing in with pleasure the unique odor of the Phillips General Store. It was part spice and part cotton cloth. Salty pickles and horse-mouth salve. Camphor and meal. Leather and kerosene. Jesse closed his eyes, savoring it. The store had near every smell and at once a smell all its own. And the memory of it was painted upon the young man's memory with indelible accuracy.

He smiled to himself. Mr. Phillips was busy talking with the drummer Pigg had mentioned. So Jesse began strolling the long length of the store. Allowing himself the luxury of letting his eyes wander where they may, wondering at the vast array of things to see.

"Don't touch nothing," he reminded himself quietly. That was the rule at the store. The storekeeper was an in-law of the Piggotts and therefore family, but Mr. Phillips—and Jesse never thought to call him anything else—made no allowances for his relations. He got mad if Jesse touched anything.

"You'll break it!" he would always shout angrily, usually startling Jesse into doing just that. He hated for folks to raise their voices at him. He might not be smart, but he could hear real well.

He would just have to remember to do what he was told and stay out of trouble. That way there would be no cause for anyone to holler.

Jesse let his eyes roam among the enameled buckets and

the scythe blades. He examined the lady's picture on the front of the bluing bottle. And pressed his nose against the glass to look at the pocket watches and fancy buttons in the display case.

It was a fact that the Phillips General Store was as close to paradise as Jesse Best had ever been. He had seen, admired, and awed over every whatnot, thingamajig, and gewgaw in the place. Still, for Jesse, it was all perpetually new and absorbing.

The city man held the storekeeper's attention as Jesse wandered through the last array of goods for sale. He paid no heed to their talk, but noted that the drummer was talking louder and louder and that Mr. Phillips said little or nothing, but continued to shake his head.

Jesse moved closer to the two as he admired the selection of pipes on the shelf with the tobacco. His pa had a pipe and Jesse could smoke it when he wanted. That is, if he smoked it outside. His sister Meggie didn't tolerate any manly vices inside her home. But Pa's pipe was simply a reed stem set into a hollowed corncob. These pipes were applewood and brier root, fancy carved. Some had real Chinese amber at the mouthpiece. Others were tipped with India rubber. So entranced was Jesse that he moved up closer. Completely forgetting the no-touch rule, he reached out his hand toward a particularly handsome bulldog bent brier with a covered nickel top.

His hand never touched the pipe, however. The sound of excited footsteps on the porch drew his attention.

"Good mornin', Mr. Bwoody!" Jesse heard a small voice call out.

"Hey there, youngun," was the answer returned.

"Good morning, Mr. Broody."

The voice was feminine and familiar.

Jesse heard the scrape of the chair against the porch boards as gray-haired Pigg rose gallantly to his feet in greeting to the young woman.

"And a beautiful morning it is, Miz Winsloe," he said.

Jesse moved away from the shelf and nearer to the doorway of the store. His curiosity of a few moments earlier slipped his mind as easily as a hog on ice. A woman was coming into the store. Jesse Best liked women.

"Can I have a candy, Mama? Can I? Can I?" the young boy was asking excitedly as he came through the door.

"We'll see," was his mother's answer.

By the delighted grin that swept the child's face, it was clear that "we'll see" was an answer in the affirmative.

The boy skipped delightedly two paces and then stopped dead still in front of Jesse.

"Hello," Jesse said warmly, smiling down at the small fellow at his feet.

"Gar," the little boy said as he swallowed nervously.

He gazed up in wonder and fright at the huge man. The child was only knee-high to Jesse. But there was more than a difference in size that caused the youngster to back up a pace and edge around Jesse with a wide berth. His big eyes were wide with fear as if he expected any moment for the man to grab him and eat him alive.

"Good morning, Simple Jess," Althea Winsloe said as she followed her son into the store. Clearly she had seen the strange manner in which her son greeted their neighbor. "How are you?" she asked. Her smile was exceptionally bright as if she hoped to lighten the sting of her son's rudeness.

Her effort worked quite well as Jesse gazed back at her, his expression near worshipful.

"Tolerable, ma'am," Jesse answered. "Right tolerable."

He bowed slightly as he made room for her to step by. Jesse closed his eyes as she passed beside him and inhaled deeply, a dreamy smile upon his face.

Jesse loved the smell of women. Old women, young women, women who'd spent the morning laboring over a tub of laundry, or women who were dressed up for Sunday with dabs of rose water behind their ears, Jesse relished the sweet redolence of them. And Althea Winsloe had an aroma that Jesse much admired. It was a mixture, of course. Not that he couldn't sort them out perfectly. And he didn't consciously even try. But he did take another deep breath, merely to enjoy it. There was the clean fragrance of yellow

soap, the smooth sweetness of fresh-churned butter, woodsmoke and sage, yarrow and hobblebush. All smells that
were very familiar to him. And there was something more,
some underlying scent that was almost beyond his detec-
tion. He couldn't describe it as sweet or spicy. It wasn't
balmy or savorous, perfumy or yarbish. But it was there. It
was always there. And no other woman on the mountain
smelled that way.

"Good morning, Mr. Phillips," she said, greeting the
storekeeper. She nodded politely to the stranger.

"Ah . . . dear Mrs. Winsloe," Buell Phillips said effusively. "You are a pretty sight as always. Oather will be so
sorry that he missed you."

Jesse's brow furrowed slightly with curiosity. Why his
cousin Oather would be sorry to miss Althea Winsloe, he
didn't know. But there were lots of things that he didn't
understand.

Miss Althea was speaking very firmly about being a
grown woman and the owner of her farm. Jesse was a little
surprised that Mr. Phillips didn't know that. He seemed to
know pretty much everything.

Mr. Phillips ignored what Miss Althea was saying and
began talking about his son, Oather. Jesse figured he must
be talking to the drummer, because Miss Althea already
knew everything there was to know about Oather, everybody on the mountain did.

His mind wandering due to the foolish nature of the
conversation, Jesse's attention was captured by Baby-Paisley.
The little boy was wistfully eyeing the licorice sticks in the
big jar on the counter.

"Can I have my candy now, Mama?" he pleaded, pulling
on his mother's skirt. "Pleese, Mama, can I have my
candy?"

Miss Althea, whose voice, to Jesse's surprise, was a little
bit shrill as she talked to Mr. Phillips, didn't answer him.
She was very caught up in the conversation about her farm
and Oather and didn't pay the little boy any attention.

The little fellow persisted more loudly and eventually had
the storekeeper himself staring down at him.

Mr. Phillips, somehow seemingly unaware of Miss Althea's raised voice and ill humor, smiled broadly at the little boy and to Jesse's near complete dumbfoundment opened the jar and handed the child a fistful of the fancy candy.

At two for a penny, licorice was dear. That last time Jesse had worked for Mr. Phillips, unloading a mule train carrying hundred-pound sacks of flour from the mill, the storekeeper had paid him only five pieces of licorice.

Of course, his brother-in-law had come back down the mountain with him the next day and insisted that Jesse get paid a man's wage.

But the storekeeper had hoped to get a day's work from him for five pieces of candy. He'd just handed Baby-Paisley twice that much, and a little fellow like him couldn't do no work much at all.

The little boy was eagerly stuffing several pieces of licorice into his mouth.

His mother, who continued speaking sharply to Mr. Phillips, didn't even notice.

Jesse's mouth watered. The smell of licorice was strong, almost like actually tasting it himself. It was Jesse's favorite candy, but candy wasn't like wages. Men don't get paid with candy.

Baby-Paisley turned slightly, glancing in his direction. The little boy's eyes widened and he clutched his licorice more tightly as if he feared Jesse might steal it.

Smiling, Jesse wanted to reassure him. But the child was not comforted. It seemed that he was genuinely afraid of Jesse. Because he was so big, and because he was different, boys and girls were often afraid of him. The older ones sometimes made up stories to scare the youngers. They made Jesse out to be the bogeyman of the mountain. That was sad. Jesse liked children a lot. He had a niece about the same age as the little boy. But his niece loved him. Baby-Paisley clearly did not.

The word *dogs* captured Jesse's attention and he glanced up to Miss Althea and Mr. Phillips. The storekeeper's expression was preachy and self-righteous. From his position, Jesse couldn't see Miss Althea's face, but the stiffness in her shoulders was evident. When she spoke, her words were crisp and cold.

"There does seem to be a great deal of interest in my late husband's dogs," she said. "Why don't you, Mr. Phillips, be so good as to get the word out to the men on the mountain that as of today, that pack of dogs is for sale to the highest bidder."

"You're selling Paisley's dogs?" Phillips sounded horrified. "You cain't do that."

"They are mine to sell, sir," she snapped. "I most certainly can."

"But your new husband—"

"I do not intend to remarry," she interrupted. "I have said that several times, but no one seems to listen. Just so that there is no misunderstanding, please let everyone know that I am selling those dogs."

She turned then, her eyes blazing with anger and her head held high.

"Come along, Baby-Paisley," she said. "I don't believe that there is a thing we want to buy in the store today."

CHAPTER
TWO

Dogs. Paisley Winsloe's dogs.

Jesse Best's mind was reeling.

"She's going to sell Paisley's dogs," he whispered aloud and then repeated the words once more in his head.

He furrowed his brow in concentration. There was something about those words that he should consider, something about them that was important. His breathing accelerated and he bit down on his lip, thinking. She was selling the dogs. The dogs were for sale. That meant that a man could buy the dogs. A man could buy the dogs. Any man could buy the dogs. Jesse was a man.

His eyes widened. Without another thought for his errand or the enormous array of wonders within the store, Jesse Best hurried toward the doorway of Phillips Store as if he was being chased by a skunk.

It had been his ambition for several years to own his own dog. A dog wasn't like a house or a farm. A man had to be smart to own those things. Even a simple man like Jesse could own a dog. And the dogs that Paisley Winsloe had were the best on the mountain.

"Simple Jess? Where you going?"

The storekeeper's words caught him in midstride. Jesse opened his mouth to explain but the words didn't come easily. It was too much to say out loud. It was too hard to bring the unfinished thoughts into words and phrases.

"I'm leaving," he answered.

Mr. Phillips raised an eyebrow and shook his head. "You

cain't go running off," he said. "What did you come here to get?"

"Huh?"

"Your family sent you here to buy supplies, didn't they?"

Jesse nodded.

"So what do they want?"

Jesse stared at him mutely.

"Come on, boy. I haven't got all day."

Almost angrily, Jesse screwed up his forehead in deep concentration.

Don't dawdle.

Don't touch.

Be wary of strangers.

Poison mushrooms in autumn.

Dogs.

Paisley Winsloe's dogs.

They were for sale. A man could buy them.

Dogs.

"Spit it out, boy!" the storekeeper said with annoyance.

Jesse gritted his teeth against the frustration. He knew. He knew. But, but what was it?

"Your sister probably put a list in your pocket," Mr. Phillips told him.

Jess nodded in defeat and pulled out the list and handed it to Mr. Phillips.

The storekeeper held it up to the dim light of the coal-oil lamp.

"Sugar, coffee, cartridges," he read.

Jesse nodded. Sugar, coffee, cartridges. He could remember it now. He gritted his teeth and shook his head. He hated having to show the note. There was nothing to do for it. He got overset and forgot to remember.

"That just happens to folks," his sister Meggie would have said to him.

Jesse hated that it mostly happened to him.

"I can get these for you, Jesse," Mr. Phillips said. "It won't take a minute."

It took a whole lot of minutes, Jesse thought. He stood on first one foot and then the other, anxious.

Dogs. Paisley Winsloe's dogs. It was all he could think about. He knew them. He had hunted with them. Old Poker, Sawtooth, Queenie, and Runt. The memory of them was sights and sounds and smells and it filled his brain until he could think of nothing else.

Dogs. Paisley Winsloe's dogs.

Mr. Phillips handed Jesse his purchases wrapped neatly in heavy brown paper.

"Thank you, Mr. Phillips," he said.

The storekeeper smiled at him. "Why don't you just look around a bit more, Jesse. Just look all your fill, while I finish my business with the city man here."

"Oh, no, sir," Jesse answered. "I got to leave now. I got business."

"Business?" Phillips chuckled. "What kind of business could you have, Simple Jess?"

"I'm buying me some dogs."

The storekeeper stared at him, stupified.

Althea Winsloe wasn't angry. Not anymore. She was cold and calculating and determined. She wasn't marrying anybody. Not Eben Baxley, not Oather Phillips, not anybody. And if the folks on the mountain wouldn't listen to her, they could sure mind her actions. She was selling Paisley's dogs.

It really was a smart thing to do, she told herself. She didn't hunt, didn't know a thing about dogs except that they ate and slept a lot. Baby-Paisley would want hunting dogs, every man did. But by the time he was big enough for hunting, the hounds they had now would be old. It made perfect sense to sell these off and get new ones when Baby-Paisley was older. She should have thought of that before. There was no sense feeding animals that she couldn't use. And it was more than simply getting rid of the dogs. It would send a message. Only the owner could sell an animal. Those hounds had been Paisley's pride, but they were hers now. They did not belong to her mother-in-law and they were not a dowry. She would do with them as she saw fit.

Her eyes narrowed slightly in distaste as she thought of

fast-talking, good-looking Eben Baxley, always about half-drunk, always laughing in that kind of nasty way.

And she didn't think much better of ponderous, slightly patronizing Oather Phillips. Especially with Buell Phillips trying to force a courtship with him down her throat.

So the men set quite a store by those dogs of Paisley's. Althea set her jaw firmly. She'd poison the whole pack before she let either of them get ahold of so much as a flea off those hounds. She'd sell them all right, and she'd sell them to someone else, that she would.

The thing that made her the maddest, however, was not really the dogs. It was folks trying to tell her what to do. She was standing up to them. At least she had so far. But it was hard for her to do.

The people on this mountain, kith and kin alike, had been telling Althea McNees Winsloe what to do for most of her life. Sweet, quiet Althea. She works hard. She's not much trouble. That's what the relatives would tell each other when they'd pass her around. Spring cleaning with Aunt Ada, then summer caring for Cousin Pugh's children. Harvesttime with Great-Uncle Nez. And winter, winter when times were hardest and food was scarce, winter with whoever was least luckiest that year. Althea was an orphan. Or at least half of one. Her mother died when she was just a baby. Her father had married a woman from the White River country. He'd left his only child from his first marriage with his family and moved off with the new wife, who wanted no reminders of a woman who had come before.

Althea had stayed on the mountain. She had been an extra child, an extra mouth to feed. Even as a little girl, she'd known that. So she'd done what she was told and she never caused trouble.

She hadn't caused trouble the year she'd married either. All that summer and fall she had worked and prayed and minded her elders. Slicked up and sporting fine clothes, Paisley Winsloe had called on her only twice before he'd asked Uncle Nez for her hand.

"He's got his own farm, Althea," her uncle had told her excitedly. "The best corn bottom for miles. He's got the finest pack of hunting hounds on the mountain and a milk cow that just come fresh. You cain't do better than that, gal."

Althea knew perfectly well that her uncle's own corn that year hadn't made doodley-squat and that his failing eyesight was taking a toll on the game he brought in. So she'd married. She'd married well. And she'd done it to save the family another winter mouth to feed.

She hadn't liked her husband all that much. But she'd been soft-spoken and loyal to him and had birthed his son. She'd minded her husband as she had her family and would have done whatever he said until the day she died. But *he* had died. That had changed everything.

She glanced down at the little boy walking beside her. Baby-Paisley was her child, the joy of her life. He would never be what she had been, the leftovers of a long-ago marriage.

She would have no other husband, not now, not ever. She would keep the farm. No other man would ever claim it as his. And when he grew up to be a man, it would be Baby-Paisley's.

That vow, of course, was easier to make than to live with. She hadn't been able to put in a crop by herself. And no one thought she needed to. She was still young enough to get her a man to do that. There was a hog to slaughter, but ham and bacon wouldn't go that long a way without fresh game to supplement the meat stores. And any man that hunted for her would be expecting something for his trouble sooner or later. She'd put up plenty of goods from her garden. But she didn't have the firewood yet to keep a blaze in the hearth. Winter was coming and she was far from ready.

Althea heard a noise in the distance behind her. She hardly had time to glance back before her young son bellowed out a bloodcurdling scream.

"He's chasing us!"

With a rush of strength that was innate, maternal, and as powerful as that of any she-bear or panther puss with a threatened cub, Althea grabbed the child up into her arms and turned to face the unknown menace, her teeth clenched, defensive and ready.

What she faced was Jesse Best hurrying up the trail behind them. At the sight of her fighting stance he stopped abruptly as if she had called for him to halt. He just stood there, waiting as her shoulders relaxed.

"He's a-goin' to get us!" Baby-Paisley wailed in her arms.

Althea looked down at her son in surprise. "It's only Simple Jess. He's not going to hurt us."

The little boy did not appear to be convinced. Althea set him on his feet and motioned Jesse to come forward.

"You startled me," she told him, not willing to explain that her son was afraid of him. "I wasn't expecting anybody on this trail."

Jesse came toward them slowly. He was a huge, almost hulking fellow with powerful shoulders undisguised beneath their covering of butternut homespun. When he was about a yard and a half away he jerked his hat off his head.

"I didn't mean to scare you or the boy," he apologized. "I didn't mean nothing." His eyes lingered overlong on Baby-Paisley as if he hoped to reassure him. "I just wanted to talk to you, Miss Althea, ma'am."

"What about?" she asked.

He appeared, at first, to be hesitant to meet her gaze. Then, as if he'd mustered his courage, he looked straight at her. His eyes were startlingly true blue. And his expression was totally free of perfidy or guile.

"Dogs," he said.

"Dogs?"

"You said you was selling the dogs."

"Paisley's dogs. Yes, I am selling them," she answered.

"I might like to buy one," Jesse said.

Althea was momentarily surprised. "You would?"

"Yes, ma'am, and I got two bits," he said.

"Two bits?"

Jesse nodded solemnly. "A day's work at a man's wages. I unloaded the mule train for Mr. Phillips. He give me two bits and five sticks of that licorice," he said, pointing to the candy still clutched in Baby-Paisley's hand. "It's my favorite."

"It's your favorite," she said. "Honey, share a piece of your candy with Simple Jess."

Baby-Paisley looked up at his mother as if she were a traitor, but dutifully handed over one strip of the sticky sweet candy, snatching his hand back quickly as if he feared the big man might bite it.

"Thank you," Jesse said to him quietly.

She watched as he brought the candy to his mouth. He closed his eyes and took a deep breath as if enthralled with the aroma alone. Ripping off just a little piece of the licorice string with his teeth, he chewed it very slowly as he seemed to focus every bit of his attention upon its sweet taste and texture, savoring it. Althea was momentarily mesmerized. She had never seen anyone show so much pleasure in something so ordinary and simple. It was his favorite.

When he finished his bite and swallowed, he allowed his tongue to run the full length of both his lips, upper and lower, before he turned his attention once more to Althea.

For some unknown reason, gooseflesh skittered up the back of Althea's neck. She hadn't realized that the morning was so cool. She met Jesse's glance for only a moment. There was something almost disconcerting about the depth of honesty in his gaze.

"You want to buy the dogs?" she asked him in a somewhat indulgent but businesslike tone.

"One," Jesse answered her. "I suspect two bits, cash money, oughter buy one."

Althea nodded thoughtfully. Was two bits what she might expect to get for a hound? Truthfully, she didn't know. She had thought to sell them together. The dogs had all been trained together and worked together. She had no idea what their individual value might be. But she really hadn't a price in mind for the pack either. One dollar for the four of them. Jesse, simple that he was, probably knew their value better than she.

Back when her late husband was courting Jesse's sister, the simple man had often borrowed Paisley's dogs to hunt. After his marriage to Althea, her husband had had no use for Jesse or any of the Best family. But she'd never heard

Paisley, or any other man on the mountain, speak poor of
Jesse's hunting skills. He could trap and shoot and run dogs,
though he'd never had any of his own.

Althea wanted to get rid of the dogs. She didn't need
them and selling them off would show everybody on the
mountain that she was pure-dee of her own mind. But she
sure didn't want Oather or Eben or her mother-in-law
or . . . or nearly anybody else to have them. Perhaps Jesse
would be the perfect person to sell them to.

But not for two bits. She needed more than that if she was
going to try to make it through the winter without cash from
a crop.

Althea brought her glance up once more to meet the true
blue eyes of the giant man who stood before her. Simple
Jesse Best was huge, dependable, and work-brittle. And he
was standing silently in front of her, waiting. He wasn't
telling her that she should sell him a dog for two bits. He
wasn't offering her advice on how she should manage her
life. He was waiting for her to tell him what she was going
to do.

Slowly the furrow in Althea's brow softened and a smile
spread across her face.

"Simple Jess, how would you like to own all Paisley's
dogs?" she asked quietly.

He stared at her blankly for a long moment, then
stammered slightly in confusion. "I—I—I would, ma'am,"
he said. "But I ain't got but two bits."

She nodded. "I know how much money you have, Jesse,
and I want you to keep it."

It took a minute for him to understand her words. When
he did, his jaw dropped open. Clearly her words were more
than simply puzzling to Jesse. She felt a momentary need to
comfort him as the young man began scratching his head
uncertainly.

"Miss Althea, I—"

"I want you to work for me, Simple Jess," she said
quickly, excitedly, grinning at him like a giggly young girl.
"I want you to earn that pack of dogs," she said.

"Earn 'em?"

"Yes. You know I didn't put a crop in this year. Winter's coming and I'll need firewood and stores and game."

Jesse nodded. "I suspect that's true."

"You can work for me," she said. "You help to get me ready for this winter and by the first snowfall you'll own a whole pack of the best hunting dogs on this mountain."

CHAPTER 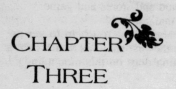 THREE

She didn't know what she'd expected. But Althea Winsloe had not expected Jesse Best to show up on her doorstep before daylight the next morning.

When the first bootstep sounded on the porch, Althea's eyes popped open. The dogs, sleeping under the porch, set up a howl.

Baby-Paisley was asleep up in the loft.

More than that Althea didn't think, she acted. She was out of her warm, cozy bower in one fluid movement. Standing on tiptoes, she jerked the twelve-gauge Winchester from its hooks above the mantelpiece and had it cocked, raised to her shoulder, and pointed at the doorway before she spoke.

"Who's on my porch and what do you want?"

There was one instant of silence. Fear beaded up as sweat on her upper lip.

"It's Jesse. Jesse Best."

A sigh escaped her that wilted her shoulders. She lowered the shotgun, surprised at the furious beating of her own heart. She hadn't realized how frightened she had been.

Quickly she unhooked the drawstring latch that was intended only to keep out critters and would have been little deterrent to intruders.

Jesse stood in the darkened doorway, huge as a bear. All four of Paisley's faithful hounds were on the porch with him, their tongues hanging out and their tails wagging happily. They knew him. They knew him to be friend, not foe.

"What are you doing here in the middle of the night?" she asked. "Has something happened?"

Jesse looked momentarily confused. "It's near dawn, Miss Althea," he said. "I'm here to earn the dogs."

Althea shook her head, disbelieving for a minute before glancing toward the distant eastern horizon. Sure enough, there was a pale silver glimmer in the distance.

"You're an early riser," she said.

"I didn't sleep much," he answered. "I was too excited about the dogs. So I come running at first light. I got special excited out here when I thought you were gonna shoot me."

He indicated the shotgun that Althea still held in her hand. It weighted her arm down as if it were made of lead. She released the hammer from the cock notch and handed it to Jesse.

"Hang this up over the fireplace and I'll get some breakfast started. Be quiet though, I don't want to wake Baby-Paisley."

"I'm awake," a little voice called from the loft ladder on the other side of the room.

"Well you might as well come on down here, then," she told him.

Baby-Paisley looked doubtful, his big eyes following Jesse as he returned the shotgun to its place. "I'll wait 'til he goes 'way."

"Simple Jess is not going·anywhere. He's working for us for a while," she said.

The little boy looked stricken, horrified.

Althea could do nothing about it. She realized that she was still standing in the middle of the room, clad only in her josie. She pulled the top buttons together, and glanced nervously toward Jesse, who was turned away from her. She'd been so frightened, she'd actually met a man at her door in her underclothes. Hastily she walked to the hook on the wall by the bed where her dresses hung. Glancing back, she saw Jesse had stooped to poke the fire and set the morning blaze to popping. She was clumsy as she gathered her workdress and swiftly slipped it over her head.

She chided herself for such foolishness. Simple Jess

was . . . well, he was simple. He probably thought no
more of seeing her than if she were his sister. He wouldn't
know or care what was a dress and what was a josie. She
was decently covered up either way. It wasn't like she'd
invited a *man* into her house when she was half-naked. Jesse
Best wasn't a man, not exactly. He was big, like a man, and
looked like a man, but . . . well, he was something else
entirely.

Althea's hair was wild and she pulled it together tightly at
the back of her head and twisted it up enough to hold it with
one big wooden hairpin.

"Have you broken your fast this morning?" she asked him
as she retrieved her apron from its hanging place on the dry
sink.

Jesse turned to look at her then. "I had some cold pone
and venison jerky," he admitted.

"I suspect it was too early for your sister to fix you a hot
meal," Althea said.

Jesse nodded. "Yes, ma'am. Meggie was still lollin' in the
bed with her man when I left."

His words brought a bright blush to Althea's cheeks. A
vision of bucking bedclothes flashed through her thoughts.
Jesse's sister had married around the same time as she and
Paisley. They had one child already. But that never seemed
enough for menfolk. Like Paisley, he probably wanted to be
making babies all the time.

But Simple Jess wouldn't know anything about that.
Surely, he only meant that his sister still slept. It was
Althea's own wicked mind that imagined lolling before
dawn quite differently.

"I don't mind the cold pone and venison," Jesse said. "My
sister Meggie ain't much of a cook nohow."

Althea smiled at him. "Well, I'm a pretty fair cook
myself," she told him modestly. "If you and Baby-Paisley
will see if those lazy hens have anything for us, I'll fry you
up a breakfast that'll take you all morning to work off."

Jesse smiled at her.

"I doan need no help gatherin' eggs!" Baby-Paisley
shouted angrily.

Althea looked up at her son, surprised. "All right," she said quietly. "You gather the eggs yourself. Simple Jess can feed the hounds. He'd rather do that anyway, I'm sure."

"Yes, ma'am," Jesse answered. With a slight nod to both of them, he hurried outside.

Althea gathered up her big bowl and spoon and commenced mixing flour and soda and water for biscuits. In the distance she could hear Simple Jess calling to the dogs. His voice was deep and sharp with authority. It had a warm, masculine timber. Althea found herself genuinely enjoying the sound of it.

Her son continued making his way down the loft ladder, his expression sullen. She didn't like to see him pouting.

"Baby-Paisley," she asked him, "why are you so rude to Simple Jess?"

"He ain't right in the head, Mama," the little boy told her dramatically. "And he's mean."

Althea began pinching off biscuits into the pot. Her brow furrowed. How much could a little boy like Baby-Paisley understand about simplemindedness? She wasn't at all sure how much she understood herself. Perhaps it was safer to merely discredit his mistaken impressions rather than explain facts she wasn't really sure of.

"That's not true, Baby-Paisley," she said.

"Is too," the little boy insisted. "He's gotta be mean. I'm the man of the house, Mama. I gotta keep you safe. That Simple Jess, the devil stole his mind and now he ain't right in the head."

"Where on earth did you hear such a thing like that?"

"Gobby Weston told me," Baby-Paisley replied. "And Gobby knows everything."

Althea shook her head. She wanted her son to have his little friends. But the bad thing about friends was that they always seemed to know so much more than parents. "Gobby Weston isn't as smart as you think," she corrected him. "The devil doesn't steal anybody's mind. And Simple Jess wouldn't hurt us. He's a nice man. I want *you* to be very *nice* to him. He's going to be here working for us every day until the winter comes."

Baby-Paisley didn't look at all pleased at the prospect. Althea put the oven pot full of biscuits in the ashes at the edge of the fire. She wiped her hands on her apron and reached up to one of the hooks above her head to retrieve the side of bacon that was hanging there.

"Are your bedclothes dry this morning?" she asked.

The little boy's face flamed bright red. "No, Mama," he said very quietly.

Althea suppressed a sigh of disappointment. She smiled brightly at her son, as if it really didn't matter.

"Would you drag them down here for Mama, honey?" she asked as she slapped the bacon onto the sideboard and began to slice it. "It'll just take me a minute to hang them on the line and they'll be dry as a bone by afternoon."

Baby Paisley nodded. His cheeks were still pink with embarrassment as he hurried to bring the evidence of his little accident down the ladder.

Althea turned back to her cooking. The thin, neat slices of bacon she laid lengthwise in the big cast-iron skillet. She refused to get mad at her son about his accidents. She knew he was trying. He hated to wet the bed, but it just kept happening. Althea had even taken to getting him up in the middle of the night and walking him to the hobblebush near the front porch, but it hadn't really helped.

"It just takes time," she assured herself. He was only three and a half. Lots of children still wet the bed at that age. And most of them, she was sure, got a switching for it. She certainly had. And the switching hadn't made things one bit better. She wasn't about to treat her baby the way she'd been treated. Not that she hadn't been loved and cared for. She had. Switching was simply the way bedwetting was handled on the mountain. It was the way things were done—just like young widows with farms remarried in a hurry. The old women were right about a lot of things. But Althea didn't think they were right about either one of these.

Unfortunately, her way with the bedwetting hadn't worked so far either. She sighed. There was something about this problem, this small recurring difficulty, that made her feel that somehow she was not quite as good a mother as she

wanted to be. She was the only parent that Baby-Paisley
would ever have. She had to be very good at it.

Jesse called the dogs by name. Old Poker, Sawtooth,
Runt, and Queenie. He knew their histories. Old Poker was
the daddy of all of them. Daddy *and* granddaddy of Runt.
He was getting pretty old now. One of his back legs
stiffened up on him from time to time. Next time Queenie
came into heat, it'd probably be Sawtooth that gave her
puppies. Course, that wasn't good. Jesse knew that. It
wasn't wrong, exactly, for a sister dog to mate with a
brother dog. It was better to put some new blood in stock,
but it wasn't *wrong* with dogs. With people it was different.
There was lots of rights and wrongs when it came to mating
and people. Jesse didn't know all of the rights and wrongs.
But he did know some of them. And he knew that it was
wrong for a man to see a woman in her josie if she wasn't
his sister or his wife. This morning he'd seen Althea
Winsloe in hers and she was neither.

Jesse closed his eyes and let his mind linger on the
memory. Standing in the doorway with that big shotgun in
her hand, she'd been real pretty. Her hair was down. It was
real long. He hadn't known that. It hung down the front of
her josie and kind of curled around those . . . those big
round places that he tried not to think about. Her . . . her
round places were really round. And they had points on the
end of them. He could see the points through her josie.

Jesse opened his eyes and ran a hand nervously through
his hair. He was getting hard down there again. He'd got
hard that morning in the cabin. He'd kept himself facing the
hearth 'til it eased off, but he'd been hard as a stone. That's
why a man shouldn't see a woman in her josie, because it
made him hard.

Even when he was keeping his gaze on the fire, he could
still smell her, Althea Winsloe. He knew the fragrance of her
anywhere. He recognized it as easily as he did her name. He
could also smell the clover-stuffed bed ticking she'd been
lying on. She'd been lying on that bed wearing nothing but
her josie.

Jesse swallowed. Miss Althea was a nice lady. She hadn't meant to make him feel that way. She probably didn't know nothing about how a man felt. But she smelled so good, and he'd seen her round parts real clear, and he just couldn't help but get hard about it.

Jesse blew a deep breath through his mouth like an overworked mule and turned his attention to the hounds that circled him excitedly. He needed to think about something else. He needed to think about something else right away. It wasn't right for him to be getting hard about Miss Althea. She was nice to him. She was going to let him earn Paisley's dogs. He'd wanted his own dog for so long now. It was like a dream that he might have one. Now Miss Althea said he could have four. And not just any four, the best four on the mountain.

He stooped down and began running his hands along the necks and ears of Old Poker, looking for ticks. Ticks were a nuisance to anybody. They could be deadly to a dog if they lodged in a place he couldn't get to. The old hound liked the attention and stretched leisurely as Jesse searched him over.

"Hey, Sawtooth," he said, crooning a little to the other big male as he sent Old Poker on his way. "Let me check your ears, boy. I ain't gonna hurt you lest I have to."

Sawtooth was a durn good dog. That was Jesse's opinion. He was the one that had faced the bear Jesse'd killed three winters ago. He'd been hardly more than a pup at the time, but he was a good tracker even then. And he was brave, a real brave dog.

For his bravery, the bear had slung Sawtooth against a tree. It should have killed him, but the dog was damn lucky. The tree'd smashed his mouth up pretty good and broken most of his teeth out. But he'd lived. And the bear didn't. That was hunting. You took a risk. If you won, you got to eat and to tell about it for years to come.

The meeting with the bear had given Sawtooth his name. It also gave him a face that seemed to be perpetually in a snarl. But Sawtooth was a good dog. And there was no meanness to his nature, which sometimes happened to a dog

that'd been hurt. He was a strong, brave hunter and Jesse
would be proud to own him.

"Come here, Queenie girl," he called out to the redbone
bitch. She'd kept her distance from him, but came eagerly
when he called her. She licked his hands, obviously tasting
the venison that still lingered. Rolling over on her back, she
let him scratch her tummy.

"Good girl, good girl," he praised her as he used his big
hands to scratch and caress her. She had more than her share
of fleas, but she was free of ticks and her ears and gums
looked healthy.

Runt, who was little more than a puppy, was jealous of
the attention Queenie was getting. He kept pushing his way
next to Jesse. Trying to get Jesse's hands to scratch his own
ears. But Jesse made the excitable pup wait his turn.

"We're going huntin' real soon, girl," he promised Queenie.
"I cain't today, 'cause Miss Althea's got work for me. But
real soon we'll be out there a-chasing." He grinned broadly
down at the dog. "Do you think you can run me down a fox,
Queenie?" he asked. "Yes, I suspect you can. I suspect you
can. I just got to get Pa to go with me and take his gun."

Runt finally got his chance. Jesse petted him as he looked
him over. He was still at that stage where his legs were
longer than he could easily manage and he was too excitable
to be much good at tracking. But he had good lines and good
blood. It would be a pleasure turning him into a hunting
hound.

Jesse let him go and rose to his feet. He glanced around
the homestead, allowing himself the time to take it all in. He
couldn't think as fast as other fellows. But he could figure
things out if he was given enough time. It was a big and fine
place. Maybe the best farm on the mountain. It was familiar
to Jesse. He had been here many times. But not since
Paisley had died. The place had looked better before Paisley
died.

The cabin was on a little bit of a rise and was shaded by
a big broad elm. The rest of the clearing was as near flat as
highlands ever got. Sitting in a dip on the east side of
Marrying Stone Mountain, the ground was low and black

and good for growing. The whole yard was surrounded by a split-rail fence, seven ties high. It was in pretty good repair, but Jesse reminded himself to look it over real careful. A bad fence was bad farming, everybody knew that.

The barn door was closed. Jesse suspected that if Miss Althea hadn't put in a crop, then it was probably just about empty. The cow was roaming freely, ripping at the grass and ignoring the few old hens that scratched around her. She had yet to set up a bellow. Miss Althea must tend to her milking late in the mornings.

The hog pen was pretty clean. The one full-grown hog watched him, snout snugged to the rails. He wasn't puny, but neither was he fine. Still, the hog would have to be scraped and butchered before cold weather set in.

The garden plot was a big one and well kept. Clearly, Miss Althea was good at raising food. Of course, there was nothing much left there this time of year except for a few tomatoes and peppers and a big patch of pumpkins. But Jesse knew with certainty that her root cellar was probably full to bursting with tubers and preserves.

The smokehouse looked deserted. She needed meat. And the hog destined for hanging ham wasn't going to be near enough.

"Yes, we're a-goin' hunting," he said to himself as much as to the dogs. "Rabbits, squirrels, possums, a deer would be nice. Yep. I'd sure like to get Miss Althea a deer."

He glanced back toward the house. It was a broad, sturdy cabin with a wide porch, a real pine floor, and tin shingles. It was a fine house. It was tight and dry and spacious. The best on the mountain. A much better house than the one his own family lived in.

Althea Winsloe was a lucky woman to have such a place. No wonder she'd married Paisley Winsloe.

He hadn't liked Paisley very much. He'd been nice to Jesse back when the fellow had been set on courting his sister Meggie. But mostly he'd been nice to Jesse when nobody but Meggie could see him. When other folks was around, he didn't act like Jesse's friend. Jesse knew what it was like to have a friend. Roe, his brother-in-law, was Jesse's friend.

Maybe it wasn't right to speak ill of the dead, but Jesse thought that Paisley Winsloe was the only friend that Paisley Winsloe had ever had.

Course, maybe Miss Althea had been his friend. They were married and had a baby after all. That was pretty friendly.

Roe said that covering a gal, a gal that was really yours, that it was a really special kind of friendship. Roe knew a lot about that kind of thing. He'd covered some gals back in the Bay State before he'd met up with Meggie. He said that with them others it wasn't too much. But when a man covers a woman that's his wife and that he loves, it was different.

Miss Althea had a baby, so for sure Paisley must have covered her. That's what married people did. And if the noise from Roe and Meggie's bed was any clue, they did it pretty regular. Miss Althea probably thought real friendly of her husband.

In his mind, Jesse could almost smell the sweet, subtle fragrance that was Althea Winsloe, and he remembered again how she'd looked in her josie, so round and womanish and with those points.

She'd been a married woman. She'd probably kissed Paisley and hugged him and let him look at her parts, all her parts. And when he got hard, she'd probably let him put his thing inside her.

Jesse closed his eyes and took a deep breath. He was hard again. And he suddenly hated Paisley Winsloe.

CHAPTER  FOUR

Althea was perfectly dressed, her hair neat and her apron around her waist as she carried the damp bed linens to the clothesline. The sheeting and quilts were no big chore, really. But the clover-stuffed tick was getting more than a little worn from its almost daily airing in the sun.

She draped it all across the cotton clothesline with unthinking precision. All the corners hung exactly even. And she actually took a step backward to assure herself that it was straight before securing the pieces from the breeze with wooden peg pins.

That done, Althea glanced across the homestead clearing. She saw her son, egg basket on his arm, searching out the secret roosts of the old hens. And in the distance she saw Jesse. He'd apparently found the milking gear and had tied Ol' Bessie to the fence. Had she thought of it, she'd have warned Jesse that the old cow was likely to kick. Now it seemed unnecessary. The often cantankerous old cow was standing complacent and unconcerned, chewing her cud, as Jesse, a total stranger, relieved her of her morning milk. Althea smiled, shaking her head in astonishment. Jesse did seem to have a way with animals.

She found herself watching him. His every movement was made with exceptional grace. Her brow furrowed slightly. She'd always thought of him as clumsy and inept. It was an assumption she had made. She thought it to be typical of simplemindedness. But as she watched Jesse from this distance, he was certain and sure. Althea shook her head, somewhat surprised. Just seeing him at work, a person wouldn't know that he was any different from any other man.

She was distracted by her thoughts as her son began hurrying back toward the house as fast as his little legs could carry him.

Determinedly, she swallowed the impulse to call out for him to be careful. He was very likely at any minute to trip and spill his basket. But Althea would much prefer broken eggs to injured pride.

"I foun' lotsa eggs, Mama!" he told her excitedly. "Lots and lots."

He stopped excitedly in front of her. Althea squatted down next to him and peered into his basket.

"That is lots of eggs," she agreed. "Shall we count them?"

He nodded eagerly.

As she touched each one she said the number.

"One."

"One," Baby-Paisley repeated.

"Two," she continued. "Three. Four."

Together they counted, Althea touching each egg as she spoke. When she got to eight, a deep adult voice joined Baby-Paisley's at the repeat.

She and the child both looked up to see Jesse now standing with them. Althea was startled but pleased. She glanced over at her son. His expression could have been accurately described as furious.

"Nine," she said finally, smiling broadly at the little boy. "You found nine eggs this morning, Baby-Paisley. That *is* a lot."

"That's a whole lot," Jesse agreed.

The child looked mutinous. "It's more than you could find," he snarled at Jesse vehemently.

"Baby-Paisley!"

The little boy grabbed up the basket and stomped off to the house.

Althea, stunned and disapproving, gazed after her disrespectful son.

"I apologize, Simple Jess," she said to him. "I don't know what has got into Baby-Paisley."

Jesse shrugged. "That's a whole lot of eggs for those few old hens," he said. "I wouldn't have even looked that long."

She smiled at him, grateful that he didn't take her son's crankiness to heart.

"I guess the chickens knew we were having company for breakfast," she said. "Come on inside. I suspect about half of those eggs were meant for you."

Althea led him to the house. He dutifully brought the milk inside and poured it through the strainer for her before stepping out to wash his hands in the trough.

Baby-Paisley was sitting at the table, silent and belligerent. Althea tilted her head toward him slightly and gave him a hard look.

"Did you wash your hands, Baby-Paisley?" she asked.

"Yep," he answered shortly, holding them up less than an instant for her inspection. "He doan get none of *my* eggs," the boy declared.

Althea's mouth thinned in displeasure. "I'm not proud of the way you talked to Simple Jess," she whispered, hoping the subject of their discussion could not hear. "He's working for us now. You don't have to be afraid of him. He's not going to hurt you."

"I ain' 'fraid of him," Baby-Paisley lied vehemently. "I doan like him and I'm the man of the house."

Althea could hear sounds of Jesse finishing up. "We'll talk about this later," she promised her son ominously.

"Does he have to eat with us?" the boy asked loudly.

"I can eat on the porch," Jesse said from the doorway. "That's what I do when I work for Mr. Phillips. He says that hired men eat on the porch."

Baby-Paisley smiled, victorious, and folded his arms across his chest with satisfaction. Althea was tempted not to wait to talk to him later.

"Absolutely not, Simple Jess," she said. "You come right on in here and take a seat at the table." She gave her son a warning look. "I hope you like biscuits 'cause I've baked up a big batch of them."

"Yes, ma'am," Jesse assured her.

Althea filled two tin plates with thick slices of crisp

cooked side bacon and set one in front of each of the two males now seated at either end of the gingham-covered table.

"You'd best enjoy this last bit of side pork," she told them. "There won't be any more until we butcher that hog."

Baby-Paisley was not concerned. Althea was grateful that her very fortunate little boy knew nothing of going hungry.

"It'll be cool enough to butcher real soon," Jesse said. "I'll ask my pa, he'll know when exactly."

Althea nodded at him. She didn't need Jesse's father to tell her when the time came for hog butchering. But there was no need to mention that to him. He was trying to be a good hired hand. She wouldn't fault him for the effort.

Althea poured a big mug of the warm, fresh milk for each of them. "I'll have these eggs rustled up in a jiffy," she promised them.

Turning toward the fireplace, she pulled the baking pot away from the ashes, lifted the lid, and with her bare hand began jerking the perfectly browned biscuits out and into her apron. She carried them to the table and piled them haphazardly upon the cloth.

"Here's something for you all to start with. Do you want sorghum or preserves, Simple Jess?" she asked as she placed the brown butter crock in front of him.

"Sorghum," he answered.

"What about you, Baby-Paisley?"

The little boy's eyes narrowed. "Preserves," he answered, his little voice full of challenge.

Althea, tamping down her growing exasperation, quickly supplied each with his choice and urged them to make some headway with the biscuits while she stirred up the eggs.

She emptied most of the bacon drippings into the grease crock on the shelf. She cracked six of the eggs into the rest of it and set the skillet inside the hearth. Squatting down next to the blazing coals, she carefully smoothed her skirts away from the flame. The eggs popped and crackled in the grease. She jiggled the frying pan slightly to assure herself that the eggs weren't sticking.

Behind her she could hear an uncomfortable silence,

punctuated only by the occasional plunk of a tin mug against the tablecloth.

Baby-Paisley's fractious behavior was wearing a little bit thin. She was definitely going to have a long talk with that young man and if she didn't get some results, that young fellow was going to be spending some time counting cobwebs in the corner.

When the whites were cooked and the yolks still soft, Althea pulled the skillet away from the flames. She continued to rotate the pan gently as she located a plate. Setting the plate on the table, she eased the circle of eggs onto it.

"Smells mighty good, ma'am," Jesse said. She glanced up to see him eyeing it eagerly. He'd pulled his spoon out of his pocket and was wiping it on the edge of the tablecloth.

"Let's see how it tastes," she said, slicing off four onto his plate.

Jesse didn't wait for further invitation, but took a big bite. Althea watched as he closed his eyes and appreciatively savored the plain breakfast fare.

"My sister Meggie ain't never cooked eggs this good in her life," he said.

Althea smiled, pleased with the compliment. "Your sister is happier at the weaving loom," she said. "I love to cook so it comes easier to me."

"It sure goes easy to my mouth, ma'am," he answered.

Althea watched him eating with such unconcealed enjoyment. She was not the best cook on the mountain, or even the second best, but she was good at it and could turn a tough piece of gamey rabbit into a savory broth. It was something she had worked hard to learn and it was good to be appreciated. It had been a long time since anyone had bothered to acknowledge her effort. Her relatives had always been fairly generous in praise. But she hadn't cooked for Uncle Nez or Aunt Ada for several years. These days the only person who tasted her wares was her son. And Baby-Paisley didn't know there was any other cooking in the world.

Her mother-in-law, Beulah Winsloe, always found fault

with any dish she presented and Orv never disputed his wife.

Paisley had enjoyed her cooking. That was obvious from the tremendous quantities of food he'd consumed. But her husband's idea of a compliment for a good meal was a hearty belch once he had all he'd wanted.

It was good to hear the words aloud. It made her feel . . . it made her feel somehow like cooking was really worth the trouble.

"What are you thinking about?"

The question came from Jesse. She glanced over at him.

"I can see that you're thinking about something," Jesse said.

"Oh." Althea blushed a little at being caught daydreaming. "I was just remembering things from the past. Old things, things that don't matter anymore."

She had intended her words to be light, but somehow as they came out they were not quite so much so. She smiled brightly at the young man to assure him that they were.

Jesse was looking at her closely. His eyes were bright blue and very serious, as if he were studying her. As she gazed into those eyes she saw what she recognized as great depth of feeling and sentiment. It was as if he knew her, really knew her and understood all that was inside. For a moment it was almost as if some pent-up something had burst within her and a flood of feelings threatened to pour out. She stared with almost desperate relief at the clear blue eyes that offered such sweet assuagement. Then she blinked in puzzlement. Just as quickly as it had come, the strange feeling departed as she realized who owned those eyes. Jesse Best, Simple Jesse Best.

"Have another biscuit," she said quickly as she turned from the sight of him at her table. She poked, unnecessarily, at the fire in the hearth. Her hands were trembling. What on earth had come over her?

She turned back to the table, but deliberately focused her attention upon her son. Somehow she couldn't quite look at Jesse. What had she thought she'd seen?

They didn't call him Simple Jess for no purpose. He was

feebleminded, weak in the brain. He could no more know her fears and feelings than he could fly. Getting out of bed so quickly this morning must have made her light-headed. Determinedly, Althea joined the fellows at the table. A good breakfast in her stomach would clear up the giddy fancies in her head, she was certain.

Darkness was almost upon him as Jesse hurried along the ridge toward home. Under the trees it was already black as night, but Jesse had no fear of getting lost. He took a sniff of the air around him. It was scented with pine and forest duff and just a whiff of woodsmoke from Ma Broody's fire. He knew it was Ma Broody's 'cause her place had more than its share of sweetgum trees and the old woman was always trying to use the soggy but aromatic culls for firewood.

The scents of the mountain were all familiar to Jesse. He'd once heard Tuck Trace brag that he could find his way home blindfolded. Jesse hadn't understood why that was a thing to brag about. Anybody ought to be able to do that. Jesse's eyes were sharp as a coon's, but the scent of the trail was always clearer than the sight of it. And while the landmarks could and did often change, the clear, distinct smells of plant, animal, and men remained the same.

Jesse knew this in the same way that he knew how folks sometimes felt. He didn't understand it. His mind was not smart enough to *understand* things, but he could know them nonetheless.

Like he knew that Miss Althea was unhappy. No, maybe unhappy wasn't quite the word, he thought. Miss Althea was lonesome. Not in the sense of being alone. She had Baby-Paisley and her in-laws and any number of folks around her. But maybe it was that she was different from them. Jesse was different, too. Maybe that was why he knew her feelings. He wished he could make it better, but he couldn't, of course. Being different just was. Not a fellow, nor a woman neither, could just stop being different. It was something that just had to be resigned to. Jesse had resigned himself, in most ways. Miss Althea would have to do it, too.

Of course, Jesse didn't know how that was to be done. It

was sort of like going to sleep, he thought. You couldn't make yourself do it and the harder that you tried the less apt you were to succeed. But somehow you'd wake up and realize that you'd been snoring away all night long and not be able to remember how it happened.

Miss Althea would be fine, he assured himself. She was just lonesome. And she had the boy to think of and no man to help her get ready for winter. Jesse'd help her. He wanted to do that, he realized. Even if there were no dogs, he wanted to help Miss Althea.

The clearing was deserted as he came up the path to the small homestead carved out of the steep side of Marrying Stone Mountain. It was not a large place and boasted only a modest poled cabin with a half loft and an add-on in the back. The familiar farm smells of laid-by crops and domestic animals mingled with the scent of woodsmoke and the vague odor of scorched beans. Home. The place where Jesse had lived his entire life.

It was full dark now and the glow of the fireplace spilled bright yellow light through the open doorway and across the porch. Jesse hurried his step as he came closer. From the edge of the porch he could see them all, his family.

Meggie, his sister, bustled nervously around the kitchen. Her face was smudged with flour and her apron splattered with grease as she hurriedly reached into the fireplace to save a pan of half-burnt, half-raw corn bread. Always a notoriously bad cook, marriage and motherhood hadn't improved her abilities. No one in the Best household had ever gone hungry, but there had been plenty of meals when they would have been quite willing to do so.

Onery Best, Jesse's father, sat at the far end of the table watching his daughter's frantic activity with curious acceptance. He was a contented man. A fact that perhaps seemed strange to some. He'd given up his life as an itinerant fiddler a quarter of a century before to become a farmer and father, two occupations for which he was not particularly well suited. But he'd loved his wife and had been loved in return. He apparently had no regret or bitterness at the fate that had left him alone and raising two children for twenty years.

Onery Best was an old man now. What hair he had left was silver as frost on walnut branches. He'd let his beard grow until it hung halfway down his shirtfront. His bad leg was propped up on a stool and wrapped tightly in an elm and vinegar poultice that was pungent enough to overpower the aroma of the dinner just cooked.

To his left sat Jesse's brother-in-law, Roe Farley. Roe had been Jesse's friend before he'd become his sister's husband. And Jesse was proud to call him friend still. Roe was like no one else on the mountain. He came from someplace far away. Roe said that the river at that place was called the Atlantic Ocean and that it was so wide a fellow couldn't see across it on the clearest day in summer.

He was a different-looking fellow than he'd been four years ago. He'd been slim and pale then, and his hands had been as soft as a girl's. Hard work and mountain life had broadened his shoulders, darkened his complexion, and callused his palms. But he seemed happier and stronger for it.

Roe was not much of a farmer, but he was learning and did better this year than last. Roe could do things that lots of farmers couldn't do. When he put his spectacles on his nose, Roe could read faster than most men could think. And he could write down music on paper, not just the words, but the sounds, too. It looked kind of like squash growing on a fence, but it was the sounds of songs. Jesse could make the sounds on his fiddle, but he knew he would never read them or write them.

Kneeling tall in the chair next to Roe was Little Edith, Roe and Meggie's daughter. Her pretty blonde curls were pulled away from her tiny heart-shaped face and temporarily confined to two long plaits at either side of her head. She was very pretty. According to Granny, Edith got the Piggott good looks. Jesse wasn't so sure about that. She really favored her daddy more than his sister Meggie. But Jesse would never dream of contradicting Granny Piggott. When she said a thing was so, it was best just to agree with her and get on with the business of living.

Jesse just stood there for a long minute, staring at the four of them. His family. The people who loved and cared about him more than any in the world. The picture was full and complete even as Jesse looked in on it. Unbidden, a vision of Althea Winsloe's dinner table came to his mind. It was only her and the little boy. The two of them sitting across the table. He with his babyish talk, she with her thoughts by herself. There was something missing in that scene.

Jesse's brow furrowed in thought, but he had no time to ruminate about what it was. Meggie glanced up at that moment and caught sight of him in the doorway.

"It's about time you got home," she said. "Are you going to just stand there or are you gonna come on in to supper?"

"Uncle Jesse!"

Little Edith stood up in her chair and heedlessly threw herself in his direction, knowing that Jesse would catch her, which he did. He hoisted her up high into the air until she brushed the shock of herbs hanging from the rafters and she giggled as the branches tickled her nose.

"I missed you *all* day," she declared as she wrapped her hands around his neck and hugged him tightly. "Nobody stops to play with me when you're not here."

Jesse nodded solemnly. "Then you know how Matilda feels when you leave her in the laundry basket and run off to the yard to play with the chickens," he said.

Edith gave a guilty glance toward the basket where Matilda, a small bundle of rags that bore a vague resemblance to human form, lay carelessly cast.

Little Edith turned back to Jesse and shook her head. "Oh, no, Uncle Jesse," she said. "Matilda likes to be left alone sometimes. She's a sickly child and needs her rest."

Jesse stared at his niece, momentarily puzzled and then his eyes brightened and he smiled broadly. "I never knew Matilda was sickly," he said.

"Oh, yes," Edith answered gravely. "She's got the consumption and some days she can scarce draw a breath."

Onery laughed heartily at his granddaughter's explanation. "Lord Almighty, that girl can tell a tale," he said, slapping his thigh. "Roe, you'd best plant a grove of hickories around this house. You're gonna need switches aplenty 'fore you get that little gal growed and gone."

"Papa don't never switch me," the little girl bragged proudly. "He says that it'd just hurt him and wouldn't do me no good at all."

"Then I might have to take up the task myself," Onery warned.

The little girl giggled as if her grandfather had told a good joke. "No, you won't," she said with certainty. "Besides, it's too late. Granny Piggott says I'm already 'spoiled beyond redemption.'"

"Well, you'd better let your Uncle Jesse sit down to eat his supper," her mother interrupted. "Or I'm likely to spoil your evening by putting you to bed without yours."

Edith and Jesse shared a look that indicated neither believed Meggie's threat. But she did allow Jesse to put her back in her chair. He washed his hands while his plate was being dished up.

"So how was your first day as the hired man, Jesse?" Onery asked.

"There's a lot of work to be done," Jesse said. "The fences and buildings have been let go since Paisley died, I guess. I got a good start on it."

He sat down at his place at the table and pulled his spoon from his pocket. Gazing down at the plate of unappetizing meat and beans before him, Jesse was reminded of the wonderful breakfast and noon meals that he'd been served at Miss Althea's. The memory of that good-tasting food made the fare presented to him even less appealing than usual.

"How about them dogs?" his father asked. "Did you check 'em over good? They might be wormy, ye know. Has she been taking care of 'em fair?"

Jesse nodded. "They look real fine, Pa," he said. "I looked 'em over for ticks and scabs and they're pretty clean."

The old man nodded, pleased. "If you take some copper scrapings from the forge—don't get no iron now, just the copper—put that in the dogs' food and you'll worm 'em better than any potion you'd think to mix up."

Listening obediently, Jesse very deliberately added *cop-*

per scrapings to the mental list of things he was trying to remember.

"What are they going to need for the winter?" Roe asked. "Have you looked the stores over?"

Jesse assured his brother-in-law that he had. Roe had more confidence in Jesse's knowledge than did his father. Perhaps it was because Roe, not knowing a thing about farming himself, had had to depend upon Jesse.

"She's going to need meat," he said. "She's got that one hog to butcher, but it won't feed the both of them if the snows is long."

His father nodded. "The way them squirrels have been hoarding, I don't think old man winter's going to let us off easy this year."

"Well, we'll have to go hunting pretty soon then," Jesse said. "You just tell me the day, Pa, and I'll let Miss Althea know I ain't coming."

The old man sighed heavily. "My leg's about to kill me, but it might loosen up some if I get it out a-romping across the country."

"I could go with him," Roe suggested.

Onery nodded. "When we have to, I'll be counting on you," he said. "But I've a need to wait 'til we have to."

"I'd like to bring her a deer," Jesse said. "I can get her all the rabbits and possoms she can eat with snares. But if you'd let me borrow your gun, Pa, I think I could bring her a deer."

"We could use some venison around this place, too," Meggie stated adamantly.

Her husband looked up at her, teasing laughter in his eyes as he feigned surprise. "I thought that this *was* venison," he said, holding up a haunch of meat.

"That's a pork roast!"

"All your cooking tastes like ambrosia to me, Mrs. Farley," her husband answered.

Laughter flittered all around the table. Even Meggie couldn't hang on to her affronted feelings for more than a minute.

"What else are you going to be doing over at the Winsloe place?" Roe asked.

"They need fuel for the winter," Jesse answered. "That's a real good-sized house. Miss Althea's going to need a lot of wood. She's been burning the brush near the house until it's nearly clean enough to plow. There's not a stick within walking distance on a snowy morning."

"Ain't her in-laws been helpin' her a'tall?" Onery asked.

"I guess not. I'll be going up on the mountain to bring down a tree. Won't be much time for curing, but it'll keep them from freezing."

Roe nodded. "I suspect so."

Jesse glanced up to see his father looking at him speculatively. The old man seemed to be choosing his words.

"What kinder tree you thinkin' to bring down, son?" he asked softly.

Jesse was just ready to dip his spoon into his plate, but stopped in midtask and swallowed nervously. He looked closely at the old man sitting across from him at the table. His father's eyes were loving and accepting, but they were serious. This was a test. Jesse's heart began to hammer.

Onery Best had voiced no complaint when Jesse had announced that he was going to be working for Miss Althea. It left more work on his father and Roe, but there hadn't been even a whisper of complaint about Jesse's decision.

But it was not that his father lacked interest. He allowed his son as much freedom as Jesse chose to take. Still there were times when he questioned his son's ability. That time was now.

Onery was worried that Jesse would make a mistake, a mistake that might hurt him and somebody else. Jesse's palms were sweating. He worried, too.

He swallowed the lump of fear that had settled in his throat.

"I'd need to get a tree that'd burn pretty clean," he said.

A long, thoughtful pause followed. His family waited patiently.

"Don't want to get nothing that's soggy or sappy," he

continued. "The wood should have a smooth grain that would split easy."

He glanced toward his father for assurance. The old man nodded.

"A red oak'd be good," Jesse said. "If it was close to another tree and neither could get a good spread going. It'd be a shame to waste a red oak otherwise."

"That's the truth," his father agreed. "But what if you can't find no red oak in close quarters?"

"Then I'd fell a hackberry," Jesse answered. "It burns near as clean as the oak, splits easy, and don't make nothing better than firewood."

Onery Best gave his son a big approving smile. "Eat up, boy," he said. "A man what earns his own living needs to get plenty of vittles in him."

CHAPTER
FIVE

The heat from the fire of the big black wash pot popped sweat out on Althea's brow. Her arms ached from the constant stirring of the wooden wash paddle. Wringing out the dripping garments and hanging them to dry was no easier. Wednesday/washday was her busiest of the week and offered some of her hardest tasks. But she didn't mind it, really. In fact, lately the workdays seemed to go faster than expected for Althea.

It was strange, the mere fact that there was another person at the place made day-to-day progress and accomplishments seem bigger and better. Truly, it surprised her that his presence was so unobtrusive. It was not as if she pretended he was not there. She was very aware of him. Too much aware. The thought came to her and she pushed it away quickly, not willing to even give it a perusal.

The last of the wash, the bedclothes, were gently boiling and the fire going low. Althea glanced up from her laundry kettle to check on her son.

Baby-Paisley was playing with the chickens. Henry, the old rooster, was now sporting a bandanna around his neck and from the shape of the stick the little boy held in his hand, Althea speculated that the old bird had just robbed a train or busted into a bank. Her son was gallantly bringing the cock to justice. She smiled. Soon enough the responsibility for this farm would be his. She wanted him to enjoy his little boy days as long as they would last.

With a light heart she let her gaze roam the homestead for a moment until she stopped to watch Simple Jess. He was over in the fallow cornfield near the house. She hadn't had an idea about putting in a crop last year. Orv and Tom had offered to do it for her. But she'd turned them down flat. As she'd turned down all their offers for assistance. She hadn't wanted their favors. She hadn't wanted their presence. It was funny that having Jesse there wasn't intrusive at all.

Except, of course, for Baby-Paisley. That child was determined to dislike Jesse and disagree and dispute every word that came out of his mouth. Of course it was hard for the little fellow, she thought. Baby-Paisley was used to adults who knew things and could be depended upon. It must be a little threatening to see a grown man whose mind was not whole. The brain-weakened were peculiar and different, almost as if they were always strangers.

Jesse was familiar, and yet he was not. He looked like the Piggotts, but he might as well have been from another mountain entirely for as well as he was known.

What did she even know about him? Althea thought quietly for a moment. She knew about *his kind*, but what did she really know about him. The feebleminded could not think. Everyone understood that. But she knew that Jesse did think. She often watched his brow furrow as he did it. The feebleminded were only oversized children; little boys in the bodies of men, that's what folks said. And yet there was nothing about Jesse Best that made one think of him as a child. It was all strange and confusing. How much more so must it be to her son? There was no way that Althea could *explain* Jesse to Baby-Paisley. She couldn't quite grasp it herself.

With a sigh, she leaned against the wash paddle and watched the ripples of strength in an endless rhythm, as Jesse moved the big long scythe back and forth, cutting the withered old cornstalks and the tall grass that had grown up around them. The field would look much better cleaned up, she thought. She'd thought several times to clean it up last spring. It was the first thing a person saw when they reached the homestead and its neglect gave a bad impression to any who passed this way. She'd decided to let it go, however.

She didn't care much what people thought and the ground would be covered with snow soon enough.

Immediately her thoughts came together and she realized the futility of Jesse's effort. She sighed loudly and shook her head. Jesse was wasting his time cleaning up the field when there were important things that had to be done. She needed firewood and she needed her hog butchered. And her hired hand was employing himself with a useless task.

She fought back her annoyance. Of course she couldn't expect Jesse to know what had to be done and when to do it. He was simple. It was her task to tell him what to do and see that he did it. He might look like a strong, dependable man. A person might forget that his silence was not thoughtfulness. But he was, after all, simple.

Determinedly she set her laundry paddle aside and began walking out to the field. She'd need to keep a closer eye on him and set out his tasks each morning at breakfast. She didn't know what she'd been thinking of, just letting him decide what ought to be done. He had a strong back and a willingness to work. Those things, however, would be wasted if he didn't receive the proper guidance and direction.

"Jesse!" she called out to him. "Jesse, come here."

His scythe stopped in midmotion and he turned toward her curiously. He braced the heavy tool upon his shoulder as if it were no more than a cane rake and headed toward her. He moved easily, with strength and grace unexpected in such a large man. He was smiling at her. Glad to see her. It was a beautiful smile. A smile that made one apt to forget that he was no ordinary man.

The heat of the day was on him and his cotton homespun shirt clung to the thickness of his muscled chest. Slightly disconcerted by the sight, Althea determinedly forced her gaze up to his bright blue eyes that looked down on her inquiringly.

"Jesse," she said firmly. "It's foolishness for you to waste your time cleaning up this field." She heard the strident tone in her voice and deliberately tried to moderate it. She wasn't angry at him. And she didn't want him to think that she was.

"All of the grass and brush in this field will be covered in snow in another month and no one will even be able to see it."

"Yes, Miss Althea," he agreed, nodding. Clearly he did not understand the meaning of her words.

"There is plenty of *real* work that needs to be done, Jesse. And I've hired you to do that work."

"Yes, Miss Althea. You're trading the dogs for my work," he said.

"Yes, I'm trading you the dogs. But I need real work, Jesse. Work that will help me."

"Yes, Miss Althea."

"You see, Jesse," she said, remembering to speak to him slowly and softly, hoping that he would be able to understand, "I'll need winter meat stores and firewood. Those are things that I can't get for myself. I'm counting on you for those things, Jesse. That's why I've offered to trade you my dogs."

"Yes, Miss Althea."

"So you should be gathering up wood and splitting it," she told him. "Or building the butchering platform for that hog."

He nodded. "I'm going to fell a tree for you, Miss Althea," he said. "There ain't enough brush around here to do you for the winter. I picked out a good-sized hackberry up on the far ridge for you this morning. I thought I'd wait until next week to cut it down. Most of the leaves ought to be off of it by then and it'll be less trouble to drag down the mountain."

"Oh," Althea said, startled. "That sounds like a good idea. That sounds like a very good idea. A whole tree? That's a lot of firewood."

He nodded in agreement. "And you may need it if the winter turns out to be a bad one," he said.

"Yes, I suppose that's true," she admitted. "Now about the hog—"

"I was wanting to ask you about that," he admitted, interrupting.

"We *will* need to butcher the hog. You were right to ask,"

she said. "I know you are probably fond of the animal, but it was raised to put meat on the table."

Jesse's brow furrowed in puzzlement. "What I was thinking to ask, Miss Althea, was if I could bring my family's hogs over here and we could butcher them all together."

Althea's eyes widened.

"Butcher them all together?"

"I know you don't like folks about much," he said, surprising her with his perception. "But it takes lots of lumber and time to build up a butchering platform and it seems kind of like double work to build one here and another at our place. Besides, it's heavy work, ma'am, dipping a hog. I don't expect we could do it by ourselves. If you're willing, Miss Althea, I could just drive our hogs over here and we could do everybody's butchering all in one day."

"Yes, well that sounds like a good idea," she said thoughtfully. "It is a lot of work for just one hog. In fact, since I only have the one, perhaps it would be better if you just drove it over to your place."

"I thought of that," Jesse said, leaning slightly closer as if relating a confidence. "But truth to tell, Miss Althea, if we butcher at our house, well—" He hesitated. "If we butcher at our house the sausage making will be done in my sister Meggie's kitchen. If it's her kitchen, Miss Althea, that means she'll kind of be the boss, if you know what I mean."

Althea did know what he meant and indicated her agreement.

"I was thinking," he went on. "That if we butchered the hogs here, why you would be sort of taking charge. I love my sister, Miss Althea, but I'm betting your sausage tastes ten times better than any she could put up."

Jesse's expression was so sincere and so much the truth, Althea found herself laughing out loud.

"What a thing to say, Jesse!"

"I'm not just thinking of myself," he assured her. "Pa and Roe and me, we're used to Meggie's cooking and we don't mind it so much. But you and the boy'd be hard-pressed to eat her recipe all winter."

Althea shook her head in delighted disbelief. "I would be pleased to fix the sausage," she told him, genuinely enchanted at the unexpected, backward, and mostly upside-down compliment. "And I'm glad that you've been thinking about meat for our winter."

Jesse's expression turned solemn once more. "Of course," he said. "This one hog won't be enough for the whole winter. I've got snares out for small game. And as soon as Pa's feeling up to it, me and the dogs'll be taking his gun out to try to get you something bigger."

"Why, you needn't wait on your father's good health, Jesse. You can take Paisley's gun if you'd like," she told him.

Jesse's eyes widened. "I could?"

"You hunt with your father's gun, don't you?"

"Yes, Miss Althea," he said.

"You are careful and safe with it, aren't you?"

"Yes, Miss Althea."

"Then you might as well take Paisley's. It could probably use a good cleaning. It's not doing anyone any good over the fireplace."

Jesse smiled at her. It was a broad welcome smile. It was the kind of smile that could make a woman forget that he was simple, not just a handsome, teasing man. "It's good for keeping strangers off the porch," he said.

Althea gazed at him curiously for a moment and then realized that he was making a joke about his first morning at work. She laughed, strangely embarrassed at being reminded of her foolishness and dishabille.

Unconsciously she checked the top button on her blouse to assure herself that it was decently closed. She cleared her throat unnecessarily.

"You are welcome to use the Winchester to hunt game," she said. "But I don't want you wasting any more time here in this field. There is no purpose in cleaning it up. So move along now."

Jesse hesitated.

"Come on now, Jesse," she said. "I suppose you can start cleaning up the smokehouse. There really is no sense in spending more time on this."

Still he hesitated.

"Jesse."

"What about the cow?"

"The cow?"

"What are you going to feed her this winter?" he asked. "There's no hay in the barn and no corn in the crib."

Althea's brow furrowed.

"I thought if I'd cut all the fields as close as is safe for the ground, it might give us enough to keep her fresh through the cold weather." He gestured toward the field around him. "Like you said, it'll all be covered up in snow pretty soon and that cow won't be able to get at it. If I cut it and stack it right, she'll have something to chew on at least. It ain't alfalfa or clover, Miss Althea, but it's grass and I suspect Ol' Bessie will be glad to have it once the ground's covered."

Althea stared at Jesse for a long moment. "I forgot about the cow," she said. Her tone was one of near disbelief. "I forgot about the cow completely."

Jesse nodded with solemn understanding. "That happens to me sometimes, Miss Althea. I have to say things over and over to myself so that I don't forget them."

"You go ahead and cut the grass, Jesse," she said.

"It won't take me but a couple more days to get all of it if the weather holds," he assured her. "Then I'll be felling the tree and cleaning the smokehouse and everything that you're thinking I should do."

"Yes, yes, I'm sure you will, Jesse," she said.

He was smiling at her still. That smile was so genuine and there was nothing feeble or weak-minded in it. His teeth were gleaming white and dimples shone in each of his cheeks, but it was his eyes, his bright blue eyes with their innocent warmth and crinkled corners that held her attention.

"Thank you, Jesse. Thank you very much," she said quietly.

"You are welcome, Miss Althea."

They just stood there across the fence from each other, silent and staring at each other. Althea felt strangely disoriented, as if she were taking sick or losing her balance. Jesse just continued to smile.

Something captured his eye and he looked away. Althea continued to graze at him, observing the perfect curve of his jaw and the bristly blond stubble upon his cheek.

He glanced back at her and hesitated, stopping to look guiltily down at his feet, and then spoke again.

"I don't like to tattle, Miss Althea," he said quietly. "But I think I need to say something."

"What?"

His smile was gone now, his tone one of sincere confession. "Your boy done chased that rooster into the pigsty and he's covered in hog wallow up to his eyebrows."

"What!"

Althea turned immediately to see her son cheerfully cavorting in the stinking mud of the pigpen.

"Baby-Paisley Winsloe! You get out of there this instant!"

Eben Baxley rolled out from beneath the porch overhang at Phillips Store. He knelt in the damp grass for a long moment and held his head in his hands as he cursed the daylight that seemed to stab like a knife through his head. He'd promised himself that he'd drink less and think more, but the previous evening he'd reneged on his pledge.

"Mornin'."

The word itself was a disagreeable sound. Eben glanced accusingly in the direction of the porch to see who dared to utter it.

Old Pigg Broody sat on a barrel, chewing a mouthful of tobacco and squinting slightly to more closely observe him. Being the object of such scrutiny did not sit well with Baxley.

"You get an eyeful, old man?"

Broody chuckled, too broad-minded to be offended and too old to be scared. "Yep, I seen worse, boy. But you do look like you got the stuffin' beat outer ye."

"You should see the other guy," Eben growled.

Pigg laughed out loud at that. "Ain't nobody seen him. His daddy says he's too beat to get out of the bed. But then that boy weren't much of a scrapper even as a pup. It's a good thing he's taken to reading the law. He's not one that could make justice with his fists."

Eben didn't bother to dispute the old man's words. Oather Phillips didn't have much of a reputation for fighting, but the fellow'd been downright mad last night and Eben had been downright drunk. That was a mix guaranteed to cause an indecent share of bruises and pains.

The taste in Eben's mouth was foul as he half crawled, half stumbled to the well. The creaking lines as he lowered the bucket sounded as loud in his ears as shotgun blasts.

Damn, he didn't want to drink anymore. He was sick to death of it. And just as surely as his mother's naggings to him, drink was to be the death of him, just like his daddy, if he kept it up.

He moaned as he pulled the water-filled bucket back to the surface. His arms ached. His thighs ached. He winced at a stabbing pain in his shoulder. Everything hurt. And he'd been the victor.

He unhooked the water bucket from the pulley and set it on the ground next to the well. He knelt before it momentarily, like a penitent, and then plunged his head beneath the surface. As he straightened he slung water in every direction, but his eyes were wide open now and he felt revived. Gingerly he felt the lines of his facial bones. Oather didn't have much of a punch, but he'd been relentless. Nothing broken, but Eben did feel like the living devil.

He was pressing a tender lip when he felt an unexpected jab from the inside of his mouth. His eyes widening, he checked his front teeth.

"Hell's fire and damnation!" he cursed. Peering anxiously down into the bucket of water, he checked his reflection. He couldn't see for sure, but it felt like half his right front tooth was missing. What remained was like a jagged saw. Eben jumped to his feet immediately.

"You got a glass, old man?" he called out to Broody. "You got a looking glass?"

The old man took the time to send a half jaw of amber spittle unerringly off the edge of the porch.

"Sure ain't," he answered. "When you get my age, young feller, you avoid them dang things like the plague."

Testing the rough edge of his tooth once more, Eben cursed vividly. Without another thought he hurried up to the store and took the porch steps two at a time.

His welcome there was uncertain and the pounding in his head relentless; still, he stomped through the open doorway without hesitation.

"Phillips!" he called without ceremony. "You got a looking glass?"

The storekeeper looked up from his book work, his expression far from pleased.

"You got your nerve showing your face in here today, boy," he said. "Oather's mama claims the boy's got two broke ribs. He can't even rise from his bed."

"He started it," Eben shot back. "You shoulda taught your boy better than to take on a feller half again his size and with more than twice his reputation."

"What in the devil were you two fighting about?" the man demanded. "Althea Winsloe?"

Eben didn't answer.

"It's not as if the gal is his or your intended. The woman ain't said who she's willing to marry. There's nothing to come to blows about."

"And there won't never be," Eben counted. "You think any woman'd choose Oather over me?"

The effect of the sneer he attempted was somewhat marred by the bruises on his face. At that moment Eben spotted the looking glass and hurried over to it.

Putting his mouth as close to the glass as he could manage, he raised his swollen upper lip out of the way to assess the damage.

"He marked me!" Eben exclaimed with furious disbelief. "I can't believe Oather Phillips has marked me for life. There's a corner broke off my front tooth sure as the world."

Phillips snorted almost proudly. "So I guess you'll think again before messing with my boy," he said.

Phillips smiled as if he took pleasure at the thought of his son involved in violent fisticuffs. As his attention returned to the present, he shook his head over the mess of cuts and bruises that covered Baxley's face. "He sure banged you up. What in the devil did you do to make that boy come at you like that?"

Eben didn't answer, but turned his attention back to the mirror. It didn't really look as bad as he feared. It felt like he'd lost half a tooth, but it was really just a corner chip. Not enough to spoil his looks. And Eben Baxley was rightly proud of his looks. Even this morning, beaten and battered, he was a handsome fellow. He was tall and a little more slim than was strictly necessary. But working and fighting had insured that his shoulders were sufficiently broad and his arms well muscled. His hair was thick and dark, the color of chestnuts, with just a bit of childhood curl left in it, enough to keep one dangling forelock carelessly drawing attention to his attractive face. Women in Eben Baxley's life twirled around his finger as easily as did that forelock.

Since the days he'd been "Mama's pretty boy," women had been important. His mother made all the rules, set all the standards, and said all that would be done. His father, often drunk and sloven in self-pity before he died, meant nothing to Eben. Nothing except an example of what kind of man not to be. Eben was strong, decisive, confident. It was a purposeful thing with him. And women were always drawn to that. He could walk into any dance hall between here and Calico Rock and know that sooner or later he could be pleating the petticoats of any woman present.

"Ouch!" Eben winced as he unintentionally broke open the new scabs on his knuckles. "Damn this. Phillips, you got any salve in this place?"

The storekeeper pointed to the shelf behind him. "It's a penny a tin. You got money, boy?"

"I got money," Eben answered. "But ain't it usual for an injured man to be treated with hospitality?"

Phillips huffed. "Buy the medicine with cash money and the hospitality will come along in due time."

With cold reluctance, Eben tossed a penny on the counter.

"A fellow'd hate to be broke and close to death in this place," he said sarcastically.

Phillips ignored the jibe and picked up the penny. He set the tin of salve on the counter beside Eben and then leaned backward to call out to the room behind them.

"Mavis! Come doctor this fellow!"

Eben blanched.

"I can tend myself," he said quickly.

"Mavis'll tend you," Phillips answered.

"I don't need her. I can do it myself."

"You talking bad about my hospitality," Phillips told him. "I won't have you going around saying I wouldn't send my wife or daughter to ye when ye had need."

Eben had no time to reply as Mavis Phillips stepped across the threshold that separated the storeroom from the Phillips's place of business. She looked straight at Eben. She looked at him hard. There was no evasiveness in her gaze, no coy lowering of her eyelids.

Momentarily taken aback, Eden faced her temerariously. Then a cynical smile took over his expression and his glance became sultry.

"Why if it isn't Miss Mavis Phillips, the prettiest little redheaded gal on this mountain."

Mavis held her chin high and her face devoid of any inkling of her thoughts as she moved toward him.

"What do you need, Mr. Baxley?"

Eben's smile became downright lecherous as he glanced toward Phillips, then leaned closer not to be overhead. "I believe, Miss Mavis, that you already know more about what a feller *needs* than a single woman ought."

He watched, satisfied, as she swallowed nervously and two bright spots of color appeared on her cheeks.

"Got my knuckles all cut up," he said more loudly. "Seems like I accidentally run into some young fool's face."

Her hands trembled as she fumbled with the lid on the tin of salve.

"Been a good long while since I seen you, Mavis," he whispered, deliberately moving closer to her. "Course, the last time I seen ye, I seen a lot."

The lid on the salve clattered noisily upon the counter.

She grabbed his right wrist before dipping two of her fingers into the rather vile-smelling yellow medicine and slapping it roughly onto his hand. Eben winced.

"Damn, woman!" he cursed. "But then you never did have much of a gentle touch. You left scratches on my back I could feel for a week."

"What are you doing here?" she demanded in a whisper between clenched teeth. "You promised to stay away."

"And I have, sugartail," he answered. "I've stayed away four long years. But I can't stay gone no longer. Haven't you heard? I'm getting married and going to live right here on this mountain."

"Don't you do it," she said, her tone threatening. "If you do I'll—"

"You'll what?" he asked. "Confess all?" He shook his head, disbelieving. "You already done that with your dear brother Oather and he cain't even get out of his bed this morning. Are you wanting me to whip your poor old daddy, too?"

She raised her chin higher, prouder. "My mama's a Piggott," Mavis reminded him. "The whole family would take up arms against you if I just spoke the word."

"And my mother's a McNees," he answered, unconcerned. "Are you thinking to start up a feud, Mavis? Is that what you want? You've heard about feuds, ain't you? Whole mountains of good, decent folks end up dead over some falling out. Is that what you want, a bunch of folks dead? Dead over your *honor*?"

Mavis blanched.

"What your honor wants is me dead, Mavis," he told her, his eyes as cold as a mountain winter. "But I'm not dying, sugartail, and I'm not giving up this chance to have my own farm here on the mountain."

"You've got no shame, Eben Baxley," she hissed. "You've got no shame at all."

"I've got shame," he answered. "If I'd a raped you, I'd be real shamed. I might be shamed enough to stay away from here. I might even be ashamed enough to let your daddy kill me. But it wasn't rape now, was it, Mavis?"

"I hate you," she said.

"Sugartail, you hate yourself," he told her. "It's time you acknowledged the corn. There's none to blame here but yourself. You made gravy before the meat was cooked. You ain't the first woman to do it and won't be the last, but it's done and for good." He chuckled without humor and shook his head. "Didn't your mama warn you about rollicking with men that never made you no promise?"

"I thought—"

"You thought if you gave it to me, I'd offer for you. That's what you thought and I know it. But I'm not *obliged* to do that, sugartail, not for you, nor any other woman that I've beat down the grass with. And I've got no such intention of marrying you, Mavis Phillips."

She shuddered. It was an involuntary movement, but he watched her struggle against it. He looked at her closely. Were there tears in her eyes? If there were she managed to hold fast against them. He wanted her to cry. He wanted her to cry and beg and plead. He wanted to leave her on her knees.

"I don't see what you've cause to complain about," he continued cruelly. "You got a pure-dee rollix off me and you admitted right out how much you liked it. It ain't like I didn't leave you with no prospects. Poor ol' Widow Plum is of an age to retire, I'm thinking. This mountain'll be needing a new, young whore and I can testify that you'd make a good one."

A tiny cry escaped her then and he looked at her. Her pretty mouth was opened in horror and he was sure that those sweet blue eyes he still saw in his dreams were darkened with tears.

On target. He'd wounded. Victorious, he stepped back and examined the greasy mess that now swatched his knuckles.

"Why, thank you, Miss Mavis," he said loudly. "This is as fine a nursing job as any I've ever had."

He turned toward the still preoccupied storekeeper busily

assessing his books across the room. "I tell you, there is something about a woman's touch that just heals a man. Don't you agree, Mr. Phillips?" he asked. "Don't you agree that the touch of a woman is kind of like a miracle?"

The old man grunted with unconcern.

Eben laughed in a way that sounded more angry than amused.

"You tell Oather that I'm sorry he's laid up in bed today. I'll be heading up to my cousin Paisley's place to see if I can offer comfort to his widow," he said. "Maybe I can get me a miracle there, too."

He turned back to Mavis behind the counter.

"It's been a real pleasure to see you again, sugartail," he whispered.

"Lord, ain't she just the prettiest little redheaded gal I ever saw," he called out to the storekeeper. "It's a wonder that you ain't got her married up already, Phillips. Cain't she find no one man to set her heart on?"

The storekeeper shrugged. "Not none that she tells me," he said.

Eben chuckled unkindly, his gaze still upon Mavis. "Women do keep their little secrets, don't they?"

CHAPTER
SIX

He'd caught two rabbits and a possum in his snares. Jesse was busy at the back of the smokehouse scraping the meat from the hide. He was happy. Miss Althea had been pleased that he'd gotten all the tall grass cut, stacked, and covered, and she'd been impressed with his catch of the day. He'd be bringing her a deer, he promised himself. If two rabbits and a possum could make her so excited, a big haunch of venison on the hoof would probably thrill her near to death.

The cool crisp scent of fall was in his nostrils and the bright colors of turning trees were all around him. His belly was full and Miss Althea had smiled at him. Yes, Jesse was happy. He couldn't resist humming a tune. As the old words came to his mind, he began to sing, the meaning of the verse as obscure as the rhyming sounds within it.

> "My gal lives at the head of the holler,
> Hi di rinktum diddle dum a day;
> She won't come and I won't foller,
> Hi di rinktum diddle dum a day;
> Geese in the pond and ducks on the ocean,
> Hi di rinktum diddle dum a day;
> Devil's in the women when they take a notion,
> Hi di rinktum diddle dum a day!"

"That's the God's truth if ever I heard it."

The unfamiliar voice startled Jesse and he jerked his chin up quickly to face the intruder, his hand gripping the scraping knife in a defensive manner.

The fellow who'd come walking upwind of him was leaning against the broad trunk of an old elm tree as if he owned the place. He smiled very deliberately at Jesse and spoke with intentional friendliness.

"Good morning, Simple Jess." The fellow glanced up to the sky and gave a rather carefree laugh as he reconsidered. "Well, I suppose that it's afternoon already. The day kind of gets away from a feller when he wakes up late, I guess."

Jesse made no comment on the time of day or the attempt at humor.

The man straightened up and took a step forward. He was dressed up good enough for Sunday. His trousers were city-made black duck and were held up with real elastic web suspenders. He hadn't bothered to put a collar on his blue striped shirt, yet he was slicked up and starched and looked as fine as a hair tonic peddler at a family reunion.

"I don't expect you remember me," he said, folding his arms across his chest and staring down at Jesse.

Rising to his feet, Jesse still clutched the knife in his hand, but the tension in him had eased.

"I know who you are," he said. "You're Eben Baxley, cousin to Paisley Winsloe."

Eben raised an eyebrow in appreciation. "Why, that's exactly right, Simple Jess. Very good."

There was something about the way the words sounded to Jesse's ears that made him think it wasn't quite praise at all.

"I seen you at Miss Althea's wedding," Jesse told him. "You was real drunk at the time."

The man's eyes narrowed and he cleared his throat. Jesse continued.

"Ain't seen you around here since."

"I haven't been around here," he said. "I didn't have no reason 'til now. I come to see Althea Winsloe."

The man glanced past Jesse toward the house. Something tightened in Jesse's chest. The need to protect came upon him as instinctual and unlearned as hunger or thirst.

"How is the lovely widow today?" Eben asked.

This was Miss Althea's baking day. By now she must

have the last loaves in the oven and she'd be letting the fire wane.

They'd eaten the nooning over an hour before. Fried catfish and hot bread. Heaven. And Miss Althea sitting across from him at the table, smiling and talking. Heaven again.

Jesse glanced with concern once more at the house behind him in the distance. He knew as if he could see it himself that inside there, Miss Althea—smelling of yeast and looking young and bright as sunshine—would be tiptoeing about her chores. Baby-Paisley would be napping as usual on Miss Althea's bed and she'd be busy with the quiet chores of the household.

"She's up to the house?" Baxley asked.

Jesse didn't answer. This man was Paisley's kin. Jesse knew that. Kin wouldn't hurt kin. Jesse knew that, too. But somehow Jesse sensed a threat from this man. He sensed a threat and he'd die, bloody and maimed, before he'd let anyone hurt Miss Althea.

"What do you want around here?" Jesse asked, nearly snarling the words.

Baxley's eyes widened in surprise. His jaw hardened and his expression turned belligerent.

"That's a question that should more likely be put to you than me," he said. "What are you doing around here, Simple Jess?"

"I work for Miss Althea," he said.

"*Miss* Althea?" Eben's features softened as he apparently found Jesse's words amusing. "She's been Mrs. Winsloe for four years, but I suspect a fellow like you don't know the difference."

Jesse did know that she was Mrs. Winsloe because she was married, but he didn't bother to explain himself. He'd always called her Miss Althea and she'd never complained a word about it. Just because a woman got married didn't mean that she became somebody else. Maybe when she got old like Granny Piggott, or got real fat like Beulah Winsloe, he might call her something else. Still, she'd always smell like Miss Althea, so it wasn't like she would ever be another person.

Eben gestured toward the gutted animals at Jesse's feet. He'd just begun skinning the possum. The rabbits lay off to the side.

"Did you get that meat with squirrel shot?"

"Snares," Jesse answered.

Baxley shook his head. "Snares take too much time, boy. I've not got the patience for them."

Jesse wasn't a boy, he was a man. For a minute he thought to tell the intruder just that. But he didn't. Baxley's opinion didn't matter to him all that much. He knew Eben to be a lazy hunter. When he used to come looking for game with his cousin Paisley, the two spent more time drinking down donk than pressing the dogs.

"Snares are clean and quick," Jesse told him. "I save the gun for real game."

"You got your own gun now, Simple Jess?" He sounded surprised.

Jesse felt the flush of embarrassment in his cheeks. He wanted his own gun. Like owning his own dogs, it had been a long-time ambition. But for now, it was still something in his future.

"Miss Althea's going to let me use Paisley's Winchester," he said proudly. "I usually hunt with my pa's but she says I can use his."

Eben Baxley's brow furrowed and then, to Jesse's puzzlement, he shook his head.

"No, I don't think so, Jess," he said.

"You don't think what?"

"I don't think you should be using Paisley's gun," Eben answered.

"I been hunting for years," Jesse told him. "I ain't going to hurt myself."

Baxley chuckled. "I wasn't worried about you," he said. "I'm thinking about that gun, boy. It's a fine Winchester and I don't want you fooling with it, maybe fouling it."

Jesse wanted to protest, but the words jumbled in his mind. He was not about to foul the gun. He knew about guns. He was very careful. He'd memorized what to do. When he carried the gun he never let his mind wander. He recited the rules to himself over and over.

Jesse sputtered momentarily and then managed to protest. "Miss Althea said!"

Eben took a step forward and patted Jesse on the shoulder. "I know she did, boy. And I'm real sorry that she got your hopes up like that. You see, Simple Jess," he said, feigning friendship, "I'm marrying up with your 'Miss Althea.' You know what that means, don't you?"

Jesse was stunned momentarily.

"Of course I know what marrying up means," he declared. "It means you live with a gal and sleep with her and get babies on her."

Eben Baxley grinned broadly. "Yep, it means that. It also means that all that she owns, I'll own. That makes the gun mine. And I don't want you taking *my* gun hunting."

"You're bespoken for Miss Althea?" Jesse shook his head in disbelief.

"Yes."

"She didn't say nothing about it."

"That's because I haven't declared for her yet. A fellow has got to do the proper thing and ask the question before the woman goes to confiding it about. I just come to the mountain last night. I'm here to do my declaring today."

Jesse felt a strange hollowness inside him. It was like a bellyache, but not exactly. It was an emptiness, the vastness of which made him feel like he wanted to cry.

Men don't cry, he reminded himself quickly. *Jesse is a man. Men don't cry. Jesse doesn't cry.*

He looked back toward Baxley. The man continued to stand before him. His stance was somehow almost threatening, almost belligerent.

"I won't take the gun if you say it's yours," Jesse told him. "I'm used to my pa's anyway."

"That's good, Jess," Eben said. "Just remember that everything on this farm is going to be mine. I don't want you taking anything."

Jesse almost nodded his assent when a thought occurred to him and he raised his chin in challenge.

"But the dogs is mine," he said. "She already give me them. That's why I'm working here, to earn the dogs."

Eben nodded. "That's what I heard." He chuckled out loud. "Lord, leave it to a woman not to know the value of the best pack of hounds on the mountain."

He slapped Jesse upon the back, another friendly gesture that didn't quite ring true,

"I know she made you a bargain, Simple Jess. And you accepted it in good faith. A man can't fault you for that. I'm willing to honor it. You ask any man within a hundred miles of here and he'll tell you that I'm as good as my word. So, Jess, you look them dogs over real good and pick out the one you want. One dog oughter be enough for you, don't you think? You pick out the one you want and I'll give it to you."

"She said I was earning the whole pack."

"Yes, but she thought you'd be working here for a long time. Mrs. Winsloe didn't realize how soon I'd be ready to get wed. Now don't worry, Jess. You'll get your dog. Whichever one you want. And you won't have to be working here much longer to get him."

Jesse's fists clenched with the need to fight. But what he really wanted was to argue. He wanted to say no. With clear crisp language cutting sharp as a knife he wanted to proclaim that the dogs were his. All of them were his. Miss Althea had already given them to him. What she'd already given couldn't be taken back, except by her. If she asked him, he wouldn't hesitate, but *she* had to ask him, Miss Althea, her own self. He wanted to say that coolly and calmly and with resolution. He wanted to make Eben Baxley understand that he wouldn't be just taking the one. The pack was his and he was taking them all.

That's what Jesse wanted to say. But he could not. Jesse's mind wouldn't work. It wouldn't order up the terms and phrases in the order needed. The only thoughts that came to him were hurt and angry ones. The only words he could conjure up were *no, no, no.* And he couldn't just say that.

He clamped down his teeth and furrowed his brow trying to force the right words, the real words, the words he wanted to say into his brain. But they would not come. It was one of those times when Jesse hated being simple. It was one of those times when he most wanted to be like other men. It was one of those times when he had to hold his peace because his mind was not their equal.

Eben was unaware of the struggle going on inside Jesse's heart. Without concern he stepped past him on his way to the house and then stopped to glance back.

"Why don't you clean up that fat gray rabbit first and then bring it up to the house, Simple Jess. I suspect the lady will be inviting me to stay for supper and I ain't had a good haunch of sweet-seasoned hare in a long while."

It had been a major battle to get Baby-Paisley down for a rest. That child was as stubborn as he was smart, Althea thought. He kept on and on. Asking questions, getting thirsty, then needing a trip to the brush, she thought he might never give up the struggle to stay awake.

She missed the old days. That's how she thought of them. Those wonderful days, almost just yesterday and yet now so long ago when she could take him to her breast and sing him a lullaby and he'd be asleep and dreaming before she could get to the chorus. She glanced over at him lying on her bed at the far side of the room and smiled.

Her self-proclaimed "man of the house" lay balled up upon his side, his short chubby thumb buried comfortingly in the depths of his baby mouth. She gently straightened the light coverlet she'd thrown over him and resisted the urge to lean down and kiss his brow.

It was warm in the room. Althea moved toward the kitchen cupboard on tiptoe. She'd been baking bread all morning and the evidence of that effort was lined up along the cooling board. Three loaves were usually more than enough for her and Baby-Paisley. But she'd made twice that much this week. Simple Jess was, it seemed, very partial to her light bread. She wanted to be sure to have plenty for him.

Althea wiped her hands on her apron and then tested the coolness of each loaf. She didn't resent the extra bit of flour it took. There probably wouldn't be enough to last through the winter—it would be turnip kraut and poor-do before they knew it—but Simple Jess was going to put meat on her table. Meat was more important than bread. With his help, they'd get through this winter. And next year . . . next year—

"Well, ain't this a scene to warm the cockles of a man's heart."

Althea started and turned with a hand pressed upon her heart to the man who stood in the doorway.

As quickly as recognition dawned, she glanced anxiously toward the sleeping child.

"Hush! You'll wake the baby!" she admonished him in a scolding whisper.

As if noticing the child for the first time, Eben nodded and tiptoed over to the side of the bed and stared down at him for a long minute.

Althea used the time to compose herself.

Eben Baxley was here. Beulah Winsloe must have sent for him. And the man undoubtedly thought they were to wed. What a coil!

Althea remembered him well. She'd met him for the first time when she was little more than a girl. He'd been a handsome, smiling fellow even then. Some of the girls had giggled and cooed over him. Maybe Althea had herself a time or two. She wasn't that easily impressed anymore.

She'd spoken with him a couple of times that short spring that Paisley had courted her. He and Paisley were carousing partners and had been since their early teens. Eben would show up on the mountain, the two would soak up a crockful of donk, and she'd not have her gentleman caller until Paisley managed to sober up two or three days later.

He looked up from his inspection of the baby and smiled at her. So handsome. Always smiling. Eben Baxley reminded Althea of her daddy. It was a memory that could not be described as fond.

He walked toward her. His steps quiet and careful. His

expression friendly and warm. She was not afraid of him. Not at all. Still, when he came to stand right in front of her, less than an arm's length away, she stepped back.

"He's a fine boy, Althea," Eben said softly. "I know Paisley would be right proud of such a son."

She nodded, mutely accepting his words.

"I know if he was my boy," Baxley continued, "I'd think myself a damned lucky fellow."

Althea raised her chin haughtily.

"There is no need for cursing, sir," she said sharply.

Eben raised a curious eyebrow and chuckled lightly. "*Damned* ain't much of a curse, honey," he said.

She looked him straight in the face, unmoved by his humor.

"It's a curse word all the same. And I won't have it around me or my child."

Eben folded his arms across his chest. His eyes narrowed and he gazed at her assessingly.

"All right, honey," he said finally. "I suspect I can bridle my tongue if your mind is set that direction."

"And you may call me Mrs. Winsloe," she added. "I am not anybody's *honey*."

His own jaw came up at that, seeing it clearly as a challenge.

"We're kin, h—Althea," he said. "Distant kin for now, but soon to be closer, I'm hoping. I cain't be calling you Miz Winsloe like you was some old crone with a wart on your nose."

"You will call me Mrs. Winsloe or keep my name off your tongue altogether," she said.

Eben sighed heavily. "All right, all right. You sure think you're the last button on Gabe's coat, now don't you?"

Althea didn't answer.

"I can tolerate that," he continued. "I'm not the kind of man that needs to make a woman think less of herself so that he can pretend he's better."

He relaxed and smiled broadly at her, taking a small step forward and almost casually leaning his hand upon the wall behind her.

"I do hope," he said more softly, "that you won't be one of them starchy women and expect me to be calling you Miz Baxley after we're wed."

"No, you won't ever have to call me Mrs. Baxley," Althea answered. "Because we are never going to wed."

She stepped away from him and busied herself at the hearth. The fire was low and nearly perfect for the last bread in the oven. She poked and stirred it anyway.

Eben chuckled again and shook his head. "Your mother-in-law said you were determined to be mulish about this."

"And I certainly am," Althea told him with a determined glance. "Not just mulish, I am downright resolved not to marry."

"Now that's the biggest foolishness I've ever heard spoken. I never thought you to be a foolish woman, Miz Winsloe."

"There is nothing foolish about not marrying up with you, Eben. I'd think it to be about the smartest thing a woman could do."

He chuckled again. His handsome smile was a sight to behold, but Althea barely bothered to glance at it. "I'm not saying that there ain't women out there that would agree with you," he admitted. "I've done broke some hearts, I suspect, and I've been known to rollix aplenty. But that wildness about me, that's all in the past. When I settle down with a woman, I intend to be hardworking and dependable so that woman will have no regret in marrying up with me."

"Well, I'm sure *that woman* will be very pleased to hear it," Althea told him. "But she isn't me."

Eben's good humor faded visibly. "Are you hoping for Oather Phillips?" he asked. "To my thinking, he ain't much of a prize. Personally, he's not a bad sort. But you take on a man, you take on his family. You'd think that a gal that already has dear cousin Beulah as her interfering mother-in-law wouldn't be so eager to take on bleating Buell Phillips as the other side of the family."

"I am not marrying Oather," she answered, sighing heavily.

"Who then? Those Broody twins are a little young for

you," he pointed out. "And Beulah would have a fit if you was to latch up with one of those drunken Weston boys."

"I just told you, I do not intend to marry at all."

"You don't plan to marry at all?" His question was offered with skepticism. "With due respect, Miz Winsloe, you are going to have to marry. And everybody including you knows it."

Althea's face flamed, but her words were stubborn. "I certainly don't know why."

"Somebody's going to have to take care of this place. You can't do it alone. Even Paisley couldn't do that. That was why he took on a wife to help him."

"And you're thinking that you want to help me take care of this place." Her tone was exaggerated irony.

"That I would," he answered.

"I've never known you to be very work-brickle, Eben Baxley," she said. "Drinking and dawdling are more true to your reputation."

Eben raised his hand as if giving a pledge. "I've not tried to deny it. But I've come to the end of my youthful ways, Miz Winsloe. And I'm ready and willing to become a dull and dutiful husband."

Althea snorted with disbelief.

"I'm speaking as honest as the day is long," he said.

Eben rubbed his hands together thoughtfully. "I can't claim to love you," he said. "Oh, I suspect I could speak some pretty words to try and turn your head. But we both would know I don't mean 'em."

He glanced up at her hopefully. As if to determine if honesty was really the best policy.

"I could tell you some pretty lies and try coaxing you into that lonely bed of yours," he continued. "I'm a pretty fair hand at lovin' and truthfully, it might be easier to win you that way than to speak the truth. But you're going to have to have a man for this farm. Even if you could manage it yourself, folks ain't going to let you do that. They want you married up."

Althea knew he was speaking the truth. But she didn't want to hear it.

"It ain't the way for a young woman to be single," he continued. "And folks don't like the idea of that boy growing up without a man."

He shook his head and told her honestly, "You're going to have to marry. Folks are going to insist on that. And it's going to be soon. I ain't perfect and I'm not claiming to be. But I am Winsloe kin."

Althea gave him a raised eyebrow, saying to him, in effect, that she didn't consider that a recommendation.

"I'm not afraid of work," Eben assured her. "I don't think you'd regret matching up with me. You might even come to have feelings for me."

Althea felt as if the room were choking her. So much of what he said was true. They *were* going to insist that she marry. All of them, Winsloes, McNees, Piggotts, the entire mountain community was set upon it. Could she go against all of them? Was she strong enough to withstand them? She never had been. Could she now? Could she for Baby-Paisley's sake?

"Mr. Baxley, at this very moment, I have all the *feelings for you* that I ever intend to have," she answered tightly.

"Now, don't go all starchy on me again," Eben said, grinning. "We've got to come to some understanding here, Althea. I said I was willing to try. I think you ought to do the same."

"Why on earth should I? You're just another fellow who wants to get his hands on this farm!"

He nodded and looked her in the eye. "You don't think that's reason enough to marry?"

"No, I don't."

"Wasn't that why you married Paisley Winsloe?"

Althea's eyes widened. She felt as if she'd been slapped. "Mama?"

Startled, she turned immediately to her son. He was sitting up in the middle of the bed, his expression pouty as he rubbed his eyes.

"Oh, we woke you!" she exclaimed as she hurried toward him. "I'm so sorry, sweetheart."

Sitting beside him on the bed, she urged him to lie down

once more. "You just go on back to sleep and we'll be real quiet."

"I doan wanna go to sleep," he whined. "Who's he?"

Althea glanced back at Eben, still standing by the fireplace.

"That's Mr. Baxley." She hesitated, wondering what more she ought to say. "He was a cousin of your daddy's."

Baby-Paisley immediately sat up again and looked more closely at the stranger.

"Did my daddy look like him?" the child asked.

Althea felt the blood drain from her cheeks. She had known, of course, that Baby-Paisley didn't remember his father, but to hear the little boy admit as much aloud grieved her.

"No," she answered evenly. "Mr. Baxley doesn't favor your daddy much. Your daddy looked more like Grandma Beulah."

Baby-Paisley's expression was positively horrified.

"Gwamma's an old lady!" he said.

Eben Baxley laughed uproariously.

Althea gave him a harsh look and he quieted, but there was still a twinkle in his eyes. He stepped to the bed.

"Don't worry, son," he said. "Your daddy didn't look one bit like an old lady."

Baxley's grin was infectious and the young boy smiled back.

"Now what, may I ask," Eben said, leaning toward him curiously, " is a big old boy like you doing lolling in the bed in the middle of the day?"

Baby-Paisley's eyes widened. "Mama makes me take a nap," he admitted.

"A nap? I thought naps were only for babies," Eben said, glancing toward Althea in feigned horror. "You're no baby, are you, son?"

"Nope."

"Then you'd best get yourself outside to play."

"Wait just a minute!" Althea interrupted as her son rolled out of the bed. "Paisley Orville Winsloe, what do you think you're up to?"

The boy stopped immediately, but his expression was mutinous.

"The man said I could go outside an' play."

"What *the man said* is what the man said, but what Mama says is the law."

The boy lowered his head and his lip protruded obstinately.

Althea glanced over at Eben. His grin was infuriating. She sighed heavily.

"All right," she said. "You can go out and play now. But you're going right to bed after supper, young man."

"Yes, Mama," he agreed, his feet fairly slapping the plank floor as he hurried out the door.

"See ya later, mista," he called out to Eben.

"I hope so. I sure hope so, son."

Althea watched her little boy's departure, nonplussed. She turned her fury to the instigator of it.

"Eben Baxley, what are you thinking of, coming into my house and ordering my child about?"

Eben grinned and stepped closer.

"I was thinking about getting the boy's mother alone," he answered with a chuckle. "Looky here, the bed's already mussed. And it be a shame to waste it."

To Althea's total surprise, he slid his arm behind her knees and easily picked her up. He laid her on the bed in one smooth motion. He was on top of her before she even had a moment to grasp what was happening.

Althea Winsloe was not for one instant afraid. Eben Baxley was teasing and she felt not the slightest moment of danger.

"I thought you weren't going to try to win me with pretty words and sweet lies," she said.

He grinned down into her face. "Actually, right now, I wasn't thinking about winning anything. I was just planning on a pleasant passing of the afternoon."

"Oh, for heaven's sake." She pushed at him ineffectually.

"It's like I said, honey," he continued. "These folks are determined that you marry. Now, you may not be thrilled about that, but I'm sure I could find a way or two to thrill ye."

"You'd do better to bring her meat."

The words came from the doorway. Eben pulled back immediately and Althea, with a little cry of horror, jumped up off the bed.

Jesse was standing in the doorway, a plump rabbit, skinned and ready for the stew pot, held in one hand.

Althea, who'd felt nothing startling or scandalous about Eben's unwanted advance, felt her cheeks turn bright red with embarrassment. His embrace had been no more enticing than a brother's, yet now, with Jesse watching, she nervously straightened her already straight clothes and clutched tightly together the already buttoned collar of her dress.

"What are you doing here?"

Momentarily he stood in silence, his eyes sharp and his nostrils flaring slightly. Then it was as if he relaxed and he looked at Althea as he always did—in that open, honest fashion.

"He told me to bring the rabbit," Jesse said, indicating Eben. "He said you'd be asking him to supper."

Althea glanced over at Baxley, still sitting on the edge of the bed. He was like a little boy caught with his hand in the cookie jar. But clearly he had somehow enjoyed being caught by Jesse in such an improper embrace. He was not humiliated. He was smiling as if something had happened between them. And he was acting as if he were proud of it.

"You are letting me stay for supper, aren't you, honey?"

His lazy grin and the way he let the sweet name roll off his tongue infuriated her. It was all Althea could do not to reach over and slap his face. But she was certain that would make things look even worse.

"Most certainly not!" She was flushed and confused, but she was adamant. "Jesse, I . . . we . . . Jesse, nothing happened, I mean . . ."

The simple young man continued to look at her curiously, waiting. She was at a loss. She turned her attention back to

Eben. He had leaned back to lounge indolently upon the bed, just as if he thought he had a right to be there.

"Get out!" she hollered, startling even herself with the vehemence of her words. "Get out of here right now! You, too, Jesse. The both of you just leave me be. I've got work to do."

CHAPTER

SEVEN

The dinner of rabbit stew had been wonderful. Jesse's appetite hadn't been the best, however, He was still confused about the events of the afternoon.

Miss Althea was going to marry Eben Baxley.

Eben Baxley was getting the dogs.

Eben Baxley was getting the gun.

Eben Baxley was getting the farm.

Eben Baxley was getting Miss Althea.

He tried not to think about that. Especially not that. He tried not to remember what it looked like. What they looked like. Eben Baxley had been lying on the bed with Miss Althea. Jesse tried not to think about it. Thinking about it hurt. Not a hurt like hammering a thumb, but a different hurt, deeper somehow.

Usually *thinking* was more of a problem for Jesse than *not thinking*. Tonight was different. Tonight Jesse couldn't seem to stop thinking, much as he tried. He would gladly have liked not to think about Eben Baxley ever again at all. But that was impossible. At least it was impossible at Miss Althea's dinner table. Baxley was all that Baby-Paisley talked about.

"Is he really my daddy's cuzzin?" The little boy's eyes were wide and excited. "Did they really go huntin' together?" he asked. "Were he and my daddy best, best friends? Does he have any little boys of his own?"

Jesse listened as Miss Althea answered every question as patiently as possible. Baby-Paisley had been totally enthralled by his brief introduction to Baxley. By the end of the meal it was clear that she was as tired of the subject as he was himself.

"Go on up to bed, Baby-Paisley," she said as she washed the remains of dinner from the boy's hands and mouth. "The morning comes as early as regular tomorrow."

Jesse rose hastily from his chair. He was not at all eager to leave. Truthfully, he could gladly have sat by the warmth of Miss Althea's hearth and enjoyed the welcome aroma of her home until kingdom come, but he reminded himself that Pa said a man didn't overstay his welcome. Jesse was a man and did what men did.

"Good night, Miss Althea," he said.

"Wait, Jesse."

He stopped. So did Baby-Paisley, who had his foot on the first rung of the loft ladder.

"Go on up to your bed, Baby-Paisley," she said. "I need to talk to Jesse about something."

The little boy looked at Jesse with narrowed eyes, but reluctantly followed his mother's orders. She waited until he was completely out of sight, although there was no question in Jesse's mind that the little fellow had his ear to the edge of the loft scurry and was listening to every word.

Jesse cleared his throat, a little bit uncomfortably, and looked at Miss Althea with curiosity. She seemed ill at ease. He wanted very much to take away the little worry line that furrowed up between her eyebrows.

"It was a fine rabbit stew, Miss Althea," he said. "Best I think I ever eat."

She acknowledged the compliment with an expression of pleasure, but the effect of it didn't reach as high as her eyes.

"Sit down, Jesse," she said quietly. "Here, move your chair close to the fire. There's a chill in this autumn air tonight."

He did as he was bid and she pulled her own chair up to sit across from him. She seated herself and smiled. It was nice, Jesse thought. It was nice just sitting here with her. She was pretty and sweet-smelling and pleasant and it was just simply kind of wonderful sitting with her.

Their eyes met and inexplicably she flushed. The color in

her cheeks heightening to a shade nearly as bright as dogwood berries.

Hastily she glanced away. She stared into the fire. Jesse followed her gaze. For several minutes the two of them merely watched the brilliant orange glow of the dying flame.

"It's so quiet," she said at last.

Jesse looked over at her, waiting for her to say more.

"After supper when Baby-Paisley goes to bed, it's always so quiet, too quiet. Sometimes I think the whole world, God included, goes to bed when he does."

Her smile was so warm, so welcoming, And it was for him, Jesse Best. Jesse felt as if some hard hurt thing inside of him began to melt.

"That's why God made music," he told her.

She raised a curious eyebrow. "Music?"

"When it's too quiet and you get to thinking that you're all alone and God's busy elsewhere," Jesse explained, "you just got to sing or play a tune or such and the music fills up the space."

"It does, does it?"

"Yes, ma'am," Jesse assured her. "If I were to start sawing on my fiddle, it wouldn't be quiet around here at all."

She chuckled lightly in agreement. "I guess that's true. And I do admire the way you play the fiddle, Jesse."

She said the last with such emphasis that Jesse felt he was almost glowing from the inside out. She *admired* the way he played the fiddle. Jesse wasn't sure if he'd ever been admired before.

"I could bring it here, Miss Althea, the fiddle," he told her. "I could play for you after supper and you wouldn't be lonely no more."

"Oh, I'm not lonely," Althea said, too quickly. "I am not lonely at all. I have my son and . . . and well, mothers never get lonely when they have their children."

Jesse nodded at her as if he understood, but he didn't. She'd said things were too quiet. Quiet was quiet, but too quiet was lonely, or so it seemed to him.

"Still, I could play for you," he said. "It wouldn't be no trouble at all."

"That's sweet, Jesse. You are very sweet."

It wasn't sweet at all. He really wanted to play for her. He wanted her to listen to his music.

"I played for you before," he said more quietly. "I played at your wedding. Do you remember that?"

"Of course I remember," she said. "You played nearly all night long and it was wonderful. Your music made it seem like a real wedding."

Jesse's brow furrowed in puzzlement. "A real wedding?" He vividly remembered the celebration. The biggest wedding ever held on the mountain. His sister and brother-in-law had only jumped the Marrying Stone, but Paisley Winsloe had invited everyone from here to yonder. The preacher had spoke words from the Bible and the ladies were all dressed in their best and smelling fine and itching to dance and sing all night. There had been food and drinks and frolicking like never before. He couldn't imagine a wedding more real.

Althea was blushing again. "Of course, it *was* a real wedding," she said. "It's just that it all happened so fast and . . . and . . ." She looked away from him, back into the flames of the fire and then down at her hands. Her words came slowly and Jesse could feel the pain in them as she spoke. "Paisley was drunk as a lord. I'm sure you remember that. And . . . and my . . . my father didn't come." Her chin came up again and she spoke more crisply. "I'd always thought that my father would come to my wedding."

She picked nervously at the hem of her apron and once more gazed sightlessly into the fire. Jesse knew she felt bad, but he didn't know why. More than that, he didn't know how to make her feel better.

"You got a pa?" he said. "I didn't know that."

Althea glanced over at him and shook her head slightly. "Everybody has a pa, Jesse. Some are dead and some are gone but everybody's got one."

He nodded. He kind of knew that, but he hadn't thought about it before.

"My pa might as well be dead for all that I see him," she said. "But he's not dead, he lives over at the White River."

Jesse accepted this piece of knowledge and silently committed it to memory. Miss Althea had a pa and he lived over at the White River.

"Maybe your pa will come for the next wedding," he said.

Her chin came up quickly and her expression quickly turned from surprise to anger. "You, too!" she accused.

Jesse was startled. "What?"

"You've got me remarried again just like everybody else."

Nervously, Jesse swallowed. Miss Althea was mad. She'd been mad that afternoon and she was mad now. Folks got mad. Folks got mad at him a lot. But he didn't want Miss Althea mad at him. He'd made another mistake. Somehow he'd made her mad. And for the life of him, he didn't know what it was.

"Eben told me," he said.

"Eben told you what?" she asked.

"He told me you were bespoke."

Althea's mouth opened. Then she closed it. "When did he say that?" she asked. "After . . . after you saw us . . . you saw us this afternoon?"

Jesse shook his head. "No, when he first walked up. He said you was bespoke and that I could only have one of the dogs."

"He said what?" She was even more angry than before.

"He said I could only have one of the dogs." Jesse was deliberately conciliatory. "And I don't mind, Miss Althea. I thought it over and one dog is plenty for me. I don't mind at all. If that's what you want, then that's what I want."

"That's not what I want at all!"

Jesse was momentarily taken aback by the vehemence in her tone. "You want me to have all the dogs?"

Althea rose to her feet and began to pace the room. Jesse watched her.

"This is more important than the dogs!" she said.

She stopped then and shook her head before giving to him

the very vaguest of smiles. She amended her words. "Well, at least it is to me."

As if having a sudden desire to share a confidence, Althea scooted her chair closer to Jesse's. She sat down facing him. Her knees were only an ax's width from his own.

"Jesse, I know you don't understand what you saw here this afternoon," she began.

He gazed at her curiously. "I didn't see nothing except you and Eben Baxley on the bed."

Althea's cheeks flamed and she covered her face. "That's what you don't understand. We . . . we were on the bed, but nothing happened. Nothing at all. Truly."

Jesse nodded. He knew it was true. When he'd walked in he'd been immediately on alert. The two of them there on the bed. Unmarried folks didn't loll around in beds together. They had been where they shouldn't be. And like a good hunter when the birds go still, Jesse'd been cautiously wary.

Trusting his best sense to guide him, he'd narrowed his eyes and sniffed the air. The scent of the place was unthreatening. There was nothing, no danger, no anger, not even the smell of lust, male or female. It had been only Althea's home and herself and Baxley. He'd relaxed then, knowing that she was safe and didn't need his protection.

"Nothing happened," she said again.

"I know that, Miss Althea."

She sighed with momentary relief and then leaned forward, her elbows on her knees. Her voice took on the cadence of entreaty. "But, Jesse, if you tell people about what you saw, they might think something happened."

He nodded again.

Her brow furrowed and her expression took on a look of impatience. "You don't have any idea what I'm talking about, do you?"

"Yes, ma'am," Jesse assured her, his tone matter-of-fact. "You and Eben Baxley was in the bed and if folks hear it they'll think you was in the bed to make a baby, but you was not."

Althea sat up, apparently startled at his grasp of the

obvious. "Yes, that is . . . ah . . . yes, that is what people might think, but it's worse than that."

Jesse listened curiously.

"You see, Jesse, a lot of people want me to get married. I don't want to. Eben Baxley wants to marry me. But I don't want to. Unfortunately, if anyone hears that I've been . . . well, if they thought that something improper had happened they might force me to actually marry him."

"You don't want to marry him?"

"No. Oh, no, Jesse. I don't want to marry anyone."

"Why?"

"Why?"

Jesse nodded.

"Because I . . . well, I just don't."

"You've got to have a reason, I guess," he told her.

Althea sighed and looked at him closely. "You want to know the truth, Jesse?"

He gave her a puzzled frown. "I wouldn't want to know a lie."

She laughed then. It was the first time he'd heard her laugh in a very long time.

"The truth is, Jesse, that I don't want another husband because of Baby-Paisley."

Jesse nodded with sage wisdom. "The boy don't like sharing you," he said.

Althea looked surprised. "Don't be silly. It's not that. It's that a new husband would want his own children and I'm afraid Baby-Paisley would just get sort of left out. He would never be the *real* son again and he would always know it."

"Why would he be left out?"

"I don't know, but that sometimes happens with step-mothers and stepfathers. My own father got a new wife and then didn't have any place in his home for me. I couldn't let it happen to my sweet Baby-Paisley."

"He's a good little boy," Jesse said. "Any man would be proud to call him his son."

"Oh, Jesse, you're so sweet." She grasped his hand in her own.

Her hand was warm and soft. It was a woman's hand.

Jesse looked down to see it. So small compared to his own and so firmly clasped around his big rough fingers. His heart began to beat faster.

"So you ain't marrying Eben Baxley," he said.

"No, no, Jesse," she said. "Not if I can help it. But folks might . . . folks might make me if they thought I'd done something with Eben Baxley."

"But you didn't do nothing," Jesse said. "And I can tell them so."

"I think it would just be better if you not tell anyone anything at all."

He nodded in agreement. "But I can tell Eben Baxley that you said I could have the dogs."

"Yes, of course you can have the dogs."

"And the gun," he continued. "Eben said I was not to borrow Paisley's gun, that I might foul it."

"He said that?"

Jesse nodded.

Althea stood up and pulled the long Winchester down from its housing above the fireplace.

"Take it," she said.

He didn't hesitate. He held the gun in his hand, the weight of it welcome to his arms and the scent of gun oil and powder like ambrosia.

"You want me to go hunting tomorrow?"

"You hunt whenever you want, Jesse," she said. "The gun is yours."

"Mine?"

"It's a gift. I give it to you. It's yours."

Jesse stared at her in disbelief.

"Even if I have to marry, no husband will ever have it. It will already be yours."

Jesse looked down at the gun, pride of ownership swelling inside him. A gun. His own gun. Jesse Best owned a gun and the best pack of hounds on the mountain. It was everything, well almost everything, he had ever wanted.

He glanced over at Althea and his brow furrowed. Thoughtfully he replaced the Winchester on its hooks above the fireplace.

"I said the gun was yours, Jesse," Althea told him.

He nodded. "It's mine, Miss Althea. I accept it. But I think I'll leave it here." He smiled teasingly at her. "It's good for keeping strangers off your porch."

The Phillips family lived over the General Store. However, there was no narrow stairway to maneuver, no real feeling of being upstairs. The building was perched on the side of the mountain in such a way that the winding path up the incline led to the back porch of the building, where one walked straight into the second floor. It was called the family porch. It was a private place away from the customers. Much needed by the Phillips family since every tinker, drummer, or resident of the mountain considered the front porch of the store building to be public property.

The family porch was overgrown in honeysuckle, creeping phlox, and trumpet vines deliberately encouraged by the Phillips females. It was a quiet sanctuary, a haven of peacefulness, an entirely different place from the hustle and bustle downstairs.

It was upon this quiet porch that Mavis Phillips found her brother Oather. He was young and strong and good-looking. With legs and arms lanky long and the sprinkling of freckles across his nose he appeared younger than twenty-four years. His hair was not the bright flame red of her own, but a deep copper color. He sat sprawled on the slat-back swing holding a slab of raw meat against the side of his face. With a grimace, he looked up her with the one eye that wasn't swollen shut.

"How are you feeling?" she asked him.

Oather moaned slightly. "I feel like some no-good rollix-chaser has beaten the stuffings out of me," he said. "I'm just hoping that he feels half as bad."

Mavis made no reply. Her brother looked up at her.

"You saw him, didn't you?" His voice was accusing.

"I could hardly help it," Mavis answered, not quite able to meet his gaze. "He came into the store. I was there."

Clearly Oather didn't like it, but, cursing under his breath, he accepted the inevitable. "I guess that seeing him can't always be avoided."

He pulled the meat off his eye and fingered the injured flesh there gingerly. "Curse him for a lowlife popskull, I wish he'd been too beaten to be on his feet for a day or two." Oather shook his head. "At least I think I taught him to keep a respectful distance from you."

There was silence as Mavis carried her basket to the doorway and set it upon the side-turned baking powder crate that served as a small table. She appeared to be concentrating completely upon her task.

Oather raised his chin and looked in her direction curiously. His one good eye widened in disbelieving recognition.

"By God, he actually spoke to you!" The angry words brought him immediately to his feet. He groaned with the sudden movement.

"We passed only a few words," Mavis assured her brother hastily. "It was nothing, Oather. Truly nothing."

The young man gave his sister a long hard look.

"Fry me brown, Mavis, if it were nothing why can't you look me in the eye?"

She whirled to face him, her expression heartbroken and her eyes bright with tears.

"I won't have you fight him anymore, Oather," she said. "I won't have any more blood shed on my account. I'm sorry that I ever told you. I should have . . . I should have . . ."

"You should have let me kill him that very day!" he said.

"Oather, the way he is, he might have killed you."

Her brother shook his head with unconcern. His teeth were clenched holding back the rage inside him. He dropped back down upon the swing in frustration and fury. "Truth is, Mavis, I think I'd rather be dead than have to live knowing what that man did to you. And him smiling. Smiling. Like you was nothing or of no account."

Mavis hurried to seat herself at her brother's side. She wrapped her arms around his waist and held him fast. They had always been close, closer than most brothers and sisters tended to be. They rarely fought each other, saving their energies for resisting the absolute rule of their father.

"Don't even talk about being dead," she pleaded. "I couldn't live if something happened to you. And it's all my doing, you know. He said I got what I deserved and he's right, Oather. That's what hurts so much, is that he's right."

"He's not right!" her brother insisted.

"Yes, he is," Mavis insisted. "I slipped off to the woods with him, knowing full well what he had in mind. I told you that. He's not blameless, Oather, but it was my failing. It's always the woman's misdeed, everybody says that. If it were some woman other than me you wouldn't fault him."

"I would, Mavis," he declared adamantly. "I would. People *say* that it's the woman's duty to put on the stops, to not allow the spooning to get out of hand. And they *say* that a man is welcome to whatever he can get. That's what they say all right. But that's not the way it should be, Mavis. It's like the law. A man's got to heed more than just the letter of it. There's the spirit, too."

"You don't think that in the 'spirit of the law' I should have said no as well?" she asked.

"You were in love with him," Oather said quietly, pushing a stray red curl away from her pretty face. "Any fool could have seen that. I've never been in love, Mavis, but from what I hear it doesn't help a person to keep their thinking straight."

"Still, I could have said no," she admitted.

"He should have walked away, Mavis," Oather told her. "Or he should have wed you. His taking the physical part of what you offered, but spurning the love that went with it, that's what I don't forgive." His voice hardened with anger. "It's what I'm not going to forget either."

"But that's what we've got to do," Mavis urged. "We've just got to forget it and get on with our lives."

Oather raised his chin, his good eye narrowed. "Getting on with your life, is that what you're doing, Sister?" he asked. He shook his head as he took her hand in his own. "I remember when we were little," he said. "We'd put on

Mama's aprons and we'd play 'house' all day every day while
Papa was downstairs in the store. Do you remember that?"

She nodded.

"And I remember that my little red-haired sister always
wanted to take care of the babies. She'd feed them and dress
them and change them. She cared nothing about playing
sweep up, or cook or churn. All that little girl wanted was a
dozen babies to tend."

Oather raised her chin with one finger and looked
solemnly into his sister's eyes. "When are you getting on
with that life, Mavis? When are you going to have some real
babies to tend?"

Mavis sighed and gazed sightlessly into the darkened
autumn tangle of honeysuckle vines, bereft of leaves or
blossoms.

"Never." She said the word so softly it was barely above
a whisper.

"You can't wed another man," Oather continued. "Because you'd be obliged to tell him why he's not the first.
Then he'd be bound to cast you off as a whore or kill the
man that wronged you."

"I'm resigned to the spinster life," she said more bravely.
"Mama and Papa need me. I'll always be here for them."

Oather shook his head. "But there's not a woman on this
earth more suited to motherhood."

Mavis didn't argue that. She didn't want to argue anything. She wanted to just sit quietly with her brother, the
strength of her life, and not think about it all. She wanted
just to not think. But that was impossible.

"If Eben Baxley would just leave again," she said.
"That's what I kept thinking. If he would just leave and this
time never come back. If I didn't have to see him. If I didn't
have to remember. But it doesn't seem as if that is likely to
happen."

"Why not?"

"He says he's going to marry Althea Winsloe," Mavis
said.

Oather raised the eyebrow on his good eye. "Althea

doesn't want to marry," he told her dismissively. "We've heard her say so time and time again."

Mavis shook her head. "And you don't want to tend the store neither, but you spend your days tending it," she pointed out. "It's like with Pa. When Miz Winsloe or Granny Piggott get their backs up about something, it happens. Althea Winsloe will be married before the snows set in. And more than likely, it'll be Eben Baxley. He'll be living nearly neighbors to us for the rest of my days."

Oather gazed at his sister. She couldn't hide the pain that reality conjured up.

"It'll never happen," Oather declared adamantly.

"I don't know how you think you're going to stop it," she said.

Oather didn't appear to know immediately how himself. Mavis had forbidden him killing Eben. Or from telling what happened and letting someone else kill him. Oather had tried warning Baxley away with his fists and had taken a severe beating for his intention. He had no idea how he would stop the donk-swilling scofflaw from moving on to the mountain. Then, slowing as if allowing the idea to take root, he drew a long, cleansing breath—a sigh, almost of acceptance.

"If Althea Winsloe has to be married," Oather said solemnly, "by heaven, I'll wed her myself before I let Eben Baxley live here and make your life a misery."

Mavis's eyes widened. "But you told Papa that you wouldn't do it. Papa absolutely ordered you to court her and you stood up to him like a cornered cat. I've never seen you so stubborn and certain about anything before in my life."

"I'm still certain," Oather said. "I don't want to wed her. I don't want to wed anybody and Papa wouldn't be able to force me to it. But before I let Eben Baxley live here and make your life a misery, I'd jump Granny Piggott herself off the Marrying Stone."

"Would you marry Althea?" Mavis asked, her voice suddenly full of hope. "Would you really do that for me?"

"I'd rather kill Baxley, but you won't let me do that," he answered.

"Oather, Oather, Oather." Mavis almost laughed as she hugged her brother tightly around the waist, relief pulsing though her with such hope she could have almost giggled. "This is going to turn out wonderful, wonderful I'm sure."

"Hmmm." Oather didn't seem as certain.

"And I don't think you'll be sorry," she continued. "Maybe Althea isn't the woman that you wanted, but she's real kind and sweet and I know that she'll make you a good wife."

"Yeah," Oather agreed without enthusiasm. "I'm sure she'll be as good a wife as any other. I had promised myself not to take one at all."

Mavis drew back a little and glanced up at her brother. Her expression was curious. "You're not going to start that talk about not liking girls again, are you?"

Oather immediately sat up straight as a shot and glanced nervously around the area. "Keep your voice down, Mavis," he hissed sharply.

"Oh, for heaven's sake, Oather," Mavis told him honestly. "I don't understand this a bit. Twelve-year-old boys say that they don't like girls. Grown men don't say that. All men like girls, that's just nature's way."

He didn't enlighten his sister, but spoke to her gravely. "Mavis, what I said to you I said in confidence. It's . . . it's a private feeling that I have. I shared it with you because I love you and you are my sister. But I never intended for you to bring it up again."

"All right, I won't bring it up, but it is just silly. I don't know why you even told me such a thing in the first place."

Oather shook his head in agreement. "I don't know why I told you either. I guess . . . I guess because you shared your secret with me, I felt I should do the same."

"But what kind of secret is that?"

"It's *my* secret. Now please, don't ask me about it again and let's not talk about it anymore," he said.

"All right. I won't mention it anymore. It doesn't seem like much of a secret, but I suppose you wouldn't want Papa to hear it."

"I don't want *anyone* to hear it," he declared with

certainty as he glanced around the area nervously once more. "And especially not Papa."

"I won't say anything. But Papa will be so proud about you deciding to marry Althea," she said.

Oather nodded and then shook his head. "I'm doing it for you, Mavis. I've spent most of my life trying to be what he wanted and failing. I'll undoubtedly fail at being a husband to Althea Winsloe, too, but if it keeps Eben Baxley away from you, that's all that matters."

CHAPTER  EIGHT

The morning was cool and crisp. Winter was just around the corner and as each day passed, Jesse worked harder and longer and faster for Miss Althea. This morning however, he was not working, or not working exactly. A sprinkling of snow and frost cracked under his feet as he made his way through the trees. He carried Paisley Winsloe's freshly cleaned Winchester, loaded and ready. No, it wasn't Paisley Winsloe's Winchester anymore. It was his own. It was Jesse Best's Winchester. The idea of that was wonderful, unbelievable. It certainly lightened the weight of it on his arm.

In front of him Sawtooth, Queenie, Runt, and Old Poker led the way through the brush. The four dogs were as intent upon their task as was Jesse. Hunting was no idle pastime, pleasant though it could be. If Miss Althea and her boy were to make it through the winter, they would need game. Jesse was determined to find some.

He watched the dogs as they worked, judging them. Old Poker may have been the veteran, but he was not leading. Jesse was aware of the way the aged hound was tagging Sawtooth, imitating his movements, following him, sniffing at places where he had sniffed. Old dogs, like old men, lose their eyesight and their hearing. Even the creature's sense of smell seemed weakened. But he didn't give up or stay to the side. The hound wanted to be in on the trail. Old Poker was trying to be a hunting dog, with none of the advantages of the species.

Queenie wasn't much better, Jesse noted. The female had grown lazy and fat over the summer. Even worse, the pads of her feet had softened from inactivity and the rough ground they now moved upon had them scratched and sore. But Queenie too had the craving for the hunt. She hurried along with a swiftness that belied the sad condition of her feet. Runt was fiesty and eager, if not very knowledgeable about his business. He had become a pet of sorts for Baby-Paisley and had had no training at all. But he showed good heart and Jesse believed he had the makings of a fine hound.

The dogs were good, very good, just as Jesse remembered them to be. And now they were his, just like the gun. Miss Althea had said so and nothing Eben Baxley might say could make it any different. He was proud to own them. Proud to be earning them. He wanted to show Miss Althea, with their help and the gun, just how much game he could put on her table.

Hunting was something that Jesse could do. It didn't require a fellow to think things through, remember rules or reason. Like playing the fiddle, Jesse could rely on his natural inclinations to lead him. Of course the gun was not that easy. He had to remember to load it, cock it, aim it. But he wouldn't need the gun until he had spotted his quarry.

A noise some distance behind him caught Jesse's attention and he stopped for a moment and glanced back. There was nothing to be seen among the thick gray tangle of undergrowth and only the faint crackle of snapping underbrush could be detected. His nostrils flared to get a whiff of scent but came up with nothing. Walking into the wind was good for stalking prey. It was impossible for the animal to sniff out anything behind him. But by the same token, the stalkers were also unaware of what might be on their own trail.

Jesse glanced at the dogs again. They had undoubtedly heard what he heard and could probably even pick up the scent. They were completely unconcerned with whatever was following them. Jesse shrugged and continued onward. If the dogs didn't mind the straggler, then neither should he. Perhaps they'd strayed through an old coon's territory and the critter was escorting them out. Sawtooth was obviously

following some other creature. Jesse hoped it was something meaty like a turkey or grouse. A fine gray winter pelt
would be nice to get and good to sell, but he was hunting for
Miss Althea and she couldn't eat a fox.

He simply had to trust the dogs. On the hunt, man and
dogs were always a team. With Jesse, perhaps this was more
true than with most. Most men, knowing themselves to be a
lot smarter than the dogs, often overruled their judgment.
Jesse, not thinking himself much smarter than anything, did
not. He often relied upon his own instincts. He therefore had
more respect for instinct, perhaps, than a man who normally
relied upon intellect. The mind of the dog was in many ways
as simple and uncomplicated as Jesse's own. He was taught
to memorize actions in places he couldn't reason, and obey
in situations that he did not understand. When he did
understand he followed his instinct. His instincts assured
him that as hunter, the dog was at least the equal of man.
And for scenting and tracking, the dog was superior.
Ignoring the rustle in the weeds behind him, Jesse continued
to allow Sawtooth to lead.

The forest of the Ozark Mountains was old and well
culled by nature. The majestic oak and chestnut trees
interspersed with hickory and pines were widely spaced, the
forest floor matted with an undergrowth of unruly shrubs
and vines. Sumac, burning bush, and dogwood were often
the hiding places of squirrel, fox, and turkey.

Jesse kept close behind the dogs. Sawtooth had become
more careful and quiet as he went forward. The other dogs
mimicked his behavior and Jesse knew they were getting
close. Moving through the brush with care and stealth, Old
Poker, nearly deaf himself, advanced low, slow, and with
silence. Even Runt was moving forward with care.

Jesse almost sighed aloud with pride. This was an
important test for the hounds, and thus far Jesse was
favorably impressed. A stalking dog had to fight his natural
desire to chase. He was to locate the prey, lead the hunter to
it, and then wait, ready to give chase only if he was so
ordered. If the animal was injured or on the run, it would be

the dogs' job to bring him around. But barking, yapping, or chasing now would only warn the game away.

Jesse stepped gingerly through the brush, guarding his step and measuring his breath. The wonderful Winchester, cool and heavy in his hands, glistened in the morning sun. He had never owned his own gun. His pa had thought it too big a responsibility for him. Owning a gun had been one of Jesse's three secret ambitions. He wanted his own gun, his own dogs, and . . . and, well, he wanted a woman. He'd never admitted those things to anyone except his brother-in-law, Roe. It was hard to believe that two of those things he had now.

Two of those dreams had been fulfilled.

His thoughts turned to the final ambition, but he pushed those ideas away. He had no time to think about women now. He was holding a gun. Guns were very dangerous and a man had to be very careful. Jesse was a man, he reminded himself. He could remember to be careful.

The blood was pounding in his ears. Each step forward was more thrilling than the last. The excitement primordial. Jesse couldn't see his prey yet. His nostrils flared. He couldn't scent it either. The dogs were spitting distance ahead at the top of a small rise. Sawtooth stopped stone still. His ears were perked so high they trembled, his legs as stiff as if made of wood. Queenie immediately backed him. Runt looked confused, but followed their lead. Even poor Old Poker held himself rigid in place.

His heart hammering, Jesse eased himself forward. He caught the smell of gamey musk in the breeze and his eyes widened. Meat. Real meat. A winter's worth perhaps. Excitement welled up inside him.

Be quiet. Don't dawdle. Take care.

Jesse moved with stealth and his hands were steady upon the Winchester, but inside he was quivering with excitement.

He wanted that meat for Miss Althea. He wanted it so much, so very much, for her, for Miss Althea.

He took his steps with great care. The prey wouldn't scent

them upwind, but it would hear and run if Jesse's movements weren't quiet.

As he reached the rise he peeked over. Even there, the smell sharp and distinct, he almost didn't see his quarry, grayish-brown among the bark and underbrush.

Behind him the snap of twigs sounded again and from the effective camouflage of nature, a white tail raised up in alarm. It might as well have been a flag of surrender. Jesse saw him. There, in the small gully just to the left, the strong, healthy buck stood tall and straight, his antlers, decorated with velvety down, six points at least. The big buck stood in majestic beauty, two half-grown does at his side, their winter coats thick and glossy with the gray of an Ozark winter.

Another snap of underbrush and they were gone, vaulting through the brush in a flash of movement that was both swift and elegant.

"Hunt!" Jesse hollered and the dogs shot out from behind him as if fired from a pistol. Barking noisily they disappeared in the direction of the buck almost immediately.

Jesse sighed nervously and began to whisper to himself. The words imprinted upon his memory from so many hunts.

"Raise the gun smooth, slow, and sure," he said. "Don't fumble."

He didn't.

"Ease back the hammer."

It made a slight clicking sound, letting Jesse know that it was ready.

"Get the line of your sights at ready, watch the world right through the middle of the little metal crook."

Jesse held the Winchester pointed directly into the empty spot where the deer and dogs had disappeared. He waited. The barking of the dogs was in the distance now. Not nearly as loud as the sound of his own breathing. The musk of deer was still strong and he let the scent fill his nostrils. He was the hunter. The deer was meat. He would bring home the meat for Miss Althea.

In his mind he saw her, not as she had been that morning, but as she might be on a cold winter day, snow barricading the cabin door and with a hungry young son at her side. The boy would not cry and Miss Althea would not fret. She'd simply put a haunch of venison on the fire and it would feed their bellies. The venison that Jesse Best brought to them.

The barking of the dogs was getting louder, closer once more. Jesse's finger curled around the trigger. He tried to still his mind from all thoughts. But the image of Miss Althea lingered.

Sweet-smelling Miss Althea with her warm smile and her so very round parts. She never looked at him mean or like she was afraid. She looked at him loving, warm and loving, like she looked at the boy. She looked at Jesse that way. And he liked it. He really liked it. But he wanted it different, too. He was not a boy. Jesse was a man. He wanted Miss Althea to see that. He wanted to put meat on her table. That's what men do for the women they love.

The barking was almost upon him. Jesse stilled all thoughts as he held the gun at the ready. Like a flash of gray and brown lightning, a deer swept into the clearing. Jesse tensed. He had no time to reason, only to know. It was one of the does. He held his fire. An instant later the buck was right behind her.

"Squeeze."

The Winchester's retort was loud in the quiet stillness of the Ozark morning. Without even so much as a startled expression, the beautiful animal, the guarantee of Miss Althea's winter survival, dropped to the forest floor. Dead with one clean shot to the heart. The second doe sailed over him and vanished into the smoky silence of the killing's aftermath.

Jesse raised the shiny, well-cared-for Winchester and sighed with relief and satisfaction. He had done it. All by himself with no other to help, no other man to remind him what to do or help him think his way, he, Jesse Best, had brought down the meat.

It's what a man does, Jesse reminded himself. *And Jesse is a man.*

The dogs surged immediately, surrounding the kill, assuring themselves that he was not about to get up and run.

Jesse almost laughed aloud with the release of tension. If he
didn't get one other piece of meat this winter, Althea
Winsloe and her son would still survive. Perhaps not in
great style, but they would survive. Jesse could almost taste
the venison roast on Miss Althea's table. He wondered if he
would really get a chance to taste it.

"Whoopee!"

The exuberant cheer from behind him startled Jesse. He
turned in surprise to see Baby-Paisley hurrying out of the
brush. The little boy had on his short pants and woolly
socks, his heavily padded winter coat making him look
strangely top-loaded. His blond curls were covered by a
gray glove hat that was big enough to fit low on his ears.

Jesse was surprised to see him. *He shouldn't be here.*
Something told Jesse that immediately. Little boys just
didn't appear in the woods. Something was wrong about
that, Jesse knew right off. But couldn't help smiling at the
little fellow's excitement and enthusiasm. He let the vague
feeling of unease pass without further scrutiny.

The mystery of the noisy critter following them and why
the dogs were uninterested was certainly solved. Baby-
Paisley must have followed Jesse from the time he and the
dogs left Miss Althea's place.

"You done kilt him for sure!" the child exclaimed. "I
didn't think you could, but you sure did."

With a whoop of victory the little boy went charging
down into the gully, a yard-length stick held before him like
a lance. He raced toward the downed animal screaming like
a wild Indian. Jesse watched, momentarily amused and then
shocked as the young boy began brutally jabbing the dead
deer with the stick.

"Take that . . . an' that . . . an' . . . "

His eyes widening and thoughts whirling, Jesse cried out,
"Stop!"

The child ceased immediately and turned toward Jesse,
stunned by the authority in his voice. The two stared at each
other. Jesse hurried down into the gully.

Jesse was agitated. The youngster was defiant.

"You mustn't do that," Jesse told him. "You mustn't."

"Why not?" the child asked contentiously. "I'm just playing. Why do I have to stop?"

Jesse's brow furrowed and he looked at the boy mutely. There was a reason. Jesse knew that there was. He searched his brain trying to find it. There was a reason.

"You mustn't," was all Jesse could think to say.

"I was just playing," Baby-Paisley protested once more, his tone taking on a whiny cadence. "The stupid deer is already dead."

Jesse searched his brain, knowing the answer was there, not being able to find it.

"You mustn't," he told the little boy firmly. "I can't say why. Sometimes I can't remember the whys of things, but I know you mustn't."

"You just doan want me to have no fun," Baby-Paisley declared, his bottom lip protruding obstinately. "You're mean. You ain't my pa. You cain't tell me what ta do! I'm having fun and you cain't tell me what ta do. You think you're like my pa, but ye ain't!"

"No, no," Jesse assured him quickly. "It's not that. It ain't like I'm your pa, it's . . . it's . . ."

Still he struggled. There was something wrong here. Something really wrong. Jesse knew that it was wrong. He just didn't know if he could say why. He became angry at himself, angry and frustrated.

Stupid mind, he thought to himself. *Stupid Jesse's mind doesn't work right. Doesn't think right.* He clenched his teeth and tightened his fists in frustration. *Stupid, stupid mind.*

Then, within the midst of his self-loathing, he noticed the hounds at his feet. They were high-spirited, but sedulous as they surrounded the kill.

"See the dogs," he said to the boy. "See how the dogs act?"

Baby-Paisley glanced down at them and nodded, puzzled.

"They don't stab or poke or tear at the kill," Jesse said. "They know to respect the meat. You've got to respect the meat, too."

Baby-Paisley looked at the well-behaved dogs, not totally convinced.

"It's nature for dogs to grab and tear at the meat. I guess it's nature for us, too," Jesse said. "To get excited about outsmarting a deer, to feel like the winner and wanting to show off or something. But the dogs have learned better and we got to, too. The kill isn't for killing. It's for food."

The little boy's brow furrowed thoughtfully, but he wasn't totally convinced. "You just doan want me in on your hunt," he accused.

Jesse shrugged. "But you *were* in on it. You've been behind us all the way from your house, ain't you?"

The child nodded.

"You were quiet in the brush and following the dogs, just like me."

Baby-Paisley nodded again.

"I took the shot, but then you didn't have the gun. I've been hunting lots of times with my pa when *I* didn't have the gun. That didn't mean I wasn't on the hunt."

The little boy's eyes widened and his look was respectful. "You mean part of this kilt deer is mine?"

"Half," Jesse answered. "There's just two of us, that makes it half. When there's more, each gets less."

Baby-Paisley broke into a delighted grin and stared down at the fallen buck with awe.

"I got meat," he declared and stepped back a respectful distance from the kill, no longer needing the childhood thrill of poking it with a stick.

Jesse smiled at him, knowing exactly how the young boy felt. He felt like a man. Jesse felt like a man, too.

But neither was allowed to linger over the moment. Jesse set the Winchester safely against a tree trunk and removed the knife from his belt. He bent down to dress the deer. As he did so, he showed the child how it was done.

He widened the wound in the animal's chest, allowing the blood to flow out freely.

"You've got to tie off the bung," he told Paisley, in the same calm, patient tone his father had always used with him. His father always talked through the gutting of an animal, explaining over and over how it was done, impressing it upon Jesse's mind. It seemed natural for Jesse to do the same with the boy. It seemed natural for the boy to follow his directions.

Jesse pulled all the innards out onto the ground and deftly removed the liver.

"Put this on a clean flat rock," he told Baby-Paisley. "We'll get your mama to cook it for you for supper."

"For me?" Baby-Paisley asked, his tone one of awe.

Jesse nodded. "It'll make you a fast runner," he said.

"I'm already fast," the child boasted. "Sometimes I can even beat Gobby Weston."

Jesse eyed the boy with appreciation. "When you can run as fast as the deer, you'll beat him every time."

Reverently, and with great care, Baby-Paisley bore the deer's liver to a cooling place on the rock. Jesse gifted the remaining offal to the dogs who eagerly shared their reward.

The little boy hurried back to the man's side as he continued to use the hunting knife surely and with deftness.

Baby-Paisley watched curiously and asked questions whenever Jesse paused in his recitation of instructions.

"How come you didn't follow da dogs when they took after the deer?" he asked. "How'd you know they'd come back this way?"

"Deer run like rabbits," Jesse answered. "They like to stay in their territory and so they run in circles. The dogs just get on the outside of the circle and make it small so they return to the spot that they started from."

Baby-Paisley accepted this notion thoughtfully.

"Why didn't you kill the first deer? It was almost as big as·this one."

"The first was a doe, a female," Jesse answered. "We need the does more than the bucks because they have the babies. She'll find herself another buck and we'll have more baby deer next spring."

The little boy pondered those words as well. "So we can kill all the buck deer 'cause they doan have babies," he said.

"No, not all of them," Jesse corrected. "Babies need daddies, too."

"Why?"

"It's just that way," Jesse said. "It takes two to make a baby."

The boy was looking at him curiously, clearly expecting further explanation. Jesse blushed a little. The child obviously didn't know about bucks and does or men and women or about the propagation of all things that crawl or walk or swim.

In truth, Jesse didn't know that much about it himself. He'd seen hogs bred and hounds mating. He'd even watched a couple of slow old turtles locked in nature's embrace one long-ago afternoon. But he had never touched a woman. He had never spilled his seed inside one.

Pa had said that he couldn't, not ever. Pa said that no daddy on the mountain would ever want Jesse for a son-in-law and that it was best if he just not think about such things.

His brother-in-law hadn't been quite so certain.

"The feelings you get in your body, Jesse, they are the same feelings that other men get and they have nothing to do with your mind." That's what Roe had told him.

Jesse was a man and he had a man's feelings. But Baby-Paisley was no man, it was years before he'd need to understand those things. There was no need for Jesse to try to explain them today.

"Be sure not to cut or scrape these hocks," Jesse told the boy, changing the subject abruptly. "And stay clear of the dewclaws. This is where the scent of the deer comes from and if you clip them with your knife you'll spread it all over the meat and give it a bad taste."

Baby-Paisley nodded.

Jesse let the boy help as he raised the kill by the backbone and shook it vigorously to free the last of the blood and guts. The little fellow had a death grip on the deer antlers and was actually more a hindrance than a help, but Jesse didn't shoo him away.

"He don't weigh near as much when you get him gutted," Jesse pointed out. "There's no way the two of us could have lifted him with all his guts still inside."

The little boy nodded in agreement. He was barely able to stand under the weight of the antlers as Jesse shook the deer to drain it completely.

This was how a man learned to dress game. It was how Jesse had learned, by helping even when he was no help. By the time Baby-Paisley was big enough to hoist a buck on his own, he'd know exactly how to do it, just as Jesse did.

"If you can help me get him around my shoulder," Jesse told the little boy. "I think I can carry him myself."

The child ineffectually patted and pushed as Jesse heaved the carcass across his broad shoulders like a very weighty shawl. Slowly he rose to his feet, gingerly balancing the weight evenly. The burden, heavy as it was, lightened considerably as he imagined how proud and thrilled Miss Althea would be with her winter meat.

The hounds, having finished their treat, were effectively cleaning the area, sated and satisfied.

Jesse retrieved the Winchester.

"Get your supper," he told the boy.

Baby-Paisley hurried to the smooth rock and grabbed up the squiggly, slippery liver. Fearing he might drop his precious booty, the little boy pulled off his hat and deposited his trophy within it.

"Come on, Runt, Queenie, Sawtooth, Poker," he called to the dogs. "Let's go show Mama what we kilt."

The boy and dogs headed into the brush and Jesse followed in their wake. The dogs knew their way home and the youngster would never get lost staying with them.

Jesse felt as excited as the little boy.

"Yep," he whispered to himself. "Let's go show Miss Althea what we killed."

CHAPTER NINE

Althea Winsloe was frantic. Her whole body trembled in anxious terror and it was only sheer force of will that kept her from bursting into tears. One minute the day had been cool and crisp and fine and he had been right there and the next minute he was gone.

"Baby-Paisley!" she attempted to call out once more. The sound came out more a croak than a cry. "Baby-Paisley, answer me!" Her throat was raw and sore from calling, crying, entreating, even begging. Where was he? Was he all right? Her baby? Her precious, precious baby?

She had tried to be methodical. She'd checked the barn, the shed, the smokehouse. She'd looked under the porch, and in the trees near the cabin. She'd climbed the ridge to scan the distant field. He wasn't there. He wasn't anywhere. Baby-Paisley had wandered off. Somehow when her back had been turned he had just strayed away.

Circles, ever widening circles, that's how searches were accomplished. She couldn't allow herself to panic, to get so frightened that she couldn't think. She had to search for him. Circles, ever-widening circles. Where was he? Where was her little baby?

She'd said she could raise him all by herself. That's what she'd told Granny Piggott and Beulah Winsloe and anyone else who would listen. She'd said she could do it alone. Althea Winsloe didn't need anybody else.

Pride goeth before a fall. Had she truly been so prideful? She could take care of him. She could. And she could watch him. She had been watching him. It wasn't that she hadn't been watching him.

Her guilt was nearly as strong as her terror. It helped, only barely, to keep her worst fears at bay. Had he fallen from a rocky ledge? Been attacked by a bear or panther? Drowned in the stream and whisked toward the rushing river? Was he lying hurt, bleeding, helpless, dying? Was he calling for his mama? Mama was supposed to protect him. Mama had promised to protect him. Could Mama protect him? Why hadn't she seen him leave?

She'd been washing. She always kept him at a distance when she was washing. It was dangerous to have a little one close to the fire pit or the boiling laundry. It wasn't her regular Wednesday for laundry. Perhaps he had known that she'd been irritated at that. Every bedsheet in the house had been peed upon and a half week to go before washday. She had been irked about it. But she wasn't angry with Baby-Paisley. She never said a word to him about it. Surely he didn't leave on purpose 'cause he thought she was angry. No, that was foolish thinking. She had done nothing wrong. Baby-Paisley had just ambled too far from the yard and was lost. She had to find him.

Circles, ever-widening circles, that's how searches were accomplished. She could not panic. She couldn't give in to fear. She must make ever-widening circles until she found her lost son. She must find him and bring him home. She must bring him home and keep him safe.

Being a mother was a big responsibility. She knew that. After those first months of endless days and midnight feedings she'd finally been able to get some sleep. But sleep for a new mother brought dreams, sometimes bad dreams, even nightmares. Her baby would be in a burning hut and she couldn't get to him. Her baby would be falling from a ledge and she couldn't catch him. Her baby would be choking and she couldn't help him. And the worst dream of all. In her dreams she would be going about her business and suddenly realize that she'd forgotten her baby and left the child somewhere. She would try to find the baby again, but she never could.

Circles, ever-widening circles. She felt like that last awful dream had finally come true. She thought of Paisley. It was not something that she did often. She could see him in her mind. Not as she usually did, dressed in his best suit and lying cold and still on the kitchen table. Today in her memory he was standing tall and straight, his stance angry and his tone cutting.

"You'll spoil that boy for sure kissing on him and catering to him," he said. "You'll turn him frothy for sure."

"He bumped his little head, Paisley. I can't just leave him to cry."

"It ain't even bleeding," he pointed out. "Mama says if it don't require sopping or sewing, don't make a fuss about it. And if he continues to cry, then give him a whallop to cry about."

"I'm not treating my child that way," she told him stubbornly.

"You should listen to Mama," he said. "You are so determined to go your own way you discount everything she says."

"Because I don't think she knows what she's talking about. This is my child and I'll raise him as I see fit," she declared.

"She raised me and I didn't turn out so badly. You forget that I have a part in this, too."

"And you want him raised like you were?"

"Yes I do. There is nothing wrong with the way I was raised. I turned into a hard worker and a good provider. I want my son to turn out the same."

"But there is so much more to life. There is so much more I want for him."

"Lord Almighty, like what?"

"Like love, Paisley. I want him to know love."

"Love? Hell, is that what this is about?" His voice was raised to an angry pitch and he was sneering. "Every argument turns out the same with you. You want love. Well, it's the middle of the afternoon, but if you want me to show you some *love*, just pull up your skirts and let's get on with it. It takes less time than arguing about it and I got a field to plow this afternoon."

"That's not love, Paisley Winsloe," she snarled right back at him. "Love is something entirely different. Apparently something that with your raising you can't understand at all. My boy is going to know that he's loved because I'm going to love him."

"You'd go against your husband and his family?"

"For my baby I would. We don't need you or your mother or the Winsloe clan."

Paisley stomped out the door, but not before delivering the final shot. "Someday, Althea Winsloe, you're going to find out that you can't do things alone and that your way is not always the best. I can't wait to see that day. I'll be laughing my head off."

She wondered if Paisley was laughing his head off now. Their son, her precious, precious son, might be there with his father right now. The thought offered no comfort for her.

Circles, ever-widening circles. Althea clutched her coat more tightly around her. She was cold from the inside. The kind of cold from which no coat could protect her.

"Baby-Paisley!" she called out once more to the still, cold silence of the morning.

Perhaps she hadn't been completely right in the way she'd raised her son. Maybe he was a bit spoiled and not always the best behaved. But he was a happy child. She wouldn't have him yelled at or struck in anger. There would be time enough when he was older to reason him out of his obstinate ways. At least, she prayed that there would be time.

The sound of a barking dog caught her attention and she stopped still and raised her head.

The dogs. Jesse had the dogs. They could help her find her baby. Dogs could follow a scent, a trail. She didn't know much about dogs, but she knew that. Jesse knew about dogs.

She abandoned her ever-widening circle and hurried toward the sound, tearing through the brush, heedless of its ripping at her skin and clothes. Jesse had the dogs and he would help her. Jesse would find her Baby-Paisley.

"Jesse!" she cried out as she ran toward the sound. "Jesse, the baby's gone. You've got to help me find the baby."

Heedless of the brush and briers, Althea was running through the woods. Rushing toward the happy sounds of dogs and laughter.

"Jesse! Jesse!" she called.

Her bonnet caught on a limb and was pulled away from her head to hang limply down her back. Her hair came loose and was wild and scraggly around her face. The hem of her skirts was alternately dragged and snagged. Her heavy cloth coat grazed the tines of an old toothache tree, rending a long deep gash in the sleeve. Althea hurried on, oblivious.

"Jesse! Jesse!" she called out. "Baby-Paisley's missing. You've got to help me find him."

It was in a small clearing that she spotted them. The dogs first came rushing toward her, yapping and sniffing. Over their heads she saw Jesse, gun in hand, a huge deer carcass poised upon his shoulders. Then her eyes widened as Baby-Paisley came into view.

"You found him!" she cried with joy. Then her hand flew to her mouth in horror as she eyed her son. The child was covered in blood. There was blood on his coat, on his hands. He carried his hat. It was dripping and bloody.

"Oh, my God!" she screamed and dropped to her knees.

The little boy, unconcerned with his mother's strange behavior, came running. He was smiling, smiling, covered in blood and smiling.

"Mama, Mama, look what I got. Look, look."

The child held out his hat, nearly shoving it in her face, and some bloody, horrible something lay inside. Althea eyed the contents of the hat in horror and grabbed her child.

"Where are you hurt? Where, honey? Where?"

Her tone was panicked and desperate as she ran her hands restlessly upon the child's body, touching, searching for his injury. Seeking the wound where the horrible thing in the hat had come from.

Baby-Paisley pulled away from her, confused.

"Mama, let me be," he insisted.

"Tell me where you're hurt, precious," she pleaded. "Tell Mama where you're hurt."

"I ain't hurt," he insisted. "Look, Mama, I kilt a deer."

"A deer?"

Althea repeated the word in a strangely vague tone as if unsure of the meaning of the word.

"Yep. I kilt a deer and this is the deer's liver and Jesse says I can eat it for supper 'cause I hunted it."

"Hunted it?"

Baby-Paisley nodded eagerly.

"Jesse took me huntin' and we kilt a deer."

Althea's eyes widened as comprehension filtered into her brain.

"He took you hunting."

"Yep and we kilt a deer, see."

Althea looked up to see Jesse Best standing there, right beside her son. The deer carcass slung over his shoulders now held new meaning. He was grinning as broadly as the little boy.

It took a moment for Althea to put the strange pieces of the puzzle straight in her mind. Her little child, her baby boy, was not injured and bleeding. He had not been crying for his mama to protect him. He had been taken from her house without her permission to go on a deer hunt. She had been left to worry and fear while the child had been traipsing through the woods with a disgusting, bloody deer liver in his hat.

The tears of terror that she had so valiantly held back now came rushing to her eyes. And with them a white-hot anger that would not be controlled.

In a flash, Althea came to her feet. Jesse's smile had faded somewhat and there was wariness in his look. It wasn't enough to halt her action. With all the force she could manage Althea slapped him across the face.

The sound was inordinately loud in the clear, cold silence of the clearing. Only her son's startled intake of breath echoed it.

"Don't you ever take my child from my home without permission!" she screamed. "Not ever. Do you understand me, you feebleminded fool!"

The clearing was still and silent for a long moment. Then Jesse's answer came calm and quiet.

"Yes, ma'am, I do."

Althea faced him for one more long minute as a tiny trickle of blood escaped from the side of his mouth and coursed down the side of his chin like a bright red ribbon.

There was something crashing in Althea's heart. Something crashing and crying, but she couldn't quite center upon it as the sharp fire of anger still surged through her veins. But as she watched the path of that bright red ribbon something pierced her heart as deeply and as surely as a skinning knife. Deliberately she turned from it.

Baby-Paisley stood wide-eyed and stunned, still holding his hat before him. Althea jerked it from his hands and threw both it and its contents into the brush. Then hastily she lifted the child into her arms and headed toward her cabin. By the time she'd left the clearing, she was almost running.

Jesse was busy skinning the deer, but it was hard for him to keep his mind on his task. He'd hung the carcass, head down, from the huge old red oak tree on the far side of Miss Althea's barnyard and he had managed to make the right cuts and proceed as he'd been taught, but he found it difficult to concentrate. He had to remember everything that he must do, but his brain kept crying out, "Stupid, stupid Jesse!" Drowning out all other words in his head.

He stopped, the knife trembling in his hands. He bit down hard on his lip and closed his eyes as he tried to force the right instructions into his mind.

Cut from the inside out.

Peel the hide down and forward.

Keep the knife clear of the hock.

Stupid, stupid Jesse. Feebleminded fool.

Jesse's bright blue eyes snapped open in fury.

"Dadburn and blast!" he ground out under his breath, using his sister Meggie's most vivid curse, the only one that he really knew.

He hated making mistakes, even little unimportant ones, and this mistake was very big and very bad. Not just because he'd looked stupid to Miss Althea, but because he had scared her. She had been really scared. Jesse could tell that. Pale and wide-eyed and near tears. She'd been really scared. She'd never have slapped him otherwise.

He should have known that Baby-Paisley wasn't supposed to wander all over the mountain. He was just a baby and of course he wouldn't be allowed. Jesse hadn't been allowed out himself without Pa or Meggie until he was nearly grown. But he just didn't think. He just couldn't think!

Jesse clenched his teeth in frustration and forced himself to continue his task. But he couldn't force away the thoughts that plagued him.

Other men would have just known right away that the boy had gone off without permission. Other men would have realized immediately that his mama would be worried and that he should rush the boy back home. But Jesse wasn't like that. He couldn't *know* things if nobody had told him, if he hadn't learned them.

Sometimes he could sense things. He remembered, now that it was too late, that he *had* sensed something. When he'd seen the little boy in the woods he'd known that it was not quite right. But he'd ignored that feeling.

Solemnly he used his right index finger to cross his heart, silently vowing to listen to those feelings from now on. The world was too complicated just to rely on what folks could tell you. Sometimes a man just had to go with his feelings on things even if he didn't understand the why of it.

Determinedly he used his knife once more to separate the fine gray hide from the dark red meat.

Cut from the inside out.

Peel the hide down and forward.

Keep the knife clear of the hock.

Don't soil the meat.

He'd skinned more meat in his lifetime than a scholar could total up on a school slate. His father had him out dressing and preparing hides long before he was allowed to hunt. It was a job that required minimum dexterity and strength; there were only a few rules to remember, and except for the blade side of the knife, there was little chance of injury. Still, it was a very responsible task. Meat that was badly dressed would taste gamey and be dark and tough. Jesse had learned his lessons well. If the meat that graced his family's table tasted poorly, the blame was invariably his sister Meggie's cooking skills.

As Jesse rolled the hide down the animal's back and over its shoulders, he felt some pride. It was a good one. Winter gray, unscarred, and downright pretty. He wasn't about to ruin it. He intended to give it to Miss Althea. Maybe she wasn't too happy about the deer right now. But she would be grateful for the meat this winter, and the hide would make a fine soft winter vest for her with enough left over for a pair of heavy-duty work gloves.

Feebleminded fool.

He heard her words again and they stabbed his heart as certainly as if he'd used his knife. He pushed the hurt away. She had been scared. And she had been angry. It wasn't that she had meant to hurt him, he reminded himself. Miss Althea wasn't like that. She was warm and sweet, just like she smelled. It was Jesse who had been in the wrong. She had cause to be angry at him. She'd called him feeble-minded. But that wasn't like a mean thing. It was, after all, very true.

Jesse remembered when Tom McNees had called him the same thing. He was just a boy at the time; his sister Meggie had been little older than Baby-Paisley was now. Granny Piggott had always called him Simple Jess, but he'd just thought that was his name. He knew he was a little different than the other children. They played with him, but he never could quite understand the games, so they gave him special duties. For troublemaking with the boys, he was always the lookout. For house with the girls, he was always the baby. And when they played hide-and-seek, if Jesse got to be It, somehow everybody managed to come home free.

But that warm spring day at the church picnic, Tom McNees had called Jesse feebleminded. Jesse had commit-ted the word to memory and that evening when they were back home he'd asked his father what it meant.

"Well, son," Onery Best said, sitting Jesse down beside

him on the wash bench that sat in front of the barn. "Feeble is just another word for crippled or sickly."

"I ain't crippled or sickly, Pa," Jesse protested. "I'm big and strong, everybody says so."

His father nodded in agreement. His expression was soulful but his words were matter-of-fact. "You are strong in your body, son, mighty strong, and ye got a right to be proud of that. I am, for sure."

Jesse smiled. It was good having his father proud of him. He wanted it to always be that way.

"But yer mind, Jesse," Pa continued. "Yer mind ain't so."

Jesse's happiness dimmed somewhat as he nodded acceptance.

"Yer thinkin' works kind of like this gimp leg of mine," his father said, rubbing the thin, emaciated limb that had once been broken and badly set. It had grown together incorrectly and left him permanently lamed. "Yer mind works about like this leg. Half the time you just have to drag it along with ya, most of the time it slows ya down."

Jesse was thoughtful at his father's words. "Did I bust my mind like you busted your leg, Pa?"

Onery Best chuckled lightly and ruffled his son's hair with affection.

"Well, yer sorter did," he explained. "When you's born, I wasn't here, you know that."

Jesse nodded.

"But what they that was there told me—and that included yer mama and Granny Piggott—was that ye came into the world with the cord wrapped 'round yer neck."

"A cord wrapped 'round my neck?"

"The cord betwixt yer mama and yerself. It got all snarled around yer neck somehow and Granny says that you practically hanged yerself just getting born."

Jesse wasn't sure he understood that, but he nodded just the same.

"It's a wonder that you lived at all. Lots of younguns born that way don't."

"But I did."

"Yep, you lived, but yer mind was injured. Like my leg,

it just couldn't be set right, and so you are like you are, and you won't never be nothing else."

Jesse considered his words thoughtfully. "So I'm feeble-minded."

"Feebleminded, simple, slow-witted, unsound. Those are all just words folks use to describe the kind of affliction you got."

"I ain't never going to be no better." Jesse didn't phrase it like a question. Somehow he already knew the answer.

"It ain't fixable, son," his father told him. "But it ain't a dying wound neither. My leg ain't never gonna be no better, but I cain't just sit around with it and say, 'Ain't it a shame I'm a cripple.' I get up and do my life my own way. I walk where I got to go, plow when they's no help for it, and if I get a little too worse for drink, I'll be dancing 'til I fall on my face. I suspect it don't look like other folkses' walking or plowing or dancing, but it does for me."

Pa looked down into Jesse's face and ran a brown, work-callused hand across the softness of his cheek.

"Ye'll just have to do with yer mind the best that ye can," he said. "If it looks a sight for humor to some folks, well, son, just don't give that no mind."

"Don't give it no mind," Jesse repeated, committing the admonition to memory.

Onery pulled the little boy into his arms and hugged him tight. "God put this thing, this gimp of yer mind, on ye for a reason of His own. What He's thinkin' is not for us to question."

Jesse saw that his father's eyes were bright with unshed tears.

"I ain't about to be questioning God," Jesse assured him quickly.

One tear did escape from his father's eye and he hastily wiped it away with his sleeve. "I want ye to always remember how proud I am that ye ere my son. And if ye just do the best that ye can with what ye got, then you'll be as good a man as any."

"Do the best that you can with what you got," Jesse whispered to himself once more as he finished stripping the hide from the deer's back. That's what he'd always tried to do. And if he envied other men for the limberness of their minds, he didn't believe them any better than himself.

Jesse carefully rolled the hide, tail to head, and set it aside. He didn't bother to salt it. He'd be making it into buckskin and that meant soaking it in wood ashes and water instead. He temporarily stowed it in the crux of the old oak so the dogs or other animals couldn't get at it.

He commenced butchering the deer. The good-sized animal would provide a lot of lean winter meat. Jesse quietly recited the steps to himself. He could not allow himself to make foolish mistakes. Meat could mean the difference between life and death in a bad Ozark winter.

He removed the shoulders first. They would be salted and smoked. Not as good eating as the hams, but plenty nourishing. Jesse laid the meat carefully in the barrow skid. It was fine venison. Miss Althea might be mad now, but she'd come around when she got a good look at this meat.

Moving to the back of the carcass, Jesse carefully removed the back-strap portions on either side of the backbone. This was the best eating on the deer. Roasted, fried, or just cut into slabs and grilled over the fire, this part of the venison was so naturally tasty, even his sister Maggie couldn't ruin it.

The tenderloins, on the inside next to the backbone, were cut out next and laid in the barrow.

Jesse cut apart the backbone near the base of the spine, separating the rib cage from the hams. The rib meat would be used for jerky. The hams would be the special prize for a special dinner.

Once the meat was cut and loaded, Jesse pulled it to the area next to the smokehouse. He salted it all down and hung it carefully on the hooks inside. It would be left to dry and cool for several days. It was not necessary to actually smoke it, but the smokehouse was convenient for hanging it and provided protection from animals and the elements.

It was late by the time Jesse finished his task. He was tired and his muscles ached, but in a way he felt better. He'd made a mistake, a bad mistake. He'd scared Miss Althea. He never wanted to do that. But he'd also brought her meat. It was a thing that a man did for a woman. Jesse was a man. Miss Althea was a woman. His mental acknowledgment of that stirred activity in the front of his trousers.

"Stop it!" he whispered harshly to his own body. It did not immediately obey.

To clean his blood-splattered body and cool the ardor that plagued him, Jesse headed to the water trough. He stripped off his shirt and began washing the scent of blood and deer from his body. The cool water washed him quickly. It took more time to chill the sparks of sensual desire that made him human and male.

From behind him he heard a soft familiar voice call his name.

"Jesse."

Startled, he turned abruptly and clumsily, almost tripping over the woman standing behind him.

"Miss Althea," he said, righting himself by grasping her shoulders. A spark passed between them, like a tiny bolt of lightning. Jesse didn't know what it meant, but he saw Miss Althea's gaze fall on the naked expanse of his damp muscled chest and he was embarrassed somehow. He hastily grabbed his shirt and pulled it on. He could not, however, concentrate well enough to do up the buttons, so he just pulled his suspenders up on his shoulders to hold his shirt more or less closed. He gave a worried glance toward the front of his trousers, hoping his present condition was not obvious. The loose, homespun butternut hid a multitude of sins.

Hastily he brought his gaze back to Miss Althea. She wasn't looking at his chest anymore, she was looking up at his face. Unlike the last time he'd seen her, she didn't look angry. Her silky brown hair was tidy again and her cheeks were no longer flushed, but prettily pink. She was standing close to him. Close enough that the strong scent of the deer that lingered around him was softened by the warm, sweet fragrance that was her own.

"I . . . I . . ." Jesse verbally stumbled as he searched his brain for something that he'd meant to say. He had something important that he had to tell her. It was something he had planned to say to her at the first opportunity. This was the first opportunity, but he couldn't remember. He searched his brain, knowing that the words were there. He couldn't find them.

"It's a fine piece of meat," he tried finally, pointing jerkily with his thumb to the smokehouse in the distance.

"Yes, it is," she said softly. "And thank you very much. It's a fine deer that you and my son brought me."

That was it, Jesse realized. He and Baby-Paisley had gotten the deer. But the little boy shouldn't have been with him. He was supposed to apologize about not bringing the boy home right away. That's what he had planned to do. He was supposed to explain that he just hadn't thought about it. That he hadn't known on his own, although he'd sensed that something was wrong. He hadn't known because nobody had told him, but now that he knew what he was supposed to do, he would always do it, next time and forevermore.

"I'm sorry." He managed to get the two words out from the torrent of thoughts that flooded through his brain. "I made a bad mistake and I'm sorry."

Her eyes widened and then she smiled. She looked so pretty when she smiled.

"No, Jesse, I'm the one who made the bad mistake and I am sorry," she said.

Jesse's brow wrinkled in puzzlement.

"Baby-Paisley told me that you didn't really take him with you," she said. "He just followed you out there."

"He told you that?"

"Yes."

Jesse nodded manfully. "He's a fine feller, that little boy of yours. Lots of times folks do things wrong and let someone else take the blame. It takes a fine character to own up to failings. You done raised that boy to be a man, Miss Althea."

"A man? He's only a baby."

"He helped me git the deer," Jesse said. "He followed me right out there in the woods. And we was real quiet, so he must be just a natural tracker."

Jesse thought his words to be a high compliment. Miss
Althea had a right to be very proud of her little boy. Jesse
hoped that she was.

"I thought he was some critter at first. The dogs didn't
pay him no mind 'cause he's familiar to them. It was just
like a man going hunting. That's what I told him and I tell
you the same."

"Baby-Paisley is much too young to go hunting," Althea
told him firmly. "But I do know now that it wasn't your
fault," she continued. "I blamed you and I struck you and it
wasn't even your fault."

Jesse's brow furrowed. "Oh, but I shoulda known," he
protested. "When I seen him, I shoulda known that he ought
not to be there."

"How could you have known that?"

"Other fellers would have known," Jesse told her solemnly. "And I almost knew myself. When I saw him, I
thought, 'This ain't right,' but I just let it go and I'm not
doing that no more, Miss Althea. I made myself a vow.
When I'm thinking that something is wrong, I'm going to
say so from now on. I promise."

"Well good, but just so you know, Baby-Paisley is not
allowed out of sight of the house without me with him."

Jesse nodded. "Are you gonna whoop him?"

Althea shook her head decisively. "I do not believe in
striking children," she said.

"It's not so bad," Jesse told her. "I been whooped plenty
of times."

"I've had my share of beatings, too," she said. "And I
don't believe they really serve any purpose. Baby-Paisley is
quilt bound all afternoon. I spread a quilt out upon the floor
and he's not allowed to move farther than the edges of it
until suppertime."

Jesse pondered her words a moment before nodding
thoughtfully. "That's pretty prime punishment for a busy
little feller like Baby-Paisley."

"And no less than he deserves," Althea answered. "I want
him to be grateful for the freedom he has of the yard. And
make him unwilling to risk it by straying away again."

Her tone was stern, but loving. Just like a mama ought to be, Jesse thought. And she was pretty, too. In fact she was sure prettier than any mama on the mountain. Jesse's own mama had been pretty, he remembered that. But somehow the way he felt looking at Miss Althea wasn't at all the way he felt about his own mama.

"Are you going to finish with being mad at him by supper?"

Althea smiled, curious. "Well yes, I suppose that I will."

Jesse gestured for her to follow and headed over toward the smokehouse. In a small pail of water just inside the door floated the ugly brown deer's liver that Baby-Paisley had carried in his hat.

Althea's distaste at the sight indicated that she found it no more appealing now than she had in the woods.

"The boy did help me get the game," Jesse said. "You slice it real thin and it'll cook up mighty fine with some onion."

"Oh, Jesse," Althea said, shaking her head. "Neither Baby-Paisley nor I ever eat organ meat. We don't like it."

"He'll like this, ma'am," Jesse assured her. "He'll like it better than anything that he has ever tasted."

"And why would that be?"

Jesse shook his head as if he didn't know. But on some level, he did.

"It's hard to explain about, Miss Althea," he said. "Boys get tired of being boys. They want to be men. I know it seems like a hurry-up thing, he's still so little and all. But sometimes a feller just need to feel grown."

"And helping to bring down the deer made Baby-Paisley feel grown?"

"It sure made me feel grown," Jesse admitted.

His expression took on a serious aspect as he searched his thoughts for some kind of explanation.

"I guess I understand it better than most 'cause there ain't no feller on the mountain that felt like a boy longer than I did," he said. "And there ain't nothing so fine as feeling like a man, even if the feeling only lasts a minute or two. He don't really want to be grown yet, but it's nice to have a taste of it anyway."

"And this stinking deer liver is going to be a taste of it?"

Jesse grinned at her. "If you're not going to be mad at him anymore, maybe you could fix him the liver. If he don't like it, after all, and won't eat it, you can always give it to the dogs."

She laughed out loud. "All right, Jesse Best, you win. I'm cooking liver and onions for supper tonight. Why don't you stay? That way, you can both enjoy it."

"I'd be pleased to take supper with you, Miss Althea," Jesse answered.

"Good," she said. "Maybe feeding you a meal will begin to make up for me slapping your face like I did."

Jesse shrugged away the note of concern in her voice.

"It didn't hurt much."

"But I broke your lip," she said.

He tentatively explored the injured area. "It ain't hardly even swelled."

"Let me see."

Althea stepped up right in front of Jesse and stood on her tiptoes. The touch of her small feminine hand on his mouth, so tender, so unexpected, jolted him somewhat.

"Don't pull away, Jesse. Let me see."

He didn't move. He couldn't. He felt frozen in place, as if his shoes were hobbled to the ground. She was warm. Sweet and warm, and the scent of her seemed to seep into his brain, making it difficult to keep thinking. Her hand was soft as it touched him. She pulled his bottom lip down and probed it gently. Jesse knew that she was just checking to see if he needed doctoring. His sister Meggie would have done the same. But it didn't feel like his sister Meggie.

She was close. So close. Jesse took a deep breath and found out that when his chest expanded, it touched hers. He swallowed nervously and took another deep breath.

Yes, it was her chest all right. He could feel those soft round parts of her, buried as they were beneath coat and clothes and heaven knows what else. Still, they just barely grazed the front of his only partially covered muscles. His reaction was immediate. He was hard. He told his body to stop that. His body didn't listen.

Deliberately Jesse took another deep breath and actually inched closer to her. She didn't seem to notice. They were round. And they were soft. His hands twitched. It was only by balling them into fists and holding them tightly at his side that he managed to control them. She was close, so close. So soft. So round. So close. Her fragrance was on him like a stain or a brand.

"It's going to be sore for a day or two, but I don't think it needs any alum or goose grease," she said.

He felt the breath of her voice upon his neck and it raised the flesh like a prickly herb.

Jesse was looking down into her face now, her very familiar face. Wide-spaced eyes. High cheekbones. And a tiny mouth that almost seemed too small for the amount of wisdom that flowed out of it. He focused his attention on that mouth, now.

"I cain't even feel it," he said honestly. All his sensation seemed to be settled elsewhere.

His heart was beating faster and faster. He tried to remember what to do. There must be a memory, a caution, a rule about what action to take with these all new, so exciting feelings welling up inside him.

Mustn't touch. Mustn't touch, he repeated to himself. The admonition kept his hands still, but it could do nothing about the expansion in his heart.

It was instinct that was prodding him now. Instinct, primordial and unrelenting. Had he not just promised not to ignore his instincts? Had he not just that afternoon made a vow to follow those feelings when he had nothing else to lead him?

"Why don't you kiss it better?" he whispered to her.

"What?"

It was surprise that parted her lips, but his instincts took it for acceptance. He leaned his head down and she covered his mouth with her own.

For an instant, a glorious instant, it was heaven. His first touch of feminine flesh against his own. The scent of her was more than a stain upon him now, it filled his lungs, seeped into his veins, and coursed through every part of his body. And the taste, the taste of her, was not sweet but unexpectedly tangy and tart. A taste that didn't satisfy but rather keened the appetite, making a man crave more.

So naturally Jesse's arms went about her, pulling her close into his embrace. Feeling the soft round curves pressed tight against him. It was everything. It was wonderful. It was perfect, for an instant.

A sound of protest came from her throat. Jesse immediately released her.

She pulled away, taking two steps back before stopping to stare at him. Her hand covered the sweet lips he had just so thoroughly kissed. Her expression was stunned and shocked.

"You mustn't do that!" It was a demand spoken in a horrified whisper. "You must never, never do that."

"It seemed right," Jesse told her in a plaintive whisper. He was having trouble catching his breath and his hands were trembling. "It seemed really right."

"But it wasn't. It was wrong," she said.

Nervously she looked away from him, unwilling to meet his gaze. She attempted to straighten her hair. She wiped her hands upon her apron.

"Miss Althea?"

"I don't blame you, Jesse," she said at last, taking control of her whirling emotions. "I must have . . . I must have led you astray somehow. But you must never touch me again."

Jesse's disappointment was palpable. "Never?" That seemed impossible. To be allowed to know how wonderful it was to feel and smell and taste her and then to *never* be allowed that again. It was so unfair. Jesse wanted to cry. It was too unfair.

"Never," Althea reiterated sternly. "Now . . . now go on home, Jesse. I . . . don't think you should stay to dinner after all."

CHAPTER TEN

The Literary on Marrying Stone Mountain was held every new-moon Friday from spring thaw till bad weather set in. After the first snow fell that cold November in 1906 most folks on the mountain had expected that they wouldn't really have a chance to get together again until the crocus were in bloom. But the first week of December was bright and almost balmy. This special gift of good weather could be ignored by no one.

Granny Piggott had her grandnephew, Oather Phillips, pick her up in a skid cart and bring with them her favorite rocking chair. Under her direction, he set the chair beneath the branches of a broad-limbed elm near the schoolhouse, where the old woman could hear and see goings-on of whatever sort were made available.

By right of age and sheer strength of will, Granny Piggott was the matriarch of the mountain. She'd always been a force of law among the Piggott clan and as of late she'd begun to tell the McNees what they should or shouldn't do as well. Those that resented her intrusion, namely Beulah Winsloe, could say little about it. Elders were accorded great respect on the mountain. And after all, it was Granny and her husband who had first settled this now well-peopled community. The two had come from the Caintuck as newlyweds. They'd carved a homestead out of a wilderness, raised a passel of children. Granny had buried her man twenty-five years earlier. If she looked as if she ruled the roost, sitting in her bentwood rocker and smoking her clay pipe, there was none who was about to tell her differently.

Granny looked upon her surroundings with sharp vision that belied her aging eyes. Not much got past her; still, she looked upon this mountain, her home for so many years, as much with scenes from memory as with scrutiny of the moment.

This wide-open space on the south side of the mountain was not cleared by man's plow or fire's wrath, but kept nearly denuded by the bulging dome of solid granite only inches under its sparsely grass-covered surface. The big rock church with its undersized whitewashed clapboard steeple stood to the east side of the open area. The church had been built by the two families that settled the mountain, the Piggotts and the McNees. The steeple remained a subject of contention between the two. The community had decided twenty years earlier to build a bell tower for calling the righteous to the house of the Lord. The Piggott family had taken upon them the job of constructing the belfry. The McNees brothers had sought a proper bell for the community to purchase. Spending the churchfolk's entire cash savings, the McNees had returned with an enormous brass bell from a near-empty Catholic monastery near Calico Rock. The bell was far too large for the flimsy steeple constructed and a near feud erupted among the congregation over whether to build a bigger tower or buy another bell. Neither side had ever triumphed in the argument and to that day the huge monastery bell sat in front of the church and the tiny steeple sat atop it.

The west part of the clearing, near the elm where Granny sat, was occupied by the tiny one-room poled-pine cabin that served as schoolhouse during spring and early summer, before the young local scholars were needed to work in the fields. It was also the center of community activities, the church, so near it, being considered too holy a place for the fun and frolic mountain folks so often craved.

Between these two man-made structures, both evidence of the mountain folk's grip on civilization, sat the Marrying Stone. The huge, upthrusting piece of white quartz, nearly four-foot square, had been a sacred place to the Indians who had once lived here. It was now a place that mixed superstition with religion. It was believed that God could see the spot clearly from heaven and that He personally blessed the unions declared there. Though many now professed not to believe in the stone's superstitious essence, not many who wed failed to take the symbolic jump from its summit.

Granny smiled to herself as the remembrance of weddings past filled her thoughts. Marriage was an important sacrament on the mountain. It was a rite of passage to adulthood and a guarantee of generations for the future. Granny was a great believer in it, and wished both its joys and sorrows upon all the young people around her. Except perhaps the young man at her side. Of him she had her suspicions.

"So yer daddy's a-saying yer to take up courtin' the Winsloe widder," she commented to Oather.

The young man nodded. "I'm going up to escort her here as soon as you're settled, Granny."

The old woman gave him a shrewd perusal and commented thoughtfully, "I was thinking you was dead-set against marrying altogether, least of all for acquiring a good corn bottom."

Oather shrugged and looked distinctly ill at ease. "I suppose I've changed my mind," he answered. "Anyway, I'd best hurry or she'll be down the mountain already on some other fellow's arm."

"That Eben Baxley most likely," Granny agreed. "He's a slick, good-looker if ever I seen one. Got a way with the ladies, that Eben has."

"I hardly think that serves to recommend him as a husband," Oather replied.

Granny hooted with good humor and slapped her knee. "No, I guess you wouldn't think that it would, but it always does."

She watched Oather's expression turn dark and her own turned to puzzlement. "I wouldn't fret on it, boy," she told him. "You don't have his charming ways, nor the Broody twins' sense of fun, or even Tuck Trace's steady ways. But I've always seen ya as a right smart feller and you treat yer mama and sister good. That's a true test of how a man will be to his wife. You see how he deals with the womenfolk he's already got."

Oather sighed with what sounded like resignation. "You can be sure, Granny, that I'll treat Althea with respect and consideration."

She nodded solemnly, and took a long smooth drag off her pipe. "I know you would. Indeed, boy, I know you would." She chewed upon her pipe thoughtfully as she considered him. "I suspect, though, that it would be a lot to expect for you to love her."

"Do you think Eben Baxley will love her?" Oather asked, venom clearly discernible in his voice.

"No, I don't imagine so," Granny admitted. "Still, it kindy seems like she deserves as much, don't it?"

Oather was saved having to answer by the boisterous arrival of Ned and Jed Broody. Just the sight of them lightened Granny's heart. It was with difficulty that she held on to her trademark cranky demeanor.

"If it ain't the two most bone-idle worthless young rollix-raisers in two counties."

Ned and Jed chuckled delightedly at her unkind description. The twins, who looked just alike and were rarely ever seen separately, hurried up to Granny with the naughty-little-boy grins that neither the intervening years nor the cares of the world would ever dim.

"I knew I smelled tobacco in this glade," Jed declared to his brother in an astonished tone.

Ned attempted to seat himself in the old woman's lap. When she swatted him away, he squatted in front of her chair. "Well, are you going to smoke without us, Granny, or are ya willing to let a couple of your favorite young gentlemen have a puff or two."

"You young varmits are big enough to get yer own pipe and pokeweed," she answered, feigning a scold.

The Broody twins only grinned more broadly. Jed took on the posture of a supplicant, begging, "Please, please, Granny. Just let me have one puff, one little puff. I don't get green and throw up no more."

Granny slapped the young man's hands and declared him a sheer loss of foolishness.

Oather, seeing the old woman was to be well looked after, took his leave and headed up the mountain. He was walking his future bride to the Literary, he announced. The very thought of which set sour in his stomach. But Oather Phillips was determined upon this. The good-for-nothing, lowlife lothario who ruined his sister was not going to marry and live as neighbor to Mavis for the rest of her life.

The subject of Oather's unhappy thoughts, Eben Baxley, watched him go from the far side of the clearing.

The Broody twins were still laughing and teasing. But not so much that Granny failed to notice Eben Baxley hurrying off down the road. It struck the old woman as interesting that rather than trying to scamper up the ridges to beat Oather Phillips to Althea Winsloe's door, Eben Baxley took off in the direction of the Phillips General Store.

He saw her before she saw him. That was fortunate. She'd been avoiding him as if he carried plague. But then, he did plan to *plague* the woman in one sense of the term.

Heaven knew that he should be up the mountain, smiling and bowing over Mrs. Althea Winsloe. He'd seen Oather Phillips heading up that way. He firmly intended to marry Althea, but this week it hadn't been his future bride that was most often in his thoughts. It had been this woman coming up the road to the Marrying Stone. This woman from his past.

Mavis was beautiful. He was struck by that as clearly now as he had been when he'd first seen her grown-up, four very long years ago. It was not just the startling red hair and the fairer than fair complexion, her skin so pale it was almost translucent; there was some other quality, some undefinable something that had spoken to him immediately. And it had said to him, You have to have this woman. You have to make her your own.

Having her had proved to be a lot easier than he'd expected. *Making her his own,* however, proved to be something that would never happen. That was her fault, he reminded himself. His jaw clenched in anger. She'd tried to put him on lead strings. Maneuver him. Force him to do what she wanted. Eben knew about women like that. Nobody told Eben Baxley what to do, especially not some woman.

He remembered that night as if it were happening all over again.

"Mavis, sweet sweet Mavis," he whispered into the soft, sweet-scented red hair that lay all around her and pillowed his head. "I love you, Mavis. I've said those words in the past, but I never knew what they meant until this very minute."

He was still inside her, warm and safe and joined. It felt so right. It was unbelievable. He'd been half-drunk for two days, celebrating Paisley's upcoming nuptials. He'd thought that after the wedding, he'd simply drink himself into a stupor and then sleep it off. He'd never dreamed that at the infare, the wedding party, he'd find what he'd been searching for his whole life long.

"I love you, too, Eben Baxley," she told him, nuzzling against him like a contented cat. "And it's wonderful. I can't believe how wonderful it is."

He rolled to his side then, but wrapped his leg around her to pull her with him. He wasn't ready to relinquish their union, but he wanted to look into her face. Her pretty pink gingham party dress fluffed like warm strawberry froth between them. The bodice of the gown still clung to her waist, the hem bunched about her hips. Her josie, however, had been discarded completely and lay with his topcoat on the cool grass beneath them. Their illicit pairing in the moonlight had been lustful and eager. But in its aftermath was warmth and affection and intimacy between them.

He grinned down into her clear blue eyes. "Wonderful?" he quipped. "Then you would recommend me to the other young ladies of your acquaintance, Miss Phillips?"

She feigned fury and began to sputter. To halt her words, as she knew he would, he kissed her. He learnedly, lingeringly, lovingly kissed her. And she kissed him back with equal pleasure.

When their lips parted once more, she sighed with sweet regret. She loved his touch, his taste, his tenderness. And she did not hesitate to demonstrate her feelings.

Eben pushed a stray lock of bright red hair away from her face as he gazed at her, his expression more serious.

"I tried not to hurt you," he said, concern clear in his tone. "They say a first time always pains the woman."

Mavis smiled up at him. "That's what I'd heard, too. I was so scared thinking about it this afternoon, I nearly gave in to cowardice. I wasn't sure I could go through with it."

Eben's brow furrowed in puzzlement.

"This afternoon?"

Mavis giggled and looked slightly sheepish. She smiled up at him under lowered eyelids, taunting.

"You think you seduced me, Mr. Baxley," she told him, her tone a teasing challenge. "Well, I saw you first. I've had my heart on my sleeve for you since I was in pigtails. When you came into the store last Thursday I said to myself, that's the fellow that I want. If I don't do something about it, some other girl is going to get him."

"So you decided to do something about it." Eben's words were strangely quiet.

"I figured I could try to get your attention, but with all the other girls, I wasn't sure that you'd single me out. And even if you did, everybody knows that you're leaving in the morning. And with your cousin Paisley married up, well, there was just no telling when we'd see you again. I decided this afternoon that it was catch you tonight or cut bait."

"So you *caught* me."

Mavis giggled then, oblivious of the abrupt cooling of the world around her.

Eben disengaged himself from her body and turned away. He began pulling up his pants.

"Eben?" An uneasy tremor had crept into her voice. "Eben, what's wrong?"

He didn't answer. He couldn't answer. His thoughts were whirling. He'd been duped, gulled, bamboozled. This woman, this woman who he thought he might love, actually love, this woman had made a fool of him.

"Oh, you're mad about being caught," she said, finally. "I should have known that you might feel that way. Men are so prickly with their pride. But, Eben, I promise you'll never regret it.".

She sat up beside him. He'd half turned his back to her, but she wrapped her arms around him and lay her head against his shoulder. "I'll be the best wife that you can imagine. I'll cook and clean and keep a place nice for you. I'm sure Papa will build us our own little house and he'll let you work in the store. Everybody knows you aren't much for farming. With your friendly talking ways I'll bet you'll be a real success at business," she told him with great confidence. "And there'll be children, Eben, think of it, our children. I want a half dozen at least. Little boys, little girls, all of one kind or some of each, I don't care. Just so they all look like you."

Eben jumped to his feet. His face was red with fury.

"Oh, you've got it all figured out and neat as a pin, don't you, Mavis Phillips. Me, my life, my work, a wedding and children, all wrapped up and tied with a little pink bow to match your dress. Well, it don't work that way, sugartail."

"What do you mean?"

"I mean good-bye, good riddance, I had a fine time, a great rollix. It was my pleasure taking what you were so eager to give."

"You can't . . ."

"Oh, sugartail, I can and I am. I'm walking away from this and I ain't never looking back. No woman is going to dictate to me, get me under her thumb. You can say frog till doomsday, but I am not going to be hopping."

"Eben, wait, let's talk about this, let me explain."

She was on her knees, wide-eyed with fear and disbelief. Eben's temper was hot and his heart was cold.

"There ain't much left to explain is there? If your belly swells up with a baby, you have my permission to call the boy Eben. But his last name won't never be Baxley. Nobody, you hear this, woman, nobody makes me do nothing I don't want."

He'd left her then. He'd turned from her and strode away

as far and as fast as he could. He'd left her there, half-naked in the woods, crying and calling after him.

He had been angry. He was still angry. He stoked that anger as he waited for Miss Mavis Phillips on the broad path from the store to the clearing.

She carried a basket of baked goods on her arm for the feed. All her attention was focused upon it for that moment. It left Eben with the luxury of observing her unnoticed.

She was not dressed in pink tonight. Pink was a young girl's color, a tint of youth and happiness and hope. Her dress was blue, steel-blue, almost gray. It wasn't a young girl's color. It was the color of a matron, a widow, a spinster. A color of sorrow and sadness. It was a color meant not to attract. Somehow on Mavis it looked attractive. She was still slim and curvy. The cruelly fired premonition of an unlawful get had proved to be untrue. Still, the intervening years had changed her. She must be all of twenty now, he thought. She was older, quieter, much more solemn. For a moment he remembered her sweet young smile and delighted girlish giggle and it warmed him.

She looked up then. She saw him on the road before her and she stopped still. She looked like a doe catching sight of the sun's glint on the hunter's rifle. She wanted to run. He could tell that she did. She wanted to run. But she didn't. She swallowed bravely and continued walking toward him.

Damned if he didn't admire her. Determinedly he thrust that unwelcome thought away.

"Evenin', sugartail," he said, stepping directly into her path.

Mavis nodded and then moved to step around him. He reached out to take her arm. She tried to pull away, but he held her firmly.

"I think I see your mama and papa coming up the road," he said. "You wouldn't want them to start questioning why you're unwilling to take a gentleman's arm."

She glanced quickly behind her. Her parents were, in fact, some distance behind her, but within sight. Resigned, she allowed him to escort her. But she held herself stiff and silent. He walked circumspectly, her hand on his arm as he carried her basket, just as if he were a benighted beau with his Saturday sweetheart.

"I do love a party, sugartail," Eben said. "Dancing and laughing and wooing the womenfolk just makes life worth living, don't it?"

She didn't answer.

"Why, I was just thinking about the last time I was here for a big night on the mountain. Do you recall that, sugartail?"

Chin high, she ignored the question. He continued his one-sided conversation, undaunted.

"Well, sure you do. You probably still think about it from time to time. All that spooning and snuggling and you under me all squirmylike. They say a woman don't forget her first man, no matter how many frolicks and fellers come thereafter."

He continued to chat, undeterred by the cold silence beside him. He spoke of the simple mountain pleasures, but always with a hint of more earthy meaning in his words.

They had reached the edge of the glade. People were arriving from every direction. A few more steps and they would be among them. His current course of conversation could continue and none would be the wiser. He might well hang on her arm all night and folks would think little or nothing of it. But nothing, nothing of substance would be said between them. Mavis stopped and turned to him.

"What do you want, Eben Baxley?" Her voice was quiet, but it was cold enough to freeze tree sap.

"What do you think I want, sugartail?"

"I haven't any idea. To hurt me? Spurn me? Humiliate me? You've already done all of those. What punishment is left?"

"Punishment? Ah, sugartail, why would I want to punish you? I want to be your swain."

"My swain?" She scoffed at the word.

"Surely so. I told you, didn't I, that I plan to marry up with Paisley's widow. She's got a fine farm for sure. Ain't no other way I'm ever going to own a piece of ground so fine. And the McNees and Winsloe clans, they are counting on me. I'm not about to let them down. But, truth to tell, I don't imagine prickly Althea will be much pleasure in beating the bed tick, if you get my meaning. Even Paisley thought she was downright chilly between the thighs and he chose her for a wife on purpose."

"So you plan to marry her and have me for your . . . your . . ."

"Whore, I guess, is the word you're looking for," he said.

Mavis swallowed thickly and held her chin ever so slightly higher. Eben smiled.

"It ain't a sweet word, or one that womenfolk like overmuch. But the truth is, Mavis, that you enjoyed me and I enjoyed you. You tried to hog-tie me to your apron strings and get a ring on your finger. You found out I'm too much a man to be led around like that. There ain't no going back, sugartail. What's done is done. But if I recall correctly, the two of us sure stir up a love storm. There's no reason we should deny each other that pleasure."

"Leave me be, Eben Baxley. I want nothing to do with you."

He eased himself closer to her, his voice a low, husky whisper. "That's what your pretty little mouth says, sugartail. But your body still warms up to me real nice. I can tell that about a woman, you know. I've had so many gals, I can tell from clear across a room when a woman's got an ache for me. You got one, sugartail. You can feel me up between your legs right now, can't you, Mavis?"

Her cold fury exploded to white-hot anger as red splotches of color stained her cheeks. She pulled away from him, but he grabbed her arm.

"Think about it, sugartail," he said. "Right now you're still plumb mad at me and can't think about nothing else. But you'll remember how good I made it feel for you. You'll remember how much you liked it. You let your mind give in to what your body already wants. I'll be ready. You just say the word and I'll fix us up a nice safe bower somewhere and I'll pleasure you till you can't walk straight for a week."

"Stay away from me, Eben Baxley," she said stonily.

"Ah, sugartail, are you trying to tell me what to do?

Didn't you learn your lesson on that already? I do what I please. Not you nor no other woman can make me do anything that I haven't a mind to."

Althea Winsloe was nearly ready to scream with frustration by the time she arrived at the Literary. Oather Phillips as escort had been an unwelcome surprise. Her mind had been in such an uproar the last couple of days that she had looked forward to the outing with great pleasure. Now it looked like it was to be just another occasion where she would be pushed, prodded, and pressured to remarry.

She didn't dislike Oather. In truth, she liked him and respected him. Even as a boy he had been kind and generous. Perhaps he had been a little too serious. But his father was forever watchful and critical of him as a child. It was difficult for a boy to be a boy, when his father was singularly determined to make him a man. If Oather had grown up to be rather reserved and distant, he was also hardworking and unfailingly polite. Any father should have been proud of that, Althea believed. And any woman should have been pleased to have him as her beau. But Althea was not pleased. Althea didn't want a beau.

"So in actuality," he was saying, "the transition of man from the singular existence in the wilderness to a grouping of domiciles in communion brought about both the need for mutual cooperation and the development of civil law."

"Uh-huh," Althea agreed lamely. She didn't know or care about what he was saying, but she had listened with as much patience as she could manage from the minute he'd stepped up on her porch.

She could hardly have refused to allow him to walk her down the mountain. But his company had taken a lot of the joy out of the trip. He was there to get her farm for the Piggotts. The strain of keeping it from him, and everybody else on the mountain, was wearing her thin.

Though they were not late arrivals, the open area between the church and the school had filled up fast. The men were gathered in small groups already well into discussions on the weather and the crops. The women were spreading pots and baskets of the dinner offering on the rough wide planks that served as the banquet tables. The children, as always full of excitement and energy, ran every which way, laughing and playing as if suddenly this important community occasion were only a simple frolic held for their benefit.

"Mama, there's Gobby Weston!" Baby-Paisley announced excitedly. The little fellow had been mostly sullen and silent during the walk. He had not been included in the adult talk and he didn't much like sharing his attention with the man from the store. "I got to go play wif him, Mama. Pweese!"

He held his little hands up in prayerful pleading. It was all Althea could do not to laugh out loud at the supplicating gesture.

"Don't you leave this clearing," Althea told her son with as much maternal sternness as she could manage. "If I start looking for you, I want to be able to find you."

"I woan wander off, I pwomise," he said solemnly.

Althea nodded her approval and the little fellow hurried off to join his friends. Truly she envied him. He was here for a fun evening and time with his friends. It looked very likely that Althea was to have neither.

As they approached the food tables, Beulah Winsloe, who appeared to be in charge, looked up. When she spotted Oather Phillips at Althea's side she eyed her daughter-in-law with disapproval.

The older Mrs. Winsloe looked ripe and ready to give the younger a significant piece of her mind. Althea was saved, however, when Myrtle Pease called out to her from the far end of the table.

"Did you bring a meat dish, Althea? We're grouping the meats on this end of the table."

"Yes I did," she answered, cheerfully putting distance between herself and her mother-in-law's black expression. "Fresh venison with possom-grape dumplings."

There were sighs of approval all around as Oather set the big cast-iron cauldron upon the table. Althea Winsloe had a reputation for being a fine cook.

"Where did you get fresh vension?" Beulah Winsloe was

quick to ask. She was still looking daggers at both Althea and her escort. Her tone was accusatory.

"Jesse Best brought down a deer for me," she answered. "He's working at my place, helping me get ready for the winter."

"I heard that he was working for you," Myrtle Pease admitted.

"Trading some hard labor for those dogs of Paisley's is the way it was told to me," Sarah Weston piped in.

"Yes, he's helping me out and earning the price of the dogs."

Mrs. Weston shook her head and gave a conspiratory glance toward Beulah Winsloe; the two were first cousins. "It sure seems a shame to me to put a fine pack of hounds in the care of an *iddjet*."

Althea felt an immediate flare of anger spark through her. "Jesse is no idiot, he's merely feebleminded."

All three of the women, McNees clan every one, nodded in agreement as Beulah spoke. "Simple Jess is feebleminded and Pastor Jay's senile. That's the kind a minds ye can get with the Piggott clan."

The woman's verbal shot was aimed directly at Oather Phillips, who as expected blushed with shame. Jesse Best's unfortunate birth injury and Pastor Jay's loss of faculties in later life were true embarrassments for the Piggott family. The belief that such weaknesses were carried "in the blood" was not a superstition easily overcome.

Oather's silence upon his family's shortcomings only served to make Althea more quick to rise to Jesse's defense.

"Well, he's certainly a great provider," she told the women. "He got this deer on his first day out and it's big enough to keep Baby-Paisley and me in venison all winter. Have your boys done much hunting lately, Mrs. Weston?"

The woman paled and then her cheeks reddened in embarrassment. The Weston boys were well known for drinking and sleeping. Farming and hunting were not their forte.

"Let's go over and say hello to Granny Piggott," Althea suggested quickly to Oather, wanting to make her escape before Beulah and her minions could recover from their well-done set down. "That old woman must be ninety if she's a day, but her mind is quicker than most folks half her age."

Oather took her arm and led her away from the table, clearly pleased.

"Thank you taking up for my family," he said quietly.

"Oh, they don't really need much taking up for," Althea assured him. "It's just that my mother-in-law is probably not too happy to see you at my side."

"I'm sure she's not," Oather agree. "But she's right about the Piggotts. We have a strange turn of people in the family. Pastor Jay, talking to himself all day long, and poor Jesse, as dumb as a stump. Meggie marrying up with that music fellow from back east. And me."

"You?"

"I'm . . . I'm . . . well, I'm a little different," he said quietly. "You know that."

Althea didn't really know that at all. She shrugged off his words. "You're just yourself, Oather," she assured him. "Nothing too curious about that."

Granny Piggott was like a queen holding court under the broad-limbed elm. She sat in her rocking chair, smoked her pipe, and sooner or later each and every person made it over to her to pay their respects. Some she praised, some she scolded. Some were singled out for special consideration on this clear December evening. Althea and Oather were among the latter.

"Well, don't you two look right standing together," she stated, with bald approval. "Come closer, come closer. I don't see as well as I used to."

This wasn't at all the truth, but they dutifully moved forward. Granny looked up at them, rocking and smiling in approval.

"Don't you two just look fine," she said. She spoke the words between a clenched grin, unwilling as she was to relinquish the clay pipe she held between her teeth. "Both of you healthy and good-looking and just about the same height. Piggott, my late husband, was just about a hair's breadth taller than me. I always think that's important," she said.

She removed the pipe from her mouth and leaned forward as if relating a confidence. The two leaned forward to better hear her soft-spoken words.

"Some women thinks that tall men is best, but my take on it," she said, looking at them meaningfully. "And I can speak plain here 'cause dear Althea has done been married. When it comes down to the man and woman thang, it's best to have a mate that sorta fits ye."

Althea felt the blush steal into her cheeks and she stifled the naughty urge to giggle at Granny's risqué words. She managed a quick, guilty glance in Oather's direction. His complexion was more than pale, it appeared almost green as if he had suddenly taken ill.

"You'd best excuse us, Granny," Althea said quickly in a protective gesture. She hastily moved away on Oather's arm. His embarrassed reaction had been extreme. Althea felt a wave of unexpected sympathy for her unwelcome suitor. She began to chatter with feigned liveliness to distract him. It was not a mannerism natural to her character and she searched the crowd desperately for the hope of aid. She spotted it in the person of Jesse Best.

"Jesse! Jesse! Hello!"

With Oather at her side, she hurried up to the Best family, just arriving on the edge of the crowd. Onery Best was a bright-eyed and jovial man whose aging body was bent and twisted with lameness. His daughter and her husband, Meggie and Roe Farley, were a handsome young couple, obviously deeply in love with each other. Their daughter Edith was about four and as pretty a little Piggot as any ever grown on the mountain.

"Miss Althea," Jesse said, apparently a little surprised by her unexpected eagerness. "Why hello."

For the last two days he'd worked quietly around her place and she'd barely spoken to him. Too late Althea remembered the improper kiss they had shared and her vow to keep her distance.

"Mr. Best, Meggie, Roe," she addressed the family politely.

Oather had leaned forward to solemnly offer his hand to Jesse's father and brother-in-law. He nodded with only the slightest hint of condescension to Jesse.

"Look! I got a doll," little Edith Farley interrupted. "Her name if Matilda. She ain't never been to a Literary before."

Dutifully, Althea squatted down to look at the pretty little girl and her doll.

"Why, she looks just like you," Althea told the child with extravagant surprise. "You both have beautiful long hair the same color as corn silk."

"Hers *is* corn silk," Edith explained more seriously. "But mine just looks that way."

"Have you come here to play with the other children?" Althea asked her.

Little Edith nodded eagerly. "I brought my doll to show 'em."

"My little boy is out there playing. Maybe you could find him and show him."

Edith looked unsure. "Boys don't always like dolls. Why don't you have a little girl for me to play with?"

Althea ignored that question. "Some boys like dolls," she assured the child.

Edith nodded thoughtfully. "Yep, maybe," she said. "Uncle Jesse likes my doll and he's a boy, sort of."

"Yes, he is," Althea agreed with a smile.

She glanced up at Jesse standing over them. He was so tall, so huge. He was looking down at the two of them so intently, his blue eyes filled with something . . . something Althea didn't understand, but could so very clearly feel. At that moment he didn't seem like a *boy* at all.

CHAPTER  ELEVEN

Jesse always loved the Literary. He loved the good food, all the laughing and talking, the music, the dancing, and the scent of the women. He loved being around all the women on the mountain at one time and just reveling in the distinct, feminine fragrance of each. This night, this Literary was different. It was as if, like a hound, his nose picked up the scent of a trail and all other smells around him were mere distracting odors to be ignored.

Althea Winsloe. Her aroma had always been familiar to him, pleasing to him. But now, it was part of him. Now he knew both her taste and her touch, and her fragrance had been inhaled into his very bones and mingled with the scent that was his own.

"You look real pretty, Miss Althea," he said, reminding himself to doff his hat.

She did look pretty. So clean and pressed and neat as she knelt beside Little Edith and looked up at him. He wanted to drop to his knees beside her, to pull her into his arms. To taste again the hot sweetness of her mouth and feel the warm softness of her round parts against his chest. He could see in her eyes the minute that she remembered. The kiss was once again as real as the day that it had happened. And once again her brow furrowed in worry and she distanced herself from him.

She turned a big smile on his family. That smile looked to Jesse not to be quite real.

"Simple Jess has been such a help to me," she said. "I am

so grateful, Mr. Best, that you've been able to spare him from your farm."

"Oh, it's pretty much Roe and Jesse's farm these days," Best answered her. "And you jest call me Onery, now. Saying that Mr. Best makes me sound like an old grandpa." He winked broadly at Althea. "And I may be that to this little gal, but I ain't such to a pretty woman like yersef."

Althea laughed a little tentatively. "I can see where Jesse gets his flirty ways."

"Flirty way?" Meggie sounded dumbfounded and then delighted. "Jesse, have you been flirting with Althea?" she teased.

Jesse stared at his sister stupidly, wondering how to answer. Althea spoke up quickly, she was almost fluttering as she made her explanation.

"It was just a manner of speaking," she said hastily. "Of course Jesse doesn't flirt. He's very polite and very hard-working, too. He's . . . he's good with the dogs."

"Jesse ought to be good with dogs," Roe said. "He's been dreaming of having his own for years."

Meggie was easily diverted and chuckled in agreement with her husband. "I think Jesse may have more in common with dogs than he does with anything walking around on two legs."

"Well, Paisley's dogs are a rare pack, I understand," Oather Phillips chimed in. "I do hope, Simple Jess, that you are appropriately grateful to Mrs. Winsloe for letting you have them."

She hadn't *given* him the dogs, Jesse wanted to point out. He was earning them. He wanted to explain that to Oather. Oather was very smart and could think very well. He would understand the difference. Jesse wanted Oather to know that Jesse was *working* to get the dogs, they weren't a gift. He wanted to explain that. But it was too hard.

"I kilt a deer," Jesse said.

His words brought good-humored laughter and his brother-in-law patted him proudly on the back.

"I heard about that," Oather told him. "In fact, Mrs.

Winsloe here made fresh venison and possom-grape dump-lings. I carried the pot from the house for her."

"Lord Almighty!" Onery exclaimed. "Possum-grape dump-lin's are my favorite. A taste for a man to savor. We'll have to get us some of those, won't we, Jesse."

Jesse nodded mutely, but he wasn't thinking about the taste of possum-grape dumplings. He was wondering why Oather Phillips had carried the pot for Miss Althea. If she had needed someone to carry it, Jesse would have been glad to do so.

"All these men ever think about is their stomachs," Meggie complained. "Here we are with all these folks to talk to and they want to spend their time eating."

Her husband laughed at her. "We can't help ourselves," he explained. "It's the only time this family ever gets anything half-decent to eat."

Meggie feigned fury and used her elbow to punch Roe in the ribs. Meggie Best Farley's lack of cooking skills were legend on Marrying Stone Mountain.

"I brought my fiddle," Jesse interjected, indicating the contents of the pillowcase that was slung over his shoulder. "I know how you like to dance, Miss Althea. So I brung my fiddle to make you some music."

"Why, thank you, Simple Jess," Oather replied. "I enjoy dancing myself. I'd be delighted to take a turn or two across the floor with you, Mrs. Winsloe."

"I'll look forward to it," Althea answered politely.

Jesse was confused about his feelings once more. He wanted to play for Miss Althea. He wanted for her to get to dance. But he hadn't thought about the obvious fact that dancing meant she would dance with a man. Somehow, he didn't like the idea as much as he had when he'd packed his fiddle.

"I hope they'll be time for dancing," Roe said. "Orv is going to debate Labin Trace on whether snakes had legs in the Garden of Eden."

"That sounds like something more akin to the preacher's domain," Onery pointed out.

Oather nodded in agreement. "That's a certainty to last half the night and I heard a rumor that someone's planning a kangaroo court."

"A kangaroo court!" Onery whistled with delight. "Who's in the soup these days?"

Oather shook his head. "I haven't got a clue, but I feel sorry for the poor victim, whoever he is."

There was sympathetic laughter all around.

Roe put his arm around his wife. "Well, we should probably make our greeting to Granny Piggott now," he said.

"She's in fine form tonight," Althea warned.

The couple acknowledged the caution gratefully and headed off in that direction.

"Let's go get something good to eat, Grandpa," Little Edith suggested.

Onery excused the two of them, and steadying himself on the little girl's shoulder, they made their way to the tables.

Without a word, Oather simply took Althea's arm and led her away. Jesse was left standing alone, staring after them. His nostrils flared and his eyes closed. He could still smell her presence. Truly, it was like she was inside him. He opened his eyes. She was still walking away with Oather Phillips. The feeling that twisted in Jesse's heart was an unfamiliar one. He didn't recognize it and was unable to put a name to it. He was bereft.

Jesse was still standing by himself a few moments later when Buell Phillips stepped up on the porch of the schoolhouse. People began to gather close around and the crowd hushed to hear as Phillips announced the beginning of the debate.

"Resolved," Phillips called out loudly. "Prior to being condemned to crawl on its belly forevermore, the snake in the Garden of Eden walked upon legs."

The crowd politely applauded the topic under consideration.

"Advocate for the resolution is farmer and brother-in-law of our preacher Tom McNees, Mr. Orville Winsloe."

Orv stepped up on the porch and bowed slightly, accepting the praise of the crowd.

"In opposition to the resolution tonight," Buell continued, "is farmer, father of four, and grandfather of eight, Labin Trace."

Trace, who was a most frequent debater and a favorite of the crowd, took his place on the porch amid loud clapping and cries of encouragement.

Phillips repeated the resolution once more in case anyone had missed it and then left the schoolhouse porch to the verbal combatants.

Orv spoke first, quoting chapter and verse and in a tone that was stiff and superior.

It was all too hard for Jesse to understand. And he was not interested anyway. Snakes didn't have legs. He knew that. He'd seen plenty of snakes. If they had legs they were lizards. Thinking about things was hard and it didn't seem to him much of a question to ponder about. So he didn't. He wandered around the edges of the crowd for several minutes. On most Literary evenings, he'd used this kind of time to slip up to the women and just stand there and enjoy their presence. Somehow tonight that occupation didn't interest him.

He loitered on the edge of one group and then another before finally seating himself in the grass next to Granny Piggott's rocking chair. He was stroking the thin layer of grass that grew there and feeling the strength of the rock beneath it.

Granny leaned over toward him, pipe gripped securely in her teeth.

"You don't understand a word they are a-sayin', do ye?"

He looked up at the old woman, his bright blue eyes wide with honesty. "No, ma'am," he said.

She gave him what passed for a clenched-tooth smile and reached over to run a gnarled hand through his thick blond hair.

"Don't pay it no mind then," she said lovingly. "In this world, boy, such as that don't matter a flit."

Jesse nodded solemnly and leaned forward as if to

whisper a secret. "There ain't no snake with legs, Granny," he said.

The old woman hooted with laughter, causing a slight disruption of the proceeding and several people to turn and look.

"I'm believing like you, Jesse," Granny said. "And I've had plenty of years to think about both sides of the argument. What you got in that sack? You carrying your own vittles with ye?"

"I brung my fiddle," he answered. "I thought I'd play for some dancing, but Oather Phillips says there probably ain't going to be time."

Granny snorted. "Dancing is just what we need."

Turning her attention back to the speakers on the porch and the crowd gathered around them, Granny determinedly took her pipe out of her mouth.

"I've had about all this yammering I can tolerate!" she interrupted.

Labin Trace had not even finished his opening statement, and appeared momentarily dumbstruck by the unexpected interruption. He looked helplessly to Buell Phillips, who immediately stepped up on the schoolhouse porch once more.

"Granny, we're having a debate here," he said.

"Lord, don't I know it," she answered tartly. "And a bigger noise of foolishness I never heard. I didn't live all these years just to be kilt with boredom."

Titters of laughter scattered among the crowd.

"Jesse here done brought his fiddle," she went on. "I'd sure druther hear him play us some music than to hear these two drone on endlessly on something that we cain't know the truth of 'til we've been called to heaven."

A murmur of agreement began to make its way through the crowd. Of course, it didn't really matter if they agreed or not. Jesse knew that Granny got her way no matter what.

Without anybody's dictum, Jesse rose to his feet and began undoing the knot tied in his pillowcase. Jesse's fiddle had belonged to his father, who at one time had made his living as an itinerant fiddler. It was a beautiful instrument with a small neck and a fine scroll, but more than that, the fiddle had perfect tone and a purity of sound that was rare. Onery Best had given it to his son with a great deal of pride.

"You've got a way with the music," his father had said. "You're the better fiddler. By that right the fiddle should belong to you."

With that instrument in his hands, Jesse made his way through the crowd and up to the porch. With reluctance and a good deal of muttering, Buell, Orv, and Labin slipped back into the crowd.

Propping the chin piece against his collarbone, Jesse drew the bow down slowly across the e-string. He adjusted the solid brass keys slightly, then let his gaze drift across the crowd. He knew them, each and every one. And they knew him. But it wasn't until he saw Althea Winsloe's face that he stopped his perusal. He closed his eyes and let the sweet scent drift into his nostrils. Pine tar. Rosin. And Althea Winsloe.

Jesse began to play.

The music was joyous and the dancing looked fun. But Eben Baxley kept himself on the edge of the merriment and didn't bother to join in. The woman he was supposed to dance with, Althea Winsloe, was not exclusively dancing with Oather Phillips, but Phillips was keeping a close eye upon her. Eben wasn't concerned. He was confident of winning her. He had a plan being put in effect this very night. Let Phillips twirl her around on the dance floor. He wouldn't have much opportunity for that in the future.

Leisurely, Eben made his way over to Granny Piggott's rocking chair. He'd yet to greet the old woman and although he suspected she didn't altogether approve of him, he knew that it would be a grievous breach of mountain etiquette to ignore her. Granny was the one woman he'd never been quite able to charm. He had no ideas as to why that was so. But his mother had once hinted that the old woman had no use for her either.

Tonight as he approached, Granny was totally absorbed in watching Jesse Best play the fiddle. Squinty-eyed and scrutinizing, she was obviously unaware that Eben was even there. He loudly cleared his throat to get her attention.

"Evening, Granny," he said.

"What? Oh, Baxley, I seen you here earlier," she said vaguely and once more turned back to contemplate the schoolhouse porch.

Her rudeness was somewhat daunting, but Eben didn't allow it to unsettle him. He followed her lead and focused his attention upon the music being played.

"That dumb Simple Jess is one hell of a good fiddler," he commented.

"Don't you curse in my presence, boy, or I'll wash yer mouth out with soap." The old woman's scold was automatic, but halfhearted. She didn't even turn to look at him. "Can ye hear that?" she asked more quietly. "Can ye hear it and do ye know what it is?"

"What?"

"The boy's playing," she answered impatiently.

"I just said that he played good," Eben replied.

"Jesse's always been able to fiddle. He's the best I ever heard. And I heard plenty of fiddlers in my time," she said. "But I ain't never heared him play like this. There's something . . . something new about it."

Eben raised an eyebrow. He had no idea what the old woman was hearing. His brow furrowed and he listened closely. He was no expert on music and it had been years since he'd heard Jesse play. There was little chance he would notice any subtle change. Deliberately, however, he began to lend an ear to the spirited sound of the fiddle. Inexplicably, as he listened his mind conjured up the image of Mavis Phillips, her eyes dreamy and her hair tousled. There was a warm, sweet softening for her inside his heart and he wanted just to hold her, safe and secure in his arms.

Silently he cursed himself. What idiocy? Holding Mavis Phillips safe and secure? What he really wanted to do, he assured himself, was to hold her down against a nice soft place, pump her pretty body until he was limp as a dishrag, and get her out of his thoughts forever. That woman was far too often on his mind these days. He needed to concentrate

on getting himself married to Althea Winsloe. When that
farm was his 'til death to part, then he could take his fill of
Mavis at his leisure. Determinedly, he pushed all thoughts
of her to the back of his mind, though he could not dispel
her image completely.

"I don't hear nothing," he said to Granny. "Just good
fiddle."

"It's like . . ." The old woman's voice was almost
dreamy. "It makes me think like . . . like I was young
again."

Eben watched, puzzled, as she stroked the blue clay pipe
in her hand lovingly, as if it were a living creature.

Her words continued quietly. "It makes me think of my
man, Piggott. Something in that playing puts me in mind of
him. Lordy, I miss that man. After all this time, I miss him
now almost like the loss is fresh upon me. Yet, I'm not sad.
No, it's a sweet kind of feeling."

She looked anxiously toward the source of the sweet
music. Granny shook her head, puzzled. "I swear he has
never played like that before. It's almost something kindy
magical. Do you feel it?"

She turned to look at him and her expression turned wry.
"No, I don't suppose you do."

Eben eyed the old woman curiously once more and then
politely took his leave. The old gal was slipping, he
suspected. At her age he supposed it was highly likely that
a bit of good music could make her fanciful.

He walked around the clearing once more. Though he had
been raised elsewhere, these folks were still his people. His
mother was a McNees. And though his feather was raised in
the Caintuck, he'd come to this mountain first to settle.
These folks were his, and yet he had never been quite a part
of them.

The evening was almost full dark now and pine-knot
torches lighted the area around the schoolhouse. In the
shadows there were youngsters playing and folks eating. A
pile of sleeping children lay together on quilts, watched over
by Eda Trace, one baby still at her breast and another
already hinted in the broad curve of her stomach. She waved

at him as he passed and he smiled back. Eda Piggott, that's who she had been four years ago, before she'd married Tuck Trace. She'd been the prettiest girl on the mountain and had known it, too. Eben had given her a good long look back then. He might have tried to spoon her, but Mavis had distracted him. Mavis. Mavis was one distracting woman.

He pushed his thoughts of her as far away as he could and contented himself to survey the dancing. Most folks had found new dash in their feet and were cavorting around as if they never had to plow or chop or haul. They were enjoying the chance for frolic. And as he looked on, Eben couldn't help but enjoy it, too.

The Broody twins were having a little friendly competition between brothers on who could swing his partner faster. The young ladies involved were dizzy with more than excitment as the laughing, charming young men twirled them in turn. The purpose of the competition was obvious to Eben and other onlookers, but unfortunately not the young ladies. The faster a girl was twirled, the higher her skirt rose in the back. The pretty young victims were dazzled and giggling as the fresh pair of scallywags viewed with impunity their lower limbs.

Onery Best was dancing like a fool. And the folks around him gave him a wide berth. His lame leg gave him a strange tilt to his gait and it seemed at any moment he might fall down flat upon his face. But he executed both the double shuffle and the pigeon wing after a fashion and the other dancers rewarded him with a smattering of applause.

Roe Farley, the city man from the Bay State, had his wife upon his arm. Farley couldn't jig for beans, but moved in a strange rocking motion that looked like drawing water from a well. He called it the One-Step and claimed it was very popular where he came from.

Two of Gid Weston's boys, obviously liquored up, were dancing with each other, as none of the ladies chose to partner them. They were not doing very well as each insisted on leading. Only their shared ineptness kept them on the floor.

Eben was grinning broadly when he caught sight of

Mavis. His smile vanished. She was dancing with Doward
Pease. Jealousy zinged through Eben's veins and he tightened his fists. Pease was old enough to be her father, he
thought angrily. Deliberately he took a deep breath and
allowed more rational notions to penetrate his incomprehen-
sible wrath. Pease *was* in fact the father of one of her
friends. And the man's wife was not fifty yards away, in the
circle of gossipers surrounding Beulah Winsloe. There was
nothing wrong in Mavis being the old man's partner. Still, if
Eben wasn't dancing, somehow he didn't want her to be
either. It was sheer foolishness on his part. Tonight he was
going to maneuver Althea Winsloe into marrying him. He
had to stop wasting his thoughts and emotions on Mavis
Phillips.

"The boy has found love at last."

The words were spoken behind him and Eben turned to
find Pastor Jay standing there. The wizened old man was
bent and gray and his eyes were dreamy. Yet there was a
solidness about the man that was somehow comforting.

"Evening, Pastor," Eben said politely.

The title no longer was a true one, of course. Pastor Jay,
whose mind had been slipping for nearly a decade, had
retired from his position at the church nearly four years
earlier. Now the pastor's flock, Eben supposed, was the
invisible congregation that he talked aloud to day after day
as he sat alone on the Marrying Stone gazing up into the
heavens.

"He's finally found true love," Jay continued. "And I
thank the Lord Almighty for it."

"What? Who's found true love?" Eben asked, both
startled and amused.

"Why, Jesse," Pastor Jay answered. "Don't you hear him
playing it? Jesse's always spoke to us most clearly through
that fiddle. Ah, he's speaking it plain. *I'm in love. I'm in
love.* That's what his fiddle is saying."

Eben raised a skeptical brow. "A talking fiddle and
Simple Jess in love?" He shook his head. "I think you're
mistaken, Pastor."

"Truth oft looks suspect and lies are believed," he told Eben sagely.

"Perhaps so, but who on earth could Jesse be in love with?" Eben asked.

Thoughtfully the old man tapped a finger against his chin. "Now there, right you are, that's a puzzle," he said. "Heaven wouldn't send just any gal for Jesse. He's a favorite, you know."

Eben smiled more kindly. "No, I didn't know. So he's a favorite of yours is he, Pastor?" Eben glanced back at Jesse, who was bowing his instrument rapidly in the yellow glow of the torches.

The old man's eyes widened in surprise. "Oh, not mine. He's not a favorite of mine. I have no favorites," the pastor proclaimed. "All the lambs on this mountain are equal in this herder's care." He sighed with pleasure as he gestured toward the handsome young fiddler once more. "Jesse is a favorite of Heaven."

Eben grinned, incredulous. "*Simple Jess* is God's favorite?"

Pastor Jay nodded with animation. "That's what they say and of course it makes perfect sense. The Good Lord did command to 'come unto me like a little child.' Our Jesse sure always does that."

"That's what who says?" Eben asked him with puzzled amusement.

"Why, the angels."

"You talk to angels?"

Pastor Jay put his hands on his hips and looked at Eben with genuine annoyance. "Well, who else am I going to talk to around here? I spend all day, ever' day, up there on that stone. Why, if I didn't have the angels to talk to, I'd have to just blabber on to myself."

Eben's grin broadened, but his words were soft as he patted the daft old man on the shoulder. "You just talk to whoever you've got a mind to, Pastor. And you give them my best regards."

The aged preacher smiled kindly at him. "That I'll do, son," he said.

"I see Tom and Orv over there," Eben continued, pointing them out. "I have some business with them and I'd best be at it."

It was a polite dismissal and Pastor Jay nodded. "Right so, you go on about your business. You're a fine young man, son. You remind me so much of your father."

Eben had just stepped away when he stopped in his tracks and turned back to the preacher.

"What did you say?"

"I said you put me in mind of your father. You are much like him, you know. Good man down at the core. A real good man at the core."

Eben laughed, but there was no humor in it. His words were hard-edged and steely. "You've got me confused with some other fellow, Pastor," he said.

"You're Baxley, ain't ye? Clyde and Dora's boy. I married them, you know," the old man said. "It weren't the best match I ever saw, but good come of it, I suppose. They had you."

Eben nodded. "I'm their son."

The pastor smiled and continued to ruminate. "I remembered you, I did. I remembered you from the funeral. It was me that spoke the words when your daddy was put in his grave. He was a fine, good man."

"My father was weak. I am nothing like him. I despise him. He was a weak man and worthless," Eben whispered harshly.

"Oh, no," Pastor Jay corrected, almost with humor. "That's what people *thought* him to be. But it was not the truth about him at all." The old man wagged a finger at Eben as if correcting a schoolboy error. "Didn't I just explain to you that truth oft looks suspect and lies are believed?"

"I remember my father, Pastor," Eben said firmly. "I remember him very well."

"But you only knew him when he was in prison."

"In prison? My father was never in prison."

"Oh, yes," the old man continued. "It was a prison all right. Drink was his prison. It held him fettered and fast."

Pastor Jay's tone softened to consolation. "Don't grieve so, son. He's free now."

Eben's eyes widened with shock and then narrowed with anger. He cursed vividly.

"Crazy old fool!" He scowled, storming away.

CHAPTER  TWELVE

Jesse Best had never fiddled better. That's what everyone was saying and Althea Winsloe couldn't help but agree. Like a house afire he'd played everything from "Molly Lockett" to "Ryestraw," and "Fisher's Hornpipe." It was all wonderfully executed and without Jesse even hesitating to catch his breath.

Althea had hardly had time to catch her own. She'd danced every dance, stopping only on two occasions to assure herself that Baby-Paisley had not gotten himself into any trouble. After an exciting evening of play, the little fellow lay spent and sleeping in a pile of quilts and like-minded toddlers near the edge of the clearing.

Althea herself was nearly breathless with exhaustion. Surely Jesse, who had played full tilt all night, must be nearly ready to drop.

Observing Jesse, however, he did not appear overly fatigued. He looked so strong and tall and masculine standing in the glow of the pine-knot torches. His fingers moved with such dexterity upon the fiddle's fine curved neck, and when he drew the bow, it was as if his body, all of it, were a part of what made the sound. He was handsome, very handsome. And he seemed so whole. That was it, Althea realized. When he played the fiddle, none could tell that he was simple, slow-witted, less than other men. Perhaps, Althea thought, that was because when he played he was not. She glanced at him once more as Oather Phillips twirled her in that direction. Jesse fiddled music from his heart, not from his mind. So when he played it, you couldn't tell that he was feebleminded. She couldn't tell it when he'd kissed her either.

The thought brought a guilty blush to her cheeks. She'd spent much time pushing away the traitorous feelings that had come upon her when Simple Jesse Best had held her in his arms. She trembled even now at the memory of it. For that one wonderful moment she'd felt safe, desired, beloved. One sweet moment, and she was so ashamed!

She had never shirked Paisley's touch, but it had never thrilled her as Jesse's had. That was because of the illicit-ness of it, she assured herself. Paisley had been her husband. He'd had a legal and moral right to her body and she'd had a legal and moral obligation to make it available to him. There was nothing legal or moral about kissing Jesse Best. It had been sin, plain as day. Breathless, heart-stopping sin. And one of the worst kind. The sin of taking advantage of a lesser creature. As the set ended, she glanced up at him on the porch. His eyes were bright, his smile was wide, and a thin sheen of sweat plastered his thin cotton shirt to the masculine contours of his body. He did not look at all like a lesser creature, and certainly not one that had been sinned against.

Determinedly she focused her attention back on Oather Phillips and the other folks who surrounded her. It had turned out to be a surprisingly pleasant evening. Her mother-in-law had kept her distance and none of the McNees clan had even mentioned marriage to her all night. Oather was an excellent dancer. He moved on the floor with such grace that Althea felt the two of them were almost gliding on ice. And he didn't, as some other gentlemen, stand too close or let his hand stray to her waist. Nor did he try to sweet-talk, tease, or flatter her. He kept himself at a respectable distance and a civil tongue in his head. He therefore proved to be a pleasant companion. She was enjoying herself. She needed this, she was sure. Her isolation and worry of the past few months were surely part of the cause of her unseemly behavior with Jesse. A fun-filled frolic away from the cares of the farm would do much to sort out her strange temperament. And she was having fun.

However, when Tom McNees, Orv Winsloe, and Eben Baxley stepped up to the schoolhouse porch and stopped the music, a sense of unease settled in Althea's heart.

"Kangaroo court!" Orv called out. "We're calling a kangaroo court."

The crowd immediately began to laugh and cheer. Althea did not. Her father-in-law was a man almost completely devoid of anything resembling a sense of humor. His calling out for a kangaroo court somehow did not ring true as an invitation to fun and games. A niggling worry skittered through her heart. Inexplicably she glanced toward Jesse. He was looking straight at her. His eyes reflected the worry in her own.

"Who's it to be, Orv?" someone called out. "Who's up for justice?"

"Has one of these young rascals been peekin' in the church privy again?" another hollered.

"Whoever it is, let's behead 'em by sunup!" a third voice joined in with laughter.

The kangaroo court was a well-loved amusement on the mountain. It had come about as a way to teach folks who had never left the mountain about laws and courts and the ways of the world outside. But it was as exciting, entertaining, and comedic as any play put on for city folks. *Defendants* accused of such humorously heinous crimes as swallowing watermelon seeds, singing to hogs, or putting wishweed under their pillow at night were tried before a jury of their peers. *Lawyers* spoke for each side of the story. And a *judge* handed out punishments.

Pigg Broody made his way to the schoolhouse porch. "I'll be a-judging," he announced. "I ain't had a turn at it in a month of Sundays."

There was a smattering of applause at that announcement. Pigg was a character any time of the day or night, but as a judge, he was unequaled in brass buffoonery.

Tom, Orv, and Eben had their heads together for a minute and then Orv spoke.

"Pigg Broody suits us fine as judge, we accept."

The old man snorted sort of offhand in acknowledgment and seated himself on the edge of the porch, his tobacco spit can beside him at the ready.

"Who you wanting to try?" he asked Orv.

"Althea Winslow," Orv answered loudly.

Pigg's eyes widened. "What's the charge?"

"Failing to remarry."

A gasp of surprise went through the crowd. Althea stood still as a stone and mute as folks turned to look at her. This was not like making a pie with green apples or collecting rainwater in a leaky barrel. There was no intent to be fun here and Althea saw no possible outcome but a bad one.

"Go arrest her," Judge Broody directed.

Tom McNees hurried toward her, the folks in front moving away to allow him a path. He grabbed her arm. Althea found her voice.

"No!" she said sharply. "Let me be. I'll not have any part of this."

"The accused never wants to go on trial," Pigg pointed out to the gathering.

"There is no reason to bring me to court," Althea insisted.

Pigg leaned forward and eyed her speculatively. "So you've remarried and just ain't tole us."

That statement was greeted with laughter by the assembled.

"I haven't remarried," she answered with deliberate calm. "But that's not a crime."

"That's for the court to decide," Orv told her sharply. "The judge and the jury can say that. The accused cannot."

Althea huffed with indignation. "The kangaroo court is supposed to be a game," she said. "This is no game, Orv Winsloe. You're up to something."

He shrugged. "I'm only up to the truth. I think these folks want to find out the truth."

"Truth is something you find in church," Althea countered, with a contemptuous glance toward Tom McNees. "The kangaroo court is not for truth, it's supposed to be fun. And this is not my idea of fun."

"Yer sure entitled to yer ideas," Judge Pigg agreed thoughtfully before taking a good long spit into his can. "But I don't think they's anything in the rules that says kangaroo court *has* to be fun. I ain't never heared of a rule like that. Did you, Orv?"

"Never," Althea's father-in-law replied.

There was a murmur through the crowd.

"Bring her up here, Tom."

Satisfaction upon his face, Tom McNees half-led, half-dragged Althea forward. She stared daggers at Tom McNees.

"You shouldn't be a party to such a thing as this," she told him in a harsh whisper. "You were Paisley's own uncle. And our preacher as well."

Tom didn't answer. Those things were true. But Althea knew that he was also Beulah Winsloe's brother and he'd been doing exactly what that woman told him all his life. Althea had no illusions about who was behind this little game and why.

She stood before the judge, her head high and her jaw tight. Althea was grateful that the torches could not well reveal her color. She felt as pale as death.

"Well, we will be needing a jury," Pigg said, punctuating his statement with a spit of tobacco. "Labin, you got shorted on the debate this evening, you want in on this one?"

"Sure, I'm willing," the man answered as he stepped through the crowd to stand on the edge of the porch.

Pigg scanned the crowd once more. "Miz Pease, how about you?"

The woman nodded and made her way to the front.

"Jesse, you want to be on this jury? You always seem to enjoy yourself a-doing it."

Althea looked up at see him standing to the left of the crowd. He'd put his fiddle back into its pillowcase and appeared wide-eyed and confused. He was looking straight at her. His expression was questioning. Kangaroo courts were supposed to be fun. Clearly he sensed that this one was not.

"He can't be on the jury," Orv interjected. "Simple Jess is being called as a witness."

"He's a witness?" Pigg's tone was condescending.

"Yessir, Yer Honor," Orv answered.

Pigg shook his head and spit his tobacco. "Well, all right, Jesse. You just stay where you are. Let's see here, ah—all right, Dora Weston, how about you?" He indicated the woman standing with Beulah Winsloe.

"It'd be my pleasure," she announced. She gave Althea a long assessing look as she passed by to take her place among the jury.

Pigg had just begun to peruse the crowd once more when Granny Piggott stood up and called out to the Broody twins.

"Ned! Jed! You take my chair up to the porch, I'm a-sitting on this jury."

"Now, Granny," Pigg interrupted. "Folks don't *choose* to sit on the jury, the judge picks who'll be on it."

Granny clamped her pipe between her teeth and put her hands on her hips. "All right, Judge Piggott Dunderwaulf Broody, pick somebody for your jury."

Pigg winced visibly at the sound of his middle name. "There're two women on the jury already," he said.

Granny shrugged with unconcern. "I'm neither a man nor a woman no more. I've lived long enough to see both sides of the question. And I've lived long enough to remember when you were still in short pants."

His Honor the judge gave a heavy sigh of resignation. "Granny Piggott for the final juror."

The twins carried her rocking chair to the porch and helped her into it. She immediately began smoking and rocking, her expression thoughtful.

"All right now. Are you the prosecutor, Orv?"

"No, I'm going to let Eben do that."

"You?" Althea's tone was incredulous as she stared at him in horror. "How dare *you* make accusations against me."

"I'm making the accusation," Orv insisted. "I'm just letting this young fellow here speak for me. He's family after all."

"*I* am family." Althea's tone was harsh with anger.

"Oh, stuff and nonsense," Pigg broke in. "We're all family of one kind er another. We're either Piggotts or McNees and most of us got in-laws on the other side. So let's not be making this into some kind of feud."

The crowd murmured agreement.

"Who's to defend ye, gal?" Pigg asked.

"I'll defend her," Oather Phillips piped in, stepping up beside her.

Althea turned to stare at him in surprise.

"Trying to please the lady, Oather?" Eben asked. His voice was heavily laced with sarcasm. "Well, it might work, I suppose. But most of us fellers know ways that are quicker."

There was a hoot of risqué laughter from some of the young men present. Oather ignored the jibe.

"I know a lot about the law," he explained, more to Althea than to the crowd. "I know the *real* law. And I think I am a worthy match for such as Eben Baxley."

Eben chuckled unkindly and addressed the crowd. "Yep, a worthy match. We can all still see the bruises on yer face."

More laughter erupted.

Phillips's brow narrowed in anger. "I don't mind fighting in defense of women."

"I suppose not," Eben answered, speaking more to the crowd than to Oather. "You're about half woman yourself."

The taunt could not be ignored. Phillips took a threatening step forward. His father muscled his way through the crowd.

"You trying to start something, Baxley," Buell snarled. "I'm here to help finish it."

"Little Oather is going to need help," Eben answered.

"Now, now, fellers." Pigg Broody rose to his feet to stand between the two threatening combatants. "There ain't nothing here to bring us to fisticuffs. And I'd think the both of ye to have sufficient taste of that recently."

The likely menace lessened, but the two young men stared daggers at each other.

"Baxley," Pigg continued. "Yer comments were dang libelous and clear outer line. Apologize."

"Apologize?"

Pigg's tone was stern. "Apologize, or I'll find ye in contempt of this court."

Eben glanced momentarily at Orv and Tom, who were watching him expectantly. Deliberately he relaxed his shoulders and let go of his breath.

"I apologize," he said quietly. "Didn't mean a thing by it, I assure ye."

"Good, then that's settled," Pigg announced. The Phillips men took a half step backward, but neither appeared particularly happy.

"Widder Winsloe," Pigg said, determinedly moving forward and directing his questions to Althea. "Do you want Oather Phillips here to defend you?"

Althea was appalled at the near outbreak of violence and angry at being in the center of it.

"No, I won't have him defending me," she said.

"Then who do ye want?"

"No one. I don't need anyone," she insisted. "I haven't done anything!"

"Then you choose to defend yerself," Pigg announced.

"I have done nothing wrong!"

"That's for the jury to decide, young woman. So we'd best be at it. You about ready, Eben?"

Baxley gave Althea a long look, it was almost kindly. He leaned forward slightly to whisper to her. "You look mad enough to spit, honey," he said. "Don't you remember I told you that starchiness is downright unattractive to fellers?"

Her answer was a furious glance that caused him to actually laugh out loud.

"No need to take on so, honey. Things are going to work out for the best."

"Call me Mrs. Winsloe."

He grinned. "Right, Miz Winsloe." He turned back to the judge. "I'm ready, Your Honor."

Pigg nodded. "Then call up yer first witness."

"I call Beulah Winsloe."

Althea's mother-in-law took the stand, which was simply

a seat next to Pigg, with the regal superiority of a queen ascending to her throne.

Eben was smiling and confident as his first witness settled in.

"Miz Winsloe," he began and glanced back toward Althea. He oozed of charm. "This is a bit confusing having Miz Winsloe as the accused and Miz Winsloe as a witness. I suspect I should call you Miz Winsloe, the elder, but truth to tell, you two don't look much apart in years."

Beulah tittered almost girlishly.

Althea rolled her eyes.

"Miz Winsloe, what is your kinship to this woman here standing accused?"

"She's my daughter-in-law."

"And your son?"

"Paisley Winsloe," she answered. "As fine a young man as ever walked these mountain paths, God rest his soul, he passed on nearly two years ago."

"Two years," Eben repeated. "That's a long time. Of course as his mother you still grieve."

She nodded solemnly. "Yes, I grieve every day. But life does go on."

"Yes," Eben agreed. "Life does go on. Now, Miz Winsloe, your daughter-in-law, does her life go on?"

Beulah's sorrowful tone disappeared like magic. "Indeed it does."

"Do you think that she grieves for your son?"

"Of course I do!" Althea blurted out angrily.

"Don't interrupt," Pigg ordered. "You'll get yer time to question the witness."

"She doesn't grieve as I do," Beulah answered.

"What do you mean?"

"I mean, I think she's sad that he'd dead, but I don't think it's the same. Why, she was only wed to him a short while. He's been my son since the day he was born."

"Ah yes, I see," Eben answered. "Now this woman," he continued, pointing to Althea. "This woman has flatly refused to remarry. Is that correct?"

Beulah nodded. Her voice took on an affronted tone. "She

told me to my face that she wouldn't have another husband."

"Because she still grieves for her husband?"

"No, that's not why at all."

"She told you why?"

"Yes, she did. She told me that she wasn't giving up that farm to anyone."

"The farm. Ah . . . that's your son's farm."

"Yes."

"And your daughter-in-law wants it for herself."

"I want it for my son!" Althea blurted.

"Wait your turn," Pigg scolded once more.

"She wants it for herself," Beulah said firmly, looking Althea square in the eye. "And she wants her son for herself, too. She don't want no interference from any man on raising her boy. She don't even want me and Orv to have any say about him neither. That farm is my son's, and that boy is my son's. And she don't want me to have no say in neither. Althea Winsloe is just selfish through and through."

"That's all the questions I have, Judge."

Clearly Eben felt that he'd won the round. He accepted the nods and encouragement of the crowd gracefully.

Pigg nodded. "You can ask whatever you like now," he told Althea.

Althea hesitated. Her mind was awhirl. She didn't know what to say. She felt naked, exposed. She felt that they were all against her. She had a right to live her life how she pleased. To do what she thought best for her son. To keep her husband's land for him. She didn't want Baby-Paisley to be some man's stepchild. She knew what that was like and she wanted better for her boy. There was nothing wrong in that. Her frustration grew. Her question came from that frustration.

"Why are you doing this to me?" she asked Beulah painfully.

"Object!" Eben said sharply. "That's not a proper question, Your Honor. This witness is a witness. She hasn't brought the accused to this court, we have."

"He's got the right of that," Pigg told her. "You got a better question, Althea?"

Nearly bristling with determination, Althea attempted to gather her wits about her, to form a plan for her defense.

"Mother Winsloe," she began. "Is every woman who becomes a widow on this mountain expected to marry?"

"No, of course not. Some are, some aren't."

"And what determines whether a widow should remarry?" Althea asked.

Beulah hesitated. "Well, her age, I suspect, and her health."

"What about her feelings? Does a woman's feelings have nothing to do with whether she remarries?"

"The feelings of her family count as much as her own," Beulah stated adamantly.

Althea let those words go unchallenged. She glanced over at the jury.

"Granny Piggott was still a young woman when she was widowed. The Piggotts didn't make her remarry. Why is the McNees family different?"

Beulah huffed. "Granny Piggott was forty if she was a day when her man died."

"That's a bald-faced lie," Granny contended, shaking her pipe at Beulah. "I barely had the rose off my cheeks."

The crowd chuckled in humor at her reaction.

"Yer outer order, Granny," Pigg told her.

"I'll put *her* outer order, if she ain't real careful," the old woman threatened.

When the chatter died, Althea asked her question again. "Why must the McNees women remarry and the Piggotts not?"

"It ain't Piggott or McNees," Beulah answered. "It's the woman herself."

"But you just said it was the family," Althea pointed out. "If it's the woman herself, then *this* woman simply chooses not to."

There was some murmur of agreement.

"Sometimes a woman don't know what's best for her and her family has to help her to do what's right."

Mumbles of concurrence for that statement filtered through the crowd.

"Help her to do what's right," Althea repeated Beulah's words. "Do you mean what's right for the woman or what's right for the family."

"It's the same thing."

"Is it?" Althea's expression was skeptical. "Do you want your grandson, Baby-Paisley, to inherit the farm that you gave your son?"

"I surely do."

"If I were to remarry, wouldn't that inheritance be in jeopardy?"

"Not if you married someone in the family."

Althea nodded thoughtfully and rephrased her mother-in-law's answer. "So you not only insist that I remarry, for my own good," she added, turning halfway toward the crowd with emphasis, "but you get to choose who the groom will be."

"Object, Your Honor," Eben interrupted. "Miz Winsloe has not insisted on anything. She's telling this court a few things about her daughter-in-law."

"Your Honor," Althea countered. "Her daughter-in-law just wants Mother Winsloe to tell the court a few things about herself."

Pigg was thoughtful. "Well, can ye come up with kindy a better way to ask?"

"All right," Althea agreed. She hesitated, thinking. "Mother Winsloe, how many times have you mentioned remarriage to me."

"I've spoke about it," she answered. "How would I know how many times? I don't go around counting my conversations."

"Well, could you make a guess?"

"I could guess, I suppose. A few times."

"A few times?"

"Well, more than a few times."

Althea nodded. She turned back to face the assemblage as she asked her next question.

"And when you first started talking about this remarriage,

who by name did you suggest as a suitable husband for me?"

Beulah's expression was cross as she turned to the judge. "I don't see how this matters nothing."

Althea still didn't look at her.

"Answer the question, Beulah," Pigg admonished.

Beulah huffed disgustedly and then answered so softly it was barely above a whisper. "Tom."

"What did you say, I'm not sure everybody heard it?" Althea prodded as she turned to face her.

"Tom," Beulah answered more loudly.

"Tom." Althea turned to face the crowd and then pointed at a rather red-faced Tom McNees, who was standing to the far side of the porch. "This Tom? Tom McNees, your brother, our preacher?"

The crowd tittered delightedly, both at the suggestion and at the much-apparent embarrassment of both Beulah and her brother.

"You know there ain't no other Tom."

"Isn't it a bit unusual for a woman to marry the uncle of her late husband, the brother of her mother-in-law?"

"It's done. Ain't no law forbidding," Beulah insisted. "Nothing vile or immoral about it. You ain't more blood to him than you were to Paisley."

"But it is a little strange to match me up with a lifelong bachelor twice my age."

"Tom's a fine, good man. He deserves a good wife," Beulah stated adamantly.

Althea feigned puzzlement. "But, Mother Winsloe, haven't you, since the day I married your son, told each and every human being on this mountain what a poor wife you think I am?"

Hoots of laughter filled the air. Althea had clearly hit the target. Beulah was an unwavering gossip and complainer. Her daughter-in-law, Althea, had long been the most frequent victim of her unhappy colloquy.

Althea let the round of amusement slowly fade out.

"So, Mother Winsloe, what was in fact the main reason

that you chose your brother, Tom McNees, for my potential bridegroom?"

Beulah sat mute for a long moment, her cheeks puffed up in anger.

"I don't have to answer that, do I?" She asked the question of Eben, but it was Pigg that replied.

"Beulah, we're all waiting to hear."

Chin high, she answered sharply, "As Tom's wife, you'd have to do what Tom tells you to do."

Althea nodded and folded her arms across her chest. "And who is it that tells Tom what to do?"

Once more the crowd exploded in laughter. Beulah's expression could have turned August to icicles. And Tom McNees's face was now so florid, he appeared in danger of having a stroke.

Althea didn't wait for her mother-in-law to try to answer that one. "No more questions, Your Honor," she said simply.

The spectators actually applauded. Althea raised her chin challengingly toward Eben Baxley. He looked less confident, but not defeated. His eyes narrowed shrewdly.

"May I ask this witness one more question?" he said.

Folks began to hush, wanting to hear.

"That's re-DI-rect, young man," Pigg answered. "You want to redirect?"

"Yes, I do."

"Go ahead," Pigg suggested.

"Miz Winsloe, you ruled out your brother as a potential husband for your daughter-in-law. Is that correct?"

"I sure did."

"Why did you change your mind?"

"That's two questions," Althea pointed out.

Pigg waved her words away. "It's redirect, he can ask as many as he pleases."

"I just need this one," Eben said, almost smiling again. "What made you decide that Tom McNees would not make a good husband for Althea Winsloe?"

Beulah looked momentarily confused as if she had no idea what Baxley might be getting at.

"Just answer truthfully, Miz Winsloe," he told her.

"Well," Beulah said. "I sort of realized that a young woman like her, still in the prime of her life, well . . . she would need a younger man. One who was more appealing in a man-woman kind of way. Or who could, you know, show her more affection."

"You mean one that she'd more likely want to be bedding up with."

A gasp of shock reverberated through the crowd. Several ladies actually screamed. Judge Broody swallowed a big jaw of his tobacco. And Beulah Winsloe covered her eyes in horror.

Althea paled so, she felt she might faint. Such things were just not discussed in mixed company. And to be discussing *her*, she felt as if she had been stripped naked in front of the crowd. Her heart trembling in her throat she looked around for help and sympathy. She found it in a pair of vivid blue eyes watching her so intently. Jesse clearly didn't know what had happened. But this unwavering loyalty, his so-very-dependable presence, was somehow a warm, soothing comfort.

"Lord Almighty!" Pigg exclaimed furiously, rising to his feet to harangue Eben. "Where do you think you are, boy? In a bawdy house or in a schoolboy sneak behind the barn!"

Tom and Orv both stepped up to young Baxley's side and were, in furious whispers, giving their representative a thorough piece of their minds.

Nearly every person present was chattering excitedly. Talking all at once, louder and louder. The sound created couldn't have been duplicated at the Tower of Babel. Althea kept her eyes on Jesse, strong silent Jesse. She knew in that moment that more than anyone present he understood her public humiliation. He understood the burn of shame that stained her cheeks.

"Hush!" Granny Piggott ordered loudly as she came to her feet. "You people act as if you'd ne'er heard of the birds and bees."

The people quieted as the old woman eyed them scornfully. "All right, young feller," Granny said, addressing Eben. "What're ye getting at? And mind you, it better be something, 'cause right now it just seems like yer up to no good."

"I *am* getting to something," Eben insisted. He turned to Pigg, who still looked rather green from his unwelcome ingestion of half-chewed tobacco. "If I could call my next witness, I think I could make it all very clear."

"I ain't so dang sure," Pigg answered.

"Judge," Eben said, deliberately using his title to pull the participants back into the focus of the kangaroo court. "This whole case is a question of whether Althea should do what she wants or follow the direction of her family and remarry. It really all hangs on what is really best for her. I think I can show that remarriage is what's best."

Pigg pondered thoughtfully for a moment, then shrugged. "Step down, Beulah. Call your next witness, Mr. Baxley."

"I call Simple Jess," he said.

CHAPTER THIRTEEN

Jesse was surprised to hear his name called. The folks were picking on Miss Althea. They were saying things to hurt her. Part of him wanted to just start slugging people. Another part wanted to run over and pull her into his arms. But Pa had taught him never to hit unless the other fellow hit first. And Miss Althea had told him he couldn't hold her in his arms. No, not ever again.

"Come on, Jesse," Pigg Broody said to him. "Come on over here and take a seat. We know you ain't ne'er been a witness before, but you've seen plenty of kangaroo courts. You know that the witnesses jest answer the questions."

Jesse nodded and made his way across the porch. He felt strange sitting by the judge when Eben and Miss Althea and everybody else was standing.

He looked closely at Miss Althea. Her expression had changed. She still wasn't happy. Jesse could tell that. But she didn't look as hurt anymore. She was worried, Jesse decided. His heart lifted lightly with further realization. She was worried about him.

He grinned at her, to show her that he was all right.

"All right, Jesse," Eben Baxley began. "Like the judge told you, all you have to do is just answer the questions with the truth. You do know the truth from lies, don't you, Simple Jess?"

Jesse was affronted. "Course I do. I been to more churching than you have, Eben Baxley."

The crowd laughed at that answer as Eben nodded

agreement. A lot of the tension from moments earlier was drained from the air.

"So all you need to do, Jesse, is tell us the truth about what you've seen and heard."

"I ain't seen or heard nothing," he said.

Laughter once more.

"Wait until I ask the questions, all right?"

Jesse nodded.

"You've been working out on Miz Winsloe's farm, haven't you?"

"I'm working to earn the dogs," he explained. "Miss Althea says they are mine, Eben. So you cain't have 'em, I don't care what you say."

"The dogs don't really matter right now," Eben began.

"They sure matter to me!" Jesse interjected.

The crowd chuckled once more.

"What I want to ask you about is Miz Winsloe," Eben said. "You've been spending a lot of time out at the farm with Miz Winsloe, haven't you?"

"Pretty near every day," Jesse answered.

"So you know just about everything that is going on there, don't you?"

He nodded vaguely. "Well, I guess so," he said, a bit of concern creeping into his thoughts. "I don't always understand all of the things."

"Now don't worry about that. I'm not going to ask you to explain, just to say what you have seen or heard."

Eben was smiling broadly, very friendlylike. Jesse's brow furrowed. Eben Baxley was not his friend, he was sure of that.

"Do you recall the day I came up to Miz Winsloe's farm?"

"Yep," Jesse answered. "I'd caught two rabbits and a possum in my snares."

Eben continued to smile. "Yes, that must have been a day to remember," he said.

Little titters of laughter could be heard in the crowd. Jesse didn't know what he'd said funny, but he smiled back at the folks as if he did.

"What did I do when I came to the farm?"

"You talked to me about the dogs," Jesse told him truthfully.

Eben sounded impatient. "After the talk about the dogs," he said.

"You went up to the house," Jesse answered.

"Miz Winsloe's house."

"Ain't no other house there."

More chuckles. Again Jesse smiled. He was beginning to relax a little. Miss Althea still looked worried. But Jesse thought he could do it. He thought he could answer the questions. There really was no trick to telling the truth. It just spilled out of a person.

"Who was up at the house that afternoon?"

"Nobody," Jesse answered. "Just Miss Althea and Baby-Paisley."

"And do you know what they were doing?"

"Miss Althea was baking bread. It was a Thursday. And the little boy was taking a nap, like he does every afternoon."

"So." Eben turned away. He was facing the crowd, but he was, it seemed, still talking to Jesse. "I was in Miz Winsloe's house alone with her while her baby was sleeping."

Jesse's brow furrowed. "Well, yeah, I guess you was."

"How long was I in the house?"

"Awhile, I guess."

"A long while or a short while?"

"I ain't got no watch," Jesse answered. "I cain't tell time, so I don't need one, I suspect."

"I was alone in the house with Miz Winsloe a good bit of time, wasn't I, Simple Jess?"

Jesse didn't quite know what Eben was getting at. But he didn't think it could hurt to tell the truth, he nodded.

"Well, yes, I guess so."

"Did you see Baby-Paisley after that?"

"Why sure."

"When did you next see him?" Eben had turned back to

face Jesse. His eyes were calculating and keen, like a fox planning a double-back trail.

"I seen him in just a few minutes," Jesse answered.

"What did he do?"

"Baby-Paisley come out of the house and went off playing," he said.

"And at that time I was alone in the house with Miz Winsloe."

He made his statement louder than necessary. It almost sounded to Jesse like some kind of announcement. Jesse glanced over at Althea. She still looked worried. He became worried, too.

"Well, yes," he said finally.

"Did that seem right to you?"

"Right?" Jess could see himself getting cornered. Somehow the words were on all sides of him and he couldn't get past. Eben was trapping Jesse with words as easily as Jesse could trap a rabbit. Jesse didn't understand how, but he knew it was happening and for the life of him he didn't know how to avoid that snare.

"Did it seem right to you that I should be in the house alone with Miz Winsloe?" Eben continued.

"No, no it didn't seem right, I guess. But I don't think it was wrong neither. Miss Althea wouldn't do nothing wrong."

"Just answer the questions, Jesse. What did you think about my being alone in the house with Miz Winsloe?"

"Well, I didn't like it," Jesse admitted. "I didn't like it at all."

Eben nodded and spoke more softly as if he were attempting to comfort Jesse.

"You didn't *know* that there was anything wrong, but even being simple, Jesse Best, you didn't like me being alone in there with her."

It was a statement that didn't seem to call for an answer. Jesse turned his puzzled gaze to Althea. She was biting down upon her lower lip.

"So what did you do, Jesse?"

"What did I do?"

"When you didn't feel right about me being in the house alone with Miz Winsloe," Eben said. "What did you do?"

"I went up to the house."

"You went up to the house," Eben repeated loudly. "You went up to the house, unannounced."

"Unannounced?" Jesse was unfamiliar with the word.

"You just walked through the door, didn't you, Jesse? You didn't knock or call out or anything like that to let the people inside the house know that you were coming."

Jesse blushed slightly. Had he been supposed to call out? Sometimes he made mistakes about the way to do things. His sister Meggie warned him about that. She said it made him look rude. Jesse hadn't meant to be rude.

"Nope. Didn't see no need to call out," he answered. "I just walk in the house when I want mostly, except in the morning when Miss Althea might be abed. She don't mind my comings and goings, at least she's never said."

The explanation was made for the other people more than Eben. Eben ignored it completely.

"Simple Jess," he said, facing the crowd once more. "Tell us what you saw when you walked into the house that day, unannounced."

"I seen you and Miss Althea."

"And what were we doing?" Eben was not looking at anybody now. He was facing the crowd, but he was staring down at his shoes as if he didn't want to meet anyone's eye.

"You weren't doing anything," Jesse said.

"We weren't doing nothing?" Eben turned to face Jesse. "Nope."

"Tell the truth, Jesse," he whispered.

"I am."

"Where were we, Jesse? Where were Miz Winsloe and myself?"

"On the bed."

There was a gasp from the crowd. Jesse looked at Althea. Her eyes were closed. Jesse wondered if she was praying.

"We were on the bed," Eben repeated.

"Yes," Jesse admitted quietly.

"Were we sitting on the bed?" Eben asked.

Jesse's brow furrowed. "No, not sitting exactly."

"Tell the folks how you caught us on the bed," Eben encouraged.

Jesse swallowed nervously. Nobody was laughing now. Everybody was listening close. As one they were almost leaning in to hear.

"Well," he said nervously. "Miss Althea, she was kindy lying down and you was bending over her some."

There were hisses of whisper coming in every direction. They were hurriedly hushed.

"She was laying on the bed and I was bending over her."

Jesse knew then what he was trying to get at. Eben Baxley was trying to make it sound like he'd been doing *that* with Miss Althea. It wasn't true. It wasn't true at all, but it was what he was trying to get the folks to believe.

"That was how it looked," Jesse stated with conviction. "But it weren't nothing."

"What happened when we saw you, Jesse?"

"You got up. Miss Althea got up, too."

"So when you walked in," Baxley stated more loudly, "Miz Winsloe and I were lying on the bed and when you saw us we got up."

"Well, yep, I guess so. But nothing had happened."

"Nothing had happened, you know that."

"Yes."

"And you know that because you didn't hear Miss Althea scream or cry out for help."

"I knew nothing happened, 'cause all I could smell was fresh bread."

Eben appeared momentarily puzzled at that comment but he didn't give Jesse a chance to explain.

"Just answer the questions, Jesse. Miss Winsloe was lying upon the bed with me and she didn't scream, or yell out for help, or try to push me away."

"No."

"Because," he said, turning to face the crowd once more, "she apparently didn't find my attentions unwelcome."

"'Cause you didn't do nothing," Jesse explained quickly. He was getting angry now. Eben Baxley was talking bad about Miss Althea. That he understood. He shouldn't be doing that. Miss Althea was good. She was very good.

"There weren't no attentions," Jesse said, his fury growing. "You're talking like you tried something and she let you, but that didn't happen."

"You're sure of that."

"I'm sure."

"Why?"

"Because . . . because . . ." Jesse silently cursed his weak mind. There were reasons why. There were good reasons why. Jesse had to think of those reasons. Jesse had to think of them now. Eben Baxley was trying to hurt Miss Althea and Jesse couldn't let him do it.

"There was nothing happening between you. I didn't sense nothing."

"You didn't *sense* nothing?" Eben's face was close and he was scornful with amusement. "Are you so knowledgeable of the ladies, Simple Jess, that you can *sense* when one has been kissed?"

"You didn't kiss her," Jesse stated flatly. "Miss Althea would have slapped you."

"You think Miz Winsloe would have slapped me if I had tried to kiss her?"

"I know she would have slapped you," Jesse answered furiously. "If you'd have kissed her she would have slapped you."

"Is that what women do?"

"It's what Miss Althea would do. And it would have hurt, too, I know, 'cause it hurt me."

"What?"

"When she slapped me it sure hurt."

"Althea Winsloe slapped you."

"Well, yeah."

Jesse looked at Althea. Her eyes were wide.

"Why would she slap you?" Eben's question was low and genuinely curious.

"Well, because I . . . I . . ."

Jesse was searching for the correct words to explain. To explain all about the deer hunt. How scared she'd been. He hadn't realized that Baby-Paisley shouldn't have been there. She was scared and hadn't meant to say such a hateful thing. He was searching for the words.

"Did *you* kiss her?"

Jesse was momentarily confused with what seemed to be a change of subject.

"Well yes," he answered. "I kissed her. She said I weren't to do that no more."

"You kissed Althea Winsloe!" Eben's tone was incredulous.

Jesse looked up to see the crowd staring at him in horror. He turned his glance to Althea. She was looking at him now, her soft, sweet little hand covering her mouth. It had been very wrong for Jesse to kiss her and now he'd gone and told it to everyone on the mountain.

"Well, yes, I kissed her. I . . . I thought it was okay," he explained. "So I did, I brung her into my arms and I kissed her. But then she said that I was never to kiss her again, never."

They were looking at him. Stunned. Disbelieving. Reproachful.

"That's the truth," Jesse said quietly. He looked at Miss Althea. She was looking back at him. "It is the truth, ain't it?"

Althea Winsloe stood alone within the middle of the crowd. Her chin was high. Her voice silent. Nobody spoke to her. Nobody dared.

After Jesse's testimony, the crowd went into disbelieving shock. The McNees family, mostly Beulah, tried valiantly to wrestle the situation back from the jury. It had been their rather obvious intent to make it look like Althea must remarry because her morals were weakened and she was in danger of being led into sin. Clearly the actual situation was worse than what the conspirators had planned to imply. And Beulah no longer wanted strangers having any say in Althea's fate.

Pigg was adamant, however. It was a kangaroo court. That's what they'd wanted and that's what they'd got. He told the jury to deliberate and the little quartet had done so for a good twenty minutes before calling Pigg over to confer with them.

Althea waited, knowing that whatever they decided, it was not going to be something that she liked. Her life was being taken over by well-meaning strangers. She would have to be very strong and determined to take it back.

It was late, very late. They should all have been home and in bed long since. But Althea was not aware of even one person who had made an early departure. The little pile of sleeping children had grown to a mountain. And Althea could only be grateful that Baby-Paisley snoozed undisturbed. His life was to be changed this night as surely as her own, but she didn't want him to see it coming. She would do all she could to protect him from it. She'd made promises to herself. Promises on behalf of her child. If there was any way on earth to manage it, she would keep those promises.

The pine-knot torches were burning low. Several had already sputtered and gone out, making the area darker, somehow more threatening. People gathered together in little groups, huddled waiting. Althea waited alone.

She gave a guarded glance in the direction of Jesse Best. He'd joined his family a bit away from the crowd. They now stood around him like a protective barrier. Roe Farley, with Little Edith sound asleep upon his shoulder, was in front, braced and wary as if ready to thwart any move made in their direction. Meggie looked just as stern, her arm draped comfortingly around Jesse's waist. Even Onery looked ready to spit nails at anyone who might be tempted to heckle, make sport, or further interrogate Jesse about what had happened.

Jesse himself looked more frustrated than angry. He knew he'd said the wrong thing. He had been trying to save her. She understood that. She understood what he had meant. It came through to her ears as clearly as the sweet tones of his fiddle playing. But poor Jesse, words were so hard for him. When it came to self-expression and phrases and hidden meanings, he would always be at a disadvantage. Eben Baxley had used that disadvantage to tangle him up. And he had told the truth. He had kissed her and he had held her. It shouldn't have happened. And for certain it was her fault. Perhaps she deserved whatever punishment was to be divvied out.

Jesse wasn't looking at her. All evening she'd felt his eyes upon her. In a way, it had seemed to comfort and soothe her. There was no soothing her now. Purposely, deliberately, determinedly, Jesse was not looking at her. She was certain that either Roe, Meggie, or his father had warned him not to.

The outcome of this night would, in its way, be worse for Jesse. Althea didn't know what her fate would be, but somehow she could get through this calamity unscathed. Jesse wouldn't be so fortunate. Jesse Best had kissed a woman and now people knew it. Whether they believed that Althea had led him on or not, parents would be warning their daughters to steer clear. The notion folks now had of Jesse Best would include not just his sweetness, his strength, and the sounds of his fiddle, but also his sexuality. For folks on the mountain, simple and sex didn't go together. That was a thing to be feared. His faintest gesture of kindness to the young girls would be suspect. And that way he had of standing quietly among the ladies as if just enjoying being near them would now make the womenfolk uneasy. There would always be that little element of alarm that perhaps at any moment he would suddenly try to kiss one of them. It was nonsense, but Althea knew realistically that was how it was bound to be.

"All right! All right!" Pigg Broody called out to the crowd. "Gather around here, we've finally got this whole thing sorted out."

Althea stepped forward bravely. She would not allow herself to be cowered by this. She felt every eye in the community upon her. She was alone. But then she always had been. Since the day her father had left her behind, she had always been alone.

Eben Baxley stepped up beside her. She glanced up at him. His expression was almost apologetic. He hadn't intended this to happen quite like it had. She knew that, and truly she didn't blame him. It was all Beulah's doing.

Althea glanced toward her mother-in-law. Beulah Winsloe looked almost as worried as Althea and she was more
upset. Althea wondered what she must think and what new
revised plans she was working on now. Her husband Orv
was by her side, looking both affronted and dismayed. Her
brother, Tom McNees, caught Althea's eye. His expression
was reproachful.

Althea raised a challenging brow. She was not about to let
holier-than-thou Tom McNees look down on her. This
whole stunt could be laid at the feet of a woman all right.
But that woman wasn't Althea, it was Beulah Winsloe. That
woman just had to have her way. Always. She wanted
control of the farm. She wanted control of Baby-Paisley.
She was determined to get what she wanted and her
interfering schemes had brought them to this pass. Althea
sighed in resignation. That was her mother-in-law and she
wasn't likely to change.

There was only one woman on the mountain who was
worse than Beulah about making folks do it her way.
Granny Piggott stood on the porch next to Pigg.

"Granny here is to speak for the jury," Pigg announced.
"Have ye reached a verdict?"

The old woman was not at all happy and was looking
Althea straight in the eye. "That we have."

"Please inform the accused," he said.

"Althea Winsloe," Granny said formally. "We, this jury,
find that you are without doubt a woman that ought to
remarry and we find you guilty of shirking yer duty to do
so."

Murmurs of agreement filtered through the crowd. Althea
purposely showed no emotion or surprise. Quietly, calmly,
she considered her next move.

Pigg was speaking once more. "The jury and I have
consulted together upon sentencing of this crime and we
feel we've come up with a fair and just resolution for all."

The crowd had gathered in closer and closer to hear.
Althea felt surrounded and squeezed. She had to remind
herself to stay calm and to breathe.

"Althea Winsloe," Pigg began. "It is the decision of this kangaroo court that you shall remarry."

The hushed voices around her seemed to concur with the judgment.

"However," Pigg continued, "we don't think it right that ye don't get a say in who the man is ye marry. Yer family has done much here this night to embarrass ye and we ain't about to reward them for their troublemaking."

Granny Piggott nodded purposefully at that.

Beulah began to huff and complain. Her husband, for once, hushed her.

"So, we give ye leave to marry any man on the mountain that will have you," he finished.

Everyone began talking at once. Beulah, Tom, and Orv were well geared up for an argument. She could hear Buell Phillips pompously hailing the decree as if it were his own. There were giggles and speculation from the young women near the back.

"What if none will have me?" Althea asked loudly, bringing the chattering crowd to still silence in one brief instant.

Pigg looked dumbfounded at the question.

Granny raised a speculative eyebrow. "Why wouldn't they?" the old woman asked, more than a hint of accusation in her voice. "Have you done worse than loll on a bed with Eben Baxley and take up kissin' with Jesse Best?"

Althea's cheeks flushed hot with embarrassment. "No. I . . . I haven't done anything else."

Granny shrugged and stuck the pipe back into her mouth before commenting from clenched teeth. "Then ye ain't much further lapsed than a lot of gals. I doubt most fellers on this mountain are going to hold that against ye," she pointed out.

There were sounds of agreement on that score.

"Perhaps the men won't be interested when they hear what I'll demand of a new marriage," she said.

Once more the silence in the clearing was eerie.

"What are you demanding?"

"No children," Althea said firmly.

Granny's mouth dropped open and she was barely able to catch her pipe before it fell to the ground. Her brow furrowed in confusion. "That's the Lord's decision," she said.

"I believe all of us here know that men and women have at least as much to do with such events as the Lord does," Althea insisted.

"You mean . . ."

"I mean that any man who marries me had better know right off that I won't bear him any children. And I won't, not ever, be a party to the making of them," she declared. "I can't make it much plainer in front of decent folks, Granny. Any man who wants to marry up with me had best be resolved to long cold winter nights sleeping on his own."

Words of disbelief ricocheted like rifle bullets through the assembled.

Beulah Winsloe sputtered. "You can't be expectin' a man to . . . to do without the . . . the comforts of—"

Althea interrupted her. "I'm not *expecting*. I am *insisting*," Althea told her. "I promised myself when Paisley died that I wouldn't wed again and I would have no more children."

"That's agin' nature," Pigg insisted. "It just ain't the way things are meant to be."

"Perhaps so," Althea countered. "But neither was the kangaroo court meant to be used for this. You *can* force me to marry. You can force me, with your mean-spirited maneuvers and nasty insinuations. But you can't make a woman, any woman, have a child against her will."

"She does have the right of that," Granny pointed out. "Not unless the feller forces hisself on her and none in my family were raised that way."

"The McNees don't mistreat women either!" Beulah insisted harshly. "But what man will marry her with those kinds of conditions?"

"I will."

The answer came from behind Althea. She turned in surprise to see Oather Phillips not a bucket's length from her elbow.

"I'm declaring for her," Oather said. "I'll marry her tonight and I'll abide by her wishes." He turned to look her directly in the eyes. "I promise that," he said softly.

The silence around them was from disbelief.

"Well, I'll be switched," Pigg Broody began, stopping only to spit a jaw full and offer a chuckle. "Feller, ere ye sure ye know what yer putting yourself in for?"

Oather wasn't given a chance to answer.

"I'm willing to wed her, too," Eben Baxley piped up.

"What?"

Disbelief bordered upon amazement.

"You surely don't mean that, son," Granny declared.

"We've been speaking plainly tonight, so I'll speak plainly here," he said. "I'm as willing to own that farm as Oather Phillips is."

"That was not—"

Eben interrupted him. "I suspect if Oather can live without the lady's favors, I can as well. Course maybe we're both thinking that she'll change her mind."

He turned to give her a wink and a grin. Althea ignored both.

"Or if she don't, well"—his glance went past her toward Oather and betrayed more than a hint of challenge—"I'm declaring for her anyway. I suspect I might be able to find other interests here on the mountain."

Oather's eyes narrowed in fury, but Granny intervened.

"Let's have no more vile talk tonight."

"Granny's right," Pigg agreed, still chuckling over the idea of fellows willing to marry without the comforts. "Enough is enough. Both you boys is willing to marry this gal?"

"I am."

"Me, too."

"All right then, Althea, which one of these fellers do you want?" Pigg asked.

Althea stared back at Pigg in shock and disbelief. She'd played her trump card and her bluff had been called. She glanced at the young men who stood on either side of her.

Expectantly, they, and the community of Marrying Stone, waited for her answer.

"It ain't good to go against your family," Beulah pointed out hopefully. "Eben is family and a friend to our poor dead Paisley. There'd be lots of gals more than eager to catch him."

"You've known my boy all your life," Buell Phillips declared, pushing his way to the front of the crowd to face her. "He's a fine prospect by any standard. Good to his mama and sister and a fine business to inherit when I pass on."

"You don't want the Phillips as your in-laws," Eben pointed out, earning him a killing look from the storekeeper.

"That Eben Baxley is a rounder and up to no good," Oather whispered quietly against her neck. "He cannot be trusted not to hurt you, or not to lie to you."

Althea's thoughts were in a whirl. Her chance was lost, her plans gone awry. There was no one to help her. No one she could count upon to be on her side.

As if suddenly drawn there by an unseen force, her gaze turned to Jesse Best. He was not avoiding her now. Whether he'd been warned or not, he watched her, his heart in his eyes. His look conveyed some message. Some message that her mind couldn't decipher. He'd been in this spot so many times, she knew. Day after day he had to make choices that he didn't understand based on truths that he didn't know. How did he do that? How did he manage? Suddenly the image came to her of Jesse in the mornings at the farm. Jesse standing tall and silent in the middle of the yard, looking all around, thinking, assessing, figuring out what to do by slow, careful deliberation.

"I . . . I can't pick tonight," Althea told them. "I can't do it."

"Do you want someone to do it for ye?" Granny asked.

"I need time. I can't just say yes, right now, tonight. I need time. No one could choose without considering it through."

Pigg's brow furrowed. "What do ye think?"

Granny tapped her pipe against her teeth pensively. "It does seem a mite sudden just standing her betwixt the two of 'em."

Momentarily the jury reconvened.

Eben grinned at her with confidence and then glared over her head at Oather.

Beside her, she could sense young Phillips's growing frustration and fury. But she didn't waste a minute of worry on it. She would do it the way Jesse did. Slowly, with due consideration she'd figure out which way to go. She couldn't just choose one of these men. Surely, she wouldn't be expected to marry without being given time to make a true choice. She didn't want to marry at all. Even children and the bedding part aside, Althea didn't want to make her life with either of these men.

Inexplicably her gaze drifted once more to Jesse. He stood still and silent, but his expression was trusting and sure. Why couldn't things just go on as they had? Why couldn't she just continue to have Jesse work for her?

That was not to be. No one was going to let life go on as it had before.

The jury turned back to face her. Althea raised her chin bravely, awaiting their judgment.

Granny's voice was loud and clear.

"Althea Winsloe will marry, all right. That we've decided. But marriage is serious business and the whole life long. She can't just be made to pick one of these fellers without giving it some thought."

Althea felt the weight of her shoulders momentarily relax, as around her the crowd began muttering their opinions once more.

"Also, these fellers got to show her what they're made of, so she has something besides their good looks to recommend them."

That caused a bit of laughter.

"But she can't have forever," Beulah complained. "Given half a chance, that girl will stall the whole life long."

"We ain't giving her forever," Granny answered. "She's

got until Christmas Day. If she ain't decided by then, it's
fitting that her family make the choice."

"Christmas Day! That's only three weeks," Althea protested.

Granny gave her a stern look. "Be grateful for what ye
got, young woman. You ain't a-likely to get a minute more."

CHAPTER  FOURTEEN

The storekeeper's family lived better than anyone on the mountain. The area above the store was neat, cozy, and well furnished. The rugs on the floor were homemade, as were most of the furniture pieces. But throughout the house, in every nook and cranny, evidence of a world outside of Marrying Stone Mountain existed. The corner of the kitchen boasted an ornately designed Acme Regal Cookstove. The cloth that covered their table was bleached linen damask, rather than homespun. The plates were white china stoneware, not tin. And while the members of the Phillips family still carried their eating utensils with them, the kitchen cupboard contained a full complement of Alaskaware knives, forks, and spoons.

The comings and goings of drummers, traders, wayfarers, and strangers had created for this family a tiny peephole on another world. Perhaps there was no intention of ever exploring that world, but simply knowing of its existence gave them a perspective unique among the people with whom they lived. It made them different. On Marrying Stone Mountain, being different was not thought altogether to be such a good thing.

On this morning, as the sunshine edged into the kitchen slantwise from the east window, groggy heads and drooping eyes were much in evidence at the Phillips family breakfast table.

Oather had already shaved before sitting down. His bruised and battered face was beginning to take on its more normal appearance. His expression was grim, determined.

Mavis still had her hair in a long untidy braid hanging down her back. Around her face masses of uncombed curls had sprouted due to the heavy moisture in the morning air. Dark circles beneath her eyes gave evidence of worry as well as sleeplessness.

Lessy Phillips was, as always, perfectly groomed and pressed. Her offering for the morning meal was tasty and sustaining and her movements were swift and efficient, but her facial expression was as weary as those of her children. It had been the middle of the night before they'd come back to the house. The dawn, it seemed, had arrived very early.

There was, unfortunately, an exception to that state of lethargy at the breakfast table. Buell Phillips was wide awake and talking a mile a minute. His family, knowing him as well as they did, remained respectfully quiet and reserved. When Buell Phillips was "having one of his ideas," it was best to keep one's own counsel and pray that the moments would pass quickly.

Which was why no opinion, in word or expression, was ventured concerning Phillips's version of the events of the previous evening.

"By God, it's as if the opportunity has just fallen in our lap," he said. "They were sure to have her married up with Baxley right and proper. They're a devious bunch, those McNees, and Beulah Winsloe could easy be first cousin to the very devil. They sure were going to sew things up last night. And Jesse Best, our Jesse Best, beat them out of it."

Buell hooted with delighted laughter.

"Who'd have believed that!" he said. "Who'd have believed it! I thought old Beulah was going to piddle her drawers when she heard the boy say it."

The storekeeper shook his head in disbelief.

He imitated Jesse's distinctive way of speaking. "She sure slapped me. Yes, I kissed her," he mocked. "She kissed me first. I thought it was all right." Phillips's laughter was hearty. "Lord Almighty! That Baxley was pale as a sheet and then mad as a hen. Here he thinks he's got such a way with the ladies with all his good looks and his charm. He tries to snuggle up to Althea Winsloe and gets nowhere. Simple Jess gets kissed."

Buell slapped his thigh. "Who would a-thought. Not me. Lord knows, I would have paid the boy to do it if it had ever entered my mind."

"I'm sure it wasn't like it sounded, Papa," Mavis said quietly. "Jesse's so sweet, it was probably just a friendly kind of kiss."

Her father huffed in disbelief. "You need to get married, girl," he said. "Learn the ways of the world. That Jesse is got the same interest in what's under gals' dresses as the rest of us."

"Mr. Phillips!" his wife cautioned in a shocked whisper.

"Beg pardon, my dear," he replied with little apology in his tone. "Nope, that gal has been a widow too long. It's time some good fellow takes her in hand before she starts leading a boy like Jesse into more than just kissing."

If Phillips's family disagreed with him, they did so silently.

Buell reached out and patted his son heartily on the back. "That's where you come in. You're going to woo her and win her. That farm is going to be Piggott ground and the Winsloes can just stamp their feet in indignation forever-more."

Oather suddenly lost his appetite and pushed his bowl of bacon-greased mush away. He gave a moment's glance toward Mavis. She looked worried, unhappy. Deliberately he steeled himself, sighing with resignation.

"I'll do the best that I can, Papa."

"I know you will," Buell assured him quickly. "I know you will. And I'm going to help you, son. I'll tell you how to go about things and you just do what I say."

Oather raised an eyebrow. He knew that it was better not to go against anything his father was thinking. When Buell Phillips was having an idea, dissenters were frequently dealt with harshly. He could follow his father's dictates to the letter. If he won the lady, everything would be fine. If he didn't, his father would have no one to blame. The problem, Oather realized, was that to insure that his sweet sister

Mavis was not forced to live the rest of her life in the shadow of the man who had ruined her life and left her like used goods, he actually had to *win* Althea Winsloe. It was clear to him that he had more chance of that on his own merit than he would ever have as the representative of his father.

"I think I should court her myself," he said, easing into disagreement in the least negative way. "She likes me, I feel pretty certain about that. I believe I can persuade her that I'd make her a good husband."

"Well, for certain you're going to court her yourself. I just know a whole lot about folks and their thinking. You just follow my lead and those Christmas wedding bells will be ringing for you," he said.

Buell leaned closer as if relaying a confidence. "You see the way it is, son, is a woman wants a man," he said. "A man who'll set her straight. One to tell her when to jump and how high."

Buell found a good deal of humor in his own words and chuckled for a minute or two before he continued.

"That Baxley," he said. "He *pretends* he's a man like that, lots of the gals think he's that way. But he's not. He's weak," Buell explained, smug in his certainty. "Just like his daddy is that one. Clyde Baxley was led around by the ties on a woman's apron for twenty years. His wife Dora was just like our Beulah, excepting Clyde weren't as easy led as Orv is. He never did get around her or loose from her, just one day he finally fell into a bottle of whiskey and never crawled out again."

Mavis raised her chin in surprise. Oather glanced at her. He knew nothing about Baxley's past, but it was not a subject in which he was interested.

"That boy, Eben," his father continued. "He was raised the same way as his father. He was just his mama's little pet." Buell shook his finger adamantly. "Boys raised by women turn out downright boneless. You can't find a man inside 'em if you search with a compass and lantern. Don't never let that happen to a boy of yours, son. You'll probably be called upon to take a firm hand with that Winsloe baby.

Paisley's been dead long enough to have near ruined him for certain. He's sure to grow up as frail as a sapling."

"He seems like a sweet little boy," Oather pointed out.

"Sweet is for girls. Sweet don't make a man of a boy. Why, when you was still toddling around here hanging on to your mama's leg, I said, 'Woman, leave that boy be, you'll ruin him.' I even threatened to take a stick to her once when she was coddlin' you," he admitted proudly, grinning across the table at his wife. She returned his regard with an uneasy smile.

"It's the maddest that woman ever got at me. But I kept her at a distance, that I did, son. You've got me to thank for that."

Oather stared at his father. The taste of bitterness was strong in his mouth. And *thank you* were not the words that came immediately to his lips. Determinedly, Oather put his feelings aside and deftly brought the conversation back to the subject for discussion.

"You're right, Papa. I'll take an interest in the boy. I just really think that for the courting, I should handle Althea Winsloe my own way," he said.

"I'm trying to help you, son," Buell said.

"I know that, Papa," Oather answered. "But I think Althea Winsloe is going to be very wary of deceit and trickery. I just want to be straightforward and honest with her."

"Well that will never work," Buell answered without the slightest consideration.

"It will," Oather said. The emphatic nature of his words added implacable rigidness to his tone. He watched the inevitable hardening of his father's jaw and waited.

"No, son," he said, evenly, sternly. "This is too important for me to leave it to chance."

"You're not leaving it to chance," Oather said. "You are leaving it to my good judgment."

His father's tone became harsh, reproving. "I think I got a pretty good idea last night of the uncertainty of your good judgment."

"What do you mean?"

"When she put up that nonsense about not having babies. You shouldn't have given in so quickly," Buell insisted. "It looked strange, mighty strange, and it's sure to have folks talking."

"I did what I did, Papa," Oather answered. "Baxley agreed to it, too."

Buell Phillips made a sound of dismissal as he turned back to his plate and used his fingers to help himself to another huge piece of side bacon. "Well, Baxley is Baxley," he said. "He has nothing to prove to anybody. You should have let Baxley say it first. It would have looked a whole lot better if Baxley had said it first."

Oather bristled and his eyes narrowed. "I don't have anything to *prove* to anybody either," he said.

Phillips made no comment on his own words, but the expression on his face indicated that he wasn't in complete agreement.

"The important thing now is to actually marry the girl," he said. "I'm the one who can help you make that happen. After you're wed you can get a child in her belly and folks will forget about what you said."

"I promised her I wouldn't do that," Oather pointed out quietly. "And I believe I have a better chance of getting her to marry me because she can believe me."

"Now that ain't totally wrong, son," Buell agreed. "You just keep telling her she's going to get her way. That's fine if she believes it. Of course, nobody's going to hold you to that."

"I thought marriages were supposed to be built on honesty and trust," Mavis piped in. Her words echoed with volumes of hidden meaning. Oather could only speculate on their wellspring. Buell waved them away.

"That's the reason you still aren't married," he speculated unkindly. "You don't understand nothing about the truth of things between men and women." He turned his attention once more to his son. "You wed Althea Winsloe and then you bed her," he said, taking a big bite of the mush. "It ain't natural otherwise and we all know it," he added, his mouth still very full.

Oather felt uncomfortable about commenting on what was natural. "Althea Winsloe may well want to hold me to my promises."

Buell shrugged, unconcerned. "By then she'll be your wife and what she wants won't matter a hoot. Look at your mother."

Both Oather and his sister did.

"Her opinion doesn't count for a thing in this house," Buell pointed out. "And she's very happy, aren't you, my dear?"

Mrs. Phillips didn't answer, she only smiled shyly and hurried to the stove for more coffee. Her husband took this as a yes.

"Just don't worry about that part of it now," Buell counseled his son. "There'll be time enough after you're wed. We've just got to see that you're wed. I'll tell you how to get there, step by step."

Oather sighed heavily and raised his chin, forced into obstinance. "I'll call on her. I've known her a long time. We are, I suppose, friends. But I'll follow no one's lead on this but my own. I'll do what I can to try to win her over."

Buell stopped eating in midbite and stared at his son in disbelief. As the reality of the unanticipated rebellion settled over him, his complexion turned florid and his expression to anger.

"Try? Try?" Buell mimicked in sarcastic indignation. "That's what you always do, isn't it, Oather. You *try*. Well, this is one time where you can't just *try*, son. You've *got* to wed her!"

The depth of his father's reaction didn't surprise Oather, but neither did his expectation in any way diminish the difficulty in facing it.

"You make it sound like life and death," Oather said, purposely moderating his tone.

"And that it is. Our honor is at stake."

Oather's eyes widened and he glanced at Mavis. She'd paled behind startled eyes. He turned his gaze back to his father, who had fortunately not noticed the exchange between his offspring.

"What do you mean 'our honor is at stake?'" Oather asked quietly.

Buell's answer was brusque. "Why, the good name of this family. We're the Piggott family, by God! We're the people that first come to this mountain. It's ours by right. These McNeeses are just breeding like field mice and taking the place over."

Oather allowed himself only a moment's sigh of relief. "Papa, these days the two families are so intermarried, folks have to *decide* which name they belong to."

"And if they have to decide, we want them deciding to be Piggotts. We're the first family here."

"Papa, that's just not important to me."

"I see it's not!" Buell was livid. "I see that for my son his name and his family's honor mean nothing."

He banged his fist on the table. The dishes jumped and clattered.

"Well, if you don't care about the McNees taking over the mountain, at least don't tell me that you weren't aware of the slight he made on your manhood."

Oather's reply was even. "I was *aware* of it, Papa, but I didn't concern myself with it. I care nothing about Baxley's opinion of me."

"What about the opinion of all the others standing there?"

"Honestly, I don't much care what they think either."

Phillips cursed lividly. "Well, I do care. Any slight on you is a slight upon me and a slight against all the Piggotts. I don't allow no slights, no time, by no one, ever."

"We can't control what other people say."

"I can," Buell insisted furiously. "And if you are any son of mine, you'll do the same. You'll command respect in this family and on this mountain, they'll follow your lead and they'll never speak a word against you."

Oather's own anger was rising. He wanted to yell out to his father that Buell Phillips was given *respect* on the mountain because Buell Phillips could give *credit* at the store, nothing more than that. He wanted to proclaim, once and for all, that he was not like his father and never would be. And he wanted to walk away from his home and never look back. He did none of these things. He stood mute and accepting as his father's wrath spewed out all over him.

"I have had just about enough disappointments from this family," Phillips declared, letting his angry gaze fall on the trio sitting with him around the kitchen table. "It's bad enough that your mother doesn't take her rightful place in this community and your sister just refuses to marry, but you, son, *you* have been the biggest disappointment to me of all."

Oather winced as if he'd been slapped.

"You are the heir to a thriving business for which you show little interest or aptitude. You've got your nose stuck in some law book ever' minute. Anyone can see that ain't natural. Now, you should have been married long since, but you don't even call on the gals. When you, for some foolish reason, decide to pick a fight with a well-known scrapper, you manage to get the life nearly beat out of you. Now here I am trying to help you with your chance at last to prove yourself—"

"I told you I have nothing to prove!" Oather roared.

"Well you may not think you have anything to prove to yourself, and maybe you don't think you need to prove anything to your friends and neighbors, but I am your father and it is damn well time that you prove something to me. You go get that woman and that farm, Oather Phillips, or you and I will see a parting of the ways."

It was full daylight, the chores done and the breakfast cleared. Althea was wiping up the crumbs and grease from the sideboard. Her mind was blank, deliberately blank. She watched the progress of her scrub rag as she cleaned the worn, pocked wood of the table. Maybe for Christmas she'd put out the tablecloth she'd gotten for her wedding from Aunt Ada. The reminder that at Christmas she would be remarried was hastily pushed to the back of her thoughts. At Christmas she'd shine up an apple real fine for Baby-Paisley and knit him the voyageur's cap. She already had the yarn dyed in blue and white. She'd make it to hang down midway on his back and finish it with a fancy tassle. She smiled thinking how delighted he was going to be.

At that moment she heard him coming down from the loft ladder and she glanced up. Today he looked dejected. The now serious, solemn, sad little fellow was dragging his damp bedclothes down the ladder.

"I peed the sheets again, Mama," he told her, shame-faced.

"Well, just put them by the door and I'll hang them out in a little bit," she promised. "Today at least they'll dry instead of freezing to the line."

He nodded, but his mood didn't lift. "Am I always gonna pee the bed?"

"Well, of course not," Althea answered, turning to survey her son's little face. "That's a foolish question. I've told you plenty of times that it will stop. It's just a matter of time. Maybe today is the very last day."

The little boy nodded, but he didn't appear convinced. "Gobby Weston says only babies wet the bed," he told her.

Althea hung the scrub rag on its nail, wiped her hands on her apron, and knelt down beside her child.

"Gobby Weston said that?"

Baby-Paisley nodded.

She tutted disapprovingly. "Well, I know something about Gobby Weston."

"What?"

"Gobby Weston isn't nearly as smart about the world as he thinks he is," she told him.

The little boy wasn't completely won over, but a quick kiss on the forehead helped somewhat. A decisive knock rattled at the door.

Althea stiffened. For one irrational moment she felt like a cornered animal. It might be her mother-in-law. Or it might be Tom McNees coming to pray for her errant soul. It could be any of the neighbors come to gawk and gossip. It could even likely be one of her prospective suitors attempting to get an early start. She didn't want to see any of them. In truth, she wanted to pretend that last night had not happened at all. She wanted to pretend it for as long as possible.

"Who's there?" she called out warily.

"Jesse Best."

Baby-Paisley broke away from her and scrambled to open the door. "Morning, Jesse!" Baby-Paisley called out excitedly. "Are we gonna work on the deer hide today?"

"Maybe so," he answered, giving the little boy a warm glance and a quick tousle of his hair. His attention immediately went to Althea. He smiled at her, a little uncertain, and just stood there, waiting. He filled the doorway, strong and stalwart and sure. The gaze of his vivid blue eyes was only for Althea.

"I come to work today, just like regular," he said. There was as much question as challenge in his tone.

"I'm glad you did," she answered. And she knew the words were the truth as soon as she heard them come out of her mouth. "Take the sheets outside, Baby-Paisley," she said as she stood up. He hurried to do as he was bid. And she waited until the child was outside to speak again.

"I didn't know if you would come back today," she said.

Jesse nodded. "I didn't know if I should," he admitted. "Pa said no I shouldn't. Roe and Meggie, too. They said that I shouldn't ever be seen on your land again. That you wouldn't want to see me. And that folks won't like me over here no more."

He looked around uncertainly for a moment, then once again straight into Althea's eyes. "I don't hardly never defy my pa, Miss Althea," he said. "But I told him I was coming here to see you. And that he couldn't stop me. I told Roe and Meggie that if you are mad at me, I probably deserve it. But I said I would be coming here, so I had to come to you, like I said I would."

"You defied your family to keep a promise to me?" Althea's question was a whisper.

Jesse nodded.

A door opened inside Althea's heart. She felt it, but she didn't understand it. The meaning escaped her at that moment, but the feel, the joy, the sweet power of the emotion pulsed through her with a gladness that was far out of proportion to the deed done.

"You went contrary to keep a promise to me." It was a quietly spoken revelation.

"I told Pa I'd take a lickin' from him when I get back, if that's what he wants. But knowing that wouldn't keep me home."

"What did he say?"

"He said he 'spected a lickin' wouldn't do no good nohow. And that I wasn't the first feller to make a fool of hisself over a woman."

"Have you made a fool of yourself over a woman?"

He shrugged and chuckled lightly. "Most folks think that I was a fool already. I just . . . I just hope you ain't too mad at me."

"Of course I'm not mad," she said. "I knew what you meant. I knew what you were trying to say."

"It's just a shame I can't say things a little better," he complained.

"Oh, Jesse, I'm so sorry."

"You're sorry? Sorry for what?"

"For . . . for everything."

Jesse was thoughtful for a long moment. "Well, I'm not sorry for everything," he said. "I'm sorry those folks made such a fuss of things last night. And I'm sorry that I said the wrong thing when I was trying to say what was right." His brow crinkled thoughtfully. "But, Miss Althea, I'm not sorry that I kissed you." His voice became quiet, almost shy. "It was about the nicest thing that ever happened to me. I mean besides having a pa and a sister and things like God gives you."

Althea felt a strange longing well up within her chest and she covered the pain of it with her clasped hands.

"Oh, Jesse," she whispered. The surge of emotion she felt was unexpected and a little uncomfortable. Like the memories of the evening before, she forcefully pushed it away. "Thank you, Jesse," she said. "Thank you. It was . . . well, I liked it, too."

He grinned at that. "You liked it, too?"

"It . . . it was a very nice kiss," she admitted.

Jesse nodded, clearly pleased with her words, then his smile turned to a naughty grin.

Althea laughed. The sound was strange and unexpected. Her mind in a whirl, her world turned upside down, she couldn't imagine that she still had the ability to laugh. But she did. And Jesse laughed, too. It was a warm, fine moment in the warmth and privacy of the snug little house. And Althea began to take heart. For the first time since the events of the previous evening, she began to believe that somehow, some way, things might actually work out.

"I am glad you're here, Jesse," she said. "I'm very glad that you're here."

"Well, I still got to earn my dogs," he said. "They are the finest pack on this mountain. It takes a lot to earn 'em. And now I'll have to do it before Christmas. Before you're to get married up."

That sobered Althea a little. But she deliberately held on to her lighter mood.

"Yes, I think it's best if you earn your dogs and take them before Christmas," she said. "I wouldn't want Eben or Oather to have them."

Jesse nodded. "No, they don't appreciate them," he agreed. "Eben's a lazy hunter and Oather don't hunt at all. Course, I don't want Eben or Oather to have *you* neither."

Momentarily Althea looked startled.

"I guess there ain't nothing to do about that," Jesse said.

Althea laughed, forcing gaiety. "Not this morning there isn't. You should have spoken up last night," she said, teasing. "You should have declared yourself as my suitor."

Jesse choked lightly and blushed scarlet.

"I couldn't a-done that, Miss Althea," he said.

"Oh, I see," she said, feigning criticism. "You aren't the marrying type then, Mr. Best? You're not interested in tying the knot?"

"It ain't that," Jesse answered quickly. "It's . . . it's . . . I don't want to make no promises I cain't keep."

"And you think wedding vows are promises you couldn't keep?" she asked, laughing delightedly.

"Not the wedding vows. I could keep them," Jesse said. "No, it's that other promise. The one not to . . . not to stir the bed with you like a husband and wife." The tone of his voice went low and soft. "If I was your man, Miss Althea, I couldn't keep a promise like that for one day."

CHAPTER
FIFTEEN

The deer hide was looking fine and worthy, though still a little green. It had been soaking in wood ash and water for several days to loosen the hair. Now that it would slip off more easily, Jesse had spread it out over a homemade tanning beam. The beam, a smooth-peeled half log, had one end flush to the ground. The other end was propped up on a sawbuck, making it waist high to Jesse and easy to work. The hair had come off easily and now with a curved fleshing knife, Jesse worked in strong, smooth downward motions to remove anything unwanted that remained on the hide.

Buckskin was not truly tanned hide. It could not be used for harness or binding because it stretched badly when wet. But buckskin was soft, pliable, and required little more than brain paste or soft soap to cure it. Deer hides made wonderful buckskin, as soft as chamois and stronger and warmer than cloth.

Jesse worked quietly, steadily, and concentrated fully on what for others might well have been a boring, repetitive task. Baby-Paisley sat eagerly beside him waiting to run for more soap or another blade. Jesse explained what he did in the same singsong recitation voice that the little boy had grown accustomed to.

"Once it is roughed and smoked," he said, "it will be pretty and strong and it will be useful to us long after we've eaten every scrap of the meat it brought us."

It was hard for Jesse to learn things. His growing-up years had been fraught with foolish mistakes and unsuccessful attempts. But once he learned a task, a word, a rule, he never forgot it. He relied upon his memory, because he couldn't rely upon his intellect. Once a thing had been worked out in his head, he kept that solution. There were too many solutions to be worked out to refigure an old one time and time again.

"What are ye gonna do with this hide?" Baby-Paisley asked suddenly, breaking into his recitation.

Jesse stopped in midmotion and thought for a long minute.

"Well, I don't know," he said. "It's half yours. What do you want to do with it?"

"It's half mine!" Baby-Paisley was startled, but clearly delighted.

"Don't you remember I told you that on a hunt the kill is shared. When there's two, then it's shared half."

"I didn't know that meant the hide, too."

Jesse nodded. "It means the hide, too."

"So whatta you wanna do with it?"

Shrugging, Jesse considered. "Well, it's a good hide. It could make a coat."

"Coat's nice."

"But if we cut it in half, there's not enough for a coat," Jesse said.

"Oh."

"So we could make gloves."

"Yeah, gloves." That appealed to Baby-Paisley.

"I got gloves," Jesse pointed out. "And your fingers are still growing."

Baby-Paisley nodded, looking down at his own mitten-covered hands. "Mama made these for me."

"So gloves don't seem quite right," Jesse said.

"Well, what else can we make?" the child asked.

"Lots of things, or we don't have to make nothing," he said. "We can take the hide to Phillips Store and trade it."

"We can trade it? Like for candy?"

Jesse's eyes widened and he laughed with delight. "It'd be a bellyache's worth of candy," he said.

The little boy laughed with him. It was undoubtedly true.

A deer hide was probably worth more than all the candy in Mr. Phillips' store.

"We could trade it for something that you and me both want," Jesse suggested.

Baby-Paisley thought about that for a long moment. "What do you an' me both want?" he asked.

"I don't know," Jesse said. "I know I don't want a bellyache's worth of candy."

The little boy giggled. "Me neither."

"Maybe we could get something for your mama."

"Somethin' for Mama? Yep, that'ud be good."

"For Christmas," Jesse said. "We could get her something for Christmas."

"Cwissmas!" The little boy's eyes were suddenly wide with excitement. "We're gonna have Cwissmas?"

"Pretty soon," Jesse told him.

Baby-Paisley lowered his voice cautiously. "Is that Santy Claus feller comin' agin?"

"He come by your house last year?"

Baby-Paisley began nodding excitedly and then abruptly stopped. "Mama said he come," the little boy said tentatively. "But Gobby Weston said there ain't no such a feller, an' he never come."

Jesse was momentarily thoughtful. He gave Baby-Paisley a long assessing look. Then turned his eyes and his attention back to the deer hide before he asked casually, "Did you check the chimney?"

"Check the chimley?"

"Yep," Jesse said. "If this Santy Claus come down and up the chimney like he's supposed, he'd get black soot all over him, wouldn't he?"

Baby-Paisley thought about that for a moment and then nodded in agreement. "He sure would. I crawled up in the hearth last summer and got real black. Mama was fit to skin me alive."

Jesse nodded. "So if Santy Claus was to climb down and then back up, why they'd be soot all over the outside of the chimney."

"That's right," Baby-Paisley agreed.

"That's how I know when he's really been to visit me."

"Has he really been to visit you?"

"Yes, lots of time," Jesse said. "But I check the chimney before I say anything. I don't want to be fooled by nobody."

"That's what I'll do!" the boy declared. "This Cwissmas, I'm a-gonna check the chimley."

Jesse smiled at the little boy. He was glad that Baby-Paisley liked him now. Since the deer hunt, the boy stayed closer to him. Daily, it seemed, they shared more. He was a smart little rascal, Jesse thought, and a fine fellow to have for a friend. But he wasn't exactly a friend. Jesse had had playmates who were much younger than he was. But what he felt for this little boy was not so much a playmate. It was something more. Something that made him feel proud of the boy and eager for him, too. Jesse didn't understand the new feeling, but it was a nice one.

Once Miss Althea was married, Jesse would miss him. Whether she took up with Oather or Eben wouldn't matter. Jesse wouldn't be welcome. At least the boy wouldn't miss him. Baby-Paisley would be too busy getting used to his new pa to even think about his deer-hunting friend.

"So do you think we should trade the hide for a Christmas gift for your mama?" Jesse asked.

"Yep," he answered. "Let's get Mama somethin' nice."

"What would she like?"

The little boy was thoughtful for long minutes. He looked all around the gloomy gray yard as if seeking inspiration. His gaze stopped on the line full of drying sheets.

"I know what she'd really like," he said.

"What?" Jesse asked.

"She'd like me to stop peeing the bed."

Jesse was momentarily taken aback and gave the little boy a long look. "I didn't know that you pee the bed."

"Doan ya see the sheets ever' day?" The boy's cheeks were bright pink with humiliation. "It's a baby thing," he said.

Jesse looked at the sheets. He *had* seen them every day, but he had not taken the trouble to think about what they might mean.

"I don't know that it's a baby thing," he said.

"You doan do it, do ya?" Baby-Paisley asked harshly.

"Not no more," Jesse answered. "Granny Piggott cured me."

Baby-Paisley's eyes widened and his attention was perked. "She cured ya?"

Jesse nodded.

"How?"

"With a penny," Jesse said.

"A penny?"

"She made me to swallow a copper penny and it cured me up overnight," he said.

"That's all?"

"That's all."

Baby-Paisley jumped up and took off toward the house.

"Where you going?" Jesse called out.

"I got a penny saved up for candy," he hollered back. "Gwanpa Orv gave it to me."

Jesse went back to his work, a smile on his face. After only a few moments the smile faded. Unhappily he remembered Miss Althea's face in the woods when she thought her little boy was lost. Jesse had done wrong then. He had scared her. He vowed not to do that again. Suddenly he was afraid that he'd done it again.

Quickly he hung the deer hide in the tree, wiped his blade on the rag, and hurried to find her. It took little more than a minute to locate her carrying water from the spring.

"Miss Althea!" he called out.

She stopped in her tracks and he hurried up to her.

"Miss Althea," he said when he got close. "Baby-Paisley was telling me that he's been peeing the bed. And I told him it could be cured by swallowing a penny and then he said that he had a penny."

Her eyes, at first puzzled, got wider and wider as he told his tale.

"Where is he?" she interrupted, her tone anxious.

"He went up to the house."

Miss Althea took off running and Jesse was right behind her. He had done wrong. He had scared her. What was it?

What exactly was it? He still wondered, but didn't stop to ask. He hurried on to the house. Beating her to the door, he held it open as she ran past.

"Baby-Paisley!" she called out. "Baby-Paisley, where are you?"

"Right here, Mama," he said, coming down the ladder, a big happy grin on his face.

"Thank God!" Althea said, dropping into a chair gratefully. She held her arms open to him and he hurried into her embrace eagerly.

"What's wrong, Mama?"

"Jesse said you were trying to swallow a penny and it scared me."

"Doan be scared, Mama. I done swallered it."

"What?"

"I done swallowed it," he repeated. "Now I woan never pee the bed agin."

"Oh, no. Oh, no!"

Althea began to pound Baby-Paisley on the back.

"Mama, stop it!" the little fellow complained.

"Cough it up, Baby-Paisley. You've got to cough it up."

"No." He pulled away from her. "I doan wanna cough it up."

"Oh, my God, what am I going to do? What am I going to do?"

"I'll go get Granny," Jesse said.

"Granny?"

"I'll go get Granny. Granny knows all the cures. She'll know what to do," Jesse assured her. "Don't worry about nothing. I'll go get Granny."

He didn't wait for a reply, but hurried out the door. The last thing he heard was two voices behind him.

"Let Mama put her finger down your throat, Baby-Paisley," Althea pleaded.

"No, Mama, leave me be. Leave me be!"

Althea Winsloe's fear had turned to frustration nearly an hour later as she stood with Oather Phillips and Eben Baxley under the huge red oak at the far side of the house, gazing up at Baby-Paisley, who had scrambled to a limb nearly twenty feet off the ground.

"I'll just climb up there and get him," Baxley was saying.

"Oh, that's a great idea," Phillips said sarcastically. "You've already chased him up in a tree. Why don't you just get him way out on a limb and maybe he'll just *fall* down."

"I don't see that you were doing much good talking him to death," Eben argued.

"Oh, for heaven's sake, both of you hush," Althea snapped furiously. "Baby-Paisley! You come down here this instant or you're going to find yourself sitting in the corner for the rest of the day."

"I ain' coming down," the little fellow answered. "He ain' shaking nothin' outer me."

"What he needs is a good dose of a hickory limb on his backside," Baxley commented.

Althea ignored that opinion.

"I won't let him shake you again, sweetheart. Just please come down. Mama's afraid you're going to fall."

From the child's pale features, it was clear that he was at least somewhat afraid of the same thing.

She had gotten nowhere with her attempts to get the baby to throw up the penny. He wouldn't let her gag him, either with her finger or with a tonic of pukeweed. She was nearly at her wit's end when Oather showed up at her door.

With his hair slicked down with pomade and the gift of a hair ribbon in his hand, he'd come calling. Immediately she told him what had happened. Oather began to patiently try to talk the little boy into agreeing to his mother's requests, assuring him that swallowing the penny would do him no good and would probably do him bad. Baby-Paisley didn't believe him.

Eben Baxley arrived during this very long discussion. He listened. Spoke charmingly and reassuringly to Althea and then offered to get the penny for her.

"I'll just turn him upside down and shake him till it comes out," Eben said simply.

Baby-Paisley hadn't liked that idea at all. When Baxley

had headed toward him, he'd skirted around him and headed out the door at a dead run.

All three adults joined in the fruitless chase around the yard. Finally, when it looked as if the little fellow was cornered, Baby-Paisley had shinnied up the tree.

"Please, please come down, sweetheart," Althea pleaded. "Mama's sorry. I won't let anyone hurt you. Please come down."

A long minute passed before his little baby voice answered. "I can't," he said.

"Why not?"

"I'm scared."

"Oh, sweetheart," Althea pleaded.

"If I move, I'm 'fraid I'll fall," he said.

"I'll go get him," Oather suggested.

"No!" Baby-Paisley seemed more afraid of someone coming up than of being stuck out on a tree limb for life.

"Baby-Paisley, you either have to climb down or someone has to come up to get you," she told him.

Whatever his answer to that question might have been, it was never heard. At that moment, noisily arriving on the trail was Jesse Best, pulling Granny Piggott on a skid.

Jesse's face was red and he was puffing from the effort. Sweat dripped from his brow. He'd shed his coat and his shirt was plastered to his body from his exertions. Granny was laughing delightedly.

"Lord, what a ride!" she called out to them. "This boy run all the way from my house, pulling me along faster than a racing horse. Whee! Ain't had such a time since I went sledding as a girl."

Jesse helped Granny off of the skid and to her feet. She was a little unsteady at first and leaned heavily on the strength of the young man at her arm. They made their way to the trio gathered beneath the red oak.

"So where's the fire?" Granny asked. "Jesse said the boy had swallered a penny. Is he a-choking?"

"No," Althea answered. "But he did swallow the penny and I can't get him to throw it up."

"Where is he?"

Althea pointed and everyone looked up.

Jesse's expression was puzzled. "Baby-Paisley, what are you doing up there?"

The little boy pointed an accusing finger at Eben. "I'm stayin' away from him!"

Granny Piggott huffed slightly and looked curiously at Althea. "That boy don't look in much danger of choking on a penny as he is of falling and breaking his fool neck!"

"Eben threatened to shake the penny out of him," Althea explained. "And he got away and took off running."

The old woman shook her head. "What did he swallow a penny for anyway?"

"Jesse told him to," Eben Baxley said, unkindly.

"What?"

Althea felt a traitor as she glanced over at Jesse. "Jesse said that if Baby-Paisley swallowed a penny he'd stop peeing the bed."

Oather shook his head. "Jesse, you know you shouldn't make up tales to little boys like that."

"I didn't make it up," Jesse protested.

Eben scoffed. "Lord knows where he got an idea like that."

Granny raised her chin and eyed Baxley belligerently. "Why, he got it from me," she said.

"Oh." The reply came from both men, and Althea, too.

"When Jesse was about nine, I suspect," she said, "Onery told me that he'd started peeing the bed. Why, the boy'd been out of diapers for a half-dozen years. I looked him over and figured it to be pinworms. Pinworms can cause that, you know."

"Pinworms?" Althea asked.

"Yep, indeed," the old woman said, glancing up at the little boy. "And there ain't no better vermifuge than copper. You swaller a copper penny and you'll kill every worm in yer gut."

"You think Baby-Paisley has pinworms?" Althea asked.

"Him? Nay," she replied. "He's still a baby. He just ain't quit peeing the bed. When the time's right, he'll quit. That's all to be said of that."

"That's what I thought, too," Althea admitted. "I tried not to make too much of it."

"And yer right," Granny said. "Making too much of it is the cause of lots of grief in little ones. But how come you didn't ask me about this before?"

"I just didn't," Althea answered.

"Did you ask Beulah?"

"No."

"You didn't ask anybody, did you?"

"I didn't think it was necessary."

"When you got a problem with your children, Althea," Granny said, "you shouldn't keep it secret."

"I wasn't keeping any secret," she assured her hastily.

Granny raised a skeptical eyebrow and then reached into her pocket for her pipe and fixings. "Yep, that's just exactly what you were doing," the old woman said. "You keep it to yourself and don't know for sure if yer doin' right and then something like this happens."

Althea felt scolded and a little bit guilty. "I wanted to handle things myself," she said.

Granny nodded knowingly. "Jesse, go get me a fire twig to light my pipe," she ordered. "Oather, you and Baxley get the things I brung on the skid and take them to the house. I need a minute with Miz Winsloe here alone."

As the young men hurried to do her bidding, once more she turned her attention to Althea.

"Lord Almighty, girl, what do you think you have family for if not to call upon with questions?" Granny asked.

Althea didn't know quite what to say.

"I know, ye don't like prying in-laws. There ain't a wife and mother, living or dead, that does," she said. "But just 'cause you don't want prying, don't mean you have to give up the helping."

"It's best not to be a bother," Althea asserted.

Granny chuckled in disbelief. "A bother? The only reason on earth why the Good Lord has let me live this long is to pass along what I done learned to the younger ones, like yourself. If I can't do that, then I got no purpose for taking up space, now do I?"

"I . . . well, I want to raise Baby-Paisley my own way," she tried to explain.

Granny nodded. "I know that. It's what your mother-in-law is all het-up about, ain't it?"

Althea nodded.

"Well, my advice then, girl, is to let the woman tell you each and every thing on her mind," the old woman said. "Listen and learn. What is worthwhile—and for all that I don't take great store by Beulah's pronouncements, there is bound to be some worthwhile—that you keep. The rest you just smile and say thank you, and forget you ever heard it."

Althea almost smiled. "Do you think Beulah Winsloe would let me get away with that?"

"It'll be tough," Granny said. "I grant you that. But it'll give her some purpose, something that woman sorely needs. And," she said, pointing to the little boy still in the tree, "it will teach your boy, by example, to respect his elders even when he don't really want to."

Althea nodded.

"And it'll make you a more patient person. A more patient person is a more patient mother, I suspect."

"I suppose you're right."

"For sure I am," Granny asserted. "And if you just *can't* go to Beulah, you come on to me. We ain't really kin, but everyone on this mountain is close to me. I ain't promising that I'll always have the answers for you, but I won't be a-telling you how to raise your boy. You'll raise him just like we all do. Trying not to make the mistakes we think our folks made with us, and then ending up making mistakes of our own that they never thought of."

Granny's chuckle was almost self-derisive. "But when you got a question or a concern, you come to me—or Beulah, if you got a mind to—we'll tell you what we think, based on the long life we've had to live. Then you either follow the advice you get, or you don't. It's still your boy and nobody can really get between that."

"All right, Granny," Althea said. "I . . . I'm sorry."

"Ain't no call for sorry," the old woman assured her. "I know how you've lived, girl. I know you been spare relation around here since your daddy moved to the White River. But you're ours now and we care about you." Granny gestured toward the three men who were hovering close by. "You're ours and we care about you, no matter which of these jackanapes you marry up with. Jesse, come light my pipe."

Jesse hurried forward with the glowing twig of green wood. Oather and Eben eased back up into the area beneath the tree also.

"Did you figure out how to get him to retch up the penny?" Oather asked.

"Well, I'd say you're not going to get him to," the old woman answered. "Just let it be," she told Althea. "Feed the little feller a big bowl of bread and greasy gravy for supper the next couple of nights. That penny'll pass the other direction. You can even put him to watching for it, to get it back."

"It won't hurt him inside?" Althea asked. "It won't get caught in his belly someplace?"

"If it was gonna catch," Granny assured her, "it would have been in the throat. If he swallered it as easy as all that, he won't have no trouble passing it through."

Althea sighed heavily, relieved. "Now if we could only get him down," she said.

"You want him down?" Jesse asked.

"Yes, of course."

Jesse walked to the spot directly beneath the branch where Baby-Paisley was perched. He held open his arms and looked up at the little fellow in the tree above him.

"Jump!" he called out simply.

Before Althea could even get a scream out of her throat, Baby-Paisley pushed off from the branch and dropped immediately into the safe, dependable, and waiting arms of Jesse Best.

CHAPTER SIXTEEN

Perhaps it *was* pinworms, or just a pure miracle, but the morning after swallowing the penny, Baby-Paisley's bedsheets were dry. The little fellow strutted around like the cock of the walk that morning. His mother could hardly keep a straight face watching him.

When Jesse arrived, the boy confidently told him that he was *cured.* Jesse didn't argue. He shared a conspiratory grin with Althea. The two of them began the morning working together to get the venison jerky hung in the smokehouse.

The rib meat of the deer had been trimmed of any fat and sliced in long thin strips. After being rubbed down with sugar and drained from a drip box for a week the meat was put to soak in a crock of brine. When the strips quit rising to the top after stirring, they were ready for smoking. Most of the deer meat had merely been hung and dried, but jerky required smoking and Jesse had gathered plenty of hickory sawdust and corncobs to do the job.

Althea was still slightly off-balance from the previous afternoon. Granny had stayed the rest of the day. She ran off the visiting suitors, telling them plainly to show up the next day ready to work.

"You want to prove you are a good provider," she'd told them. "Then you'd best show up and help provide something."

She spent her time at the Widow Winsloe's home peeling beets, rocking in the chair, and entertaining Baby-Paisley. She also apparently felt it was her duty to offer Althea help and advice.

"Well, the only wisdom I can offer about men and marriage is don't expect no changes after the wedding day," she said. The old woman shook her head and waved the stem of her pipe in Althea's direction. "Menfolks is most steadfastly set in their ways. Many a well-intentioned woman has wed up with a fellow she thought she could make a better man and spent the rest of her life not succeeding at the task."

Granny tapped out the spent tobacco and cleaned the pipe bowl with her finger. "But if you can give a man a good reason for doing something different," she continued, "it'll go a lot further than nagging or tears. Men like to think of themselves as reasonable."

Smiling, Althea shook her head. "Thus far I haven't seen anything about my remarriage plans that I would think of as particularly reasonable."

Granny chuckled and nodded in agreement. "There is something about a woman sitting pretty on a fine piece of land that'll get folks into her business in a whipstitch."

Her expression sobered and she eyed Althea shrewdly. "You're going to have to marry, just as sure as the world. You got any preference in them fellers?" she asked.

Althea shook her head. "You know I don't, Granny. I really don't have any feelings toward either of them."

"Well," Granny sighed with resignation. "It ain't the best way of starting a marriage. But you wouldn't be the first to start from nothing."

The old woman continued to rock back and forth, her expression thoughtful. "That Eben Baxley, he's not a bad feller," she said. "Though don't you be telling him I said that. He ain't half bad and he's going to straighten out in time, I've no doubt of it."

Althea gave her a skeptical look. "If you say so, Granny."

"And I do," she said. "He'll keep a woman a-laughing, Eben Baxley will. If she ain't crying, that is. Either, and a little of both are highly likely with that one."

Granny tapped the pipe stem against her teeth as she pondered. "Either, and a little of both," she repeated. "Now, that Oather, well you know I like that young fellow mighty fine."

"He's always seemed like a really nice man," Althea said without enthusiasm.

The old woman chuckled. "Oh, he's *real* nice, especial nice. It wouldn't be so noticeable in another man, but it stands out on him 'cause his daddy is such a failed-dough biscuit."

"A 'failed-dough biscuit?'"

Granny nodded her head with conviction. "Hard as rock outside and not baked all the way through."

Althea laughed delightedly at her description.

"That Oather, well there is no telling what that boy is, or will be, until he gets out on his own," Granny said. "A woman marrying him would be getting a pig in a poke for sure. Ain't no telling in this world how he's to turn out. And if he never gets shed of Buell Phillips, that man will be running him and the woman he marries till he draws his last breath."

Her brow furrowing, Althea was momentarily puzzled. "You think I should marry Baxley then?"

"No, I ain't saying that," Granny replied, packing a new wad of tobacco in her pipe. "Truth is, I don't much envy your choice, girl. But you done lived with Paisley Winsloe. I suspect you ain't got a lot of stars in your eyes about the joys of marriage."

Althea chuckled without humor. "I suppose you're right. I have given up the silly notions I once had about love and romance. I know there's no truth in that nonsense."

"No truth in it?" Granny tutted in disapproval. "I wouldn't say that, girl. Next time you're in church, you cast your eyes on Polly and Newt Weston or Grace and Labin Trace or Jesse's sister Meggie and her Roe Farley. There's truth to it, young lady, and a-plenty. But it don't happen for all and some throws it to the scraps as quick as it comes their way."

As the darkness came on early, Althea invited Granny and Jesse to stay for dinner.

Granny took a seat and put away her pipe. Althea expected the old woman simply to rest from her busy afternoon. Granny Piggott surprised her, choosing instead to entertain Baby-Paisley, leaving his mother free to cook without him underfoot.

Granny folded and tied a dishrag till it resembled a doll, whom she called Little Mary. When Baby-Paisley protested that boys didn't play with dolls, Granny looked surprised and told him that Gobby Weston did.

Won over, Baby-Paisley sat on the rug in front of the old woman's chair. Granny set the *doll* on the arm of the chair, carefully spreading out the dishrag's *skirt,* and in a little squeaky voice, supposedly the doll's, she told Baby-Paisley a story. It was about a chicken named One-Wing who got up in the tree and couldn't get down. The little boy was wide-eyed, listening.

When Jesse had come in, cleaned up and his hair still slicked back with water, he'd sat at the table, ostensibly waiting for his dinner. But Althea noticed him listening, too. He'd glanced over at her and smiled.

"Granny can sure tell a tale," he pointed out.

The old woman could tell a tale, indeed. And after supper, Baby-Paisley had begged another. Granny made it short, but not short enough. The little fellow had fallen fast asleep before it was through.

"I'll take him up," Jesse said.

Althea watched him easily managing the ladder with the little boy in his arms.

"There's something that looks right about that," Granny said suddenly.

"What?"

Granny pointed in the direction of the disappearing twosome. "There's something right about Jesse Best with a child in his arms. I'd never thought of it till I saw that little fellow land in them this afternoon. I always thought that Jesse wasn't smart enough to be a husband or father," the old woman said. "But now that I think about it, being good at those things don't take a heap of knowledge. It takes more feelings than learning. Jesse ain't been slighted on that account."

"No, he certainly has not," Althea admitted. A strange

tingling commenced inside her. She pressed her lips together, attempting to make the curious feeling stop. She glanced guiltily at Granny, hoping the woman had noticed nothing amiss.

Gratefully she saw the old woman's attention was still focused on the two people disappearing up the loft ladder.

Granny was nodding and spoke thoughtfully. "Yep, I suspect I'd better get to thinking about finding a bride for Jesse. There's bound to be a woman somewhere who can love a man for what he is, not how he thinks."

The next morning, as she squeezed the salty brine out of the strips of venison, she was reminded of Granny's words. She looked up at Jesse, carefully hanging each long thin piece of deer meat on dowel rods so that they did not touch each other. He probably could be a husband, she thought. Some not very bright girl would surely be lucky to find such as him.

Jesse worked with the certainty and confidence that Althea had grown used to. Jesse had struggled to learn the tasks that he knew. Once mastered, however, he never forgot them and he rarely allowed his concentration upon them to slip. If his quietly whispered instructions to himself were a little unusual, Althea didn't find it particularly annoying. Jesse worked steady and sure, long after others had tired, and he always seemed quite happy to do so.

That was what was best about working with him, Althea decided. He did his share and more. And he did it with such a light heart as if work itself was not a burden, but a privilege. *Maybe*, she thought, *he knows better than the rest of us.*

Her brow furrowed in concentration and she bit down on her lip again thoughtfully. That not-very-bright girl might not be able to appreciate Jesse as he deserved. Perhaps he needed someone who could do more than just accept him, someone who could admire him.

"Good morning!"

The call made them both turn and look. Althea rose to her

feet and shaded her eyes with her hand as she stared into the morning sunshine to see Oather Phillips walking across the yard toward them.

His hair was slicked back as he reverentially doffed his hat and offered a little bow to Althea. He was not dressed in his Sunday suit, but his working clothes were of good quality and they were clean and neatly pressed. He'd obviously come a-courting, but with Granny's admonition he was ready to prove his worth as a hand also.

Baby-Paisley, who'd been sitting in the dirt near the smokehouse, relating the tree adventures of One-Wing the Chicken to Runt, jumped to his feet and called out to the new arrival.

"I didn't pee the bed!" he bragged.

"Baby-Paisley!" his mother shushed him. "That is not a thing to be discussing with strangers."

Oather Phillips seemed more amused than disapproving of the little fellow's enthusiasm. He smiled warmly at Althea before turning his attention to the child.

"Jesse must have been right," Oather said to the boy.

Baby-Paisley nodded enthusiastically. "He's right 'bout lots of stuff. Just 'cause he ain't smart, doan mean that he's dumb."

Oather and Althea exchanged glances before looking over at Jesse. He blushed, embarrassed, but obviously pleased with the little boy's words.

"Baby-Paisley and I are friends," Jesse said, by way of explanation. "Guess he ain't scared of me no more."

Oather nodded in agreement. "How are you this morning, Mrs. Winsloe?" he asked Althea. "You look very lovely, if I may say so."

The words seemed so stilted and rehearsed, Althea had to stifle the urge to giggle. Sitting as she was, with her arms up to the elbows in the salt brine crock, she was sure that she could be described as most anything but lovely.

"I am very well, sir," she managed to respond politely. "And yourself?" she inquired. She felt more than a little foolish with the forced formality.

"As you see, I've come dressed to help," he said. "Taking Granny Piggott's advice, I suppose."

"I'm afraid today's chore is both messy and malodrous," she warned.

Oather shrugged as he rolled up his sleeves, apparently eager to take up the task. "But venison jerky is such fine eating, Mrs. Winsloe," he said, "that the temporary unpleasantness is well worth the outcome."

Readily she agreed with him.

To Althea's surprise the morning passed quickly and was especially pleasant for her. Hanging the venison was basically a two-person endeavor. One person to fish the strips out of the brine and the other person to hang them so that absolutely the most of the meat would be exposed to the smoke. Oather worked with Jesse and Althea found that what she was most called upon to do was make conversation and bring out coffee.

She did give some consideration to leaving the men to their task and going on to some other needed errand, but the sun was high, the wind blustery, and the narrow area around the smokehouse too inviting.

They had finished the hanging and were setting the fire when she excused herself to start the noon meal.

"You must stay to eat with us," she told Oather.

"It would be my pleasure," he said. "But only if it is no trouble."

Althea was about to assure him, politely, that it was not, when Jesse intervened.

"Nooning with Miss Althea will about make it even for the work you done," Jesse pointed out. "You got to stay. You don't want the woman to feel beholding."

Oather's face turned a vivid scarlet with embarrassment. Of course, it was part of the courting process for the female to feel beholden to the gentleman. Oather was clearly as embarrassed as if he'd been caught at it. Althea wanted to laugh, but managed to resist the impulse.

Oather put such a polite face on everything. It felt so unnatural, so constrained. He was much aware of the rules of etiquette. Somehow she found Jesse's more honest assessment much more to her liking.

But it was Oather to whom she might well find herself married, she reminded herself. She must compare him to Eben Baxley, not Jesse Best.

Eben Baxley arrived when the menfolk, Baby-Paisley included, were just pushing back their chairs from the table. Purposely he had ignored Granny Piggott's totally unsubtle advice to arrive early and be ready for work. He had his own plan for winning over the Widow Winsloe and he wasn't going to have to break out in a sweat to do it.

He made little more than a perfunctory knock on the door before barging into the room.

"Good morning, Althea honey," he said. "It's your devoted swain come to call."

The lady in question was bent over retrieving the coffee-pot from the hearth. Eben was openly admiring of the view and sorely tempted to apply a playful swat to her round feminine backside. It was Jesse Best's critical, penetrating gaze as much as his own good sense that caused him to forgo the opportunity.

As Althea straightened, she turned to face him. He watched her eyes narrow, but he was not concerned.

"Don't call me *honey*," she said sternly.

He gave her what he knew to be his most charming grin. "Beg pardon, ma'am," he replied.

Once more his eyes were drawn to Jesse. The simple fellow's expression was, as always, somewhat vague. But there was definitely still a sense of disapproval. Deliberately he pulled his gaze away to glance across the room at his truly sworn rival, Oather Phillips. With more scorn than deference in the gesture, Eben tipped his hat.

"Well, if it isn't Phillips," he said snidely. "Buell's *boy*."

"Baxley," Oather replied.

The civil greeting was anything but. Eben grinned. There was certainly no goodwill between the two of them. And that was fine with Eben Baxley. He didn't like being made a fool of by Mavis Phillips. He liked it even less that Oather

knew about it. Sure, he'd got some revenge on her. Some
would say she was treated badly. But Eben was not ever
going to be led around and maneuvered. He was not weak
like his father.

Turning to hang his hat and coat on the nails by the door,
Eben saw Oather's in that place. He pulled them down and
replaced them with his own. Casually he tossed Phillips his
property.

"Here's your hat. What's your hurry?"

His face red with fury, Oather rose to his feet. Eben
wondered if the fellow was ready for another fight. He saw
Phillips glance in Althea's direction and immediately begin
to rein in his temper.

Clearing his throat, Oather spoke rather more loudly than
necessary to Althea. "I'll be taking my leave now, Mrs.
Winsloe. It has been my pleasure to assist you with the jerky
making and I hope that I will have the honor of sampling the
same come the cold weather."

Althea thanked him just as politely.

Oather, rather formally, took Althea's hand in his own and
bowed over it as if he was set to give it a kiss. Eben was
grateful that he did not. It was all he could do not to burst
out laughing as it was.

"If I might return on the morrow, perhaps I can aid Jesse
as he begins working on the butchering platform."

"Yes, that would be fine, Mr. Phillips," she assured him.
"And thank you for your help with the venison."

"To be of service to you, ma'am, is ever my ambition,"
Oather answered.

"Lord save us!" Eben blurted out. "He'll be spouting
poetry in another minute." He leaned impudently, one hip
against the doorjamb. Oather leveled him an angry look. He
grinned back.

"Good day, Mrs. Winsloe," Oather said. Turning to the
other occupants of the room, he nodded to them as well as
he took his leave. When he stepped past Baxley, it was as if
he were keeping his distance, hoping not to be soiled.

Eben chuckled, rather unkindly, as if the sight brought

only humor. He pushed away from his position and made his way to the table.

"You got anything left over, honey?" he said. "I ain't even had breakfast yet this morning."

"Don't call me *honey*," Althea said once more.

"Widder Winsloe," he answered. "You wouldn't let a man go hungry, would you?"

Huffily, she picked up a tin plate and began to pile it with the remaining food. Eben glanced across the table at Jesse, who had remained seated. He remembered the unpleasant revelations of the Literary evening and found that it didn't set well with him at all.

"Didn't expect to see you here today, Simple Jess," he said. "I figured old Onery would have kept you out of sight for a few days until folks get over the shock of things."

"I work here," Jesse answered. "Miss Althea needs me to come and help."

Eben smiled. "But not for very long," he said. "By Christmas Day, she won't be needing to see you anymore." He glanced toward Althea. She didn't meet his gaze. That was good.

"I'm earning my dogs," Jesse said.

"Yes indeed," Eben replied. "You get the dogs, Jesse." He leaned closer and whispered loud enough for everyone in the room to hear. "But I get the bride. We won't be seeing you around here after Christmas Day."

Althea banged the plate of food down on the table in front of him. "Jesse is my friend and neighbor. He has been a great help to me in getting ready for the winter. Jesse will always be welcome in this house."

Eben raised his eyebrows and grinned broadly. "I know how fond of the feller you are, honey," he said. "Why, I'm thinking we should change his name from Simple Jess to Kissing Jess. What do you think about that?"

Bright red blooms of shame heightened the color in Althea's cheeks. The target of his teasing, however, just continued to stare at him. Jesse Best was too stupid to know when he was being made a fool of.

"Stop makin' fun of Jesse!"

That order surprisingly came from the small boy seated on the opposite side of the table.

"Jesse is my friend," he announced. "Doan you say nothing agin him."

"It's all right, Baby-Paisley," Jesse intervened. "He ain't saying nothing. He just thinks he's being funny. Fellers are sometimes wrong about that."

Eben let Jesse's assessment pass without comment. "Well, how are you this morning, Baby-Paisley?" he asked with exaggerated friendliness.

"It ain' morning," the little boy replied. "It's plum noon and we already et."

"But I haven't," Baxley told him. "And I am extremely fond of your mama's good cooking."

Eben retrieved his spoon from his trouser pocket and took a bite of the food Althea's table offered. "This is good, honey," he said. "This is real good. It's going to be a lucky man who marries such a fine cook."

Both Jesse and Baby-Paisley glared at him as he ate, but Eben didn't let it bother him. Having long had a reputation as a black sheep, he knew well how to laugh and smile in the face of disapproval. He didn't hesitate to do so now. He filled the lengthening silence around him with pleasured sounds of *mmmmm* and *ahhhhh* as he oversavored the delectable fare.

"I doan like you!" Baby-Paisley said suddenly and with such childhood certainty that it was momentarily heart-stopping. "I doan like you at all."

"Baby-Paisley!" Althea scolded immediately. "We do not talk to guests in our house that way. You apologize this minute."

The little boy looked mutinous, and Eben was glad for the opportunity to save the day.

"It's all right, honey," he said to Althea. "The boy's just being honest, aren't you, son?"

Eben's easy agreement threw the child into confusion.

"I know you don't like me, Baby-Paisley," Eben continued. "It saddens me a little because I knew your daddy. But I don't blame you for it."

He reached across the table to pat the boy on the head. Baby-Paisley drew back, but Eben pretended that he didn't notice. "You don't know much about me, do you, son? And what you do know, well, there ain't much in there to like."

Baby-Paisley's brow furrowed in puzzlement. Eben saw Jesse's expression turn suddenly wary as if he sensed a trick. Deliberately he didn't look at Althea. A mother, whether she was bear, coon, or woman, would protect her cub. Eben didn't want to stir up her ire.

Setting down his spoon, he leaned back in his chair and smiled broadly at the little boy. It was his best and most winning smile. He knew it would be hard for the little fellow to resist.

"Sometimes," he continued more softly, "you can be wrong about a feller. Has that ever happened to you?"

Baby-Paisley didn't answer. Eben continued.

"Have you ever thought you didn't like somebody only to find out that you do?"

The question was well thought out and well crafted. Yesterday he'd picked up on the story of the child's newfound friendship with Jesse. He didn't see any reason not to use the facts that he knew.

The boy's face looked thoughtful for a moment before Eben saw him give a quick glance toward Jesse.

Eben smiled again. It was going to be almost too easy.

"Baby-Paisley, go look in the pocket of my coat," he said.

The little boy hesitated.

"Go ahead," Eben urged him. "There's something in there that I brought for you."

Reluctantly the child went over to the nails by the door. He had to stand on the doorstop to reach the coats, but within a minute he pulled out the surprise gift that Eben had brought him.

"What is it?" he asked, holding the fluffy piece of brown and white hide before him.

"It's a deer tail," Eben answered. "It's a deertail from the biggest whitetail buck I ever seen."

The child turned it over in his hand a couple of times. He was clearly wary and not too much impressed.

"It ain' the color of the deer me an' Jesse kilt," he pointed out.

"That was a winter deer. Deer in winter are gray. It's springtime when they turn brown like that. Isn't that right, Jesse?"

He didn't give the other man time to formulate his answer.

"In the winter when they are gray they are pretty easy to shoot," he said. "They are cold and sluggish. About anyone can get a shot at a deer then. In the springtime when they are brown like that and just full of vinegar, it takes a real man to kill one."

"Where d'it come from?"

Baby-Paisley walked over to stand near Eben's chair. His wide eyes were focused with growing appreciation on the prize he held in his hands.

Eben had traded the Broody twins for the deer tail just that morning. It had cost him a chipped knife blade and a picture of a big fat woman shucked down to her drawers and corset, but he knew it was going to be well worth the price. It was going to win him a bride and a farm and a little boy's loyalty.

"Well, Baby-Paisley," Eben replied with deliberate casualness. "Your daddy and I killed that deer together before you were born."

"Gar," the little boy replied. His eyes widened and he looked down at the deer tail in newly realized awe. He looked up to his mother questioning. Eben was confident that she couldn't dispute him.

"Did my daddy kill this deer?"

Althea stepped forward and looked at the tail. She was obviously skeptical and gave Eben a penetrating look. It was meant both to question and to warn. Keeping his expression benign, Eben stared back at her, almost daring her to deny his story. She and Paisley hardly knew each other before they'd wed. Althea could no more speak for where he'd been or what he'd done than she could read his mind.

"Your daddy and Mr. Baxley did use to hunt together," she answered her son finally.

"My daddy kilt this deer," Baby-Paisley whispered with near reverence.

"Yep," Eben told him, warming up to the story. "Your daddy shot that deer. Not many men could have done it. Maybe Dan'l Boone or some such feller as that. But not many that ever lived on this mountain."

"Dan'l Boone?" Jesse's tone was astonished. Even he had heard of the great hunter's accomplishments.

Eben lowered his voice deliberately to a storyteller's tone. "I remember that day as clear as if it were yesterday itself," he said. "We'd been up high on the mountain trailing that buck, your daddy and I."

Eben shook his head as if he could hardly believe the tale himself.

"Lord it was warm that day, and game was as scarce as silver dollars. We'd about given up as we'd followed him down into the Squaw's Trunk narrows. I figured it was for sure no use, we'd be going home hungry."

Eben pointed across the room as if he were back in the woods on the fateful day.

"Suddenly I spotted that buck way off in the distance," he said. "Eighteen points it had and its antlers gleaming like sunset through cattails. I hollered out to Paisley, 'There's that darned buck.' Pardon, ma'am," he offered as an aside to Althea for the curse word.

"I didn't even lift up my gun 'cause it was so far away." Eben shook his head once more. "Your daddy, Baby-Paisley, he just raised up his Winchester and shot that critter straight through the heart at better than five hundred paces."

"Gar!" the little boy said again, completely enthralled.

Eben glanced around at his audience. Althea's attention was focused completely upon her son, her expression was caring and sorrowful.

Jesse Best looked very puzzled and confused. When Eben met his eye, he spoke. His tone held neither scorn nor skepticism, but was merely a stated fact.

"Paisley weren't all that good a shot," he said.

"He was that day," Eben said quickly, defusing the potential of doubt raised. "That day he was the best shot I'd ever saw." He turned his attention once more upon the boy. Baby-Paisley was now stroking the deer tail almost lovingly. He was completely enraptured by the story of the father he didn't remember and the tangible evidence of his skill and bravery. The child had no difficulty in believing such a tale of the man whose blood he carried.

"Well, son," Eben said, continuing. "Your daddy killed that deer and he gave me that tail as part of my share. I've carried that a long time. Always hoping that someday, I might get as good a shot."

Baby-Paisley nodded with understanding.

"That deer tail's always brought me luck, but I thought to myself, now that boy of Paisley's, he really should have this. That's what his daddy would have wanted. So I brought it for you, son. It's a gift."

"Oh, Mama! Mama!" The little boy began to jump up and down excitedly. "It's mine, Mama. It was my daddy's and now it's mine!"

"That's wonderful, sweetheart," she said, a little less than enthusiastically. Then slowly, like a snail crawling up a spicebush, the stalk of uncertainty began to bend with the weight of joy. Eben Baxley had pleased her son, he'd made the boy smile, she wanted to believe it, so she did.

"Thank you so much, Eben," she said. "It is a wonderful, wonderful gift for Baby-Paisley."

"Where can I put it, Mama? I wanna see it always. Always," he said, beginning to hop around excitedly as he held his treasure next to his heart. "Where can I put it?"

"Well, maybe we can hang it up here in the house," she suggested.

"But I want Gobby Weston to see it, Mama," he said, still bouncing around the room. "I want everybody to see it. My daddy kilt a deer and I got its tail."

"Why don't you wear it on your hat like Dan'l Boone," Eben suggested. "Maybe your mama could just sew it on there and everybody could see it every time they see you."

The little fellow's eyes widened. "Yes, yes I'll wear it like

Dan'l Boone. My daddy kilt a deer like Dan'l Boone. Yes, Mama, pweese, pweese."

"Well, all right," she said, smiling at her son lovingly. "Bring me your hat and I'll sew it on."

Althea reached for her sewing basket. She was happy. Eben was, too. The little contrivance was innocent enough, he reminded himself. It wouldn't hurt the boy, any boy, to think well of his daddy. And it wouldn't hurt his suit with Althea if she saw that the boy took to him. He liked children. He could be a good father. At least he knew what a good father was supposed to be. The exact opposite of the one that he'd had. She wanted to raise the boy her own way. That was all right with him. He'd keep friendly with the child and let the raising be her concern.

Althea positioned the deer tail to the hem of the little boy's gray glove hat, allowing it to hang down along the back of the neck. It was not exactly like Daniel Boone's coonskin, but it was eye-catching and the little boy was thrilled. Almost dancing around the room, he rattled on excitedly about his daddy, his deer tail, and Daniel Boone.

"No!"

The word spoken loud and forcefully had emerged from Jesse Best. It startled all three of them.

Althea, Baby-Paisley, and Eben all stared at him in surprise. He was staring at the deer tail against the glove hat. His expression was foreboding and fearful.

"Don't put the deer tail on his hat!" Jesse stated emphatically.

"What's wrong, Jesse? What is it?" Althea looked at him questioningly.

"Don't put the deer tail on the hat," he said again.

"The boy wants it on the hat," Eben told him.

"It shouldn't be there," Jesse said. "Don't put the deer tail on the hat."

"Why not?" Althea asked him.

"I . . ." Jesse hesitated uncertainly. He looked at Althea searchingly. Clearly he was upset, but he was puzzled, too, and frustrated. "I don't know, but—"

"Oh, good Lord, Jesse," Eben dismissed him arrogantly. "You're telling Althea what to do, but you don't know why."

"You don't think he should wear the deer tail on his hat, Jesse?" Althea clarified his protestation.

"It ain't good," Jesse said. "It's wrong. It's not . . . I . . . I don't know why, but it ain't good."

"You're not making any sense," Eben protested, anger building up in him. Obviously Jesse didn't believe the deer-killing story and he didn't want the boy to have the tail. Sure it was a lie, but the lie wouldn't hurt the boy. He'd paid the Broody brothers enough to keep them quiet and nobody else knew the truth except Paisley Winsloe and he wasn't likely to come back from the dead to dispute Eben's word. This was a great plan to win Althea over. Once the boy accepted him, she would, too. He wasn't about to let Simple Jesse Best foul this up for him.

"It's the boy's gift," Eben stated sternly. "He can do with it what he wishes."

"It ain't good to wear it on his hat," Jesse said, his tone certain, but his expression furrowed with worry and puzzlement.

"I want the deer tail on my hat," Baby-Paisley announced. "It's mine. I wanna wear it on my hat."

Jesse shook his head. "No, Baby-Paisley, no," he said.

The little boy stuck out his lip mutinously. "I thought you were my friend," he said to Jesse accusingly. "I wanna wear the deer tail on my hat."

Silently he appealed to Althea. With helplessness, she glanced once more at Jesse and then at Eben and at her son.

"I don't know, Baby-Paisley," she said. "If Jesse thinks . . ."

The little boy's face was crestfallen. He clasped his little hands together in a semblance of prayful supplication. "Pweese, Mama," he pleaded. "Pweese, pweese, pweese."

Surprisingly, Eben could feel the child's hurt. He wished for an instant that he hadn't ever bought the deer tail, then he pushed the thought away. It wasn't Eben that was hurting the boy here.

"I can't believe you'd listen to Simple Jesse Best about what to do with your own child," he said to Althea, almost angrily. "I hear all the time that you won't let anyone tell you what to do with your boy. Now I find out that you'll take advice from the lowest thinker on the mountain."

"I value Jesse's opinion," Althea answered defensively.

"More than your son's happiness?"

"Of course not!"

"Pweese, Mama, pweese, pweese," the little boy continued to beg.

Althea weakened once more. She looked at him uncertainly, and then back at Jesse.

"Do you have any *reason* why Baby-Paisley shouldn't wear the deer tail on his hat, Jesse?"

"I . . . I just know that it's something bad," Jesse answered, shaking his head.

"It's something bad because it's something *I* gave to the boy," Eben snapped angrily. "He doesn't like me getting between him and you two," he said to Althea. "Can't you see that? He's just angry because he wishes it were him that was going to marry you and not me or Oather."

"That's not . . . it's . . . I don't know why but—"

"All right, Jesse," Eben continued ruthlessly. "Tell the truth, now. We know you kissed Althea. You want to marry her, too, don't you? Deny that. Deny it if you can."

Jesse stumbled over his words.

"Deny it! Deny that you're jealous," Eben taunted once more.

"I . . . I . . ." Jesse's flush was guilt-ridden.

"You're just jealous 'cause you can't have her." Eben's tone dropped to an accusing whisper. "You've kissed her and pressed up against her and probably dreamt about her at night, but you can't have her, not ever."

Jesse's obvious culpability stunned him to silence.

"You can't have her," Eben went on cruelly. "You can't have her. You can't have the boy, you can't have any of it.

You can't have what you want, so you're trying to take something away from Baby-Paisley."

"No, no, it's not that."

"It is that and you can't deny it!"

"Stop badgering him," Althea snapped at Eben.

Silence fell all around them.

Baby-Paisley's expression was still pleading.

She looked at her son and then she turned to Jesse. Her voice was calm, her words coaxing.

"Jesse, can you think of any reason, any real reason why Baby-Paisley can't wear the deer tail on his hat?"

Jesse was determinedly gathering his composure. Eben had shamed him with the unspoken truth. Of course Jesse wanted Althea. Jesse was male and human and he probably got himself to sleep at night pretending he was between her thighs. Eben could almost pity the fellow, if he hadn't come to cross-purposes with him.

Jesse spoke finally, his words slow and certain. "Something is not good about it, Miss Althea," he said. "I don't know what, but something is not right. I know it."

The two looked at each other for a long time. Althea and Jesse, just staring at each other as if they were communicating on some other level than the one of words. The moment dragged on. It dragged on so long that Eben felt an unexpected spark of annoyance twist up inside him, but he managed to hold his tongue.

"Pweese, Mama." The little beseeching voice was barely a whisper.

Althea reached out and straightened her son's bright blond curls. "All right, sweetheart," she said at last. "I'll put the tail on the hat."

"Whoopee!" Baby-Paisley cried out excitedly. "I got my daddy's deer tail. My hat'll be like Dan'l Boone!" He began to bounce around the room once more.

Eben couldn't help but grin at the youngster. He felt a little like dancing himself. He didn't know why he was so pleased, but he was. It was as if he had been in a kill-devil fawnch and he was the only fellow left standing.

Still smiling, he turned his attention to Althea. She was still looking at Jesse.

"You're just confused on this one, Jesse," she told him. "I suppose it will look funny, but there isn't really anything *wrong* with Baby-Paisley wearing a deer tail on his hat."

The big, simple man nodded, but he didn't look convinced.

CHAPTER
SEVENTEEN

Hog killing, by its very nature, was a social event. But when the word got around that Althea Winsloe, with the help of Jesse Best, and only two weeks left before she picked a husband, was about to slaughter her hog, folks had to be actually told to keep their distance.

With both her suitors and their families intent upon being there, Granny Piggott felt called upon to limit the gawkers to herself alone.

"I'll be telling any news that needs to be told," she assured the uninvited and disappointed.

Beulah Winsloe, of course, could not be kept away. And she insisted that her husband and her brother be there to ensure that Eben Baxley was shown to good advantage.

Buell Phillips, hearing that Beulah would be present, showed up with his wife and his daughter. Even if his foolish son, Oather, was not allowing him to direct the courting, he was determined to see that the young man didn't ruin his chances.

Because Jesse was in the middle of things, and because the Bests also had two hogs to kill, Onery, Roe, Meggie, and Little Edith made their way to Althea Winsloe's place that morning.

Jesse was especially glad to have his family with him.

"I don't want to forget anything," he told Roe. "But I don't want any of the other folks reminding me either."

His brother-in-law nodded, understanding. "I'll be right next to you, Jesse," he promised. "Of course, I'm no expert on this either."

Jesse grinned at him. Roe had been all over the world and knew about things that people on Marrying Stone couldn't even imagine. But he was not well versed in farming, hunting, or the way of getting by on the mountain.

It was just a little before dawn when they arrived at the Widow Winsloe's place. Three separate cook fires illuminated the place in the gray light. It was a perfect day for hog butchering, clear and still. It was cool enough to keep the meat, but not so cold as to endanger anything to freeze. Buell and Beulah were already on the premises, their respective families in tow. Tom and Orv, with some assistance from Oather, had the fires going. Althea was pouring hot coffee into every cup raised in her direction. Mavis and her mother were busy salting the various pails and pans that were to be used. Granny Piggott set in her rocking chair, watching the activities and offering advice.

"Well, I see the Bests are finally here," she commented loudly. "I know that this tardiness is your fault, Onery. Them children is Piggotts through and through and Piggotts are always on time for the work. Ain't that right, Oather?"

The young man smiled, clearly pleased. He gave a quick glance toward Beulah, whose face was a mask of furious indignation, and didn't bother to answer. The statement was not meant for him or the Bests. Its purpose, in the event that anyone failed to notice, was to point out that Eben Baxley, true to his typical behavior, was nowhere in sight.

Jesse missed the implication and felt called upon to defend his family.

"Pa's leg ain't no good in this weather," he pointed out. "And we come farther than the Phillipses or the Winsloes."

"Well, we weren't about to start until we could see what we are doing," Althea assured him quickly. "Do you want some coffee?"

Jesse nodded and fished his cup out of his towsack. Miss Althea's coffee was much superior to his sister Meggie's and well worth the wait.

Visiting went into full swing once more as the women began discussing the tasks of the day and debating the proposed sausage recipes.

The men's concern was more for the weather. There was a cold spell coming. Onery Best could feel it in his bad leg. A real norther, maybe a blizzard, he told his listeners. But it was hard to tell how far off it might be. It was a good thing that pork didn't require the hanging and drying of other meat.

Baby-Paisley, bright-eyed with the excitement of the morning, hurried over to Edith Best. Since she was the only child to play with, her status as a girl was less of a detriment. She'd brought her doll, Matilda. Baby-Paisley showed appropriate scorn for such a plaything, then proceeded to tell both of them the latest he'd heard of the adventures of One-Wing the Chicken.

Jesse wandered among the groups of chattering people. He was still a bit of a scandal, having admitted to kissing Miss Althea. But most of those gathered had little fear or revulsion for him.

He watched Baby-Paisley and Little Edith playing together in the yard. They were both so smart and happy and laughing. It gave him a warm feeling inside.

As Baby-Paisley turned to run in the other direction, Jesse spotted the deer tail attached to his hat. Jesse's smiled faded. There was still something wrong about that. Something that pulled at him, worried him. But Althea didn't think so and Eben didn't think so. And Baby-Paisley did truly enjoy having a hat like Daniel Boone. Purposefully Jesse pushed back his misgivings and turned his attention elsewhere among the crowd.

He walked around and through the people gathered, catching one sentence here, and another there. He made no attempt to join in conversation. He liked to talk with one person. When it was too many people talking at once, it was just too hard to keep up with what was being said.

Jesse's heedless circuitous path around the yard had him ending up, as he often did, very near Miss Althea. He closed his eyes and breathed in the so familiar fragrance of her. It was as dear to him as wildflowers in bloom on the meadow, or the vague milky memory of the scent he recalled of his mother.

But the smell of Althea Winsloe had a new effect upon him. Since the wonderful kiss they had shared the whole of her fragrance seemed almost a part of his own self. And something about it elicited a sultry sensual reaction. He closed his eyes and let his mind wander. He thought of the taste of her mouth, the softness of her lips, and the nearness of her round woman parts so close to his own.

The stirring began in the front of his trousers again. He wanted to run his hand across the plaguey ache, but this was neither the time nor the place. He was not alone, he was in the middle of folks. Touching yourself when people were around was rude. His sister Meggie didn't have to tell him that for him to know it. And he was here to work, not to daydream. His intention was to walk to the water trough and cool himself before he acted up any more. The words he heard between Mavis Phillips and Miss Althea stopped him. They had moved away from the rest of the women and except for Jesse behind them, their conversation was completely private.

"Have you decided which one you are going to pick?" Mavis asked very quietly.

"I haven't decided," Althea answered her.

"My brother . . . my brother is a wonderful man," Mavis told her. "I know that he will always treat you well."

"I'm sure he will."

"But you're leaning toward Baxley, aren't you?" Mavis said.

"I truly haven't decided," Althea assured her. "But, Eben, well, he's not so bad as I once thought. And he is very good with Baby-Paisley."

"Oather likes children, too."

"Yes, it's obvious that he does," Althea agreed. "But, well, honestly, choosing Eben might make Beulah less angry with me. And your father . . . Well, your father can be rather absolute in his thinking. One in-law like that seems to be enough."

Mavis's expression was fraught with worry. "Althea, I can't really explain this, but it's very important that you marry my brother. He's the kind of man who can be whatever you want him to be. Please, please, don't discard him out of hand."

"I haven't, Mavis," Althea assured her. "I told you, I really haven't made up my mind. And I'll think about what you've said."

"Thank you. And, Althea, I just hope that you will be happy," she said.

"It's good to hear someone wants me to be happy," Althea told her. "I've begun to think all that anyone wants is for me to be married."

When everyone was full of coffee and the party atmosphere clearly in swing, Granny Piggott broke into the revelry.

"Who's going to do the killing?" she asked.

"Orv usually kills our hogs," Beulah announced after she gave one last glance toward the empty path. Eben Baxley had yet to arrive.

Her husband's eyes widened as he heard his name. "I thought Baxley would be here and—"

"Orv can hit them and Tom can stick them," Beulah interrupted quickly. Her unhappiness with Eben's failure to appear was well hidden. Clearly she was unable to control young Baxley as she wanted. It was an ever-piercing thorn in the woman's side. "Go ahead, Orv. You and Tom will kill them," she said.

The two aging men glanced at each other uneasily. Hog killing required the strength and agility of youth.

Tom's expression was doleful. Orv cleared his throat uneasily. "I ain't so steady or strong as I once was," he admitted.

"I brought my hammer," Jesse answered. "I think I can get them in one blow apiece, if you want me to try?" He directed the question to Althea. It was, after all, her farm and her animal.

"I've brought the .22," Buell proclaimed a bit pompously. "That is the modern way and would be just as quick and a lot more sure than Jesse's hammer."

"I don't think it's necessary to fire a gun this early in the morning," Beulah protested lamely.

The two appeared ready to commence argument on the point when Granny Piggott broke in.

"We cain't spend all day here with the two families fit to fawnch on ever detail," she declared with a snappish lilt to her tongue. The old woman seemed prepared to make a personal decree, but Jesse stopped her.

"This first one is Miss Althea's hog," he said, not quite understanding why the other people were even offering their opinion. "So we'll do whatever she wants done."

The correctness of his words quieted the crowd momentarily and they all looked expectantly at Althea. She hesitated, taken a little aback. So naturally, she turned to the only person sure to have only her interests in consideration. She turned to Jesse.

"What do you think we should do?"

Jesse paused thoughtfully a moment before answering. "Let's use the pistol. That way there's no chance of suffering," he said. "I can stand right behind the shooter with my knife."

"All right," Althea agreed immediately.

That Jesse had made the decision was obvious to everyone but Jesse. Hence the strange looks that he received as he moved through the crowd toward the hog pen were a puzzlement to him.

In the last week, with the occasional help of Oather and Eben, Jesse had built a table-high platform with a high pole and a dragging ramp next to the hog pen. A huge cast-iron potash kettle filled with water boiled rapidly on the ground fire pit at the end of the platform. Jesse surveyed the water. Wood ashes and pine tar had been added giving the color a milky appearance.

"Do you think it will do?" he asked generally.

A discussion among the men ensued and ultimately resulted in a bit of rosen added to the blend.

Jesse removed his coat and hung it on a fence post. The shirt he wore beneath it was worn and near threadbare. Hog killing was messy work. The other men did likewise. Buell handed the pistol to Oather. The young man stared at it for a moment, looking quite pale. It was well-known that the younger Mr. Phillips didn't care for guns, hunting, or shooting.

"I'll do it," Jesse's brother-in-law Roe suggested. He took the pistol from Oather and followed Jesse as he opened the gate to the hog pen.

"SOO-EEE pig!" Jesse called out as he held out a nice, fresh carrot before him. "Come here, now," he told the healthy well-fed young hog. "We know you're hungry."

By necessity the hogs had not been fed since the previous morning. Eagerly the big swaggering swine belonging to Althea hurried over to the proffered carrot. Jesse gave it to him and watched him chomp at it. He smoothed the rough hair on the pig's face and scratched his snout lovingly. Jesse had kept and cared for the hog for several weeks now. But hogs were raised for food. They were not family.

Jesse dipped a thumb in the mud and then made a print on the swine's forehead, just off center and a little above the eyes.

"See you in heaven," Jesse said gently.

He stepped back only a pace and pulled his knife. Roe, his hand trembling slightly, placed the muzzle of the gun directly upon the muddy thumbprint. The sound of the shot was somehow muffled in the morning air. The hog dropped immediately without so much as a squeal of pain or a grunt of acknowledgment.

Jesse moved up beside Roe as he handed the gun back to the men behind them. Roe and Oather then rolled the carcass on its back and Jesse used his knife to stick it. Blood began pouring out like flood waters.

"Don't waste any of that," Granny cautioned as one of the salted pans was passed up. The old woman's recipe for bloodwurst was the most prized on the mountain.

Eben arrived unfashionably late. But just in time to see Roe and Jesse kill the hog. Silently he cursed himself. He should have been here. The McNees and Winsloes expected it of him. He expected it of himself. And he'd awakened in plenty of time. Beulah would have never left the house that morning if she hadn't thought him right behind them. But he had dawdled, not purposely—well, yes perhaps purposely. Knowing he was to spend the day with *her*, that *she* would be there, it had slowed his step.

Mavis Phillips. He saw her immediately, of course. She was standing with her mother. That wild red hair was forced into a tame little braid that she wound tightly at the back of her head. As if by some extra sense, she knew his presence and raised her eyes to meet his gaze. She flushed and immediately returned to her task, pretending she had not seen him. Just as he pretended that his heart did not beat faster at the sight of her.

Daily, with heedful planning and deliberate care he courted Althea Winsloe. Yet daily, his thoughts were only for Mavis Phillips. She was in his musings, in his dreams. Truly, she had never left them. But somehow distance had proved an ally. Eben had begun to worry about the wisdom of choosing to live so near her. If he were to win Althea Winsloe, the sight of Mavis ever so near might well prove to be more self-torture than revenge.

He could win Althea. He was more certain of that than ever. The boy thoroughly liked him now. Althea found him amusing and he believed she was learning to trust him. Oather's courting was determined, but there was a cold deliberateness about it. He was no more at home on the farm than Eben himself. And marriage to him would mean a constant battle between Buell and Beulah. Althea wanted freedom from interference. Oather couldn't give her that. Eben would. It was all he could give.

Baby-Paisley caught sight of him and came running. His glove hat on his head, the deer tail bounced in the breeze.

"We done kilt the pig," he said excitedly as Eben swept the boy up in his arms. "Where was you?"

"I was on my way," Eben answered. He'd grown genuinely fond of the little boy who was so artless and unrestrained. Paisley had gotten a good deal when he'd chosen to marry a woman like Althea, he thought. A man could do worse than a woman who could raise a fine son.

"Let's find your mama," Eben said.

The child pointed. "She's got the coffee," he said.

"Did you get to have coffee?"

The little boy shook his head solemnly. "Mama woan let me dwink it," he said. "But Gobby Weston says he dwinks it all da time."

"That's probably 'cause his mama ain't got no cow," Eben said diplomatically. "I bet he'd drink milk if he had it."

"I dwink milk ebberday!" the boy bragged.

Althea did still hold the coffeepot, though it was empty. "I'll make you some more," she said, although her attention was firmly fixed upon the three men pulling the hog up the ramp to the platform.

"Don't bother," Eben told her. "I know you want to watch the butchering."

"Maybe Granny or Mrs. Phillips—" Althea turned to ask one of the older women to make the coffee for her. She didn't immediately see either of them, but did spot someone else.

"Mavis? Mavis, could you make some more coffee for Mr. Baxley?"

She looked up, obviously a bit startled. Eben watched her as she moved toward him.

"My goodness she's pale," Althea whispered to him. "It must be all the blood. It bothers lots of folks. But I had no idea that Mavis had a weak stomach."

Eben didn't answer that he thought perhaps it was not the killed hog but the man wanting coffee that had drained the color from the young woman's face.

"I'll take that," Eben said, grasping the handle of the coffeepot.

Althea let it go gratefully and turned back to the action on the platform. Jesse and Roe had tied the hog's back feet together and were lowering it, headfirst into the boiling water. Moving the hog up and down to keep it from cooking, the scalding liquid would loosen the hair from the hide.

Eben turned his back on the work and walked toward Mavis. He watched her raise her chin high. Strangely, he felt a sense of pride in her. He didn't cower her, not even now. She refused to be lowered to the woman he had made of her.

"This is real nice of you, sugartail," he said with nasty sweetness when they reached the cooking fire, far out of earshot of the rest of the crowd.

"Aren't you afraid I might poison you?" Mavis asked, her eyes narrowed.

He grinned at her. "Not really," he answered. "There are a lot of women I'd think capable of such as that. But not you. You're not direct enough. You'd want to coax a man to death, use your wiles on him."

He watched her swallow the lump in her throat and knew he scored another hit. Somehow, it didn't please him as much as he wanted it to.

"Is that what you want, Eben?" she asked finally. "Do you want me to be straight, honest, and direct?"

He shrugged. "It would sure be an unexpected change," he said.

"All right," she said. "I want you to give up the idea of marrying Althea Winsloe. I want you to let Oather have her."

He grinned, unkindly. "You want me to let Oather have her? Why should I do that?"

"Because . . . because, I don't think that you really want her. I don't think that you really even want this farm. I've not seen any real interest from you in even that."

"What do you think I do want?"

"I think you want to hurt me. You want to move here, right up the path from where I live so that I can see you every day and never have you."

"I think you flatter yourself, Mavis. You think the world revolves around you. But as for me, I don't hardly give you a thought."

"Please don't marry her, Eben," she said. "Please don't do it."

"You're jealous," he accused with an evil chuckle. He folded his arms across his chest and glared at her contemptuously. "You planned on me being your husband and now you can't stand to think some other woman is going to have what you gave up so much to get."

"I'm not asking for me," she said, nearly choking on her own words.

"Then who are you asking for?"

"I'm asking . . . I'm asking for Oather."

"For Oather?" He hooted with laughter. "Now that's a real good one, sugartail. I'm supposed to believe that Oather is dying for love of Althea and I'm standing in the way. That brother of your ain't got no interest in her at all. I'd swear there ain't a drop of hot blood in the feller. He treats her just the same as he treats you or his mama. When he promises not to beat the bed ticks with her, I can almost believe it myself."

"Oather has got to marry her, he's just got to."

"And why is that?"

"It's . . . it's his last chance. Papa is really set on it. He's said things, terrible things."

"Saying terrible things is a way of life for your father," Eben answered.

"No, there's more to this. So much more, I don't even understand it. But I'm afraid. I'm afraid if Oather doesn't manage to win her, well, I don't think Papa would ever forgive him."

"Yep, that daddy of yours, he is one man that sure has to get his way. I guess that's where you get it. You just have to make things turn out like you want them. Too bad for you that I'm not a man to be led around by apron strings."

"I'm begging you, Eben," she whispered desperately. "I'm begging you to let Oather have her. If he marries her, then he will have proved to Papa whatever it is that needs proving. Please, Eben, it means nothing to you."

"What about my pride, Mavis? You never seem to recall that I have pride."

"You can do it without much fuss. You don't have to let him win, just step aside. Please, Eben. The farm means nothing to you. She doesn't mean anything to you. It could mean everything to Oather."

"Everything?"

Her expression stricken, Mavis nodded. "Oather talks about leaving. He talks about it all the time. If he and Papa have another falling out, I'm afraid he'll go. We won't be a family anymore. I couldn't live with that. Please, Eben, I'm begging you. Isn't that what you've always wanted? You've always wanted me to beg."

She was begging. He could see it in her eyes, in her stance. Somehow it wasn't as welcome a sight as he would have imagined. She was really scared. She was really worried about her brother. Eben was convinced that nothing else could make her come to him this way. Nothing else could make her beg him again. She'd begged him on her knees that day so long ago. He'd walked away from her then. He knew that she never planned to humble herself to him again. But she had. Begging and pleading for her brother.

Eben glanced over at the butchering platform. He didn't see Oather, but he knew he was there.

Deliberately he turned back to stare at Mavis, forcing his expession to remain unmoved, frozen. The thaw inside him was growing, but he forcibly kept his face cold.

"I don't see any reason why *I* should help you," he said.

"If . . . if you will," Mavis hesistated. "I'll . . . I'll let you. I'll let you have me again."

"You'll what?"

"I'll let you have me again. I . . . it's all I have to offer. You say you want me for your . . . your something unlawful on the side. I won't be that, Eben, if you marry Althea. I swear that I could never forgive myself if I did that to her. But if you'll let Oather have her, I'll . . . I'll be whatever you want me to be."

"You mean you'll be my whore."

"Yes."

Angry heat swept through Eben as if he himself had just been dipped in boiling water.

"Damn you, Mavis Phillips. Damn you once more," he cursed. "You're at it again, ain't you? Trying to make things go your way. Trying to control me. That's what you want to do. You want to control me, tell me what to do. Run my life. I'm not that kind of man. I'm not weak. I'm not led around by a woman's skirt. Not me. Not ever."

The venom in his voice made her tremble.

"I didn't mean . . ."

"I know exactly what you meant. You meant to get your way, just like you tried before. But this time I call the shots. I make the rules. You want your brother to have that woman, well, you're going to have to stop giving orders and start taking them. Do you understand me? You'll not be telling me what, or when, or how. When I say frog you're going to jump and the only question you're allowed to have is how high. Do you understand me?"

"Yes." Her voice was a tiny whisper.

"Come on."

"What?"

"You want to be my whore? Well, I'm ready to take my whore right now. You do what *I say*, you come on right now, or you just forget about your brother altogether."

Eben turned and began to walk toward the woods. He didn't look back. She would come or she wouldn't. Fury still filled him. He hated her. He hated her. She had used her body to try to control him. And she wanted to do it again. Well, he would not be controlled. He would control. He would control her and her body.

He heard her come running up behind him. He continued to climb. Away from the path, away from the people, he continued to climb away from the restraints of the community and she was right behind him.

In a break in the brush, he saw the bent grass where an animal had bedded down. They were a goodly distance from the Winsloe cabin and completely alone. He turned to her. Grabbing her arm he pulled her to him roughly.

"Are you ready to be my whore?" he asked. "Are you going to do what I tell you, when I tell you? Are you willing to heed whatever I say?"

"Yes."

He reached over and pulled at the pins in her hair, deliberately jerking at them.

"Your hair should be loose and wild," he said. "A whore ought to look like one. That's what I've always thought."

He pulled at the collar of her dress and forced his hand down the neck of her bodice, managing to get a rough grasp on her breast.

"Your teats ain't very big, sugartail," he said. "Most of my whores has got bigger teats than you."

Her eyes were closed. She was pretending this was not happening, he was sure. She was going to let him do what he wanted and pretend she wasn't there. He was not about to let her get away with that.

He stepped back from her.

"Drop your drawers and pull up your skirt," he ordered. He was determined to make her accountable for what was happening to her.

She didn't meet his eyes. She fumbled a moment with the yards of brown calico. When they were gathered about her waist, she pulled at the drawstring of her pale cotton underwear. Hastily she stripped them down and stepped out of them. Black stockings covered her legs from the top of her boots to just past her knees. Above that she was pale, pink skin and dainty red curls.

Eben undid the buttons on the front of his trousers and pressed her back against a tree.

"I know you're ready. Whores are always ready." Clasping her buttocks in his hands he raised her up and wrapped her thighs around his hips. His teeth were clenched in anger. With not so much as a kiss on her cheek he rammed himself inside her.

She cried out. It was a cry of physical pain, but also one of humiliation. He had hurt her. He had really hurt her. It was exactly what he had wanted to do. It was what he had wanted to do for a very long time. He rammed again and again. He was hurting her. He was hurting her. That's what he wanted to do. So why were tears running down his cheeks?

In an instant, the angry, frustrated desire he had felt fled. In its place was only shame and despair. How had they come to this? How had something so beautiful come to this? It wrenched at his aching heart, wounding him. He had loved her. He had really loved her. And it was all spoilt. It was all ruined. It was all gone forever.

Eben moaned like an animal in pain.

"Oh, God, Mavis. Oh, God, I am sorry," he whispered. He buried his face in her hair. "I am so so sorry."

And he wept.

CHAPTER

EIGHTEEN

The men worked on the hog with easy camaraderie and the skill gained from years of meat tending. After being dipped for several minutes into the hot water, first one end and then the other, the hog was laid out on the platform and the men gathered around. With bell-shaped scrapers they removed all the loosened hair from the carcass in rough abrading movements reminiscent of shaving.

Oather, who had nearly worn himself out helping to dip the hog, made his way over to the water bucket. His face was reddened from exertion and he was dripping wet with perspiration. Althea scooped him a ladle full of the cool, refreshing liquid. He accepted it gratefully.

"It's hot work," he commented.

Althea readily agreed. "Yes it is," she said. "I had forgotten."

Initially she'd thought she could butcher the hog with only Jesse to help her. Now, seeing how much just pure physical strength was involved, she wondered how they ever would have managed. But, she thought, they would have. If Jesse had needed to hoist that hog up and down by himself, he would have done it. Anything she ever asked him to do, somehow he did.

Her eyes followed her thoughts and she watched him then, up on the platform. Turning and moving the hog as he was bid, he was the youngest and the strongest of the men there. And they depended upon him to do the heavy work. She wondered if they realized that. When they went home this evening, would they be aware that without the strength,

willingness, and biddability of Jesse Best, their work would
have been much harder? Althea was pretty certain that they
rarely gave him a thought at all. If asked, most would say
that they *let* Jesse help. Or that the boy *did what he could*.
They took him for granted. They all did, Althea realized,
including herself. His value to the community continued to
be errantly minimized, because Jesse himself was underes-
timated. He was different. He was like no one else. He was
not an equal. Did that make him less? ·

No, Althea thought to herself. Not necessarily.

Jesse worked, vigorous and eager, upon the boards of the
platform he had built. He was actually quite tall, but the
sense of his stature was lost while he stood alone. So well
built and robust, Jesse appeared much in proportion, with
none of the long lankiness associated with great height.
Only with other men at his shoulder was an onlooker made
aware of how far his head was from the ground.

His thin cotton shirt was now plastered to his muscles like
second skin. His pale blond hair was damp with perspiration
and glowed golden in the eastern sunshine at his back. He
was strong and virile and excitingly male.

Jesse stood now, laughing at something someone had
said. His hip cocked to one side, he stood arms akimbo, the
thick curves of his chest and thighs outlined in the bright
glow of morning. Totally without vanity or cognition, he
was beautiful like a snow-covered mountain or a tree draped
in autumn colors is beautiful. It was a beauty so natural, so
artless, that it was possible to stare in silent awe and wonder
of it.

And in many ways that was what Althea did. Entranced,
she watched him. Her throat went dry. A deep, primitive
longing welled up inside her. Against her will she recalled
once more the taste of his kiss. He was no practiced lover,
but it *was* his love, as natural as his beauty, that had drawn
her into his embrace as easily as had his arms. And it was
that authenticity that had kept her there, reveling in the
pleasure of it. Now, as memory assailed her, her heart beat
faster. She trembled.

Her marriage had in no way prepared Althea for the

sensual desire that now pulsed through her. She had been dutiful and willing. Her late husband had been lusty and eager. Her fulfillment in his arms had only hinted at the mysteries that now begged to be revealed to her body.

She remembered Jesse's words. "No, it's that other promise. The one not to . . . not to stir the bed with you like a husband and wife. If I was your man, Miss Althea, I couldn't keep a promise like that for one day."

Althea felt the words as she thought them. They sizzled through her like foxfire on an autumn night and settled in her low, very low. She swallowed nervously and bit down on her lip.

Jesse Best stood upon the platform, smiling, happy, easy in his body, nonchalant, unaware of the stirring he roused within this woman. Unaware that he was an object of desire.

"My God, he is beautiful." The words, spoken in near reverence, came from the man standing next to her.

"Yes, he is," she answered languidly from her sensual trance. "Oh!" Her horrified little squeak came immediately thereafter. Althea looked over at Oather, shocked that he had read her thoughts, and such wicked thoughts, too.

Oather stared back at her, his eyes wide in equal alarm. It was as if he too were aghast at his own words.

"I . . . I meant the pig," Oather stammered hastily.

"The pig? Oh, me, too," Althea quickly agreed. "The pig. I was thinking about the pig."

"It's a beautiful pig, ma'am," Oather assured her.

"Yes, that's the best-looking pig we ever raised."

"Yes, you . . . you can be proud, Mrs. Winsloe, very proud. That's one of the finest swine ever on this mountain."

"Yes."

"Yes, well, I'd better get to helping," Oather said, still unhealthily pale and anxious to hurry off.

"And me, as well," Althea answered, eager to busy her own hands. She had been thinking indecent thoughts about Jesse Best. She was so shocked at herself, dismayed with her own lustful musings. Contending with her own mortification, she gave no thought to Oather Phillips' strange behavior.

After the hide was completely scraped clean, the butchering began. The hog carcass was raised on the pole and split open on both sides down the belly and along the backbone to make it cool faster. Washtubs full of innards were removed and given into the care of the women.

Every portion of the animal would provide some useful purpose from the snout for headcheese to the hooves boiled into gelatin.

Onery asked for the bladder. Once it was rinsed and clean, he utilized a piece of straw to blow it up. Then he tied it off and gave it to the children for a ball.

"This coffee is purt-near boiled away," Granny complained as she moved the pot from the cooking fire. "I don't 'magine anyone'll want to drink it the consistency of sorghum."

"I'll make some more," Althea promised. "As soon as we have another fire free."

All of the freshly dug fire pits were covered with cooking cauldrons of cast-iron potash. To be safe, healthy, and useful, every portion, every piece of the carcass had to be rinsed, soaked, cooked, or all three. It took the help of all the women to make the task go quickly.

Althea's ladderback chairs had been brought outside and set at intervals around the women's work area. Planks were laid from one ladder to the next forming worktables and temporary storage shelves.

Granny had taken up the grinding of the organ meats. They would be mixed with the jowl and the ham trimmings and spiced with sage and thyme for sausage. Althea was washing the intestines. They were to be turned inside out and saved in salt brine to use for the casings.

"Mavis was making that coffee for Eben Baxley," Althea mentioned casually. Glancing around, she did not catch sight of him with the other men. "I don't know where he got off to."

"Well, where's Mavis?" Granny asked.

"I don't know," Lessy Phillips admitted. "I just looked up and she was gone. It isn't at all like her."

Althea shrugged. "I think she may have taken to the

brush. She looked just positively pale when I saw her earlier."

"I know just how she feels," Meggie Best admitted. "I love your bloodwurst, Granny. But I swear, I thought I would lose my breakfast when you asked me to mix the salt in it."

Granny humphed agreeably. "Well, Mavis ain't got your excuse."

All the women looked at Meggie questioningly. Granny answered for her.

"It seems our Meggie done stumped her toe agin," Granny said proudly.

There was laughter and murmurs of approval.

Althea's jaw dropped in surprise and then she giggled and hugged Meggie delightedly. "When is the big surprise?" she asked.

"Spring," Meggie answered with only the slightest blush of embarrassment. "About mid-March as best I can judge it."

"Lucky you," Lessy Phillips told her kindly. "I carried all mine during the heat of summer and I don't recommend it."

"All of them?" Beulah huffed in disgust. "You only had two. I birthed six live children. And I buried them each and all, including my dear Paisley, the only one to live past childhood."

The women looked at each other uneasily. Beulah Winsloe's exceptional misfortune was well-known and evoked a sense of empathy throughout the community. But it was just plain bad manners to talk about dying children or miscarriage around a nesting mother.

All women knew the chances. Meggie Farley would know them, too. Half of the babies born wouldn't live through their first winter. And half of those who did would never get past childhood illness. Measles, smallpox, whooping cough, and scarlet fever lay in wait and filled the boneyard behind the church house with tiny little graves. A woman took her heart in her hands to give birth to a child. Yet knowing the risks couldn't keep a woman from taking them.

Granny broke the uneasy silence. She too had outlived most of her children. She chose to counter the smothering solemnity with humor.

"This Meggie of ours is a smart gal choosing to carry her baby in the wintertime," the old woman said. "She can grow as fat as she pleases and none of us will be there to tell her she's looking more like a milk cow than a mama."

Her words at first brought a startled silence. Then Meggie laughed, grateful for the lighthearted intervention.

"Well, my husband can tell me, I suppose. But I hope he doesn't," she quipped.

"That man?" Granny shook her head. "That one is so stuck on you, he ain't seen ye clear since the day you wed."

Granny's teasing was light and fun. But everyone knew that Meggie and her Bay State man were very much a love match.

"The worst thing that will happen," Granny postulated, "is that you'll get so big you won't be able to get out of bed. And, mark my words, once you're in that bed, that man'll be in there with you."

Meggie blushed brightly as the women around her giggled at the naughty insinuation.

"Course," Granny continued, "nothing worse can come of it. He done got a babe in yer belly, the fiddler is paid up for a spell, so this lollyin' is plum free."

The women hooted with laughter.

"Shame on you, Granny," Althea scolded without ire. "You've got Meggie's cheeks as red as that scraped hog."

"It ain't my doin'," Granny insisted. "It's the gal's own naughty mind that's put her to blush."

The teasing continued for several more minutes as well-meant congratulations were handed out by all.

"I'm so happy for you," Althea told her. "And a little bit envious, too, I guess."

"Envious?" Meggie asked. "You want to be the one who feels like she's about to puke?"

"Well, not that," Althea admitted. She smiled and motioned toward the children still racing around in riotous good fun. "Our little ones are getting so big now. Baby-

Paisley will hardly let me hold him. And he's far from helpless these days."

Althea shook her head in disbelief as Meggie indicated her agreement. "As much trouble as it is," Althea told her. "The suckling and the dirty britches and no sleep of a night. I'd still love to be starting all over again."

Meggie beamed and nodded in understanding.

Beulah Winsloe snorted unkindly. "And there ain't nothing agin that, Althea Winsloe, except your own foolishness. That Eben Baxley will make a right fine father. If you wed up with him at Christmas, you can have a babe at your breast by fall."

Althea blushed, wishing that she'd had the good sense to guard her tongue more wisely. "I have agreed to marry come Christmas Day," she said. "But do not expect me to change my mind about having more children because I will not."

"Well, you should," Beulah told her forcefully. "You're still young enough to bear a dozen. And to not do it is a crime against heaven and I'm sure Pastor McNees would agree with me."

No one could argue that. Tom McNees was never known to disagree with his sister.

"And it's your duty to the boy to have more children," she said.

"My duty? To Baby-Paisley?"

Beulah nodded self-righteously. "That child could well learn not to be so selfish if he had brothers and sisters with which he had to share."

"My son is not selfish," she defended staunchly. "You're his grandmother. You should know that about him."

"Maybe if his *mother* didn't keep him so close, his *grandmother* might know him better," she sneered.

"I bring him by to see you every week!" Althea replied.

"And he stays right by your skirts nearly the whole time," her mother-in-law accused.

"For heaven's sake, Beulah," Granny Piggott intervened. "Don't go on so. Baby-Paisley prefers his mama, 'cause he's a little boy. Just a little boy, and a very good one at that."

"He does seem to play with other children," Meggie added, indicating the two playmates who were joyously kicking around the pig bladder ball while the dogs barked and chased after them.

Beulah was momentarily silenced, but it was clear that she didn't like it much.

"Well, Meggie," she said finally with a snide look toward her daughter-in-law. "I am happy that *you* at least are planning on having more children."

"Yes, thank you," Meggie answered.

"Perhaps if you're lucky it will be a boy this time," Beulah suggested. "I'm sure your Mr. Farley is hoping for that."

"Not necessarily," Meggie answered.

Beulah looked momentarily puzzled. It was a visibly deliberate expression. Then she nodded sagely. Her tone dripped sugar. "Yes, I suppose you're both scared you might get one like Jesse."

There were gasps of disbelief from several of the women.

Granny Piggott's face hardened to fury and she looked ready to give the quarrelsome Mrs. Winsloe a thorough set down. Meggie Farley, however, didn't give the older woman an opportunity.

"No, we are not scared that we might have a child like Jesse," she said. Her voice was calm and completely without anger or venom. "In all honesty, I don't worry a minute about it."

Meggie raised her chin and looked Beulah straight in the eye. "Being simple is not something that was carried to Jesse in the blood, it was a thing that happened to him when he was born. It could happen to any child. It could happen to the children we have now. A bad fall or a bump on the head or a spell of apoplexy can injure the mind of anyone, anyday."

The truth of her statement was sobering to all.

"But even if it were something in our family," she continued, "something that we could expect to see again and again in our children, I wouldn't be scared by it. Jesse is a strong, loving, generous man. He works hard. In some

ways harder than other men, because things in this world
don't come easy to Jesse. He is good and fair to everyone
that he meets. That isn't something that comes any more
natural to him than it does to you and me. I don't believe, as
some will say, that he's touched by angel spirits or not all of
this earth. I believe he is every bit as human and as fraught
with human frailties as the rest of us. He is not special or
favored or a better man than others you'll meet, but he is
every bit as good as any. I am proud to call him my brother.
And I would be just as proud to have a son or daughter who
was like him."

"Amen!" Granny agreed loudly.

"Yes, amen," Althea said, taking Meggie's hand in her
own. "Your brother is the most genuine, honorable, trust-
worthy man I have ever met in my life. You just know that
if Jesse makes you a promise, he will keep it."

"Yes," Meggie answered. "Jesse will."

Eben didn't quite know what had happened. He had
Mavis Phillips just where he wanted her. And suddenly, that
wasn't where he wanted her at all. He tried to stop the tears.
Desperately he tried to stop his tears. Men didn't cry. It was
weak to cry and Eben was never weak. Never. Still he cried.
His face buried in the mass of sweet-smelling red hair, he
wept with grief that came from so deep inside, he feared that
all his life's blood might begin to pour out.

He could hear himself repeating, "I'm sorry, I'm sorry."
But he could come up with no other coherent thought.

He pulled out of her body and away from the tree,
releasing Mavis from his grasp. He was loath to let her go,
but he had to. He expected her to run away. He wanted her
to run away. Amazingly she did not.

She wrapped her arms around his waist. She held him.
Eben rested his cheek on the top of her head. Inside he was
still shaking. He had wanted to hurt her, shame her, destroy
her. Somehow it was himself whom he had hurt and shamed
and destroyed.

"I am so sorry, Mavis. I am so so sorry."

She pulled her head back slightly and looked up at him.

He felt too sick to meet her eyes. He tried to glance away, but she didn't let him.

"It's all right, Eben," she whispered to him. "It's all right."

She eased her hand along his nape and into his hair. Ever so gently she urged him closer until his mouth met her own.

It was a kiss of forgiveness and a kiss of healing. It was warm, soothing, pleasurable. Eben didn't deserve pleasure. He felt that he should resist it. But he could not. He needed her kiss. He needed her.

"My Mavis," he murmured. "My own beautiful Mavis."

The taste of her was as he remembered and as he had dreamed. There was nothing of bitterness in it. It was sweet and fresh, and oh, so very right.

Slowly she sank to her knees and he went with her. Their embrace was closer there, closer to each other and closer to the earth beneath them. Mavis pressed her body against him and feathered tiny biting kisses along his neck and throat.

Eben moaned. The sting of shame was slowly being supplanted by the hot flare of desire.

Her hands, her soft feminine hands, moved across his arms and chest, seeking, surveying, and scorching him as if she were carrying fire.

She met his lips once more and deepened the kiss with teeth and tongue. She eased him out of his coat and slipped his suspenders from his shoulders.

He moved closer, seeking her warmth, her comfort. But his hands stayed still. He had hurt her with his hands, with his body. He didn't want to hurt her anymore.

So effortlessly did she find the buttons on his shirtfront and so hastily did she do away with them. Touching his bare flesh with such obvious yearning, such obvious pleasure, he was nearly overwhelmed.

Eben was hard, urgent. He wanted to clasp her to him once more, to press himself tightly against her. But he did not.

When she brought her lips to graze his chest, he gasped with the thrill of it. She kissed and teased and tantalized her way across him, stopping only to take his nipple in her teeth in a not-too-gentle love bite.

Eben cried aloud. It was an animal's cry, a cry of need. His eyes were closed tightly against the loss of control that seemed so near. His erection was hard, pulsing, aching. He moved back from her slightly, not wishing to embarrass her with its evidence.

His well-meant action garnered an unexpected reward when Mavis slid her hand down his chest and into his trousers. When her fingers closed around him, Eben's eyes came open.

"Mavis?" he ground out. It was a plea as much as a question.

She gave him no answer, but only looked into his eyes, her own dark with passion, as she continued to caress him. She touched him, not with great skill or expertise, but with a desire to please him. And please him she did. With strong, straight strokes she urged him further and further until he was too near the brink.

"No more, Mavis." He grasped her wrist. "I can stand no more."

She moved back from him then, gazing up at him, her eyes wide, almost curious at the wildness she had unleashed in him.

Eben, still holding her hand, brought it up to his mouth. Tenderly, with near reverence, he kissed her palm.

"Thank you," he said simply. "Thank you."

Slowly, she smiled.

He had barely a moment to catch his breath and regain control when she raised her hands behind her neck to reach the buttons at the back of her dress. His heart pounding, Eben watched her as she got them undone. Deliberately, she peeled away the store-bought brown calico bodice and bunched it at her waist. Covered only in her lace-trimmed josie, her bosom was firm and high.

"Look at me," she said softly.

Eben was looking. His gaze was riveted upon the full round orbs, their dark pink points pressed so formidably against the cotton.

"Beautiful," he answered in awe.

Mavis tossed her wild red hair out of the way and with one daring finger she pushed the left strap down off her shoulder, slowly, so very slowly she drew it down, revealing the bare flesh underneath. When the top half was revealed and only the lace trim covered the nipple, she stopped and looked at Eben.

His mouth was dry, so very dry. He licked his lips.

Leisurely, as if she herself were savoring the moment, she pulled the thin cotton down farther, revealing the full smooth round hillock of her breast. He had never really seen her before. Their night of regretful passion had been in darkness. He had not really seen her, not as he saw her now. The soft pale flesh was so very naked in the morning sunlight. So plump and feminine that reaching out to touch it was so tempting. The hard pink nipple seemed to be pointing straight at Eben.

Mavis reached out her hand to him. He came forward only so much as he dared and she stroked his slightly bristled cheek.

"Come take what you see, Eben," she said.

She smoothed his coat beneath her and lay back in the tall grass. She pulled him to her by her words, her eyes, and the touch of her hand on his cheek alone.

Eben leaned down upon her, eager but uncertain.

"Mavis?"

With her own hand she raised her breast as if presenting an offering. Eben could not resist. He took the hard pink nipple into his mouth. The taste, the texture, the temptation of her, was exquisite. He suckled her eagerly, thoroughly, insatiably. It was as if he were feasting upon life itself.

And Mavis was not passive at this sensual breakfast. As his mouth sought such sweet sustenance, she squirmed beneath him. Tiny cries of pleading and pleasure urged him on.

When her questing hand once again found his rigid reaction, he pleaded for mercy against the soft flesh of her breast. With a moan, he rolled onto his back, pulling her atop him. Together they fought valiantly against the tangle of clothes that constrained them. Freed at last, she hesitated only an instant before mounting him.

She was wet and eager and ready. When she impaled herself upon him Eben ground his teeth against the sheer pleasure of it.

She rode him uneasily at first, as if unsteady in her gait. But as passion heightened, their pace proved in accord. Eben gripped her hips, meeting and melding as the momentum increased.

He forced himself to close his eyes. His senses were overloaded. The sight of her above him, face dazed with passion, hair wild and flying, bosom bouncing as she strained toward fulfillment, had him perilously skirting the brink of his desire. He didn't want to spill his seed and leave her without pleasure. But it was Mavis, not himself, who was in control. It was if he could only hold fast to her and let her do her will with him.

His eyes came open when he reached his peak. He cried out her name. And he could only be grateful that he saw the same maelstrom reflected in her own expression.

It went on an eternity as the forceful, gasping clenches of her body again and again and again pumped him dry.

She collapsed upon his chest. She was breathing. He was breathing. They were both alive. Just barely. That wild red hair was everywhere. It was wonderful. It was glorious. It was oh, so dear.

Moments passed. Sweet moments. Moments of oneness. Moments unmindful of the past. Eben felt right. He felt good. It had taken the cessation of pain to let him know how much he'd been hurting.

"Mavis, I love you," were the first words he spoke.

She raised up to look down into his eyes. "I've confessed before," she answered finally.

Suddenly she was almost shy again. She moved away from him. Inexplicably eager to right her clothes.

"Rest with me, Mavis," he pleaded. "Rest with me a moment."

She didn't meet his gaze, but she went into his embrace.

"We've been gone a long time," she said. "They might come looking for us."

"Then your father would make us marry," he said. He meant it as a kind of joke. Somehow it was not funny.

She was silent for a long moment. "No one can make you marry me," she said.

He held her more tightly then. Unexpectedly he felt a sense of sadness, of loss.

"I'm sorry that I hurt you like I did," he said. "I was angry, very angry. But that was no excuse. I am truly sorry."

"Yes, I know. You said so already."

"But I was crying then," he said. "I was crying and I never cry. I haven't since I was a boy."

"It's a day for the unusual," she answered quietly.

The silence lingered between them.

Finally she pulled away. "I have to go."

He stood up with her as she retrieved her drawers from the base of the tree. She didn't put them on in front of him, but tucked them in her pocket. Eben buttoned the back of her dress.

"You had me," he said. "You *had* me."

She turned back to look at him.

Eben's words were thoughtful. "I was none of it. It was you. You had me just the way I tried to have you."

Her brow furrowed. "I . . . I'm sorry?" It was as much a question as an apology.

He shook his head. "No, no. It was . . . it was heaven, Mavis. It was so . . . so much more than I ever . . . well . . ." He couldn't finish.

Her answer was an almost smile.

"I've got to get back."

"Yes," he agreed. "I'll circle around and return by the up-mountain path."

She murmured assent and began walking away.

"Mavis!" he called out to her.

She turned to face him once more.

"I'll keep the bargain," he said. "I mean about your brother."

She pressed her lips together and nodded. He thought she

would say no more, but at the last minute she turned and spoke to him.

"The first, what you did to me," she said, "that was for my brother. This last . . . that . . . that was for you. And for myself."

Before Eben could answer, she was gone.

CHAPTER  NINETEEN

There were only four days to go before Christmas when Jesse got permission to take Baby-Paisley with him down to Phillips' store. The little boy, deer tail bouncing on the back of his cap, proudly carried the buckskin hide tucked under his arm. The day was bright but very cold. The norther that Onery's bad leg had predicted was upon them. The two were heavily bundled up, their breath coming out of their mouths in bright white clouds.

It had been all Baby-Paisley could do to keep from bragging to his mother that they were going to trade the hide for a Christmas present for her. He'd been as jumpy as a possum in nettles for over a week. Biting his little baby tongue a half-dozen times a day, he had managed, somehow, to keep his secret. But by the time they arrived at the front porch of the store, he could wait to tell it no longer.

"Jesse and I gonna trade dis deer hide for a pwesent for my mama!" he announced excitedly as he hurried up to the two men standing together on the front step.

From the expressions on the faces of Oather and Buell, Jesse could tell that the conversation they were having was not a happy one. Buell looked bullheaded and determined. He had been doing most of the talking, the tone of his voice brooking no dispute.

Oather had been listening, that could hardly be avoided, but he appeared almost repulsed; still, his expression was determined.

Baby-Paisley's welcome distraction was greeted by him

effusively. Oather turned his full attention on the boy as if grateful to him for the timely interruption.

"Trading for a present for your mama? Is that so?" he asked, grinning broadly. "What kind of present are you going to get for her?"

"A Cwissmas present," the child answered.

"Well, that's a really nice idea," Oather told him. "That is a really very nice idea. Isn't it, Papa?"

Buell Phillips looked at them speculatively and shrugged. "Christmas presents are meant mostly for children," he said.

"But we can get Mama something anyway," Baby-Paisley assured Phillips. "Jesse said we could."

Buell huffed disparagingly, indicating his feeling that Jesse's opinion was of no account. But he didn't comment.

"Is it from you or Jesse?" he asked the boy.

"From both of us," Baby-Paisley answered. "We kilt da deer together, so we share the hide."

Buell nodded thoughtfully. As an idea sprang forth and bloomed in his mind, he turned to smile craftily at his son.

"I'm sure Oather here could help you pick out something just real nice for your mama," he said. "Why, he's really family, too. And though the gift would be from you and Jesse, Oather could surely see that you got a fine present for Mrs. Winsloe. This store has anything and everything a young woman might want or need. And if you add Oather's name as one of the givers, he could really get it for you at a sweet price."

Oather, obviously not appreciating his father's meddling, hesitated before he answered. "Well," he said finally, his own expression shrewd, "I suppose I could do that."

"You could?" Baby-Paisley was excited.

"And the present you choose wouldn't be any old picked-over item that Mrs. Winsloe has seen a dozen times. It could be something completely new."

"Completely new?"

Oather nodded. "There's a drummer here today. Come in on a pack mule loaded-for-bear yesterday afternoon. He's got women's folderal and gewgaws a-plenty. Is that what you're looking for?"

Baby-Paisley nodded enthusiastically.

Oather grinned before glancing back at his father, who didn't look a bit happy at all. "Jesse, you trade that hide direct with the drummer. You'll get more of its worth for it that way."

"I will?"

"Yes indeed you will," Oather assured him.

Jesse was surprised. He thought a hide was worth what a hide was worth. It hadn't occurred to him that some might pay more for it than others.

"Why, thanks, Oather," Jesse said. "We cain't make you one of the givers, of course. Mr. Phillips is all wrong about that. This deer hide is Baby-Paisley's and mine alone. But it'd sure be nice of you to meet us up with this drummer fellow."

"I'd be delighted," Oather said.

Buell Phillips cursed under his breath. "You'll never make a businessman," he snarled to his son in whispered fury.

Oather shrugged. "If I marry a fine farm, maybe I won't have to be a businessman."

Buell snorted, but much of his venom had disappeared. "I just don't understand a bit of you. Always reading them dang law books and thinking about life when you ought to be living it. I've said it before and I'll say it again. You get that Winsloe gal or I'll be wanting to know the reason why."

Oather raised an eyebrow. "The *reasons why* were never your strong interest," he said.

His father's expression looked puzzled; Oather quickly turned his attention back to Baby-Paisley and Simple Jess.

"You'll find something nice for that mama of yours," he assured them. "And be sure to dither on the price as long as you dare."

Baby-Paisley readily agreed, without truly understanding. Jesse's brow furrowed with concern. It would be hard enough just to find the right present. He couldn't imagine remembering to dither for it, too.

He was about to say as much when Baby-Paisley hooted

with excitement and his attention turned elsewhere. He saw Eben Baxley coming up the path.

"Mista Eben!" the little boy called out. He took off running in that direction as fast as his short pudgy legs could carry him. "Mista Eben, Jesse and me gonna trade our deer hide for a Cwissmas pwesent for Mama."

Jesse watched as the little boy flew into Baxley's arms. Baxley was laughing and spun him around in the air while the child squealed with delight.

The deer tail had eased the barriers between the two. But it was only the beginning. Eben appeared to genuinely like the boy. And Baby-Paisley, fatherless, craved all the male attention that he could get. Completely gone from the child's mind was the early distrust of this man who once wanted to shake a penny out of him. Eben Baxley was now his father's cousin and his father's best friend, a man the boy somehow saw as very like his father must have been.

"What is he doing here?" Oather's question was low and malevolent.

Both Beull and Jesse looked at him curiously.

"I guess he's come to the store," his father answered.

"I don't want him here," Oather said.

"Well we'd rather have him here than up at the Winsloe place," Buell said easily. He chuckled a little to himself and lowered his voice slightly as if passing on a confidence. "Truth is, I wouldn't be surprised if he's got his eye on our Mavis."

"What?"

"The last few days," Buell told him. "When you're up a-courting on the mountain, that one comes in and just wanders around the store. He stays for hours sometimes."

"He's spoken to her?"

"I ain't seen them pass so much as a word," Buell assured him with a shake of his head. "As well they shouldn't, him being declared to Mrs. Winsloe just as yourself. But I've seen him watching her." Phillips nodded sagely. "And from time to time, almost as if it's against her will, I've seen her looking back."

"I don't want Baxley around Mavis," Oather declared

furiously. "I don't want that no-good within a half mile of her."

"Well, I don't know why not," Buell said. "It'd be the best thing in the world for him to get stuck on our girl. You'd get that Winsloe farm easy, fair and clear."

"But what about Mavis?"

Phillips waved his concern away. "That girl makes up her own mind, always has," Buell answered. "And truth is, I'd sooner see her wed to a fence post as not wed at all."

"Not to Eben Baxley." Oather spat the name out like a curse.

"That Baxley wouldn't be such a bad son-in-law," his father speculated. "I love the way he ignores old Beulah; he don't fight against her, he just don't pay her no mind. Puts that woman in her place, he does." Buell chuckled at the memory. "He's got a way with people, too, and the gift of gab. With a little practice he could easy-talk bees into buying bird nests."

Oather's face was black with fury. He looked ready to spit fire, but he did not. Whatever he might have said to his father was forestalled by the arrival of Eben, Baby-Paisley in tow.

"Morning, Buell, Oather," he said. "Morning, Jesse."

Two of the three men nodded to Baxley politely. Jesse noticed that Oather only glared at him.

"What are you doing around here?" Oather's question was contentious, hostile.

Eben shrugged, deliberately unconcerned with young Phillip's enmity. "This is a store, ain't it? I just come to buy something."

"Whatcha gonna buy?" Baby-Paisley asked.

Eben chucked the child under the chin.

"Got to get me some shot," he answered. "I'm a-thinking to go hunting and I ain't got nary a cartridge one."

"What you hunting?" Jesse asked him.

Eben pursed his lips, appearing indifferent. "Whatever gets in my way, I guess," he answered.

"I saw a fresh rub up near the Sweetwood Meadow," Jesse told him. "Looked like a big one."

"Another deer?" Baby-Paisley asked excitedly. "Mista Eben, are you gonna get another deer for my mama?"

"Well, I suppose I could," Eben answered the little boy. "You think your mama would like that?"

"She liked it when Jesse brung her one," the boy said proudly. "She kisst him for it."

Jesse blushed. The Phillipses looked unhappy. Eben laughed out loud.

"You think she'd kiss me if I brung her one?" he asked.

Baby-Paisley nodded eagerly.

"Well, maybe I will then," Eben said. He looked up at the men on the porch with more than a hint of challenge. "Maybe I will."

"You'll have to beat Oather to it," Buell Phillips said suddenly.

Both Eben and Oather stared at the man in disbelief.

"Oather was just saying this morning that he was going hunting for some meat for Mrs. Winsloe."

Turning his attention to the younger man, Eben's gaze was skeptical. "I've never known Oather to be much on hunting," Eben pointed out.

"You don't know everything about my boy that you think you do," Buell replied snidely.

"Papa, I—" Oather sounded momentarily uncertain.

Buell interrupted him, unwilling to let his son speak. "Jesse," he said. "Maybe you could take Oather up to that meadow, see if the two of you can find that old buck."

"I wanna come," Baby-Paisley cried, Jumping up and down. "I wanna come. I wanna come."

Jesse was puzzled. It was so confusing when everybody talked at once, and this conversation was especially so.

"Oather don't like to hunt, Mr. Phillips," Jesse said, somewhat surprised that the man's father didn't realize that. "He ain't never liked it. It ain't his way."

Eben laughed delightedly.

Buell looked ready to spit.

"I wanna go. Lemme go." Baby-Paisley continued his pleading as he bounced enthusiastically up and down. "I wanna go huntin'!"

Oather appeared both perplexed and unhappy. Eben's laughter had taken on a taunting quality and his father's machinations and prodding had pushed him square into a corner.

"I don't like hunting," he said finally to Jesse. "I don't find it relaxing, but I *can* hunt." He emphasized the last words and directed them to Baxley. "If Mrs. Winsloe would like another deer for her winter meat, I can certainly get one for her."

Eben hooted. "I'd like to see that. I'll bet you ain't got nothing bigger than a rabbit in your life."

"A bigger animal is an easier shot," Oather argued.

"So speaks one who ain't shot it."

"I wanna go. I wanna go huntin'," Baby-Paisley continued to beg.

Eben nodded to the boy. "I want to go, too," he said. "How about it, boy, you and me tag along with Jesse and Oather here. We'll see who can get a deer and who cain't."

"Yep, let's see who can get a deer and who can't," Baby-Paisley agreed loudly.

Jesse's brow furrowed. "Miss Althea don't want him hunting yet," he said. "She thinks he's too young."

"Oh, Jesse, pweese," the little boy begged.

"I'll ask her," Eben promised. "I'll ask your mama myself," he promised.

"Whoopee! I'm goin' huntin'!" the little boy hollered.

It was after much discussion, purchase of ammunition, and agreement to meet at the Winsloe place at dawn, that Jesse and Baby-Paisley finally got to speak with the drummer about Miss Althea's Christmas present.

As he'd promised, Oather introduced them. The man's name was Hiram Huckabee, and after being questioned by Baby-Paisley, he admitted that his mule's name was Sweetheart.

Oather whispered to Jesse that he had a very good hide and not to take anything less than what he wanted for it.

Jesse nodded solemnly as Oather added, "Don't let him

talk you into anything and dither about the price as much as you can."

"Dither."

Jesse repeated the word to himself as often as he could think about it. But it was hard to keep thinking about it. His mind was still filled with the morning's talk. He was uneasy about the hunting trip.

He loved hunting and he always wanted to go. As soon as he'd seen that big rub up in the Sweetwood Meadow, he'd thought about taking the dogs up there to peruse the place. The excitement of the tracking, the pleasure of the dogs, the cool bite to the morning air, he *wanted* to go. But, Jesse couldn't help thinking, this particular hunting trip was not a good idea.

Eben and Oather were not happy with each other. In fact, Oather's sentiments seemed pretty close to downright hatred. Jesse knew that men hunting together, if not family or friend, should at least be neighborly. These two were openly fractious and quarrelsome. They seemed as intent on getting each other as getting the deer.

And Eben's near promise to Baby-Paisley was also troubling. After his last outing, Jesse was almost certain that Miss Althea would be raked over hot coals before she'd let her baby boy go out in the woods on a deer hunt.

Jesse had suggested hopefully to the boy that maybe they should ask instead for him to go with Jesse one day to check the snares. Miss Althea might not like that too much either, but at least there would be no guns and a specific destination. Baby-Paisley was not easily turned. Eben Baxley said that he could go deer hunting with them. The little fellow was certain that it was going to happen. He even had the opportunity to mention the upcoming adventure to Gobby Weston, who happened by the store with his father, picking up supplies. Jesse was pretty sure Miss Althea's answer was going to be no. He was also fairly certain that Baby-Paisley would not take that decision too well.

So it was with a worried mind and more than little distraction that Jesse finally rolled out the newly cured buckskin for the traveling drummer.

The fellow was sharp and city-dressed with shiny shoes and a fancy straw hat. He smoked a long smelly cigar that made big plumes of blue-gray smoke everywhere and tainted the fragrance of every piece of merchandise he carried. Jesse could tell that the man was strictly a lowlander by the way he carried himself. But it was obvious as he ran his hand appreciably across the deer hide that he'd been through the woods a time or two.

"It's a fair hide," he said, damning with faint praise. "For a winter hide, it's right fair."

"We want to trade it for a Cwissmas present for my mama," Baby-Paisley told him. The little boy's mouth was full of licorice. The formerly swallowed penny had been retrieved and spent for the candy that was the favorite of he and Jesse both.

"Now that's a fine idea," the drummer agreed, smiling through the teeth that clenched the cigar. "Did you shoot this buck yourself, little feller?"

The drummer chuckled at his own suggestion.

"Jesse shot it," Baby-Paisley answered proudly. "But we was on the hunt together. So the hide is half mine."

"Is that so?"

"Yep," the little boy answered. "When they's two a-huntin' the deer is shared by halfs."

"That's a fact," the man agreed.

Baby-Paisley was bright-eyed and warmed up to the subject. "Tomorrow, I'm goin' huntin' agin. With Jesse and Mista Oaffer and Mista Eben. I gonna go huntin' for another deer."

"Another deer?"

He nodded eagerly. "Jesse done seen his rub up in the Sweetwood Meadow, so we goin'. See this deer tail on my cap? My daddy done kilt dis deer. Mista Eben was with him when he done it. I gonna kill lots of deer just like my daddy."

"Well, and good luck to you," the drummer said. "Maybe when I pass this way again, you'll have another hide to trade."

"Pwobably so," Baby-Paisley agreed seriously.

"So what kind of thing does your mama like, boy?" he asked. "Does she crave piece goods? Or maybe something to lighten her chores."

The child looked puzzled and shrugged. "I doan know," he admitted.

"We'll know what we want when we see it," Jesse assured the trader quickly. "We're sure to recognize the perfect thing right off."

The traveling man nodded, pursing his lips in thought. "Well, all right, boys. I got lots of things any female alive would just love to have," he told the two of them. "I got dress goods and ribbons. I got perfume and rouge—just like city women wear."

"Miss Althea ain't no city woman," Jesse told him.

The drummer smiled and deftly rolled up the buckskin, stowing it with his own things, as if the trade for its worth had already been made.

"I got jewelry," the man told them. "Fine things. Fine things, for certain. And I'm sure a man can't get a woman far enough back in the woods that she don't crave jewelry."

To illustrate his point, the trader opened a slim fabric-covered box that was loaded to the brim with bracelets, necklaces, rings, and spangles of all kinds.

"This is pretty," Baby-Paisley said as he held up a shiny locket. "Look, Jesse, it's got shiny rocks in it."

Jesse did look and gave a little sigh of awe, as entranced with the glittering object as Baby-Paisley.

"Them stones is genuine cut glass," the trader told them. "Ain't no way you can dig something like that up and shine it. No, sir, those are made by man and no other way."

The man pulled out a ring, wearing it on the first knuckle of his index finger. "See this, boys?" he said. "This is real pewter. As fine a ring as you're liable to find west of the Mississippi."

"Mama ain't got no ring," Baby-Paisley told him. "You think we should get her a ring, Jesse?"

Jesse shrugged uncertainly. "What else you got?" he asked.

"Lots of things, boys," he answered. "More wares and

whatits and wahoos than you ever laid eyes on in all your life."

The drummer didn't lie. He opened his pack and let them look at his merchandise. The two went through it, slowly, painstakingly. They didn't find what they wanted. Later he unloaded his mule. They went through all of those goods, too. Jesse and Baby-Paisley, each as curious as a coon, examined every strange pot and bottle, every length of piece goods and metal button, every bristly hairbrush and box of face powders.

"Look at this!" Baby-Paisley would squeal with delight.

"Ain't that something," Jesse would answer with sincerity.

The drummer began to scratch his head and check his pocket watch.

Baby-Paisley liked and wanted to buy almost everything that he saw. Jesse was just as fascinated, but had yet to see the one thing, that one exceptional thing he knew that Miss Althea would want more than any other.

As the morning dragged on into afternoon, they divided all of the drummer's wares into two piles. The potential purchases in one and the cull list in the other. The cull list was large. But the potential purchases were plenty, too. They began to go through the items once more.

Closely they examined a gold-filled lady's watch with a pretty pattern of birds and flowers on the front.

"Mama could pin this to her dress for Sunday-go-to-meetin'," Baby-Paisley pointed out.

"Or she could tie a ribbon to it and keep it in her pocket," Jesse suggested.

Momentarily they both looked enthusiastic.

"Can you tell time?" Baby-Paisley asked Jesse.

He shook his head.

"Me neither," the little boy admitted and added the watch to the pile of discards.

A fancy sash buckle with a rose-colored finish caught Jesse's eye. "What kind of animal is this?" he asked the drummer.

"It's a dragon."

Jesse's brow furrowed. "We don't have any 'round here like this one," he said.

"It's a mythical beast," the drummer explained with a little chuckle.

Jesse nodded solemnly. "Don't know the place. And I don't expect Miss Althea's ever been to Mythica either."

Baby-Paisley was delighted to find a huge stack of cards with pictures on them. Each card had the same picture printed on it twice.

"These are mighty fine," Baby-Paisley exclaimed.

"They're stereoscopic pictures," the trader told him hopefully. "It's a series called the *Wonders of the World*. Does your mother have a stereoscope?"

"What's a scaryoscoach?"

The drummer sighed. "Obviously she doesn't have one," he said.

Jesse found a mouth organ and Baby-Paisley eagerly blew in and out on it trying to make music. He was not too successful, unless one considered success getting spittle dripping down his shirt. But he enjoyed himself very much and danced around happily.

"We could trade for this. You could play the fiddle and I could play the mouth organ," the little boy suggested.

"Would that be a present for your mama?" Jesse asked.

Baby-Paisley shrugged. "Sorta," he said hopefully.

He looked at Jesse. He looked at the mouth organ. With a sigh of defeat, he put it in the pile of the unwanteds.

With fervor, they continued rummaging through the ladies' goods. They examined numerous rolls of nine-cent wallpaper, some had unusual designs and patterns, most had flowers.

They were appropriately amazed at the newfangled spring-loaded clothespins. They looked at white bonbonet lace and a china silk fan.

There were a requisite number of corsets, wire bustles, and black cotton stockings. Jesse hurried Baby-Paisley through these, thinking him too young to wonder at the mysteries of women's underwear.

"Hey, what kinda bullets is these?" the little boy asked,

holding up an open box of strange-looking cartridges, wrapped in papers.

"Those are ladies' antiseptic suppositories," the trader answered hurriedly, taking the box out of the child's hands. When both his customers continued to eye him curiously, he added simply, "They are not quite the thing for gift giving."

The two oohed and ahhed over a celluloid comb with genuine rhinestones, considered the practical uses of a huge tin of boot blacking, and discussed at great length the possibilities of the pretty pair of four-hook lacing chamois gloves.

The trader, who was now chewing on his second cigar, was becoming short-tempered. Originally he'd intended to out-dugan the simple man and little child from a good hide. He no longer thought about cheating. He only wanted to get the transaction over with so that he could get on with his business. He had still to show his wares to Phillips and he hoped to be off the mountain by daybreak the next morning.

"What's in this jar?" Jesse asked.

The trader sighed heavily and read the words on the label below the picture of the voluptuous woman with the very tiny waist. "Bust Food. Developed in France."

"Bust food?" Jesse grabbed back the jar curiously. Twisting off the lid, he peered down at the white, creamy substance inside. It smelled like lilacs, but it looked a lot like lard.

"Women are supposed to eat this?" he asked, astonished.

"Not eat it," the man said, testily. "They rub it on their . . . their . . ." He glanced uneasily at the little boy. "They just rub it on. See," he said, pointing to the words on the side. "It says, 'Feeds, plumps, and nourishes scrawny tissues. What nature has denied, Bust Food will endow.'"

"They rub it on." Jesse shook his head disbelieving. "That would be something to see."

"Yes indeed," the man agreed and then cleared his throat a bit nervously. "So what is it you fellows want?" he said. "I can't be here worrying with you all day long, you know."

Jesse sighed heavily. "What do ye think, Baby-Paisley?" he asked. "Have you seen just the right thing yet?"

"I like everything," the little fellow answered honestly. "What do you think, Jesse?"

"The combs are real nice," Jesse said thoughtfully. "And the locket really shines in the sunlight, don't it?"

The little boy nodded in agreement.

Jesse sighed and shook his head at the drummer. "I don't think real fast, mister. Can we just look at things a little bit longer?"

The man checked his pocket watch in exasperation. "Boys," he said, "I'm here to sell my goods to Phillips. I need to do that today, 'cause by morning I'm riding my mule out of here. I'd love to spend the rest of the day just letting you riffle through my wares, but I got to be up on the White River country day after tomorrow."

"You're going to the White River country?"

"That's where I'm heading."

Jesse's brow furrowed. He closed his eyes tightly trying to think. The words, thoughts, and memories jumbled inside his head like the wild rush of a flooding river. And his heart was suddenly beating like a drum. Then he knew. He just knew. It was just what he'd hoped would happen. He'd find the perfect gift and he'd know it when he saw it. Jesse became so excited he forgot about dithering completely.

"How about if we trade that hide for you delivering a message for us up there," he said.

CHAPTER TWENTY

It was worse than Jesse imagined it would be. Althea was adamantly opposed to Baby-Paisley accompanying them. All of Eben's sweet talk and reassurances didn't move her resolve one bit. Baby-Paisley threw a rip-roaring tantrum, throwing himself upon the ground, kicking, and screaming.

In truth Jesse felt sorry for the little fellow. He'd been more or less promised that he'd get to go, and he'd even bragged to Gobby Weston about it. It was a loss of stature. Jesse understood that. Still, he kept his thoughts to himself as he helped Althea get the boy in the house. His bad behavior was getting him "bedposted." Jesse lifted up the corner post on the bed and Althea slipped the child's shirttail under it. The little fellow would be sitting right there until his mother decided differently.

By the time Jesse reached the door, Baby-Paisley's anger had turned to tears of frustration. Jesse fought the desire to go back and hug the boy. He glanced over at Althea and saw in her anguished expression that she wanted to do the very same thing. Without thinking about it, Jesse held out his hand to her. When she placed her own in his, he squeezed it comfortingly.

"You're doing what you think is right," he whispered. "That's what good mamas do. He's lucky to have a good mama."

She managed to smile, if just a little bit. Jesse wanted to hug her, too. He managed not to do that either.

"We'd best be going," he said. "I don't know if we'll bring you back more meat, but we can sure try."

"Be careful, Jesse," she said.

He released her hand. Unexpectedly she straightened the front of his coat and buttoned the top button for him. It was an intimate, loving gesture. And she was standing so close. The fragrance of her was upon him again. It was all her, uniquely her. It was heaven. Jesse swallowed.

"I'll be back soon," he promised.

She nodded and he hurried away. He was trembling.

"Well, finally!"

He heard the exclamation as soon as he got outside.

"We thought you were going to take all day," Eben complained.

"Baby-Paisley was upset," Jesse answered.

Eben huffed. "A good bit of hickory limb would have done that situation a lot of good."

"For him, or for you?" Jesse asked, still shaking from the emotions that had assailed him in the cabin.

Oather hooted with laughter. "He got you there, Baxley. This whole thing was your fault. If you hadn't told the boy he could go, we wouldn't have even had to start out at the Winsloe place."

Eben had the good grace to look chagrined. "Let's get on with it," he said gruffly.

"You don't have to come along, Baxley," Oather said venomously. "You aren't really that welcome."

"Oather Phillips, I wouldn't miss the sight of you making a fool of yourself for anything in the world," he answered.

Jesse just shook his head and turned his attention to the dogs. At least he could count on them to do what they were supposed to do. He gave a familiar whistle and they hurried up ahead, ready and eager. He'd been working with them every chance he got and was more than pleased with the way they'd come around.

Sawtooth was still, by far, the best. But Queenie had lost a good deal of her lying-around fat and she was hunting better every time they went out. Runt was learning. And Old Poker kept up as best he could and was willing and ready to back the two other dogs whenever and wherever.

The dogs were his now. Althea had told him that he could

take them home with him. He hadn't done so, partly because of the boy. He hated to separate Baby-Paisley from Runt. And partly because it took away any reason for him to show up at her place. There were three days to go before she married up with one of the two men beside him. Those were three days Jesse Best was not willing to waste.

"You sure you remember how to fire that thing, Oather?" Eben pointed to the fancy new Marlin repeater that he carried.

"I got one shot for the deer and one for you," Oather threatened. "So you'd better stay out of my line of fire."

Jesse gazed in disbelief at the two fractious men. They were arguing as if they were alone, so Jesse tried to pretend that he couldn't hear them. The fact that he could hear them perfectly and that he didn't like a thing that he heard was beside the point completely.

The Sweetwood Meadow was on the far side of the mountain near the peak. The area, whether by long-gone settlers or Indian farmers, had been partially denuded and cleared. The abandoned spot had been taken over by the first growths of forest, herbs and grasses, milkweed and thistles, and the short stubby sweet wood cedars from where it got its name. The spot was especially good hunting for foxes and quail. But it was very possible that a whitetail deer might venture that way.

It was a good long walk, which under normal circumstances would have been pleasant for Jesse. The two angry men beside him, however, precluded any enjoyment of the cloudy cold morning.

"I don't want you hanging around the store," Oather said to Eben. "I've told you before, but I'm warning you now, I don't want you around there."

"I don't see no signs posted there," Eben argued. "It seems to me a feller can loll about wherever he has a mind to."

"I think we both know why I don't want you there," Oather said, his eyes narrowing hatefully. "You've done enough already. I want you to leave her alone."

Jesse wondered curiously who *she* was that Eben was to

leave alone. Could he mean Miss Althea? She didn't spend much time at the store at all. It was very puzzling.

Eben was silent for several moments. When he spoke again his tone was quieter, serious, and more thoughtful.

"I don't think I can do that, Oather," he said. "And I think it's time that we let go of this feud and dealt with each other honestly and honorably."

"Honorably?" Oather huffed in disbelief. "You don't know the meaning of the word. You've trod on our honor about as much as I'm going to stand. I don't know what I'll do about it. But mark my words, I ain't allowing anything more."

"I've been thinking a lot about things," Eben continued calmly. "I've been thinking about how things are, and what I've done. And I've been thinking that I'm going to let you have Althea."

"You're what?"

Jesse stared at Eben, just as surprised as Oather.

"I'm going to let you have Althea," he continued. "I know that you want to marry up with her real bad. I guess it would please your daddy a lot, so I'm stating here that I'm stepping aside."

"What are you up to?" Oather's voice was low and menacing.

"I ain't up to nothing, really," Eben said. He glanced around at the woods as if searching for something to hold his interest. "I talked with your sister," he admitted quietly. "And she convinced me that I should just step aside."

"You talked to her!" Oather's tone was furious. "I told you not to talk to her."

"I know that you did and I confess that you're right about that, I have no right after . . . after what happened way back then. Truly I should have kept my distance but, well, we was kind of thrown together at the hog killing and she actually spoke first."

Oather's eyes narrowed and his expression was suspicious.

Eben continued. "Mavis wants you to marry Althea," he said. "She knows it will please your father and that you really want to please him. And she thinks that maybe it will make you happy and she wants to make you happy."

Oather sneered, his reply was rife with sarcasm. "Mavis wants to make me happy, so *you* want to make me happy, is that the tale you're telling?"

"I ain't telling a tale at all, Oather," Eben assured him. "I'm just saying I'm stepping back and you can have Althea Winsloe and the farm and the all of it. I don't care nothing about it anymore."

"Well, thank you very much." Oather's tone had slipped from merely sarcastic to downright acerbic.

"Anyway, the point of this is," Eben finished, "you don't have to get this deer today. We all know you hate hunting. Jesse and I can bag it and we'll just tell Althea that you brought it to her. In another week you'll be wed and it won't make a lick of difference."

That seemed reasonable to Jesse.

"And what do you get from this?" Oather asked angrily. "My sister's honor? Her pride? Her life?"

Eben didn't answer.

"It's no trade, you mangy lowlife. Mavis is worth a lot more to me than marrying Althea Winsloe. Besides, I don't think you've won yet. I'm going to get this deer on my own and she's going to choose me over you. Then you can just go to the devil in the quickest conveyance."

"For lordy sakes, Oather, I'm trying to help you," Eben complained. "Mavis wanted me to."

"Well, I don't want you to. And I don't want you doing any favors for Mavis. If it weren't for you she might be happy now."

"Yep, she might be, if she weren't so damned worried about you."

Oather was startled by the accusation. "I don't know what you're talking about."

"You and your father, fighting all the time. The old man doesn't think much of you. You think you've got to prove yourself to him. Lord Almighty, Mavis loves you both and she's scared to death that the two of you are going to have a falling out that can't be repaired."

"You don't know nothing about me or my father or Mavis," Oather told him.

"I hurt Mavis," Eben acknowledged honestly. "I did plenty to her. I admit that. I'll even admit to hating myself for having done it. But it ain't me that's hurting her now, Oather. It's you. It's you and your father, not able to come to terms with who you are."

Eben's shots were right on target. Oather's anger floundered to uncertainty. "I suppose you're an authority on that. How long did it take you to come to terms with having a father who was a shiftless, worthless bum?"

Eben winced as if he'd been slapped. "A good long time, Oather," he answered. "A good long time. But I will tell you this. It's something that I just learned. My father was who he was. There's bad in him that I share and there's good in him that runs in me, too. There ain't nothing I can change about either of that. But my life is my own. I can't live up to him or live over him or even live like him. This life is mine and I've got to do with it what seems best for me."

Eben stopped Oather in his tracks and looked him in the eye. "You're a smart feller, Oather. Everybody on the mountain knows that. But sooner or later you're going to have to learn that you just can't be whatever it is your daddy wants of you. You're going to have to learn to be what manner of man that you are."

"Don't you be lecturing to me."

"I'm not lecturing, I'm trying to talk truth to you. I . . . ." Eben's attention was momentarily diverted. "Did you see that?"

Oather's gaze followed Eben's. "What?"

"I saw a deer in that thicket, I think," Eben said, pulling his gun to the ready.

Oather did the same. "This is my deer, Eben Baxley," he snarled. "Don't you dare take a shot at it."

Eben ignored him and cocked his rifle. "Oather, you ain't got a shot off since you were a boy, there ain't a chance in this world for you to hit nothing."

"I said it was my deer," Oather snarled, readying his weapon. "It's my deer and I'm going to get it."

Both men held their guns aimed at the thicket, hammers drawn, eager and watchful.

Jesse was confused. His gun was still at his side and his brow was furrowed. With flaring nostrils he checked the air for scent. Eben couldn't have seen a deer. They were downwind from the thicket. Jesse knew he should be able to smell a deer that close and downwind.

He glanced down at the dogs. They hadn't even hesitated at the spot. Sawtooth was in the lead, his nose to the ground, Old Poker was right beside him. Neither showed interest in anything behind him. Runt was tagging along after. And Queenie was also heading straight ahead, unconcerned with either side of the path.

"There!" Eben cried aloud.

Jesse saw it, the white flash of a deer's tail. He pulled in the scent again. He glanced at the dogs. He looked back at Eben and Oather, both taking aim.

He knew then. Suddenly, clearly, he knew.

"NO!" he screamed, jumping toward the two men. "Don't shoot!"

Throwing himself in the firing line, Jesse pushed the rifles aside. Eben managed to hold his fire. Oather was not so quick and the gun flashed and fired; the bullet sped past Jesse's ear, hitting a nearby shagbark.

"What the devil?" Eben asked.

"Jesse, are you crazy? I could easily have shot you!" Oather's shock immediately turned to fear.

"There ain't no deer," he told them. His face was pale as death and his eyes were big as saucers.

"We saw it," Eben answered. "We both saw its tail a-flashing."

Jesse turned to the silence of the woods and hollered out in fury.

"Come here this minute!"

There was a crash of breaking underbrush and then a moment later a small boy emerged from beyond the forest path. His eyes wide, his step hurried as he answered the authoritative voice that called him.

"Oh, my God!" Oather cried out.

Eben stared in disbelief.

"We could have killed him," Oather whispered in horror. "*I* could have killed him."

Jesse walked straight over to Baby-Paisley, his eyes narrowed in fury. He jerked the deer tail–decorated hat from the child's head, grabbed the little fellow by the arm, and pulled him to the path.

"What are you doing here?" Jesse asked angrily as he squatted down to look at the boy eye to eye.

"I wanna go huntin'," was Baby-Paisley's answer.

Jesse handed the cap to Eben. "Get rid of this," he ordered.

Eben did as he was bid, ripping off the deer tail and throwing it as far as he could into the brush.

"How'd you get away from your mama?" Jesse asked.

"I ripped my shirt and snucked out when she went to get water," he admitted.

Oather Phillips had dropped to his knees upon the path and was vomiting. "I almost killed him. I almost killed a little child," he kept saying to himself.

"Do you know that your mama is probably scared to death right now?" Jesse asked him. "She's probably running and crying and looking for you."

The little boy hung his head guiltily.

"Your mama loves you more than anything else in this world and you hurt her," Jesse accused. "Do you understand that? You hurt her."

"I didn't mean to," the little boy said lamely.

"Men don't do that," he said sternly. "Men don't act that way. They don't run off or hurt the women that loves them. That's not the way men do. If you want to be a man, you can't do that neither."

"I'm sorry, Jesse," he said. "I'm real sorry."

"That sorry belongs to your mama, Paisley Winsloe," he told him. "I'm taking you back to her. I'm taking you back this very minute."

The little boy nodded, understanding.

Jesse pointed his finger gravely at the boy. "And don't

you never, *ever* run off from your mama again. Do you understand me?"

"Yes, Jesse," he answered.

Jesse sighed heavily. "You scared me, too," he said. "I love you and you scared me, too."

The little boy began to cry. He threw himself into Jesse's arms.

"I'm sorry, Jesse. I'm real sorry," he whimpered.

Jesse hugged the boy to him tightly. His own eyes welled with tears. He couldn't ever let anything happen to this little boy. Not ever.

When Jesse rose to his feet, he set Baby-Paisley on the path before him. "You've got to go face your mama now and take what you deserve."

The little boy nodded bravely. "Yes, sir," he said.

Jesse turned to the two men with him. Eben was standing silently by. Oather was still doubled up, retching.

"I've got to take him back down the mountain," he said. "Miss Althea will be worrying herself crazy."

Eben nodded. "Go on, Jesse. I'll get Oather home," he said.

"This is the most foolhardy notion you've come up with yet!" Buell Phillips was raging as he paced across the room of the living quarters above the store. "You can't just up and leave."

"I can, Papa, and I am," Oather replied adamantly, his voice raised as loud as his father's. "It's what I should have done years ago."

The women in the house were quiet. Mavis was crying, almost silently. Lessy looked on and listened, apparently resigned. She'd packed her son a sack of vittles for the path. It was what a mother did when her son left home.

Oather was collecting his things, determinedly, efficiently. He was gathering together what he would not leave behind.

"If you think that you can just up and walk out of here whenever the spirit moves you, well, let me tell you this," Buell shouted, "you won't be welcomed back here like the prodigal son in thirty days."

Oather raised his chin in cold defiance. Today he was not to be cowered.

"Don't worry, there will be no need to kill the fatted calf, Papa," he said. "I won't be back in thirty days. I may never be back."

His mother stifled a gasp. Mavis moaned.

Frustration made Buell curse vividly. "There just ain't no talking to you. And there ain't no sense in this, no sense at all."

"There is every sense, Papa," Oather told him. "I almost killed someone today. Do you understand what that means to me? I almost killed an innocent little boy. Why? Because I was trying to be something that I am not."

"You were trying to get meat on the table," Buell said with rough rationality. "Accidents out hunting happen all the time. And this time nobody was even hurt."

"*I* was hurt," Oather answered. "I was hurt. I hate hunting. We both know that. I haven't carried a gun to the woods in years and we both know why. After the last time you forced me to go out, even you knew there was no sense in it. I don't like killing animals. I can barely bring myself to eat the food that's tainted by them. I suspect I could do it if we were starving or desperate. But we are neither and neither is anyone that we know. I didn't go out there to put meat on anyone's table."

Buell couldn't argue that.

"I went out there today because it was what you wanted me to do. I went out there for you, Papa."

His son's declaration was disconcerting. "All right, all right, you don't have to hunt," Buell told him hastily. "I won't ever ask you to do it again."

"Maybe you won't ask that of me, Papa," Oather said. "But I know you'll always ask more than I can give. I went out there to prove that I'm the kind of son that you really want. But we already know the truth about that. You've been ashamed of me since the day I was born. I can't live up to what you want from me. I never have been able to, I never will be able to."

"I've never said that!" Buell snapped, incensed.

"You didn't have to *say* it," Oather answered. "I'm not like any man on this mountain. I think I've known that since I was a little boy. I'm not like any of them. And, Papa, I'm not like you. I've tried and I've tried, but I'm just not like you."

"So what does that matter?"

"It matters, Papa. It matters, because it matters to you."

The truth of his words momentarily halted his father's tirade. "Oather, don't leave like this." His still gruff voice had turned pleading.

"I have to, Papa," Oather said, more softly.

"No, no you don't," he insisted.

"I do," he said firmly. "I'm not like any man on this mountain, but I believe, no I think I *know*, that there are men like me. There are men like me somewhere and I'm going out there to find them."

Buell Phillips stood and stared at his son. His father's expression was so bleak, so heart-wrenching, that his son was momentarily torn.

Oather steeled himself not to give in to the need to please, to comfort.

"I don't ask you to love me, Papa," he said. "Or even to understand me. But I do ask you to let me go without a fight."

Gesturing toward his mother and sister, he pleaded, "Can't you see they're hurting, Papa? I'm hurting, too."

"You think I don't hurt?" Buell asked.

"I guess you do, Papa," Oather answered. "I guess it hurts not to have the son that you want."

"You *are* the son that I want!"

"No, Papa."

"Listen to me! Listen!"

"I've been listening all my life," Oather answered.

"But you'd best listen now, 'cause I've never said this even to myself."

Silence filled the room. Everyone was listening. All of them. Listening. Waiting. Buell swallowed nervously. His face twisted in anguish as he sought the words.

Visibly, Buell's anger turned to determination. He appeared ready to speak, then he hesitated and directed his attention to the women.

"Mavis, Mrs. Phillips, could you please leave the room? I've important things to talk over with my son."

Mavis, her handkerchief clutched in her hand, looked ready to do as she was bid. Lessy Phillips surprisingly pulled out a chair from the table and seated herself.

Her husband's eyes widened in disbelief.

"He's my boy, too, Buell Phillips," she declared. "I'm not going to cower in the next room while you browbeat and berate him."

"I'm not going to browbeat or berate him," Buell answered gruffly.

She raised a brow in speculation and kept her seat.

"This is a personal discussion between a man and his son," he insisted sternly. "You've no call to get between it, Lessy."

"Maybe I have exactly," she shot back. "Maybe if I'd got between the two of you twenty years ago there'd be a bridge across the distance today."

"Woman, I—"

"Yell 'til you're hoarse if you like," she interrupted. "I'm not going nowhere."

Buell sputtered ineffectually for a moment and then leaned closer to his wife.

"Lessy, I'm not going to holler at the boy," he said quietly. "I don't want to drive him away."

"You can't drive him away, Buell," she answered. "He's leaving on his own. That's what's bothering you. You want him to make his own decisions, but when he does, you can't let him live with them."

"Do you want him to leave?" Buell asked incredulously.

"It doesn't matter what I want," Lessy answered. "It's his life, Buell. It's what *he* wants that matters now."

"But—"

"There are no buts about it," she insisted. "We raised him the best we could. You did your best. I did my best. Now he's grown and is what he is. It's time we simply got out of his way."

Buell looked over at his son. The two men were equal in height and could look each other straight in the eye. They did that for one long moment.

"I think it's too late for me to get out of his way," Buell said finally. "I think he's already gone around me."

Oather nodded almost imperceptibly.

Buell looked toward his wife. She was silent, but her expression showed agreement.

"Then there isn't any reason why I shouldn't stay," she said.

Mavis sat down too and stared at her father. Buell looked from one to the other. His gaze then swiveled to the young man these two women of his had sworn to protect. He sighed heavily in frustration, deflated.

"You win," he said finally. "All of you, you win." He dropped into a chair himself, as if too tired and worn to fight another minute.

The signs of dejection did not sit well on the man's features. He sat and stared at the work-callused hands on the table before him. Oather could not bring to mind a time when his father looked this way. His usual powerful personality and strong vitality seemed to have fled him. He looked suddenly to be old.

Buell Phillips raised his head, defeated, to watch his only son as he continued to pack his personal belongings.

"You say that you are different," he began finally. "Well, that's not news to me, son. I knew that long before you did."

Oather stopped his packing in midmotion. He stared, almost disbelieving, as his father continued.

"I could see it when you was just a little boy. I didn't know where it came from or what it was, but I knew it was there."

Oather's expression registered surprise, confusion, wariness. His father went on.

"I knew it, son, and I railed against it." Buell clenched his fists, emphasizing the words. "Later, as you grew, I began to suspect that I did know what it was. What manner of man my boy was going to be. I may have lived all my life on this mountain, but I ain't ignorant of the ways of the world."

He turned his head then, to look at Oather.

"I began to know and I fought against it," he said. "I did everything I could do to make it not so. But people just don't stop being what they are. I know that, I've always known it, just as you have."

Buell Phillips and his son Oather stared at each other. Both felt pain. Both felt suffering, and saw it in the eyes of the other. But something more could also be seen. Honesty. For the first time between them, honesty.

"You and I, we've always known it," Buell said. "Just like we've both known that you would have to leave this mountain. That you would have to find another place."

Oather nodded.

Buell studied his hands once more.

"I worked all my life to make something to give you, son. But the only legacy I can offer you that might make you happy is to give you your freedom."

Lessy Phillips began to cry.

"I have to go, Papa," Oather whispered with a pained glance toward his mother. "I hate to leave, but I have to go."

His father sighed heavily. "You're right, son. Your mama and your sister are bound to grieve a bit over it. Don't fret about that. We can expect no less from the women that love you. But you do have to go. You're right about that."

Buell Phillips looked old at that moment. An old man, tired and beaten. He looked around the table at the woman he'd taken to wife nearly thirty years earlier and the two strong healthy children that she'd birthed for him.

"You're right about most everything," he said. "But there is one thing that you aren't right about, Oather."

His son's expression was curious.

"You seem to think I'm ashamed of you and that I don't love you. In that you are dead wrong."

"Oh, Papa."

"You are my firstborn, my only son, my flesh and blood. I loved you, son, from the first minute I heard your baby's cry. And I've loved you every minute since. You think you haven't been the boy that I wanted." Buell shrugged. "Well, I know I ain't been the father that you wanted neither. But please, son, wherever you go, whatever you do, please know that I love you and that I always have and that I always will."

CHAPTER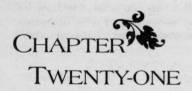

TWENTY-ONE

Christmas Eve was crisp and cold. Snow was falling sporadically in light fluffy flakes. The fire in the hearth had been banked, but the loft of the Winsloe cabin was still plenty warm. Althea wrapped a warming rock in soft cotton flannel and placed it in the bottom of Baby-Paisley's shake-down cot.

"Now if your feet get cold, you just warm them down here on this rock," she said.

"Yes, Mama," he answered. "Do you think Santy Claus is gonna come here, Mama?"

"I suspect so," she told him. "But you'd best go to sleep. If he thinks you're still awake he'll head out to some other little boy's front door."

"He doan come by the front door, Mama," Baby-Paisley explained. "He comes down the chimley."

"Oh, yes, I think I heard that," Althea admitted.

"And, Mama," he said, "doan you worry if Santy Claus doan bring you no pwesent. He brings for children mostly."

"Yes, I heard that, too."

"I think you're gonna get a pwesent from somebody else," he hinted.

"Oh?" Althea smiled at him. "Well, that would be really nice. Now you go to sleep."

She kissed her handsome little son on the forehead and watched him close his eyes.

"Good night, Mama," he said.

"Good night, Baby-Paisley."

Althea made her way down the ladder. The house smelled

like Christmas already. She'd spent all day making sweet cakes. Baby-Paisley's sock hung from the ledge of the fireplace. Smiling at the sight, she retrieved the new voyageur's cap from her sewing bag. It had proved to be a good choice. With the deer tail ripped from his glove hat, the headgear had lost all of its former appeal.

Althea shook her head. She could just be grateful that the deer tail hat was the only casualty of the hunting disaster.

She had been frantic when she'd come back to the cabin to find Baby-Paisley gone. She'd known immediately that he'd followed the hunters. But she hadn't listened to their plans. She'd had no idea in which direction they had headed.

She had wandered around aimlessly calling his name for close to an hour when she heard the shot fired up the mountain. Her heart had gone straight into her throat and she'd hurried in that direction.

She'd met Jesse and Baby-Paisley coming down. Her boy's cheeks were tearstained and his expression sober. Althea had no idea what Jesse had said to the child, but whatever it was, somehow it had soaked in.

She didn't get the whole frightening story until later that day. By the time she did, she was more able to control the fear that shuddered through her with an unholy coldness.

"I know you doan believe in whippin' me, Mama," Baby-Paisley said with sincere sobriety. "But I sure done earned a lickin' and I'm willing to take it if you wanna gib it to me."

Althea was rendered speechless by this declaration. Jesse came to her rescue.

"I suspect if the boy knows he deserves a licking," he said, "then he's already learned the lesson the licking was meant to teach."

"Yes, yes, I suppose so," Althea agreed.

Baby-Paisley had certainly been on his best behavior since. Althea folded the cap as tiny as she could and stuffed it into the bottom of the stocking. Then she pulled out a shiny red apple she'd been secretly saving in the soap barrel.

She added it to the booty, being careful that the weight of it didn't pull the sock to the floor.

It worked, she was proud. She was glad Baby-Paisley believed in Santy Claus. Althea never remembered any such person visiting her as a little girl. Not much was made of Christmas and there were never any presents. Occasionally someone would suggest that her father might return for the holiday. He never did. That story was no more real to Althea than Santy Claus.

The dogs set up to barking out in the yard. Althea's brow furrowed curiously. She heard a light tap on the door.

Althea expected no one at that time of night. It had to be bad news. Concerned, she hurried to the door. She opened it and was surprised to discover Eben Baxley standing there.

Althea folded her arms across her chest and glared at him, unhappily.

"What are you doing here this time of night?" she asked.

"I have to talk to you," he said. He appeared thoughtful, his brow furrowed in concern.

Althea sighed heavily and shook her head. "No," she said. "I'm not talking about it, not tonight. I've made up my mind, all right. I know who I'm going to marry, but you'll have to wait and hear it tomorrow at the Marrying Stone like everybody else."

"Let me in, Althea," Eben said. "Things have happened. Things you can't know."

His tone was sincere and compelling. Curiously and with resignation she opened the door wider and allowed him to pass.

Eben wandered around the room for a minute, ill at ease. He seemed different, less certain of himself. It was, Althea thought, a change for the better.

"May I sit down?" he asked.

Althea raised an eyebrow. "You usually just make yourself at home," she pointed out.

"Not anymore," he said.

Eben seated himself at the table. Althea sat across from him. His unexpected visit was puzzling and his unusual behavior more so. Things had happened, he'd said. Althea waited patiently to hear what those things might be.

"Oather has left," Eben said finally.

"What?"

"Yesterday. Oather left the mountain. He and his father had a row about what happened with Baby-Paisley, about the deer, about life, I guess about everything. They made up, or at least that's the way Mavis tells it. But Oather left anyway."

"I can't believe it," Althea admitted.

"Those two are just oil and water," Eben said. "They don't understand each other, never have and never will. Buell has such set ideas about what a son of his should be. And Oather just hasn't ever been able to live up to that."

"Oather's a different kind of man," Althea agreed.

"That poor feller has been under his daddy's thumb forever, and this, well, this was the last straw, I guess maybe for both of them."

"Maybe it's for the best," Althea said thoughtfully. "Oather's different. He's always been different from folks here on the mountain. Maybe somewhere else he'll find folks that are more like him."

"That's what Mavis said. She said that she wants Oather to be happy and that he has a better chance to be happy living somewhere else."

"Mavis is a wise young woman," Althea said.

"I hope so," Eben replied. "And I think she and Mrs. Phillips are resigned to his leaving, though they are both pretty torn up about it."

"It must be so hard to watch your son walk away and wonder if you'll ever see him again."

Eben nodded. "He promised he'd write them a post. Maybe if they hear that he's happy somewhere else, it will ease their minds a lot."

"Yes, it probably will."

"Anyway," Eben said evenly. "The fact remains that Oather is gone." He swallowed nervously. "If you've chosen Oather for your husband, well . . ." He raised his hands helplessly.

Althea nodded, realizing his point. "I didn't choose Oather," she said simply.

"Oh."

The silence in the room was thick. Eben ran a hand through his hair, mussing it. Then his concentration seemed to be completely devoted to a tiny line in the crocheted Christmas tablecloth that Aunt Ada had given Althea for a wedding present. He ran his fingernail over it again and again, gathering the words to speak.

"Mrs. Winsloe," he said, finally. "I hate to have to say this."

He hesitated. Clearly he did hate saying it.

"I really admire you a great deal. I haven't always, but I do now."

"Thank you, Eben."

"When Paisley told me he was going to marry you, well, truth to tell, I didn't think much of it at first," he admitted. "I thought he just wanted a wife and a house of his own away from his mama. I understood that really clear. I guess because my mama is just a whole lot like his. I suspect it runs in the family."

He said the words jokingly. Althea shared the humor with him.

"I never thought you were too special a woman or anything," Eben continued. "Just somebody to marry up with when no one else was around."

Althea looked at him. Eben was obviously chagrined at his own words.

"Over these last weeks," he tried more formally, "I've got to know you a good bit. You're a hardworking woman, Mrs. Winsloe. And a loving and caring one. That little boy of yours is as fine a little feller as I've ever met. He's a better legacy than Paisley Winsloe even deserves to have. Anyway, what I'm trying to say is that I do admire you and I believe you would be a fine woman for a man to wife. But, I . . ." He stumbled momentarily over the words. "I don't love you, Mrs. Winsloe, and I don't think that I ever will."

"I don't love you either, Eben," Althea told him.

That statement seemed to offer him some relief. "I didn't

used to believe that love was so all-fired important," he admitted. "But lately I've come to the conclusion that it is. It's more important than approval or prosperity or even pride. I think you're a fine woman, ma'am, but I cain't marry you."

"Eben," Althea said quietly, reaching across the table to pat his hand comfortingly. "I didn't choose you either."

"What?"

"I didn't choose you either," she repeated.

"You didn't choose . . . but . . . who . . . ?"

"I told you that I made up my mind," she said. "But I'm not telling a soul until tomorrow morning at the Marrying Stone. I appreciate you coming here. I appreciate your honesty. But it's late and I'll be saying good night."

Eben rose to his feet, clearly stunned by her words. His expression was still puzzled as he stopped at the door.

"Who?"

"Good night, Eben."

He was still shaking his head as she watched him disappear into the cold snowy night. She hugged herself and grinned. It was all working out better than she expected. She shook her head. She should have trusted her instincts a long time ago.

She glanced once more at Eben walking in the distance. That man was going to turn into a real genuine human being. Althea thought she could see all the signs for sure.

Althea was awakened from a deep sleep by a sound that wasn't familiar. She waited in the dark, still and listening. There was somebody on the roof.

The name Santy Claus came first to her thoughts and she pushed it away. There was something, some varmint or somebody very real, up on her roof. The dogs weren't barking. Surely they couldn't sleep through that racket. Did they not sense danger?

Althea threw back the covers and jumped out of bed. Without bothering to stop for clothes or shoes she hurried out the door. In truth she didn't sense any danger either. Just curiosity. The snow had stopped falling. There was about two inches of the fresh white stuff on the ground as she stood in the yard in her flannel josie and barefeet.

She stared up at the roof of the cabin, startled to see Jesse Best climbing down the outside of the chimney.

"What are you doing?" she asked.

"Shhhhhh!" he hushed her.

She came closer as he reached the ground. She saw that his hands and feet were covered in dirty black soot.

"What are you doing?" she asked again.

"I'm leaving proof that Santy Claus was here," he answered.

"What?"

"Gobby Weston told Baby-Paisley that there wasn't any real Santy Claus. I thought it might be nice for him to believe a little while longer. So I told him that to find out for sure, he should check the chimney Christmas morning to see if someone had been up and in there."

Althea laughed and shook her head. "Jesse Best, you are going to make some lucky boy the most wonderful father," she said.

Jesse shrugged. Then he looked at her and his expression grew puzzled. "Aren't you cold?" he asked. "You ain't got on no shoes and hardly any clothes."

"I'm freezing," she admitted. "Come on."

"Oh, no, Miss Althea. It's late and night and all."

"You've got that soot all over you," she pointed out. "Come inside and wash up."

Hesitantly he followed her into the dark cabin. She lit one tallow candle on the kitchen table and found a dishpan that she filled with tepid water.

"I've already banked the fire," she explained.

"This is fine," he said, pulling off his coat and hanging it on the nail by the door.

Jesse started to roll up his sleeves.

"Here," Althea said. "You've got soot on your cuffs, too. Take your shirt off and I'll brush it out."

A little uneasily Jesse removed his shirt and handed it to her. His ribbed woolen union suit clung to his upper body like a second skin and he acted a little shy as if he felt exposed standing in front of Althea that way.

She examined the dirty cuff for a moment and then walked over to the water bucket and dipped the shirt in it.

"Don't get it wet," Jesse pleaded in an astonished whisper. "I got to wear that home. If it's wet, it'll freeze."

"The sleeves were dirty, Jesse," she told him. "There's no way to get them clean except with water. Here, I'll hang it up and you can just wait here until it dries."

Jesse's expression was more than a little concerned. Deliberately he turned his attention back to the dishpan of water.

Althea hung the damp shirt in front of the fireplace. It was a big shirt that belonged to a big man. The blaze in the fireplace was banked. Althea knew full well that it would be nearing morning before the shirt could possibly be dry.

She turned back to Jesse who washed and washed. His expression was a bit suspicious and it was as if he had no idea what else to do.

When it was obvious that there was nothing left to wash off but his skin, Althea walked to his side carrying a dry towel. He reached out to take it, but instead of handing it to him, she proceeded to dry his hands. They were big, muscular hands that had left bear-size prints on the sides of her chimney. They were hands that had tended her stock, slaughtered her meat, and carried her son. Althea Winsloe wanted those hands.

"It's mighty dark this time of night," he said.

"Yes," Althea agreed. "It is very dark. And we're all alone, Jesse."

She watched him swallow nervously.

"Baby-Paisley is just up in the loft," he said.

Althea nodded. "He's a sound sleeper of a night," she told him.

Jesse was clearly ill at ease. Althea didn't feel so confident herself. She was nervous, wary, biting her lip. She'd made her decision. She would have to go through with it. And with a man like Jesse, she'd have to make the first move.

She stopped drying him and hastily hung the towel on the back of one of the ladderback chairs. She reached for his hands and held them in her own.

"Your hands are very big, Jesse," she said.

"I'm big all over," he answered honestly.

"I'd imagine you could hold a lot of things in these hands," she said.

"Yep, sure," he agreed.

Hastily, not giving herself time to give in to cowardice, Althea brought those big masculine hands toward her and laid them against her breasts.

Jesse's sudden intake of breath was telling. He stood there, silently. Her bosom in his hands. He was as still as a stone.

Momentarily Althea panicked. Was she wrong about him? Was he really just a child in a man's body? Was she asking more than he could give her.

"Miss Althea," he said finally, his voice very quiet. "Are you going to slap me?"

She released her breath. She hadn't realized that she had been holding it.

"No, Jesse, I'm not going to slap you."

He nodded slowly. "Then do you mind if I squeeze these instead of just holding 'em?"

She almost laughed, but it was more from nervousness than amusement. "Just don't hurt me, Jesse," she answered.

"I'd never want to hurt you, Miss Althea," he said. "I don't want to hurt nobody, but especially not you."

His huge palms clenched lovingly, tenderly at her soft round orbs.

Althea's heart began to pound. His touch was not tentative or shy as she had expected. He touched her as if he relished it. He touched her as if she were a finely tuned fiddle and he was charged with the task of making music all night long.

Althea had expected it to be pleasant. She had expected to enjoy his attention. She hadn't thought it would set her quaking inside.

Jesse ran his thumbs across her nipples. He pressed them and then squeezed them between his fingers.

"This feels real good," he whispered a little breathlessly. "Are you sure you ain't going to slap me, Miss Althea?"

"No," she answered, finding it difficult to inhale and exhale properly herself. "I'm not going to slap you for anything, Jesse."

"Then I'd like to kiss you," he said. "I'd really like to kiss you real bad."

"Kiss me, Jesse," she said. "Kiss me real bad."

He did.

It was like before when their lips had met, only tonight it was better. His mouth was eager, hot, questing. His hands were strong and sure and exploring her with fervor and pleasure.

"I love the way you kiss me," she whispered into the side of his throat.

"I ain't never kissed no one but you, Miss Althea," he admitted. "Is this for sure the way to do it?"

"Oh, yes, Jesse," she said, bringing her lips back to his own. "I think this is exactly the way to do it."

He deepened the kiss then. Opening his mouth wider as if he wanted to lure her into it. In fact, he was sort of pulling at her, sucking at her lower lip and her tongue. It sent shivers down her neck and arms. Inexplicably she pressed her bosom more firmly into his hands.

"You sure don't need no bust food," he told her.

"What?"

Jesse squeezed her breasts ardently. "I just love your round parts, Miss Althea. They are just about the best things I ever felt in my life."

He proved his enthusiasm for them by kneading, manipulating, and caressing until Althea was standing on her tiptoes, every muscle in her body straining to give him better access.

"Oh, Miss Althea," he said finally, removing his hands from her body. "This is the most fun I ever had in my life."

He was breathing as if he'd just run up the mountain, pulling Granny Piggott on the skid.

"Don't stop," Althea pleaded, having found the activity as pleasurable as he had himself.

Jesse let his hands skim along her back and drop to graze lightly against her buttocks.

"Can I . . ." He hesitated.

"You can rub my backside if you want," Althea told him, any earlier shyness disappearing as impulsive amatory need heightened her senses.

"I'd be happy to rub your backside, Miss Althea," he said. "But what I really want is to sort of rub your front side against my front side. I'm as hard as a stump and throbbing and aching like a sore tooth."

"Oh! Oh, all right I—"

He didn't give her time to say more. Jesse clasped her round buttocks in his hands, raised her closer to his height, and pressed hard against her, rubbing from side to side.

Althea gasped.

Jesse moaned.

"This feels so good," he said. "This feels real good."

"Oh, Jesse I . . . I . . . oh, oh, my—"

He was kissing her again. Kissing and pressing and squeezing all in the same moment. Althea was light-headed, she was nearly dazed. It had been so long since she'd felt like this. It had been so very, very long. She realized that she had never really felt like this.

His mouth was everywhere, her lips, her cheeks, her throat, her chin. He seemed to crave the tender flesh on the nape of her neck beneath her ear. The touch of his mouth there seemed to sizzle through her body like recurring bolts of homemade lightning.

Jesse wasn't satisfied with the pressing of their bodies close together. He grabbed her behind the knee and began to raise her leg as he leaned her back over on the table. It did bring them closer. Intimately closer.

"Not on the table, Jesse," she pleaded as he ran an eager, searching palm up the inside of her leg. "Take me to the bed."

Jesse stopped still as a stone. He reared back slightly to

look into her face. His vivid blue eyes were wide and shining in the dim light.

"Miss Althea," he whispered. "If I take you over to that bed, it ain't going to be just for kissing and rubbing. I'm going to want to 'put my best foot forward' as the fellers say. I'll want to be inside you, in between your legs."

"That's what I want, too, Jesse," she answered.

Jesse jerked her up from the table in such a rush that the candle teetered dangerously, making the light flash strangely around the room. In three long strides he had her back to the clover bed tick. He leaned over her, slaunchways on the one-poster.

"If you're going to change your mind, it'd be best to do it now," he warned.

"I'm not changing my mind," she said.

He sighed. It was a sound of both relief and gratitude.

"What you got on under this josie, Miss Althea?" he asked.

"Nothing," she answered.

"I'd like to see that," he said, pulling at the hem of it. "I think I'd really like to see that."

They managed to get it over her head and Jesse threw it, unconcerned, to the floor. In the dim light of the distant candle she was naked and Jesse Best was looking at her like a starving man at a community supper.

"You are beautiful, Miss Althea," he whispered in near reverence. "So beautiful I can hardly look at you."

Jesse ran his big, masculine hand from the curve of her throat, over the gently swelling mound of her breast, down the narrow stretches of her belly, and into the soft curling hair at the juncture of her thighs.

"Jesse!" she squealed, startled at the sensual eruption that he elicited from inside her.

He took her pleasured cry as permission to do as he willed. And his will was to consume her.

With his whole body Jesse began to caress her, his hands, his legs, his knees, his lips. There wasn't a part of her that he didn't want to touch or taste or nuzzle against.

Althea found herself unable to remain ladylike or dignified under this onslaught. She had always *allowed* Paisley to possess her. With Jesse she squirmed and whimpered and begged for his attention. She was clutching and clinging and urgent against him.

"I think I can't wait," he told her, fumbling at the front of his trousers.

Althea pulled at his buttons herself, managing to grabble through the layers of butternut duckins and ribbed wool.

"My God, you're holding it!" Jesse exclaimed in disbelief.

"Inside me, Jesse," she pleaded. "Let's put it inside me."

He didn't argue.

She led him to the entrance, but as soon as he pushed inside, he took back control. His first thrusts were strong and powerful, pushing her across the bed until her head lolled over the far side. Then as if realizing the error in his ways, he grasped her firmly by the hips. His thrusts remained forceful but she was able to meet him.

Again and again he pushed inside her. In the beginning it was all hot passion and no cadence. Then, from nowhere, the two found a mutual rhythm and moved in sensual, spiraling intensity.

"Oh, Jesse! Oh, Jesse! Oh, Jesse!"

Her voice got louder and louder as she approached the precipice. As they plunged over, he muffled her cry with his kiss and buried his own inside her as the essence of his passion pumped into her like a teeming flood of liquid fire and steam.

It was several minutes afterward before either could speak. Althea still lay across the bed, her head hanging off in thin air. Jesse at last noticed her uncomfortable position and pulled her back onto the bed and into a sitting position in his lap, her knees on either side of his hips, their bodies still connected.

She sighed against him, laying a hand lovingly upon his chest. They kissed. Not passionately now but playfully. He bounced her teasingly on his half-flaccid staff inside her. Althea gave him a playful bite on his neck. He reciprocated with one on the peak of her breast.

She squealed. They laughed. They looked into each other's eyes.

"I love you, Miss Althea," he said. His words sobered the tone of the moment.

She sought to get the lightness back.

"You didn't take your clothes off, Jesse," she commented. "That's downright rude with me here naked as the day I was born."

He shrugged. "I was so busy, I forgot," he admitted.

She started to tease him again, but he held her shoulders and looked at he solemnly. There were words that had to be said. And he was not going to wait to say them.

"Miss Althea," he began. "I know you're going to marry up with Eben or Oather tomorrow. Everybody on the mountain knows that. I ain't a great friend to either of them. But truth to tell, we done wronged them here."

"Do you think so?" she asked.

Jesse nodded with regret. "If I was one of them and thought you'd spent this night, this last night of your widowhood, bouncing the bed with another man, Miss Althea, I wouldn't be happy about that at all."

"You wouldn't?" she asked, feigning surprise.

"No, I sure wouldn't."

"You'd be jealous, then?"

"Well, sure I would," Jesse said. "But that ain't the half of it. Miss Althea, I ain't never done this before and don't know much about it. But I don't think a woman, nor a man neither, should . . . well I don't think that folks should do this with different people. There's something special about it. Something that sort of makes the two doing it mean more to each other afterward."

Althea smiled at him and tenderly pushed a lock of tousled blond hair out of his face. "I think you may be right about that," she said. "I think you mean more to me every minute, Jesse Best."

"So what I'm thinking," Jesse continued, "is since we done did this, and either of them two fellers are sure to be derned unhappy about it if they were to know, well, maybe you should just marry up with me. 'Cause I ain't unhappy about it a'tall."

"Are you asking me to marry you, Jesse?"

His face was solemn and serious.

"I know I ain't smart, Miss Althea. I don't pretend to be. It's something a feller can't lie about. But I can be a good husband to you, I know it in my heart. I got a good strong back. I can get you game. I can keep up this farm. And I care about your boy. I care about him a lot. But I'd never get between the two of you. Miss Althea, if you'll marry up with me, I promise to listen to you in the things I don't know about. Work for you 'til my back is broke and my fingers is down to the bone. And love and care for you until the day I die."

"Oh, Jesse, that's the most beautiful marriage proposal I've ever heard in my life," Althea whispered.

"But there is one thing," he said.

"What?"

"I can't promise not to do this with you. Now that I done it, well, I like it even more than I thought I would. So there might be more babies, Miss Althea. Unless there's some other way to stop them, there might be just a whole lot of babies."

"Jesse," she said. "Can you promise me to always love Baby-Paisley and treat him equal to any child of your own that I might have?"

"Well, sure I can. That ain't much to promise."

"It's a lot, Jesse. You don't know how much. And I know that you always keep your promises."

"Then you'll marry me?"

"Yes, Jesse, you're the one that I chose. I decided the other day when you brought Baby-Paisley home from that hunting trip. You're the only man that I'll ever love. You're the man that I want to marry."

He pulled her close and kissed her. Happiness and joy settled around them like a warm cloak. And gentleness spurred passion. His kiss deepened and a soft, low moan eased out of his throat.

He wiggled on the bed beneath her, letting her feel the resurgence of his passion inside her.

"I'm ready to do it again," he said plainly.

"You can't do it twice," she answered, giggling.

"Why not?"

"You just can't," Althea told him. "Men do it one time and then they rest up for a day or two."

"I think I'm rested up enough," he told her.

"Jesse, I know what I'm talking about," she said with confidence. "I was married for over two years. And I know all about it. You can't be ready to do it again."

He proved her wrong.

CHAPTER  TWENTY-TWO

Pastor Jay was the first person at the Marrying Stone that Christmas morning. He'd had a dream about an angel visiting the night before and he knew there was to be a wedding. He'd dressed in his black frock coat and even combed his long gray beard. There was going to be a very special wedding and he wanted to be there to perform it.

The Broody twins arrived next pulling Granny Piggott on the skid. She was heavily bundled in her lap robe against the cold bite of the wind. The old woman wouldn't have missed the outcome of the kangaroo court for anything.

Neighbors, friends of the principles, and the merely curious poured into the snowy clearing around the Marrying Stone.

Beulah and Orv Winsloe arrived, with Tom McNees in tow.

Pastor Jay had busied himself cleaning the snow off the stone.

"What are you doing here?" McNees asked the old man.

"I'm here to perform a wedding," he answered.

"No, Pastor Jay," Tom told him with just a hint of exasperation. "I'll be doing the ceremony. I don't know how you even heard about it."

"Angels told me," Pastor Jay answered.

Tom McNees glanced back at his sister. Beulah rolled her eyes.

"I even know who's marrying up," the old man said. "And a finer match, I ain't never seen."

"Eben and Althea will be a good pair all right," Tom admitted.

"Oh, it ain't Eben," Pastor Jay informed him.

Tom shook his head. "Oather's done left the mountain," he answered. "Now why don't you see if those Broody boys can find room for you on Granny's skid. We don't want you catching a fever on a frozen morning like this."

The Bests arrived shortly thereafter. Some people were surprised to see them. They weren't directly involved and Onery rarely ventured out in the cold weather with his bad leg.

In truth, the family wasn't sure what they were doing there either. Jesse had sneaked back in the house before dawn. Little Edith was sleeping like the baby she was. And Onery had been snoring loudly. Roe and Meggie were awake, but they were making so much noise of their own, they didn't hear Jesse's furtive movements.

With none the wiser, Jesse had risen for breakfast with the rest of them and announced that the entire family would attend Miss Althea's wedding. He refused to explain, or to hear any protests. Curious, but trusting, the family made their way to the Marrying Stone.

Gid Weston arrived with several of his boys; they were half-drunk already with the holiday celebration. Laughing and happy, they were ready for a wedding.

Pigg Broody was there, too, but he was a lot less pleased about it. He roundly cursed the cold weather and suggested to Granny that most folks married in the springtime for good reason.

Eben Baxley arrived and stood on the edge of the crowd. Lots of attention was focused in his direction, lots of speculation about what he might be thinking. But no one came up and spoke to him, not even Beulah Winsloe, who was just about to bust her buttons with pleasure over the apparent success of her well-laid plans.

The Phillips family was not there and was almost conspicuous by their absence. Some speculated that Buell was a sore loser. Those more kindly disposed thought the family might still be sorrowing from Oather's leave-taking and uninterested in the happy festivities.

Althea Winsloe, Baby-Paisley at her side, was the last one to arrive. The little boy was all bright cheeks and exuberant smiles as he sported his new blue and white voyageur's cap.

Eagerly he pulled away from his mother and rushed through the crowd searching and finding Jesse.

"Santy Claus come," he said excitedly. "I checked the chimley, just like you said. They was soot marks on it. Somebody'd been climbing there for sure."

"Did he leave you anything?" Jesse asked.

"This cap, ain't it wonnerful, and an apple all to myself!"

Jesse was suitably impressed. "That Santy Claus feller is some nice guy," Jesse said.

The little boy looked around eagerly. "Is Mama's present here yet?" he asked in a whisper.

"Not yet," Jesse answered.

He took the little boy's hand and the two walked back through the crowd to Althea. Baby-Paisley took his mother's hand, but held on to Jesse's as well. He stood between them, connecting them.

"Well, let's get on with it before we all freeze to death," Pigg Broody suggested crankily. "Althea Winsloe," he said, slipping into his Judge Broody voice. "You're supposed to choose your husband this morning. We're all here to see the wedding. Are you ready to choose?"

She smiled broadly. "I'm not only ready," she said with a pleasant laugh, "I'm as happy and excited to be getting married this morning as any bride who ever walked up to this stone."

Her words sent a murmur of heightened speculation through the crowd. Had Eben Baxley worked his woman-pleasing wiles on a gal once more? Was this kangaroo courting going to turn into a love match?

"Well, let's be official now," Pigg said, punctuating his words with a spit of tobacco. "Name yer bridgegroom."

"I choose," she began and hesitated dramatically before turning her head toward the man beside her. "I choose Jesse Best for my lawful wedded husband."

A gasp exploded from the crowd. Everyone began to talk at once. People were stunned with disbelief. Eben Baxley laughed out loud and shook his head. Beulah Winsloe was spitting fury.

"Do something!" she ordered her brother.

"What?"

"Anything!"

Althea stepped into Jesse's arms and he pulled her close. He wanted to kiss her, to kiss her really good. But he wasn't about to do that with all these people standing around.

Tom McNees stepped up on the Marrying Stone and raised his hands to quiet the crowd.

"We can't allow this," he announced. "We cannot and will not allow this to happen."

Silence settled in.

"There isn't anything you can do to stop it," Althea told him.

"It's against the Bible," Tom said.

A hush went through the crowd. Granny was the expert on family. Pigg Broody the expert on kangaroo court. But the pastor of the church was the undisputed expert on the Bible.

"What do you mean it's agin the Bible?" Granny asked.

"It's writ in the second book to the Corinthians 'be ye not unequally yoked together,'" Tom answered. "Jesse is simple. Althea is not. That's about as unequal as it can get."

The crowd stood silent, considering the truth of his words. People began nodding. They weren't equal and if that was what the Bible said, who could argue. Tom McNees was the preacher. He ought to know.

"That ain't what it says!"

Pastor Jay stepped through the people and stood before the stone, staring up at Tom McNees. "That ain't what the Good Book says at all."

"Pastor Jay!" Beulah exploded angrily. "You just keep talking to your angels. Let our new preacher speak to his congregation."

"I've let him speak," the old man answered just as angrily. "I've let him speak plenty. Most of the time he's speaking for the Lord, but right now he's speaking for you, Beulah Winsloe."

A startled murmur drifted through the crowd.

"The Bible don't say that Jesse can't marry Althea," Pastor Jay told the people loudly. "You say you're taking these words from the Good Book, but you just can't take some words and leave the others. It says 'be ye not unequally yoked together with *unbelievers*.' Jesse's no unbeliever. He's simple and there ain't no argument about that. But in his way he's as believing as any man here. And I dare any to deny it."

Nobody did.

"Well, even if the Bible don't speak against it," Beulah insisted angrily, "as the girl's family we can't let it happen."

"I don't know why not," Pastor Jay answered.

Beulah turned away from the old man and appealed to the crowd. "He's simple. All their younguns could be simple as well!"

"Now, that ain't the way of it," Granny called out. "We don't know why one is touched in the head and one is not."

Beulah disregarded her. "The McNees family ain't got nothing like this in our blood. You Piggotts," she said, indicating both Granny and Pastor Jay. "You don't mind it so much, 'cause it's part of you. But our folks is clean of this affliction and I won't let this gal bring it among us."

The crowd immediately began to divide up into two camps. Piggotts and McNees. Jesse turned to look at Althea. He was scared. And he could see in her eyes that she was, too.

"What's happening?" he asked. "I cain't understand when they all talk at once."

"We'll go away, Jesse," she said to him quietly as the battle of words raged around them. "If they won't marry us, we'll go away until we find someone who will."

He nodded, but she looked unhappy about the prospect. Jesse needed to say something, to do something.

"What's happenin', Mama?" Baby-Paisley looked out among the angry voices of the crowd curiously. From the corner of his eye he spied a group of strangers coming up the path and his mouth formed a little O of delight. "Jesse, Jesse," he said excitedly. "Is them Mama's present?"

Jesse gazed in the direction of the approaching men. Althea did also, curious. As recognition dawned her eyes widened in disbelief.

"Daddy?" she whispered the word as if it were unfamiliar to her own ears. "Daddy!" she called out louder.

All around the clearing voices hushed one after the other as people realized what was happening. Althea took a step forward, then two, then she was running into the arms of the man who was her father. "Daddy, Daddy, what are you doing here?"

She wrapped her arms around his neck, hugging him closely. He hugged her back, clearly startled at the young woman in his arms.

"Althea! Is this my little Althea?"

"It's me, Daddy," she answered eagerly. "It's me."

"My heavens, you are the image of your mama, darling. I would have known you anywhere in the world."

"What are you doing here?" she asked, still stunned almost disbelieving.

"Why, I got a message from a couple of fellers named Jesse and Paisley. They said you was getting married on Christmas morning and that you wanted me to be here."

"Jesse and Paisley? They got a message to you?" she said.

"It's our Cwissmas pwesent to you, Mama. Jesse tol' me it was the thing you wanted mostest in the whole world."

Althea looked down at her little son, standing so eagerly beside her.

"Yes, yes," she said. "Jesse remembered. It is the thing I've wanted most in the world. Oh, Daddy, this is Paisley, or, well, we call him Baby-Paisley. He's your grandson."

The man looked down at the little boy and ruffled the child's hair. "Well, I'm very pleased to meet you, Baby-Paisley, my grandson."

Althea turned to the man behind her. "And this is Jesse. Jesse, this is my father, Jubal McNees."

"Jesse." The man offered his hand. "Thank you boys for

sending me the message. Last time she got wed up I didn't hear about it 'til it was all over."

"I wrote you," Althea said.

He gave her a long curious look and then shook his head. "I cain't read, darlin'," he answered quietly. "I save yer letters till a penman comes 'round and he reads them all. Sometimes we get two years' worth of news in one night."

"You can't read? I never realized." Althea just stood staring at her father. "I can't believe you've come to see me," she said. "After all these years, I can't believe you're here."

"I should have come before," he said. "I should have come years before," he said. "I guess, well, I guess the years just got away from me."

"But you came today," she said.

"Lord, yes, as soon as I got the word from that peddler man, I hustled up some grub and yer brothers and we walked all night and all day to get here."

"Brothers?"

"Yes indeed." Jubal turned to the men standing behind him. "These is your brothers. There's Wendall and Cotton, that tall one is Howell and this mean little devil here is Bill-Tommy."

"Hello," she said lamely, then, "Hello! I have brothers!"

"That's what you got, Althea," her father said. "I didn't have no other little daughter ever but you."

"Where . . . where is your wife?"

"Nettie? My Nettie's been dead ah . . . going on five years, ain't it, boys."

The quartet nodded in agreement.

"Why didn't you send for me?" Althea asked.

"Why didn't I send for ye? Why, you was here with all the folks. The White River is rough country, hardscrabble living. That's why we didn't take you with us in the first place. Afterward, well, you was settled in and happy here. I didn't think that you'd want to come our way."

"Oh, Daddy," she whispered, pulling on his coat sleeve. "I thought . . . I thought . . . oh, never mind what I thought." Althea smiled and smiled until she laughed out loud. "You're here now, Daddy, and that's all that matters. Daddy, I'm going to get married."

"So who you marrying?"

The folks around who had watched the family drama from the sidelines now hurried in to confront the newcomers.

"She thinks she's marrying up with Simple Jess," Beulah Winsloe informed him. "But we're putting a stop to it."

"Beulah? Beulah Winsloe?" Jubal asked. "Lord, I wouldn't have known you."

"Her daddy is here now. A woman has to do what her daddy tells her, that is in the Bible," Tom McNees announced.

"Tom McNees?" Jubal seemed surprised. "You've taken up preaching?"

"The McNees are standing together on this," Beulah Winsloe said pointedly to Jubal.

"The McNees stand together on what?"

"We stand agin bringing the blood of the feebleminded into our family!"

The crowd reaction was a roar.

"Jesse's troubles ain't in the blood, Beulah Winsloe," Granny Piggott protested. "And I ain't going to listen to you saying so."

"Good day to you, Granny," Jubal said, doffing his hat. "You don't look a day older than the last time I seen ye."

"I was old as dirt even then," the old woman admitted. "Are you going to let Beulah Winsloe tell your daughter who to marry?"

"I got a right!" Beulah began arguing. "She's my boy's widow."

"No, you don't and I won't listen," Althea answered back.

Within a minute everybody was talking at once. The din got louder and louder and louder—each word drowning out the others until nothing, nothing could be heard but the noise.

Jesse Best covered his ears in self-defense and then raised his hands to heaven and screamed.

"HUSH!"

Startled, they did.

Jesse turned to face Jubal McNees. "I am going to marry your daughter," he said. "The problem is that I'm simple. I don't deny it. Everybody knows it. But Miss Althea loves me and so does Baby-Paisley. They love me and I've already promised to take care of them. We are going to marry. We would like your blessing, sir. But we are marrying just the same."

"Is that so?" Jubal's tone was challenging.

"It's so," Jesse answered evenly.

Jubal looked at Beulah. "He wasn't so simple that he didn't know to send for a feller when his daughter was getting married," he said. "If you'd have been that bright, I'd have been here for her last wedding."

Beulah's mouth dropped open in angry disbelief. The crowd hooted with laughter.

Jubal McNees looked down at his daughter, a young woman that he hardly new. "This man, Althea, this simple man, he suits you?"

"He suits me, Daddy."

He smiled at her. It was the handsome smile that she'd always remembered, the smile that she'd always dreamed of seeing again. Jubal raised an eyebrow and then spoke loud enough for all to hear. "If he suits my Althea, then he'll suit the rest of us."

Eben Baxley watched the wedding of Althea Winsloe and Jesse Best, shaking his head in disbelief. He should have known she was going to pick Jesse. It hadn't even occurred to him. And it was right in front of him all the time.

Pastor Jay performed the ceremony, Tom McNees having stormed off in a huff with Beulah and Orv. Althea's father gave her away and after they'd repeated their vows, she and Jesse jumped off the stone, the official declaration of being man and wife on Marrying Stone Mountain. And they did it as happily and eagerly as it had ever been done.

And Jesse had kissed her, too. In front of her father and Pastor Jay and practically the whole congregation, he'd kissed her. And it appeared to Eben that the two had had a little more practice than folks had heard about.

Althea invited the whole crowd back to her place. She'd made extra Christmas cakes, she announced, and there were plenty for everybody. Baby-Paisley, reveling in the attention of his new uncles, was regaling all within hearing distance of the evidence on his chimney of Santy Claus coming to visit.

With her father beside her and Jesse's hand in her own, Eben watched Althea Winsloe, the owner of the finest corn bottom on Marrying Stone Mountain and probably the best chance Eben would ever have for a fine farm, walk away from him.

"Told ye so."

Eben glanced, startled, to the man who'd slipped up beside him.

"Hello, Pastor Jay," he said.

"Didn't I tell you that Jesse was in love?"

"Yes, Pastor Jay, I believe that you did."

"I ain't claiming no powers, now," the old man insisted. "I cain't see into the future or any such nonsense as that. Them angels, though, sometimes they tell me things."

"So you've said."

"Well, get on about it," Pastor Jay urged him. "I cain't be waiting here in the cold all day."

"What are you talking about?"

The old man gave a long-suffering sigh. "Eben Baxley, we both know what I'm talking about. Now get on with your business. I'll be waiting here when you get back."

Eben gave the old man a strange look, bid him good day. As he started walking away, he shook his head.

"Crazy old man," he said to himself.

Inexplicably, Eben started to whistle. He went down the wide road that this morning was a slippery slope away from the Marrying Stone. Then up the small, hardly recognizable trail along the side of the store until he came to the family entrance where the Phillipses lived. He waited. He stood alone in the cold waiting. It seemed that he had waited a very long time. Thinking. Waiting and thinking. Finally the back door opened and, wearing a heavy work dress, boots, and a shawl wrapped around her shoulders, Mavis Phillips emerged on the porch, broom in hand.

"Morning, Mavis," he called out as he walked toward her.

She stopped to stare at him. Then raising her chin proudly, she answered, "Good morning."

Without another word she began to sweep the porch.

Eben waited. She didn't speak but her expression was troubled.

"I heard you're getting married this morning," she said finally.

"Yes, I am. I believe that I am."

She hesitated a minute in her stroke and then continued her sweeping.

"Don't you think that I should?" Eben asked her.

She glared at him.

He shrugged. "I just wanted your opinion."

"I don't know why."

"What you think matters to me."

"What I think?" she asked furiously. "I'll tell you what I think. You're always saying that you don't let anyone tell you what to do and that no one can make you marry anyone. But that is exactly what Beulah Winsloe is doing, making you marry."

"No," he answered. "I believe Beulah's given up on making me do things. I only marry the woman of my choice. Course, I don't think she'll be unhappy about it."

Eben sighed with satisfaction.

"Oather probably will be, but he'll get over it eventually."

"I doubt that Oather would even care," she said. "We may never see him again."

"But you'll hear from him. And he'll care all right. That's the kind of feller he is. He loves you and cares about you and wants only good things for you. He and I have that in common. So eventually I think I can win him over."

"Why would you even want to?"

"Well, it's just not good form to have a brother-in-law that doesn't like you," Eben answered.

"A brother-in-law?" Mavis looked at him, confused. Then her eyes widened.

Eben grinned.

"Pastor Jay is waiting on us. If we don't hurry, I'm afraid we'll be the first couple to jump the Marrying Stone over a frozen body."

And it was cold out on the Marrying Stone. But Pastor Jay didn't notice. He was busy talking to himself, or rather to the angels.

"Well I just worry about the boy. —He's different, always has been. But when you know a person from the time he's a baby, you cain't help but take an interest. —You can show me his future? Now that's a neat trick if I ever heard one. Let's see you try. —Why yes, I see it. I see it now. Ain't this pretty. What a beautiful place. The boy looks so happy. All those friends around. Everybody laughing. What a wonderful place. Oh, Lord, it's not what I think, is it? —It's Heaven, ain't it? Poor Oather dies young and goes to Heaven. —It's not Heaven. Then where is it? —New Orleans? Hmmm. Sure looks like Heaven from here."

Our Town

...where love is always right around the corner!

<u>All Books Available in July 1996</u>

_*Take Heart* by Lisa Higdon

                    0-515-11898-2/$5.50

In Wilder, Wyoming...a penniless socialite learns a lesson in frontier life—and love.

_*Harbor Lights* by Linda Kreisel

                    0-515-11899-0/$5.50

On Maryland's Silchester Island...the perfect summer holiday sparks a perfect summer fling.

_*Humble Pie* by Deborah Lawrence

                    0-515-11900-8/$5.50

In Moose Gulch, Montana...a waitress with a secret meets a stranger with a heart.

Praise for Pamela Morsi and her delightful novels . . .

RUNABOUT

Tulsa May Bruder thinks she's doomed to be the town wall-flower . . . until she looks at Luther Briggs and sees a face she's known forever in a whole new light . . .

"Pamela Morsi writes about love and life with laughter, tenderness, and most of all, joy."—*Romantic Times*

WILD OATS

Cora Briggs and Jedwin Sparrow come from very different parts of town. But when it comes to love, it doesn't matter what the neighbors say . . .

"A book to get lost in!"—*Rendezvous*

GARTERS

Sensible Esme Crabb set out to find a husband—and found the task more difficult than she ever expected. But falling in love with Cleavis Rhy was easier than she ever dreamed . . .

"A story as warm and wonderful—and sexy—as a feather-bed on a winter night."—LAURA KINSALE

MARRYING STONE

Meggie was an Ozark girl and Monroe an educated Easterner. But it doesn't matter where you come from—because love is a world of its own . . .

"Morsi's down-home touch lends charm."

—*Publishers Weekly*

SOMETHING SHADY

Gertrude Barkley and Mikolai Stefanski had lived in the same sleepy town for years. But it would take a scandalous discovery to make them see one another in a whole new way . . .

"A refreshing new voice in romance."—JUDE DEVERAUX